I0693023

FATHER PRESIDENT

Margaret Bailey

Copyright © 2015 Margaret Bailey
All rights reserved.

ISBN: 0986243523
ISBN 13: 9780986243523

Other books by Margaret Bailey

Diamond in the Sky—set in Leadville, Colorado, in 1895, its two lovers depend on the success of the spectacular Ice Palace built to help the silver mining town through the bust that followed the establishment of the gold standard.

Waves of Amber, First Wave
A fictionalized memoir, this story reveals how Hong, a Vietnamese refugee, and Margaret, an American teacher, manage to become family to each other despite cultural and age differences.

Waves of Amber, Second Wave
Four more refugees join the fragile family life of Hong and Margaret and nearly tear them apart.

Waves of Amber, Third Wave
Another wave of refugees throw the now enlarged family into chaos again. Only love, loyalty, and determination can hold them all together.

Stephanie's Search
A man disappears into the Colorado Rockies, and two broken people try to find him, thinking he holds the key to solving their problems. All proceeds from the sale of this book are donated to the Summit County, Colorado, Search and Rescue Group.

ACKNOWLEDGEMENTS

My sincere thanks for their suggestions and advice go to Janet Lane, Vicki Kaufman, Karen Duvall, Shannon Baker, Gail Rowe, Michael Phillips, Jameson Cole, and Bonnie Smith.

ACKNOWLEDGMENTS

CHAPTER ONE

F ather Paul Greer walked down the side aisle of St. Simon's
  Church, kicking at the hem of his cassock to cool his legs
before entering the stifling confessional. He passed through
rays of red and yellow light and turned his face away from the
stained-glass window they came from. Usually the windows lifted his spirit, but today their colors were shafts of flaming acid
that burned into his conscience, into the doubts already smol-
dering there. Every step he took was a lie, a false promise from
a priest who had no right to judge the sins of others. After the
confessions he'd stay and pray for help.

Already a dozen parishioners waited in the pews, their
heads bowed in prayer. Nearest the confessional knelt Laurel
Broussard, the acknowledged beauty of the parish. Her head
was not bowed, and Paul knew her gray-blue eyes had followed
him from the door of the sacristy.

He groaned silently and passed her with his head lowered.
Out of the corner of his eye he saw the wavy blond hair billow under a black lace *mantilla*. Her full lips followed the beads of her

rosary in an automatic Hail Mary, but her eyes moved with him. In her mid-thirties now, she was the unhappy and frustrated wife of an antique dealer in the French Quarter who had disclosed his homosexuality years ago, only weeks after their marriage. Her confession was always a protracted ordeal, and she never went to Father Morreaux.

Paul hoped she'd wait till last with her disturbing litany. He pulled open the door, stepped in, and sat down in the dim, hot-cotton air of his narrow booth. The smell of old dust and mildewed varnish—to him, the odor of layered guilt—threatened to close his throat.

He heard the creak of the kneeler behind the thin wall on his left. His hand went automatically to his forehead for the sign of the cross but sank again without completing it. He leaned his head on the back of the confessional, fingering the round red scar on the back of his right hand. It brought him back to focus.

He heaved a sigh and tugged at the warped panel that separated him from the penitent. Stuck as usual, it let go suddenly and slammed into its housing. The bang echoed from the other side of the church.

Before the echo died, Laurel was speaking. "I can't stand it anymore, Father," she started, crossing herself.

He closed his eyes in resignation and kept his head rigidly toward the front of the booth. He could not show emotion during a confession.

"They've had the application for years now. If they won't grant the annulment, I'll leave the church and get a divorce, I swear I will," she went on. "You have to help me. Can't you call the archbishop again? I'm going out of my mind."

Paul's fists tightened. He couldn't tell her it was long past time for the eighty-seven-year-old archbishop, who'd never quite given up the Latin mass, to retire and let someone more progressive take over. "Now, Laurel, we've been over all this before. You know the church's stand..."

"What about *your* stand, Father? Or don't you have one? Do you priests have any feelings at all for what we suffer, or do you just turn those in to the bishop when you're ordained?"

"Have you tried offering it up? God never gives us more..."

"...than we can bear," she finished, her rising voice edged with bitterness. "Yes, He does, Father. I don't know why you haven't figured that out. It's more than I can bear. All my friends have families, babies. I want a real life with a real man. I want children. I swear I could do without the rest if I could just have one baby before it's too late. But Justin won't touch me. I do everything I can to make myself attractive to him, just till I get pregnant. I buy underwear that makes even me blush..."

Paul closed his eyes again, feeling her desperation. She was near the breaking point.

Laurel went on, adding detail unusual even for her.

To block the images of black lace on creamy skin, Paul focused on his role as a priest. *You're only a receptacle,* he told himself, clenching his fingers around the fabric of his dark cassock. *This means nothing to you.* Still, it was harder to breathe now. The close, muggy air mixed with the odor of Laurel: her sweat; the open, fresh smell of her perfume or shampoo; a breath mint.

When she paused for breath, Paul hastened to stop the graphic descriptions. "Those are not sins in the framework of marriage, my child. Did you have something you wanted to confess?" Through the grillwork he heard her hopeless sigh, saw her intertwined, clenched hands go up to her chin.

It was a few seconds before she answered.

"I've been with another man."

"You've been unfaithful to your husband?"

Laurel sniffed. "Husband," she spat out in a whisper. "Doesn't that imply he should treat me like a wife? But yes, in the eyes of the church, I've been unfaithful. I slept with another..., well, sleep isn't exactly what we did. I happened to sit next to him at an afternoon movie. Somehow our arms were touching during some pretty torrid scenes, and one thing led to another. I couldn't help myself any more. It's not as if I hadn't had the chance before, but I never gave in. We went to his place and did it till he had to leave. He touched me in places..."

Paul listened unwillingly, guiltily, hardly able to distinguish between her confession and the conjuring of his aching libido. When he tried to change focus, all that came to mind was the sweat running down his chest to his groin. The walls closed in, compacting the heat. He pulled at the Roman collar, rigid even in dampness.

"This is serious, Laurel. You must pray and keep yourself out of the occasion of sin. You must not see this man again. Now, for your penance..."

Her head lowered until her clenched hands were on her forehead.

Paul heard her take a deep breath but could hardly hear the words that followed.

"There was one other thing, Father."

Paul waited, moving his head just enough to take a good look. She'd never been this drawn into herself before.

She breathed nervously again. The words came haltingly, like so many drops of water before a dam breaks. "I've been... having...lewd thoughts...for some time now. Months. I can't help it. They're about..."

"You don't need to tell me that. The thoughts are the problem, not..."

"They're about you, Paul. I'm so sorry. But I can't hold this in any more. I try so hard to turn them off, but everywhere I turn I see you. I don't come to your mass every morning to pray. I need you. You hand me the communion but I feel you caress my face, run your hands down my neck, over my shoulders and breasts. I'm so ashamed. Ever since we worked together on the Christmas baskets last year. I fell in love with you, and I can't get you out of my mind. And you felt something, too, then. I could see it..."

Her head came up and their eyes locked.

In a flash he knew. The guilt. The guilt layered with the mildew in this confessional was his, not hers, nor even that of the thousands of sinners who'd knelt here before her. Guilt because he responded to her in this way, but far worse guilt because his whole self had become a lie. His breath came harder, but Laurel was in full spate, and he heard every word, replayed every nuance of the desire he'd felt.

Her voice lilted happily now, even in a whisper. "Remember when we were loading baskets that night it was so cold? And we'd been laughing together like two lunatics over the story my uncle from Chicago told us about being in church and not realizing he didn't have his pants zipped till the middle of mass, and he started to zip them up at the same time the girl with the wide skirt came back from communion, and she got her dress caught in his zipper? Remember how we laughed together, Paul? Remember bumping into each other on the way back into the building? Then I took off my coat and caught you looking at me, and I could tell by your face you suddenly saw me taking off the rest. I knew you wanted me. And you looked away and then went out of the room for a few minutes. Oh, God, Paul, I knew it was wrong, but I wanted to throw my arms around you, tell you it was..."

Both his arms flew out and banged the door open. Paul jumped and ran past the waiting sinners, past the stations of the cross, past the sweet-sad faces of saints and angels, and out at the back of the church. Behind him the door slammed on its ancient hinges. Before him the blast of mid-town New Orleans traffic and mid-August heat struck him like a blow to the stomach. And suddenly he was a nothing, a lost cipher between the vast, fluctuating madness of the real world and the ancient stone fortress of rigidity that was the Catholic Church.

His priesthood whirled about him: the years of vicarious suffering with his parishioners, of dispensing penances and platitudes that merely glossed their problems over, of trying to ignore his own frustrations and doubts; and with every turn the uneasy past, spinning in the white heat, crashed against the truth of Laurel's statement. He *had* wanted her. Not loved her. Just wanted the feel of her skin, her soft body, the curving and the secret parts. He still wanted her.

Behind him the church door slammed again.

"Paul!" she called.

Without looking back, he ran around to the side of the church and past it to the rectory. In his room he stripped off the cassock and the Roman collar, put on his tan shorts and a plaid shirt, and ran down to his Escort station wagon. His hand shook so wildly he was hardly able to shove the key into the ignition.

CHAPTER TWO

A gray roadway rushed away beneath the wheels of the Escort, but Paul saw only the mottled gray of a cold marble floor an inch from his eyes. He was lying on his stomach, his forehead resting on his hands, hardly conscious of the six other young men being ordained with him. Chants and incense and the drone of the organ thickened the air above him.

He felt nothing. No elation. No anticipation. No accomplishment. He should soar in ecstasy now, but there was only—what? A tinge of fear that he had made the wrong decision? No! The priesthood was right, it was his destiny. God had called him.

And then fifteen years had rushed away as fast as the roadway vanishing behind him. Where had they gone? Why had God's voice faded to a whisper behind the din of life? Where was God in all the pageantry and stone and the wispy smoke of snuffed candles? Had there ever been a God to hear the prayers and the pleas for mercy? Had Paul the priest ever done God's will or only the Church's bidding? When had he substituted a desire to make a contribution to the world for his vocation? It had happened so slowly, as the realization grew that much of church law made its people's lives harder.

The setting sun dipped below his visor and blinded him. He pulled it lower and realized with a start that he'd been driving for hours. He had no idea where he was, though he was heading west on an interstate. He had no recollection of driving onto it, of the places he'd passed, nor even of the speed he'd been driving.

A few minutes later a sign flashed by on the edge of the interstate: Welcome to Texas. Now he knew where he was. He had no idea where he was going.

The round welt on the back of his right hand ached, and he realized he'd been worrying at it for miles, trying to rub off the old reminder of his failed faith.

He could still see thirteen-year-old Ricky Thayer in the white surplice and red robe, his pug face looking down on ten-year-old Paul Greer as they changed after serving Easter Sunday Mass.

"You don't really believe what Father Muldaney said, you dope," Ricky sneered. "Everybody knows that's just stuff they tell you so you don't lose your faith."

"I do too believe it," said Paul, "If you have enough faith, you can do anything, you can walk on fire, just like he said."

"Oh, yeah? How strong's *your* faith?"

"Plenty strong." Paul puffed up his little chest.

The other altar boys stopped changing to listen.

"You wanna prove that?" asked Ricky.

"Sure."

When they'd all hung up their vestments, they went out to the huge live oak tree at the back corner of the church parking lot. They ducked under its sprawling, low branches into dark green air that smelled of humid bare dirt and old pee.

Ricky took a cigarette and a folding book of matches out of his pocket. He lit the cigarette while the younger boys looked on with envious awe.

Paul watched, terrified of the orange-red glow at the end of the cigarette.

"Okay," said Ricky, leering at him. "Let's see if your faith is strong enough for this." He grabbed Paul's right wrist and drew the hand toward him. Ricky's left hand lowered the cigarette slowly while the other clamped tighter and tighter.

Paul felt the first heat when the cigarette was still an inch away. He jerked his hand, but Ricky was stronger.

"See," crowed Ricky. "You got no faith at all."

Paul clamped his jaw as hard as he could, and every muscle in his body went rigid with it. "I do, too." He balled his hand into a fist and forced it to hold still.

"You think this isn't going to hurt?"

"Not if I got enough faith," he said through his teeth. He squeezed his eyes shut and prayed.

The older boy twisted until Paul was behind him, unable to move or to see the cigarette.

And then it hit. Paul screamed in pain and flapped his hand below Ricky's grip. But Ricky didn't let go.

Other hands grabbed Paul's fingers and held his hand.

The cigarette came again. The smell of burning flesh drowned the other odors under the old tree. Paul fainted.

When he came to, he was alone, looking up at the dark canopy of branches, with his head resting against one of the many exposed roots. Next to him, a bent and dead cigarette butt lay in the dirt.

His hand hurt like the fires of hell, but his tears were for his failure.

Failure. Paul felt the word rush through memory and sweep up fifteen years: failure to help people with their troubled lives, failure to feel the ecstatic closeness to God that had sustained him through the seminary years. What had it been for? For a headlong flight to nowhere.

He stared up at the interstate junction from a gas station where he found himself standing at a pump. South to San Antonio. North to Dallas... North. For the first time it occurred to him where he might go. He looked around for a phone booth.

Exhausted from the long drive into a vacuum of tomorrows, Paul walked on stiff legs into an apartment building in southeast Denver. He looked down the list of tenants and found D.A. Greer, 504. David Anthony Greer. He hardly knew the brother he hadn't seen in years except at his parents' funerals. A few sparse words in sporadic e-mails, that's what they'd become to each other after so much closeness through high school. What kind of man was he now? Did he still go by the name Danny, which Paul had used as a toddler because his mother's full "David Anthony" was too big a mouthful?

Did he still live by his old motto, "Do it all and do it now"? Meaning hell-raising and women and the pot that made him so unpredictable. He'd been aloof at his father's funeral, still smarting from Paul's "preachiness." And only slightly more cordial at his mother's.

Paul stopped on the top step. He shouldn't have come. It was too much to ask an estranged brother to take on a priest in crisis. Too much strain on himself when he all he wanted was time to think. If he hadn't called ahead, he'd turn around now and keep driving. He'd just visit overnight and keep going. He took a deep, nervous breath and pushed the doorbell. Almost instantly the door buzzed. He made his way through the small lobby and tried to smooth his rumpled, stale clothes as he rode up to the fifth floor.

Danny was waiting at the elevator. He reached in and yanked Paul out into a bear hug. "By God, little brother, I'm glad to see you. Let me look at you."

He let go and they looked each other over, smiling out of two almost identical sets of deep blue eyes.

Paul's throat caught. This was the last kind of reception he'd expected.

Danny shook Paul's shoulders affectionately. "You're still thin as a fishing pole. You're not even balding, you louse," Danny complained. "Look at me." He ran his right hand over thinning black hair and his left down a small beer belly. "'Course, we always knew you got more of Mom's genes than Dad's. Come on in." He looked back into the elevator. "Where's your stuff?"

"I didn't bring..."

"Right, we'll bring it up later." He put his arm around Paul's shoulder. "Let's get you a cold beer. You look like you could use one. Long drive. You could've bowled me over with a ping pong ball when you called. What're you doing out here anyway? Vacation?" he asked, propelling Paul through the apartment door.

"No. Danny, I..."

Danny stopped and his eyes fixed Paul intently. "You what?"

"I...didn't bring...anything."

"What do you mean?"

Paul's mouth dried up, but he had to get it out sometime. "I left."

"You left what?"

Paul raised his sweaty hands, as if they held an answer, but they were shaking visibly and he wiped them on his shorts. The answer would make his decision definite, permanent, and nail him to the terrifying uncertainty.

"You left what? The priesthood? The church?"

"Both." Paul swallowed. "I think."

"What?! Jesus, Paul, after all these years? That's great. I thought you were going to tell me you were in some kind of trouble. 'Course, that'd be my bag, not yours. Tell me about it. No wonder you look so racked up. I thought you were just tired. Must be pretty scary."

"Scary? That's like saying *ripple* when you're caught in a tsunami."

"So, you're telling me you walked away with the clothes on your back? Just like that?"

"*Ran* would be more accurate."

"This I gotta hear. You want a shower first, before you talk, or a beer?"

"Shower, then beer."

"Use anything you need. The bathroom's through the bedroom. Poke around in the drawers till you find some fresh clothes."

Paul buttoned a shirt that ballooned around his chest, took a beer from the large stock in the refrigerator, and joined Danny standing at the railing of the balcony.

To the west the gray-purple silhouette of the Rockies serrated the horizon from north to south as far as he could see. The cloudless sky, gray-gold along the peaks, showed three points of light—two jets passing each other in the last sunlight, and the evening star. Rush hour traffic on the other side of the building had subsided; cooler air was descending; and in the brief moment that was neither night nor day, the world seemed to be at peace.

The telephone rang.

Danny answered it inside, started to come out again and then turned back.

Leaning against the balcony railing, Paul tried not to listen, but Danny's voice carried clearly through the sliding screen door.

"Look, Floyd, I told you a month ago the EPA was not willing to re-open those negotiations. The Arapahoe Aquifer is a dead issue...Oh, come on, we've been through that before, and I'm busy right now..."

When he spoke again, his voice took on the aggrieved patience of a teacher with an obtuse student. "It's too close to the surface. The impact study showed it's immediately under downtown and large sections of the interstate. There's no way to guarantee there won't be sinkholes that could occur without notice. And in the future it may be the only source of clean drinking water. The recharge time for all the Colorado aquifers lies somewhere between 1,000 and 10,000 years. Didn't you see the results of the survey?" Danny listened for a moment. "I can't help that. *I* didn't tell you to put your money in...Who?...I thought they were in oil...So what if they have the drilling equipment already available? Their only interest in water is their own greed. They're a raunchy crowd, Floyd. I'd advise you to dissociate yourself... Sorry, old buddy, our history doesn't mean...You tell them from me that I'm not intimidated. And don't call me about this again. You want to talk to me about other things, you call the office."

Danny joined Paul again and slammed the handset down on the wrought iron table between his patio chairs. He breathed deeply and took a large swallow of beer. "Sorry, Paul. That used to be one of my best buddies in my grass 'n coke days. He's been bugging me for months. So much for old friends, huh?"

"Yeah," said Paul, wondering how Danny felt about "old" family.

Danny watched him absorb the sunset for a few minutes. "I pay half again as much rent as people on the other side of the building, but it's worth it," he said, gazing at the gold light.

Paul tried to recapture the sense of peace. "I see what you mean."

"Come on, sit down and tell me what's going on."

"I don't know if I can talk about it. And I don't want to burden you with my problems." As he sat down, Paul grabbed the armrests to stop the shaking.

Taking a long swig, Danny regarded him over the beer can. "Confession's good for the soul. How many people have you said that to?" He set the can on the table and leaned forward with his elbows on his knees. "Look, Paul, I know we haven't been close for years, and it's my fault. But we're still family, right? And *I'm* the big brother. There's nothing you can't tell me. I'm the last person in the world with the right to judge you." He reached across, put his hand on Paul's knee, then slapped it fondly and settled back in his chair.

Paul looked at the knee, clenched his hands in his lap, and put his estrangement aside. He forced the words to come. "It's been building for years," he said, staring at his hands.

"The celibacy thing? I don't know how you put up with that nonsense as long as you did."

Paul closed his eyes. Laurel's last confession flashed through his mind in devastating detail. Absently, he rubbed the burn scar and tried to blow the smell of guilt-mildewed varnish from his nose. "I just ran," he whispered.

He looked up at Danny, hoping the dusk covered the shame that made his face hot. "In the end, lust was the catalyst, but it wasn't really the reason. I just couldn't keep handing people bromides I knew would never cure their pain. Teaching guilt, especially over things I felt the church needed to change. Promising a salvation I wasn't sure of anymore." He bit his lip. "I'd even begun to see communion as a cannibalistic act. Eating the body and blood. Human sacrifice. I'd give those innocent children a host and say, 'Body of Christ,' and they'd answer 'Blood of Christ.' It turned my stomach. The only priestly thing I still liked doing was weddings."

Danny gazed at him for a minute. "I wish I could say I'd left the church for such noble reasons. And yours *are* noble reasons. *I* just didn't want to believe the things I was doing were sins, 'cause I wasn't about to give them up." A nostalgic smile played across his face. "Way too many soft female beings to discover, oh, yes, the lovely women. And altered states to explore."

Alarm pierced Paul's focus on himself, along with the old resentment of what Danny's hell-raising had done to their parents. "You still do drugs?"

"No, no more drugs. Honest." Danny held his beer can a little higher and took a swig.

Paul tried not to frown at what he hoped wasn't a substitute addiction. "I used to worry a lot when you went to Chicago. Prayed every night for you. Maybe that's part of what propelled me into the priesthood."

Danny raised his eyebrows and grinned. "Afraid you'd follow in your big brother into a quagmire of depravity?"

Paul heaved a small snort of irony. "God knows, I imitated everything else you did. I was relieved as hell when Mom wrote you'd done the rehab, gotten your law degree and gone to work for the ACLU. Real sorry to hear about your divorce, though."

"Thanks. 'Course, the ACLU was years ago. I work a good bit for the EPA now, especially water rights. And I've been with the Population Connection for four years."

"The what?"

"Used to be Zero Population Growth."

"Oh, yeah, I think I heard the bishop mention that once."

Danny rolled his eyes. "Probably in the same breath as *plague* and *pestilence.*"

Paul grinned. "'Damnation' was the word, I think."

"So what are you going to do now?"

The question slapped Paul sharply back into the vacuum of uncertainty. He struggled for breath. "I don't know. Look for some kind of job, I guess. Maybe teach again later on, but right now I don't want anything... demanding. I have a lot of sorting out to do. About..." He couldn't make himself say it.

Danny's voice came without its usual bombast. "God? Did you leave that, too?"

Paul clenched his hands till the knuckles were white. His voice shrank to a whisper. "I don't know. I'm afraid to ask the question. If that's all gone, I don't even know what I am. Or how to distinguish right from wrong."

Danny rotated his can until the beer swished. "That's the part I remember, too." He thought a minute. "I guess throwing over the church *and* God leaves a...a kind of void that you have to fill with a personal ethic. And some of the church's 'shalt nots' were right on target. You won't throw them all away."

Danny lapsed into his own past for a minute and then shook his head. "I wish I'd discovered my own ethic before I did myself and some other people a lot of harm. You'll be fine, Paul. You're a better man than I. You always were. You don't need the crutch of the church to be a good man. Or a God either, if that's where your thinking takes you, believe me. You have my support. For ethics and honesty, give me an atheist any day."

"Atheist..." Paul could hardly say the dreaded word, and it came out slowly. He forced his hands to relax and looked out toward the fading light.

"In the meantime," said Danny, "you stay here as long as you like. The old sofa makes into a bed that doesn't dislodge too many vertebrae, and we'll get you some clothes tomorrow right after I get back from work. You need money to get you started? I don't have much, but I can spare a little."

Though his eyes stung and a lump formed in his throat, Paul managed to say, "No, that's the one problem I don't have to worry about for a while. I didn't get much of a stipend, but everywhere you go as a priest, people give you things free, so I didn't get to spend much either. I wrestled with my conscience a good bit about keeping what I had but then decided I'd earned it. And thanks, Danny."

"Well, that's settled, then. And why don't you take tomorrow to drive up in the mountains? They have a healing quality about them that'd do you good."

Danny went back inside for two more beers. "There's just one thing," he said, settling in his chair again after a long swig and a gaze at the dark silhouette of the mountains against the last light. "Saturday I have to leave town for a few days. Convention in Clearwater, Oklahoma."

"A population convention?"

"No, my party. It's August, you know. National political conventions."

Paul stared in surprise. "I know the Republican convention starts in a few days in Seattle. I thought the Democrats were going to Miami. When did they move it to Oklahoma?"

"They didn't. I'm in the Earth Rights Party. We chose Oklahoma because it's centrally located, and we thought the name Clearwater was symbolic."

"The Earth Rights Party? Never heard of it."

"Not everybody has. It was formed after the country's embarrassing performance at the environmental summit in Brazil in '92. But you'll be hearing a lot about us soon. We're small—okay, minuscule—but growing, especially after George W's abrogation of every environmental treaty we ever signed and his cavalier attitude toward the environment. We're registered in every state. Want to join?"

Paul laughed. "Well, I can't stand either of the others, so why not?"

"Wow. That was easy." Danny's smile turned sheepish. "This one's a real commitment for me, Paul."

Paul gave him a sidelong look. "That doesn't sound like the Danny I remember."

Danny nodded. "I know. News flash. But I really am serious about the environment and trying to save what's left of a beautiful earth. I don't know many of the other party members yet, so I'm looking forward to the convention." He clapped Paul on the shoulder, drained his beer and went for another.

Paul gazed at the emerging stars above the mountains and felt some the terrifying uncertainty lift from his shoulders. Danny would help him for a week or so, at least till he got a job and could figure out how and where to spend the rest of his life. Danny's life was stable now, wasn't it? Just like in the days at home, although the beer drinking brought back memories of the doper Danny, irresponsible and totally unpredictable.

Still, what choice did he have? Paul allowed himself a little of the old feeling of safety.

CHAPTER THREE

P aul slid a long application form onto the plain folding table in the Lord and Taylor's store at Denver's Cherry Creek Mall. He sat down and tried to see himself clerking in the shoe department he'd passed on his way to the personnel office. It was no more difficult than visualizing himself selling used cars or sporting goods, or driving a taxi in a city he didn't know—jobs he'd already been denied before they'd even given him a form to fill out. At least the store had done that much.

The Denver economy had been uninterested in him for three days. This application would probably be a waste of time, too, but he certainly couldn't give up without a try, especially as this one was a full-time job with benefits. And if he had to work weekends, fine. He thought of the long string of Saturday evenings he'd spent sitting in a confessional listening to doubt and frustration and pain. His spirits rose slightly. He pulled the form closer and began to fill it out.

Name: Paul Thomas Greer
Date of Birth: June 22, 1956
Education: Diploma, Jesuit High School, New Orleans,
Louisiana
> B.A., Theology, History, International
> Affairs, Current Events, Loyola
> University, New Orleans
> M.A., World History, Georgetown
> University, Washington, D.C.

Work Experience:

A surge of adrenaline pumped up his heart rate. He could simply fill in his teaching job at St. Simon's. There was no blank to fill in his ordination. He could just leave it out. They weren't interested in... Well, actually, they might check with the school and find out about his abrupt departure.

That raised a depressing thought. He had to call and let them know he wasn't coming back. Guilt flooded him for the hundredth time, and his burn scar itched. He cast about for guidance.

What had Danny said? You had to be ethical.

Paul got up and paced behind the other applicants, all years younger than he. No more subservience to the church laws: he didn't have to be obedient to anyone, he didn't have to be poor, he didn't have to be celibate. What *did* he have to be to maintain his sense of decency? Honest. It was a place to start.

He sat down, breathed deeply, and wrote:

> Paper route, age 11-15
> Parish priest, St. Simon's parish and
> School, New Orleans (Ex-priest)
> Teacher, History, Current Events,
> International Affairs, St. Simon's
> School for boys, New Orleans

It looked pathetic. He had absolutely no training in sales of any kind.

An hour later a pleasant looking woman opened the office door. She held a clipboard and peered out through round glasses. Her broad hips bulged at the sides of a thigh-length pink vest.

"Mr. Greer?" she said, scanning the applicants.

When Paul stood, she stepped forward and shook his hand. "This will just take a few minutes," she said to the others and waved Paul into her office.

I knew it, thought Paul.

"I'm Alberta Wynne," she said as she closed the door. "This is an interesting application, Mr. Greer, to say the least. Ex-priest. When did you leave the priesthood?" Her hips wiggled under the pink fabric as she walked ahead of him.

Paul sat down in the chair she pointed to, stunned by the question. He felt his face go red. "Saturday."

Ms. Wynne froze halfway to a seated position in the chair next to him, changed her mind, and walked around the desk. She took off her glasses, and her hazel eyes pinioned him like an insect to a display board. "So this would be your first real job."

Paul stared back and forced himself to smile.

She set his application aside. "Well, I'm sure you understand, we prefer applicants with experience."

Paul felt his shoulders slump and stifled the desire to slide off the chair into a praying position. "Look, Ms. Wynne, I can assure you, you wouldn't regret hiring me. I really need this job."

"I imagine you do," she said, "but I suspect all the others out there would say the same thing, and I wish I could give them all jobs."

The set of her shoulders and the grip she had on her pen told him she'd made up her mind.

Paul nodded. "Of course. I'm sorry I wasted your time. If there'd been any jobs in anything besides sales and computers and taxicabs in the want ads, I would have applied elsewhere." He stood to go, but allowed himself a parting shot, since he wasn't going to get the job anyway. "I never knew people thought the work of a priest was *un*real." He turned toward the door.

His hand was on the knob when she said, "All right, Mr. Greer. Wait a minute. I didn't mean to insult you."

Paul heard paper riffling, and when he turned back, she was frowning at his application again.

"Your educational record speaks for your intelligence; you're ridiculously over-qualified, but untrained. So I can't offer you the full time job we advertised. But I may be able to take you on part-time in men's shoes as a kind of probation. Eight dollars an hour plus four percent commission. I'd have to check with Mr. Roberson, the general manager. If he agrees and it works out on both sides, you could re-apply for full time in a few months. Would that suit you?"

Paul was at the desk again by now. "Yes, it would, and thank you."

"Well, with your record, I feel we can at least count on you for integrity."

Without thinking, Paul reached down, grabbed her hand, and shook it. "You have my word on that."

"Mind you, I'm not promising anything. And I know Mr. Roberson seldom hires part time help. He's of the old school, convinced part-timers have no loyalty to the company. There's not much chance he'll pass on this, but I'll put in as many good words as he lets me. I'll call you as soon as I know."

Paul's hopes sank again, but he thanked her and left, walking past the other hopefuls. Well, he thought, back to the classifieds.

CHAPTER FOUR

D anny left his room at the Redneck Inn, reeling slightly from a six-pack already gurgling in his stomach. He walked across the dust-blown highway to the site of the Earth Rights Party's first national convention. According to a sign leaning in the wind, the drab, one-story building housed the Clearwater billiards parlor, the Jehovah's Witnesses, the Elks, the quilting circle, and the VFW. He detoured into the billiards room to fetch a beer and then went into the meeting hall to do his part for the earth.

The hall was a square cavern of dreadful acoustics and opti-mistic proportions—room for at least three hundred, half again the current population of Clearwater. About two hundred of its brown aluminum and vinyl chairs stood in uneven rows that made Danny feel seasick. The sixty or so members sitting mostly at the back emphasized the emptiness of the room.

He made his way along a dingy side wall, where a row of tables offered name tags; party information; and brochures from Mom

Earth, Save the Seas, Greenspeak, Earth Patrol, and a number of lesser-known organizations.

He skirted the podium at the front, above each corner of which a cluster of red, white, blue, and green helium balloons sailed on drooping strings. A two foot sign hung from the front, announcing ERP. Behind the strings, two men were fiddling with a microphone, one in a suit, the other in overalls.

Dismay sloshed in Danny's stomach with the beer. He turned to appraise the gathering. So few people for a convention. Not that he'd known what to expect, but this was certainly a let-down. Nothing like the other conventions. Of course, the big parties had all the money in the world to spend—and spent it for glitz and fanfare. If *his* party had that kind of money, they'd spend it buying up endangered lands. Still, they could have sprung for a small band.

About a dozen or so newcomers sat down, singly or in small, awkward groups, joining those at the back.

A deafening screech shocked Danny and shattered the few tentative conversations of the delegates, who slapped their hands over their ears. It was sliced off and replaced by a hollow drone and then silence.

"Sorry, folks," shouted the man in the suit. "We'll get the sound system going in a few minutes."

Danny looked around to check out the females and began to feel out of place. Most of the delegates looked like left-over dopers, the types who live in psychedelically-painted school buses. Now the collection of home-made campers he'd passed on the outskirts of town made sense.

One of the few people besides the man at the microphone who looked halfway mainstream was a woman sitting at a table on the other side wall under a big "Membership" poster. She was a Helen of Troy compared to any of the other ladies.

He smiled and took another swallow of beer, thinking, *yes, yes, might as well sign Paul up with the membership chairman. Oops, chairperson. Chairdoll. Tsk, tsk, no, chairlady. Definitely lady.* A lady with his own interests at heart.

She was scanning the crowd hopefully and brightened as he approached. When she looked up, her earrings danced, small beaded patterns with tiny silver feathers dangling from them. A necklace with a pendant showing a beaded white buffalo hung over her plain blue blouse.

"Would you like to join the Earth Rights Party?" she asked in a voice as smooth as black velvet. She was in her mid-thirties, had long, straight black hair and intense black eyes.

Danny set his beer can on the table, bent down to her, and beamed. "I'm already a member, but I want to sign my brother up. Nice to meet you. My name's Danny Greer."

She leaned away from him, glancing at the can that teetered on the edge of small pile of cards. "Yes, fine, here's the form. All we need is his name, address, and phone number."

Danny wrote on the index card and held it out so that she had to take it from his hand. He waited a second to let go, but she didn't look at him. She perused what he'd written.

"Good, another member from Colorado." She moved his beer can with thumb and index finger and slipped the new card under the others. "Thank you," she said with a this-conversation's-over smile and peered around him for other potential members.

Danny broadened his smile until his cheeks hurt. "That's actually *my* address. In case you ever want to get in touch. My brother's just moved in with me temporarily."

"Aha. That should be no problem, as long as he keeps us informed. You know, of course, we don't have a primary election like the big parties. Whoever is nominated here will be our candidate. So your brother has plenty of time to get himself registered with a permanent address before the general election."

"Right. Well, nice meeting you...Emma," he read from her name tag. "If you like, we could meet afterwards..."

She cut him off. "No, thanks."

She still hadn't looked directly at him, but Danny wanted to look in those black eyes. There was something about them...

The man in the suit tapped on the microphone and dismissed the man with the overalls.

"Okey doke, folks, let's get this convention on the road." He waved his hands above his head, clapped in the manner of a cheerleader, and then turned red. "How 'bout if you folks at the back wander on up this way. Just in case the sound system starts acting up again and I have to shout. Ha ha. Come on, now. I don't bite or anything."

While the bulk of his audience got up and moved forward a few rows, he took off his suit coat and threw it on a seat in the front row. Sweat crescents lined the armpits of his shirt.

"Okey dokey, folks. I'm Gordy Johnson from Pensacola. I know you've heard of me 'cause you all got letters from me announcing the time and place of the convention. So now you can put a face to the name." A short, slender man, he stepped from behind the podium. A spaghetti spot graced the bottom of his dolphin tie, but he covered it with his hand. He gave them a big smile and rotated his head to show them both profiles. "Now, I suppose you've all had a chance to read the platform."

Three ladies with various shades of blue hair and the aura of retired teachers nodded to him from the front row. The rest of the delegates peered sheepishly at each other's materials to see what the platform looked like. On the right of the room, a tall bald man half rose from his chair, reached across to the table under the big "Platform" sign, and slipped a stapled sheaf of papers off it. Next to him another followed suit, then several others; and the movement flowed across the room like a stadium wave, followed by an embarrassed titter.

"Well," said Gordy through a light electronic squawk, "we'd better take a few minutes to read through it, then."

Danny cast another smile in Emma's direction, but she got up without noticing him and started for a seat among the delegates. Danny headed for the platform table.

CHAPTER FIVE

P aul kicked his shoes off, stretched out on Danny's bed with a cold Coke, and clicked on the small TV on the dresser. He pulled his legs up to massage his aching feet. Two days of standing on the job, and he was exhausted. You'd think Lord and Taylor's could lay some rubber mats behind the cash registers.

A small rush of guilt passed through him. He should be grateful, *was* grateful for the job, even if the general manager had made it clear he'd allowed him to be hired against his better judgment and would watch him with eagle eyes. Still, mats would be nice.

Standing for an hour at mass was never like this. A high mass flashed back, compressed into an instant's crushing memory: the organ, the choir, the incense, the chanting of the prayers, the hush that enveloped the ritual of communion, the jingling bells as he raised the host. The bells changed tone and screeched to a crescendo. He blinked. The TV was blaring a fanfare for some used car lot.

He switched to Channel 4 for the news. Maybe he'd get a glimpse of Danny at the Earth Rights convention.

Royce McClain faded into view from a booth above the convention center in Seattle, his finger pressed against the studio speaker in his ear. Below him thousands of delegates in straw hats milled about, seeking their seats and jiggling placards announcing their candidates or their states. A Sousa march blared from a dozen mammoth speakers hanging from the ceiling, flanked by huge nets of balloons. Glitzy bunting, streamers, and helium balloons, all in red, white and blue, festooned the platform. Cameras panned the crowd; their images moved at sickening speed on the enormous monitors.

The cameras focused briefly on the bitter face of Clive Jaubert, Speaker of the House, who had been inched out in the primaries by the environmental vote in California. He was about to climb up to the platform. He noticed the camera on him, flashed a smile, and turned to glad-hand a delegate.

"Good evening, and welcome to the ABS news, coming to you from the Seattle Convention Center," Royce McClain began. "As you can see, the air of expectation is feverish, with the convention only two hours...

Paul ignored McClain's comments on Joseph Landsdon, the aged senator from North Carolina, who was vying for the candidacy with George Carrington, the rising star from Minnesota. Instead he watched the chaotic activity in the background. So much hoopla, he thought. Looks more like a high school pep rally than a political convention. What on earth does this have to do with government? The party could spend the money to do so many good things.

He watched the entire half-hour broadcast for news of the convention in Oklahoma. He switched channels during commercials. No one mentioned Clearwater or the Earth Rights

Party. Nor the Libertarians, the Socialists, or the Prohibitionists, who always fielded a candidate but never got a passing word from the media. And then when the League of Women Voters rubber-banded a sample ballot to your doorknob, you got a shock over the dozen or more parties out there promoting candidates you'd never heard of.

The Earth Rights Party. Represented in every state. Paul remembered now and laughed aloud. He'd just joined it, if Danny had carried through. Probably too late for poor old mother earth, anyway.

Still, one party was trying to prolong her life. It deserved as much support as the big parties that were in the pockets of special interests, no matter how loudly they claimed otherwise. Well, at least the Earth Rights Party had a serious, non-profit agenda. Now he was glad he'd told his brother to add his name to the list of intelligent people, like Danny. What could it hurt?

Their convention had to be more appropriate to the democratic process than this.

The telephone rang, jarring him.

"Look, Danny," said a grating voice, "you're gonna have to..."

"Excuse me, this is not Danny. He's in..." Something caught at Paul's mind. "He's out of town for the weekend. You want me to give him a message?"

"Yeah, tell him Floyd called. Tell him to watch his back."

The connection clicked off, and Paul laid the handset on the bedside table, frowning.

CHAPTER SIX

Even with beer sloshing in his brain, Danny finished reading the platform before most of the delegates and looked around, feeling the disappointment settle in his chest again. What a Party. Most of the people looked as frayed and out of style as the clothes they wore.

The face of a middle aged woman caught his eye. A perfectly ordinary looking woman, only her face had something that made him look closer. Knitting his forehead, he examined all the members he could see from where he sat as they looked up from their reading. They had something in common. There was an intensity about them, and something else he couldn't find a name for. Serene determination, maybe? Now there was a beer induced description. Something earthy. Maybe they'd all been trees in a previous life.

Certainly, he had no right to judge them personally, but as national voters, they'd be a sorry lot. And there weren't enough of them to stir up a grass root in sandy soil.

The loudspeakers spat out a dry *phht* when Gordy Johnson tapped the microphone.

"Okey doke, delegates, everybody finished with the platform by now?"

Most of the delegates nodded. A few latecomers glanced around and headed to the table under the platform banner.

"I move the platform be accepted as written," said a voice from Danny's left, the stirring, dark voice of Emma, lovely membership chairlady.

"Secon' the motion," he shouted and turned to give her a smile of total agreement and warm-hearted support. She was not looking. He drank the last of his beer in a great draw and set the can on the empty chair next to him.

"Is there any discussion?" asked Gordy.

An arm in a mauve sleeve went up in the front row, and Gordy nodded at it.

"On page three, paragraph 11, subsection 4 there's a mistake in the spelling," squeaked one of the school teachers. "It's not enviro-ment, it's enviroNment."

"How 'bout if we all stand up and introduce ourselves as we contribute to the discussion?" asked Gordy.

The woman rose, her face flaming. "May-Belle Washburn, delegate from Great Falls," she stammered. "And these are my friends, also members, Lisbeth Chesterson and Maggie Brownell."

Lisbeth and Maggie shushed her with flapping hands and great tittering.

"Okey doke, thank you Mabel, let's all make that correction, page...?"

"Three. Paragraph 11. Subsection 4."

Gordy flipped through the pages. "Gotcha. Everybody got that?" he asked as he penciled in his change. No one else made a move.

A girl in a short black leather skirt and an embroidered peasant blouse stood up a few seats from Danny. "I'm Marianna," she said, turning completely around. She looked as if she expected everyone to recognize her.

"Marianna...?" asked Gordy, waiting for a last name.

"Just Marianna. See, I'm going to be a rock star singing to Mother Earth." She waited a second. "After the meeting I could audition a couple of pieces for you, like maybe for TV spots and stuff."

The young bearded men around her clapped, and someone jingled a tambourine.

"That'd be nice," said Gordy after two perfunctory claps. "Was that your question?"

"Uh, no. I just didn't get something on page nine. I wanted to ask what an aquifer is. So I could maybe use it in a song. If I can think of something to rhyme with it. And why the government should control all of them."

Gordy thrust his hand in Emma's direction.

She stood and turned to face most of the delegates. "An aquifer is underground pool or rock saturated with water, often water that's been trapped there for thousands of years with no source of renewal. As water supplies all over the world diminish or become too polluted to drink, there's increasing talk of tapping the aquifers. Because they're the last source of clean water on Earth, we don't feel they should fall into the hands of people who will simply sell water to the highest bidder. If we have to use the water at all, which is not without risks, it should be there for everyone."

"Like, wow," said Marianna and sat down.

"Any other discussion?" asked Gordy. "No? Aha, the gentleman in the very back row."

The delegates turned to the back.

"Abel Martinez, from Deming, New Mexico," said the man. He was wearing a T-shirt with "I ain't fer fur" across the front. "This section about undamming all the rivers and banning irrigation from them, putting them back in their natural state— are you talking about the Colorado and the Rio Grande and all like that?"

Gordy looked over at Emma, she looked at the man sitting next to her, and they nodded. "You bet we are," said Gordy.

"You'll never get the Colorado farmers and ranchers to go along with it. Nor the people that get their power from the dams. Not to mention California. I figure that's prett' near the whole Southwest. It'll never fly."

Gordy Johnson took on the air of a teacher to the very young. "Well, Abel, this is a long term goal and none of these planks in our platform will work until we get the population under control. And, of course, we got to shut down all those cities leaching water from the rivers and aquifers that have already been tapped to build golf courses and gambling meccas in the middle of the desert. *Then* there'd be plenty of water to let them flow naturally." He caressed the delegates with his eyes like a benevolent father.

"Besides," said a raspy voice from the middle of the room, "we're never gonna get *elected*, anyway."

Emma was on her feet immediately. "That may be true, sir," she said, her voice full of indignation, "but that doesn't mean we don't take this seriously. We might waken a few people to the plight of the Earth, on which we all depend. While we're still such a small party, that's a perfectly acceptable goal."

Danny turned to applaud Emma's fervor, clapping all alone, but she was still looking at the skeptic.

"Yes, indeedy," chimed in Gordy as the not-fer-fur man sat down again several shades darker than before and the doubting Thomas scratched at his eyebrow. "So, is there any more discussion of the platform? No? Sure? Well, let's put her to the vote then. All those in favor..."

Every hand in the room went up.

"Good, the platform stands as written and corrected for spelling." He clapped a couple of times and a ragged applause followed.

"Okey doke, I guess we can get on to the issue that's bated our breath for months: who's going to represent the Earth Rights Party on the ballot?" He stood back from the microphone and gave a slyly modest smile.

May-Belle put her hand up as far as her shoulder, and Maggie reached over and shoved it as high as it would go.

Gordy smiled broadly and recognized her, "Ah, the good Mabel from Sioux Falls. You have a nomination?"

"May Belle, *Great* Falls. No, I just want to say, well, you know how much scandal there was in Washington a few years back, lady-stuff, if you know what I mean..."

"Can't hear you," yelled Danny.

"She's talking about all the sex scandals," Gordy thundered through the microphone.

Danny reached up and massaged his scalp a little, trying to rub out the stupid phase that sometimes came when he'd over-shot a six-pack.

May-Belle turned to face the audience, scarlet-faced from her mauve collar to the roots of her blue hair. "We all know what happened with Clinton. Well, maybe not the youngest of you. I just think we ought to be sure we nominate someone with an impeccable reputation. Even if we're not going to carry the election, the press might give us a little attention, and we don't want to be embarrassed by our own candidate."

"Any discussion?"

"I agree," squeaked Maggie and Lisbeth in unison.

No one else said anything.

"I nominate you, Gordy," said the man next to Emma.

Gordy beamed, but the smile faded quickly. "Thanks for your confidence, Steve, but I...ah...find I must...ah...respectfully decline the nomination."

"But I thought..."

Danny laughed aloud and was suddenly the target of all eyes. "I got a candidate for you if you want one who's squeaky clean. My brother. He's just out of the priesthood. A pristine candidate for a pristine world, that's my brother Paul Thomas Greer."

"You can't do that," Emma cried. "He just this minute joined and he isn't even here. You don't know if he'll run."

"Of course he'll run. What's the problem? There's not a snowball's chance in hell he'll ever be elected."

The ain't-fer-fur man stood and shouted. "Listen, we know what a lot of those priests have been up to. It was in all the news. You sure your brother wasn't one of them?"

Danny turned to face him with his hands up, palms out. "I guarantee there's no sex scandal attached to him. He's the finest man I know."

"He sounds nice to me," chirped May-Belle.

Emma glared at Danny and began thumbing feverishly with her companion through a notebook. For a minute the riffle of pages was the only sound in the room. "It doesn't look like it's against any of the by-laws for him to run," she admitted through clenched teeth.

"Why don't you tell us more about your brother, uh...what did you say your name was?"

Danny hauled himself to his feet and felt his knees go weak as noodles. He should have passed on the last beer. "My name's Danny, that is David Anthony Greer, from Denver. My brother has just left the priesthood. He's a very intelligent man, has degrees in international affairs or political science, something along those lines. So even if, by some fluke, he got elected, he'd at least be knowledgeable."

"I second the nomination," said May-Belle.

"Okey doke, nominated and seconded," said Gordy. "Paul... he has the same family name as you?"

"Greer."

"Greer."

"That has such a nice ring, don't you think? We might even win with a name like that on the ballot," said May-Belle.

"Well, are there any other nominations?"

"I nominate myself," said Emma after a pause.

"Good, why don't you tell the other delegates something about yourself, Emma?"

"My name is Emma Light in the Lodge, and I'm three quarters Achappassi and one quarter Shoshone. Native American. I grew up on the Buffalo Creek Reservation in Wyoming, where I now practice law. I often represent the tribe, but lately I've also moved into environmental and other issues. I'll tell you right now that I'm not popular with loggers, miners, or polluting industries. I believe literally in the Earth as Mother and I'm serious about doing what I can to save her before we destroy her with our so called 'way of life.' If I'm nominated, I'll do everything I can to get our word out to the people." She sat down to a respectful hush.

Danny turned and looked at her until Gordy said, "Okey doke, thank you, Emma. Now, any other nominations?" He looked around the room. "No? Sure?"

Abel Martinez shouted, "I move the nominations be closed."

"Second."

"All in favor...well, that seems to carry. You two want to leave the room?"

Danny looked back at Emma. She ignored him and started to rise. Annoyance rose in his throat. "I cast my vote for my brother," he said, getting up.

"I cast mine for myself."

They walked down separate aisles and went out into the corridor. Emma leaned against a poster charting a 1983 Red Cross contributions contest, her arms folded stiffly across her chest. She was staring past her denim broomstick skirt at soft moccasin boots with silver buttons.

"Hey, loosen up, Emma. Can I buy you a beer while we wait?"

"No."

"Listen, I believe in trying to save the earth. After all, I *am* in the party, too, just like you, and so is Paul. He told me to sign him up. But like I said, and that other guy, too, we're *never* gonna get elected, at least not this time around. So why sweat it?"

"*I* still won't be a throw-away-candidate."

"Aha." Danny bent over to look in the angry eyes still glaring at the floor. There was just something about them that he knew he'd see if she'd just look back. When she turned her head away, he shrugged and went for another beer.

When they re-entered the hall, they were greeted by a smattering of applause.

"It was mighty close, but congratulations, Paul...well, Paul's brother. Paul Thomas Greer is the Earth Rights Party's candidate for president," Gordy declaimed.

Danny sat down, feeling a little guilty about Emma. But before he'd pursued that thought, another struck him like a maul. What was Paul going to say about this?

Emma sat down and stared into her lap.

"So, I guess we'll have to open the floor for nominations for vice-president since Paul isn't here to choose a running mate." Gordy looked expectantly around the room. "Doesn't anybody have a nomination?"

Danny looked up from his contemplation of Paul's certain wrath and said, "I nominate Emma."

"Second," said every other delegate.

"Okey doke, we got Emma down. Any other nominations?"

"Closed."

"Second."

"All in...carried. All those in favor of Emma say 'aye.'"

"Aye" came back in chorus.

"All opposed?"

Silence.

Danny grinned at Emma, certain of her gratitude for his conciliatory gesture and her position on the slate. She answered with a chilling smile and turned to say something to her companion.

CHAPTER SEVEN

"You did *what?*" Paul exploded, dropping his slice of home-delivered pizza. It landed half on his plate and half on Danny's glass table top. "Are you out of your mind? You must have been falling-down drunk to come up with an idea like that."

Danny lifted his hand to interrupt, but Paul leapt to his feet. He paced off the confines of the apartment in huge strides, ranting and slicing the air with his arms. When he ran out of steam, he stopped and jabbed his finger toward the phone that was sitting on the arm of the sofa. "You get on that phone this instant and tell them I decline the nomination. There's no way in hell I'm going to have my name on a nationwide ballot for president."

Danny put his hands up, palms out. "Hold on, Paul. It's no big deal."

"What do you mean, 'no big deal'? I have enough on my mind right now. I can't 'deal' with it." He grabbed the phone and it dinged as he slammed it onto the table. "Undo it *now*, you hear me?"

Danny set his shoulders. "Just calm down. Really. There's no way you'd ever be elected. We just want to run a candidate so the world begins to realize we're here. In a few years we may be a force to be reckoned with, but right now, you said it yourself, hardly anybody's even heard of us. You don't have to do a thing. Not a single thing. You don't have to give a speech, shake a hand, kiss a baby..."

"I don't care. Did it for one minute occur to you what this might do to my ex-parishioners?"

"Your parishioners?" Danny frowned in concentration. "Oh, I guess it didn't. To tell the truth, I don't remember all of it. I do remember laughing at something."

Paul knew that look. It meant Danny remembered more than he was admitting. He growled and shook his head. "Of course not. It was just like the old days, wasn't it, when you'd do something utterly insane and then hardly know you'd done it? Think, Danny. How would you feel if you even imagined someone who knew your deepest sins was sitting in the Oval Office? I won't do it, you hear? It's absurd." He turned his back on Danny and breathed hard, trying to focus on the silhouette of the mountains in the dusk. "Whatever possessed you to do this to me?" Paul turned back and stared down at him, waiting.

Danny chuckled. "Well, as a matter of fact, I do remember this little old lady who was concerned about all the sex scandals a few years back, so I proposed you as one candidate..."

Paul twitched from his head to his feet. "What?! The one candidate who's never had sex?! Why don't you just take out a national advertising campaign," he shouted. He waved his hands to write the headlines in the air, 'PAUL GREER, NO SMEAR,' 'MY BROTHER THE VIRGIN.' You had absolutely no right to do this."

Danny got up and put his hands on Paul's shoulders. "Listen, Paul, I admit I was a little drunk and I apologize. It popped out as a joke..."

Paul batted Danny's arms aside. "A JOKE? Are you..."

"...but it's done, you're already our candidate. And it's really nothing, I promise you. You're never going to be in the Oval Office. You'll be nothing but a faceless name at the bottom of the ballot and no one will even look at it, even ex-parishioners. You know how people feel about independent candidates and splinter parties. What with both major parties against them in Congress, they'd never get anything done. This country isn't ready to elect a third party and probably never will be. Just be cool and think about it. Give it till tomorrow night."

Paul narrowed his eyes to suspicious slits. "What's tomorrow night got to do with it? What else haven't you told me? Not that it matters. I'm not having my name on that ballot."

"Just meet the vice-presidential candidate. She's from Wyoming. She's a knock-out, Paul. You'll really like her. She's dead serious about all this save-the-earth stuff, way more than I am. She's very sincere. Dedicated. She could even be an ex-nun. Willing to sacrifice everything for what she believes. You can identify with that, can't you?"

"Are you telling me she's coming here?"

"Well, yeah, driving through on her way home. It took some doing to get her to agree to meet you after...ah, with her busy schedule and all. When the nominations were settled, I worked with her and the party chairman on advertising strategies, a couple of speeches..."

"What speeches? I thought you said..."

"*You* don't have to give them. She's going to take them on, just a couple of appearances with the Sierra Club, stuff like that."

"Forget it. Tell her not to come."

"I can't. Come on, Paul. At least do that much for me. If you meet her and still want to back out, maybe she'd be willing to replace you, and I practically had to beg her to come. I...ah, I sort of wanted to see her again, anyway. This one's different, Paul, I swear."

Paul heaved a disgusted sigh. "I might have known there was a woman in this fiasco. If she's coming, I'll have to meet her. But don't think some 'knock-out ex-nun' is going to make me change my mind. She could parade through that door with a marching band and a thousand flags. I still want my name off that ballot."

CHAPTER EIGHT

"Get that, will you?" Danny yelled over the drone of his razor.

Paul pushed the buzzer to release the door in the lobby, wiped the last crumbs of grocery-store fried chicken from the table, and checked that three of Danny's four mismatched glasses were clean. He yanked Danny's suit coat off the back of a chair, threw it into the bedroom, and went into the hall.

The elevator door slid open to a tuneful chime. A woman much smaller than he but with a willowy figure in a Mom Earth tee-shirt and frayed cut-offs stepped out and looked up and down the hall. She gave him a faint, forced smile.

"You must be Emma," Paul said, riveted by the sparkling onyx of her eyes. "I'm sorry, I don't think Danny told me your last name."

"Light in the Lodge."

His mind stumbled over the unexpected phrase. "I'm sorry, I didn't catch that."

She looked exasperated and raised her voice. "Light - in - the - Lodge. Emma Light in the Lodge. I suppose he didn't tell you I'm Achappassi, either."

"A chap of sea?"

"Achappassi, an Indian tribe. Reservation in Wyoming," she explained without much pretense at patience.

Stunned at his need to put things right with this woman, he said, "I do apologize, Miss Light in the Lodge. I'm not from here and things of the West are still strange to me."

She looked at him sideways, as if trying to run his words through an internal lie-detector test.

He smiled. "Would you know what this old Louisiana swamp rat was talking about if I threw in *beignets* or crawfish *bisque* or *bayous?*"

"No," she said after a second, smiling now.

"I don't think I've ever heard a name that had a more beckoning, welcoming ring. You must be very proud of it."

She regarded him for a minute, looking for a hint of sarcasm, then put out her hand. "I am. Glad to meet you, Paul. Please, call me Emma."

They shook hands. He'd never felt such a shock; her hand and the intense eyes hit him like a jolt through jumper-cables, but he hardly had time to react before Danny rushed from the apartment, still slapping after-shave onto his face.

"Emma," he cried, wiping his hands on a handkerchief. "I see you two have already met. Come on in and let's have a drink."

Emma's manner froze. "I don't drink."

"We can make coffee or tea," said Paul.

"No, thanks. I just came by because it was on the way and your brother insisted I meet you. Anyway..."

"And aren't you glad you did?" Danny interrupted. "Great guy, this Paul, isn't he?" Danny took her arm and steered her into the apartment.

"...I can't stay long," she continued, speaking over her shoulder to Paul. "I still have a seven hour drive ahead of me. I won't get home before one o'clock as it is, and I have to work tomorrow."

"Emma's a lawyer," Danny explained. "Why don't we all sit down?"

"Struggling," she added. "And what do you do?"

No one sat down.

"Shoe salesman, struggling, too. I guess you know..."

"That you just left the priesthood?" she asked gently. She stared openly but not unkindly at him. "I can't imagine starting life all over at...your age. I'd never be able to get in step again."

Paul shifted feet and swallowed to keep his voice even. "It is a...well...a big adjustment."

Emma leaned forward a little. "That was brash of me, Paul, and I'm sorry. My big blunt lawyer's mouth. All I can really say is I admire you. It must have been hard. I'm sure you'll be fine. Danny tells me you have degrees in international law and political science."

Paul glared at Danny for a second and returned to her. "World history, actually. I hope he didn't tout my degrees as qualifying me in any way to run for president." He rolled his eyes and shuddered. "My God, the very words knock me off my feet."

Emma's brows shot up. "I didn't think priests could say, 'My God.'"

"*Ex*-priest. The *ex* does a lot to loosen things up, but not loose enough for this insane idea..."

"Which was none of his doing," Danny interrupted. "I admit it was a stupid impulse, but what could I do once his name was out there? And what harm can come of it?"

Emma put both fists on her hips. "You might have withdrawn the nomination when you realized I was serious about it."

"Wait a minute," said Paul. "Are you saying you actually wanted to be on the ballot?"

"I ran against you."

"Dammit, Danny, *why* didn't you take my name out?"

Danny shrugged and grinned apologetically at Emma.

"Listen, Emma, this is great!" said Paul, "You can run. I don't want to be a candidate. It's too absurd to contemplate. You run. With my blessing. I'll vote for you. Danny can be vice-president."

Danny gripped Emma's arm lightly. "Hey, that's a solution. We can..."

Emma pulled her arm free and shook her head in annoyance. "This is all a waste of time. In the first place, our literature has already gone to press with our names the way they were voted at the convention. In the second place, Gordy's already e-mailed the slate to the election commission. And in the third place," she said, glaring at Danny, "this is nothing to you but a game combined with a little woman hunting. And nothing to you," she said more softly, glancing at Paul, "but a...a nightmare. And maybe you won't do any harm, but I might actually have done some good if I'd been the candidate. Even second on the slate, I *will* try to get our platform over to the public." She looked at her watch. "Now, if you don't mind, I won't waste any more of our time. I've got more pressing things to do than bandy words with a beer-breath playboy and a throw-away candidate." She was gone before the men could say a word.

Paul looked at Danny, whose jaw hung agape. He clapped his own mouth shut and went after her.

"Hang on, Emma," he cried, hurrying down the hall. "That was pretty cruel."

When Paul caught up with her at the elevator, she was studying the plaid carpet, her face red, her lips pressed together.

"Listen," said Paul, "Danny may have been over-interested in you, and if he did anything that was offensive, I apologize. But he means you no harm, I can assure you. He's a good man. A little flighty, maybe. But...ethical. In his way," he ended lamely.

Emma shrugged but looked him in the eye. "That may be, but it doesn't matter. It's not his interest that bothers me. It's the drinking. I've seen too many lives pickled in whiskey bottles and beer cans. I'm terrified of alcoholics." She looked away. "Of turning out the same way."

"I know how devastating alcoholism is. Maybe your terror is a healthy thing." He put a hand up to touch her shoulder but dropped it again when his heart lurched.

Emma nodded. "Maybe."

"Look, I know Danny has a drinking problem. I'm going to confront him with it. Soon. I've done some of that in my line of work."

She smiled. "Selling shoes?"

He smiled back. "Right. So if we all have to see each other again, maybe he'll be different. I know he really..." Paul could not bring himself to say how much Danny had wanted to see her.

She laid a hand lightly on his arm. The warmth of it shot instantly to his scalp and his toes.

"Listen," she said, "I'm sorry I insulted you. I know you had nothing to do with the nomination. Even when Danny suggested you, it was clear the idea had bounced off the top of his head. And tell Danny I didn't mean to lash out like that. Just don't let him think I'm interested, okay?"

Her eyes drew him in like a gentle vortex that would transport him to a place of serenity.

He got in the elevator to escort her to her car. From the fifth to the first, he watched the digital display count off the floors, fruitlessly willing his lump of a tongue to speak, profoundly aware of the lovely roundnesses under the loose Mom Earth tee-shirt and the cut-off jeans. He escorted her to her ancient white Toyota pick-up, where she turned her sparkling black eyes on him again.

"I'm glad I met you, Paul. I doubt we'll see each other again, but I wish you luck in your new life."

He grinned and ran his hand through his hair. "Well, if nothing else, I can see I need lessons in keeping a conversation going with a woman who's not wearing plain blue clothes and a little veil."

Laughing, she climbed into the pick-up, rolled down the window, and shook his hand. Then she was gone.

Paul gazed after the truck until it rounded a corner, started toward the building, stopped, and then walked into the little park across the street. He stroked the palm of his right hand with his left, feeling her hand in it again and trying to process the shock it had given him. He thought back sadly over the wasted years, when he'd simply omitted all the phases boys work through on their way to manhood. He had no idea how to deal with the sensation of a woman. Not that he'd ever see her again. A wrenching thought, but maybe a blessing in his present state.

From the balcony Danny watched Paul, remembering the scene in the hall when he'd come out to greet Emma. The atmosphere between her and Paul had been electric—until he'd broken the flow and she'd shut down. It's a sure bet she doesn't like *me*, he thought. But she seems to like Paul, all right. And his attraction to her is thick as a banana daiquiri. Hardly surprising. Fifteen years with no female companionship. Too unnatural to contemplate. So what could be more natural than a little help from a big brother? Danny smiled into the west.

CHAPTER NINE

As the day waned, Paul returned to the apartment to find Danny sitting on the balcony, beer in hand, probably his second since Emma left. Tension buzzed through him, making him wish there were a way to avoid this. He'd have to ease into it.

He sat in the other patio chair. "She said to tell you she was sorry for lashing out at you."

Danny responded with a huge shrug.

The action surprised Paul. "What's with the shrug, Danny? I know she means something to you. And I don't think it's just because you're both dedicated to saving the environment. Maybe it's just that...intensity she has."

Danny's expression slid into a strange, knowing smile, but he said, "Well, maybe I did come on a bit strong. Or the lady just doesn't like me. You can't woo 'em all, you know."

Paul forced a laugh. "No, I don't, as a matter of fact. Want to hear what else she said?"

Danny winced. "Nope."

"Tough. She said it's not so much your come-on as the drinking that turns her off."

Danny lifted the can. "What, a few beers?"

Paul clenched the armrests to give himself nerve and prevent his voice from flying up an octave. "We both know it's more than a few. Listen, Danny, I've been wanting to say something almost since the day I got here. Only it's hard to do when we haven't even seen each other for so long. Now that I've found my brother again, I just don't want to, well, make any mistakes with you."

Danny stood up, set the can on the table with exaggerated deliberateness, and stepped to the railing. "So don't, then," he said through clenched teeth, facing west.

Paul got up on knees that had gone soft and leaned over the railing to face his brother. "I have to. I care too much, even if I didn't owe you for saving my life the last week and a half. Look, Danny, I've counseled a lot of people with drinking problems."

"I don't have..." Danny said loudly and then clamped his mouth shut. "...a drinking problem," he finished with strained control. His hands were on the railing now, knuckles white.

Paul gulped and forced himself to go on. "You do, Danny. I've heard all the denials and all the excuses. I know you think your 'few beers' are okay because they're not drugs or hard liquor, but you're drinking a great deal. You might consider the idea that you just switched addictions."

"Yeah, yeah, I know. But believe me, I got it under control."

Paul couldn't stop a quick breath-laugh. "Control? Was it under control when you made fools of both of us in Oklahoma?"

A sheepish look flitted across Danny's face. "Okay, that was a lapse." His face hardened again. "Nothing like that will ever happen again. I'm telling you, it's not a problem."

"How do you know? Have you ever tried to quit?"

"I don't need to. I know I can."

Now Paul had him at the place where Danny would have to accept a challenge or admit he was an alcoholic. But he also knew Danny wouldn't simply agree to prove himself. He'd always needed the darer to challenge himself as well. Or offer a reward. Like...what? What on earth could Danny want from him?

He felt Danny looking at him from the corner of his eyes, wondering why the argument had halted.

Paul looked at the sky that had grown dark since they'd started to argue. He drew in a deep breath through thinly drawn lips. "Okay, I'll make a deal with you. If it's like you say and this whole stupid thing really goes unnoticed, I'll leave my name on the ballot if you'll stop drinking until the election's over. Those ought to be equally scary propositions. No, I take it back. Leaving my name on the ballot is a hell of a lot scarier." He put his hand out for Danny to shake. "But I'll do it if you do your part."

Danny dodged the handshake and let out a too-hearty laugh. "Now that's a fine excuse."

"What?"

"You mean you don't know that your lovely lady running-mate is the real reason you're suddenly willing to stay on the ballot? You just want to see her again."

Paul's mouth fell open and he backed away. His hand dropped to his side.

Danny pressed his advantage. "Don't deny it."

"I...guess I can't. Not the attraction, anyway. I hadn't even considered seeing her again. But I'll still take my name off the ballot if you can't stop drinking, and I don't care what kind of chaos it throws your party into."

Paul held his hand out again.

Danny looked down at it, trying to ignore the vibration that had taken over his whole body. What was shaking him up? Fear? Certainly not fear. For sure, he had it all under control, even if the beer left in the can was calling out and his tongue was tingling in response.

The charged atmosphere between his brother and Emma hung in memory like the Northern Lights. No, just keeping Paul's name on the ballot wasn't enough. Danny stuck his hand out without touching Paul's. "Here's the deal I'm willing to make. You also go out with Emma if the opportunity arises. That's your part of the bargain."

Paul squinted at him with amazement. "You're trying to play matchmaker? That's absurd. I told you last night, I can't deal with a woman in my life right now."

"So you're afraid of women. Perfectly understandable after half a lifetime of repressed libido. Jeez, Paul, you just knocked over the walls of an institution that kept your very manhood chained down. How are you going to learn to deal with it if you cloister yourself away behind your own fears?"

Paul paled visibly in the light coming from the living room. "I'm not afraid..."

"Aha!" cried Danny. "Just like I know I don't have a drinking problem. So what's the harm if you see her again?"

Paul regarded him suspiciously for a long time. "Meet her again. Not go out with her. That's all I can promise."

"Okay."

"If the 'opportunity rises,' like you said. Not if you manufacture some 'opportunity.'"

"And you leave your name on the ballot."

"Okay."

"Fine," Danny said, a lot more airily than he felt now that the bargain was closing. "I know I can quit. You run for president and I'll run for sober."

They shook hands and stood for a moment with their arms around each other's shoulders, squinting at the Rockies that had disappeared under the stars.

"I'll just finish this beer, then," said Danny when they turned to go inside.

Paul grabbed it off the table. "You just shook my hand on this," he said. "The bargain started at that moment."

Danny snatched the can and pulled Paul into the kitchen. He poured the remaining beer down the sink with his free arm stuck out in a gesture of defiance. The beer fizzed on its way into the drain. Danny controlled his face and vented his dismay by squeezing the can until it buckled with a tinny clank. He hoped the action looked triumphant. "Satisfied?"

Paul nodded. But then he said, "I hope I'm not going to regret this."

CHAPTER TEN

Emma drove up I-25. By the time she reached the Wyoming border, she'd put Danny completely out of mind and Paul— almost. Imagine starting a new life at—what, forty? Forty-five? He'd had that church to shelter him, make decisions for him all those years. Probably be a total loss, no matter what he tried to do. Or maybe not. He was intelligent enough. Masters degree in world history and he ends up selling shoes. Hopelessly inept when it came to the realities of living, no doubt. Too bad, he had a nice air about him. And a pleasing face under the black hair. She shook her head. By the time she passed Douglas and turned onto highway 59, she'd forgotten him, too.

Her mind ticked off the familiar sights of the southern end of the reservation, barely visible in the starlight: the single erratic oil well that paid the tribe about $10,000 a year, the scattered trailers surrounded by rusting cars and an occasional sweat lodge, the plain boxes of BIA housing areas, and the glint of bottles and cans in her headlights. Farther north she could sense Twin Circles Butte and the reddish cone outcroppings that always reminded her of volcanoes on a tiny planet. She reached Big Sleep a little after one.

She pulled up to the side of the general store left over from a town that had died before the reservation was established and now housed her practice. She started up the outside stairs to her second story apartment. In the dark she stumbled over a pair of legs. She fell forward as a hand shot up and caught in the strap of her backpack and another shoved at her right shoulder. She and the intruder fell down the few steps she had just climbed. She got in one good blow to his ribs.

"Mmmph, ow, that you, Emma?"

"Pop? For God's sake, have you lost your mind? What are you doing on my steps in the middle of the night? It's too cold for you to fall asleep out here."

Raymond Light in the Lodge struggled to his feet, holding to the handrail and his daughter. "I came..." he started. "Uh, I came to...seems to me there was a reason."

"Come on up, Pop, you're already here. You might as well have a cup of coffee before you go home."

She switched on the light she hadn't thought she needed. Her father squinted and put his hand over his eyes. She gathered up her back pack, took his arm and led him up the stairs. "You look awful, Pop. You've been selling your commodities again to pay for the drink. How long has it been since you ate a decent meal? You're killing yourself, you know that, don't you? You gotta quit..."

"Now I know what it was. I came to tell you to watch out for Earl Rides. He really has it in for you now." He let her pull him up the stairs. "You better lay off that stuff about the casino."

"I can't lay off it, Pop, you know that."

"He sounded like he knew ways to make you back off."

"What do you mean? He can't do anything to me."

"He can see that no one comes to you for any law work. And he's taking all the tribal stuff to Frank Three Crow. I heard them talking about it when I was sweeping the hall outside his office just...yesterday? What's today?"

"It's not day, Pop, it's the middle of the night. And thanks for the warning, but Earl's not going to make me knuckle under."

"Your mother told me you'd say that."

"She knows you're here? Okay, come on, I'll put a blanket on the sofa and you can spend the rest of the night there. But I'm kicking you out at seven. I have to be downstairs by eight."

In her office on the ground floor the next morning, Emma opened the mail that had collected in her absence, all bills and junk mail. She checked her calendar. Frank Three Crow was scheduled to come in at nine-thirty about the Texans who'd shot three prong horns out of season on the reservation. She took out the file she'd started and sat down at her desk. When Frank didn't show, she wrote up the minutes of the convention in Clearwater. She cleaned the office and read two issues of *USA Today*. No clients presented themselves before lunch. She took down her EPA guidelines and searched for a law, even the vaguest directive that would be valid, any hook on which to snag the building of a casino on the reservation. There was none.

No clients presented themselves after lunch. By quarter of five she was ready to close her practice for the day, but Earl Rides sauntered in, looking slick and imposing, as usual. His hair hung from the nape of his neck in a long pony tail, and a brand new black leather vest accented his red cowboy shirt.

"Much business today?" he asked, smirking openly.

"None at all, but I guess you knew that or you wouldn't have asked, would you?"

"Nope. I could be good to you, throw a little your way."

"No thanks. I know what you want in return. In the end, it'd cost me my self-respect."

"Come on, Emma. What's it to you if we put up a casino out on the edge of the reservation?"

"Strange, you know, I was just asking myself the same thing: what's it to Earl if we put up a casino?"

He leaned toward her, glowering. "Lucky for you there's no one else here. I can pretend I didn't hear that." He sat down on the edge of her desk. "Look, it's not as if the land could be used for anything else. It's nothing but an old meadow. There's not a tree on it that'd have to be cut, there's not an endangered species within miles of it. It's on the very edge of the reservation. And think what it'd mean for the people. Jobs. Money in their pockets."

"I *am* thinking of what it'd mean to the people. Or, to be more accurate, what it'd *do* to them. I know you've been talking to the tribal councils on other reservations. I know their casinos take in enough to pay as much as $25,000 a year to every man, woman and child in the tribe without their having to lift a finger. But have you seen the people, Earl? Have you asked what's happened to the rate of alcoholism since the casinos came in? Have you asked what percentage of the addicted gamblers are tribal members? Have you asked what happens to people who never have to lift a finger?" She pointed to the front of the office. "Look around you. Are your people fulfilled in any way, even without a casino? Do their eyes look full of purpose when they spend their food stamps, pick up their commodities, or move into BIA housing? The dole provides them with everything but pride."

"Now, don't get started on that old soap-box about rescinding the treaties. They promised to take care of us as long as the rivers flow. Dammit, Emma, they took everything away. We got a right to get something back, and more than the lousy surplus flour and the tasteless cheese and the Spam they send to the commodities warehouse."

"I know we have the *right*. I just think we've come too far from the days when people had to work to survive, when their lives had meaning. And I *will* fight you on this casino. I'll speak before the council, and I'll talk privately to the other members. But I don't delude myself about how the vote's likely to go. So I don't know why you would want to ruin my practice over this."

"You do know, Emma," he said, already heading for the door. The beadwork on the back of his belt read "Rides 'em."

"God, Earl, that was years ago."

CHAPTER ELEVEN

Just home from work four days after Emma's visit, Danny was pacing the floor in his room, loosening his tie as he spoke on the phone.

"Dammit, Floyd, the aquifer is a dead issue, and I told you not to call me at home again. Now let me make those two things clear one last time. Are you listening? Number one: The Arapahoe Aquifer will never be handed over to oil companies that want to branch out, nor, if I can help it, will any other aquifer. Number two: Do not call me here again. I'm going to have this number changed to one that's unlisted, so don't even try." Danny clicked off the telephone and flung it on top of his suit coat on the bed. His hands shaking in anger, he slipped into his old habit and started toward the kitchen for a beer, but the phone rang again almost instantly.

"Goddammit, Floyd, have you ever heard of telephone harassment? You can go to jail for that, and believe me, I won't bat an eye at filing charges..."

"Excuse me. I'm not Floyd," said a soft but stunned voice that couldn't be lying.

"So? Who're you? Some minion of his?"

A short silence followed, and Danny imagined two angry feminine eyes staring at the receiver before she answered.

"My name is Caitlin Pascoe. I'm a reporter for *The Popular Probe*. I'm trying to reach...uh...Paul Greer of the Earth Rights Party."

Danny froze on the way to the kitchen. Ah, shit. The press. He had a sudden foreboding of things reeling out of control. "Gordy Johnson's responsible for this, isn't he? Just like him to sic the paparazzi on me."

"I *beg* your pardon, sir. I'm a respectable reporter for a perfectly respect..."

"Hey, don't get in a huff. It was a joke. What did Gordy tell you?"

"That you're the presidential candidate for his party. What I want..."

His mind racing for tactics, he said, "No, hang on there, ladybug. I'm not Paul."

"'Ladybug'?" she asked, clearly miffed. "Well, manbug, what *are* you? Some minion of his? If you are, perhaps you could arrange an interview. I can come..."

"I'm his brother Danny. And I can tell you my brother's not going to grant you an interview, Miss...Pascal?"

"Pascoe."

"He's a very private person."

"A what? Is this some kind of joke? There's no such thing as a private person in politics, Mr. Greer. Surely your brother knows that."

"Of course, and he knows political campaigns are all about maximum public exposure. Look, it's a long story. If he were here, I'd let him explain why..." Danny winced at the image of Paul's anger if he had to explain so much as his name to a reporter.

But this reporter wasn't going to be put off. "Surely we can work something out. I was hoping to interview both him and the vice-presidential candidate in the next few days."

"Emma, too?"

"Yes, a kind of forum."

"A forum? Not possible, she's not even from around here."

Danny didn't hear the next thing the reporter said because he was busy rethinking his answer. This angel of a ladybug had just handed him a viable excuse to bring Paul and Emma together again. "Listen, Miss Pascoe, maybe I was hasty. And I apologize for my abruptness. Sincerely. I thought you were someone else."

The edge of her voice softened a bit. "Obviously. Apology accepted. So can we work this out?"

"For the sake of airing the party's philosophy, why don't we go ahead and set up a time, and if Paul absolutely declines the interview, I'll call you back.

"Good. Shall we say next Tuesday?"

"No, not that soon. Give me a week or ten days. He needs some advance notice for his...ah...work schedule. And I need time to set it up with the vice-presidential candidate, too."

"No need. I'll take care of that. How about Friday, September fourteenth?"

"No, better give me Thursday if you can. He can take Thursday evenings off more easily. Over dinner sound good?"

The reporter hesitated. "No, that wouldn't work well for me. The mike would pick up all the ambient noise of a restaurant."

"Well, how about dinner first and then the interview here?"

"That'd work. Mr. Greer, what do you know about the other splinter parties? I was thinking of a panel of candidates from all the small parties."

"I don't know anything about them, but I'm certain Paul won't be willing to sit in on anything more than a simple interview. Mind you, I doubt I can even talk him into that, but I'll do what I can. Give me your number. I'll be in touch." He jotted down the number, switched off the phone and threw it on the sofa.

This time he made it to the refrigerator and grabbed a beer. He had his finger on the pop-top, straining to pull it up. His hands were shaking. They shook a lot lately. He ground his jaw, slammed the can back on the refrigerator shelf and shut the door. Damn Paul anyway. Dammit. Dammit. He could do this. He stood for a minute with his head resting on his arm against the refrigerator door before he reached in and grabbed a Coke. A beer would do a lot more to cool his anger at Floyd, to help him think how to convince Paul to do the interview, to stop the intermittent shaking, and to ease the general distemper he'd felt for some days. Okay, since the night he'd promised to quit. Jesus, he'd just mouthed off at a woman with a voice as tropical-soft as a ripe mango. One he might even meet. And Paul was going to give him hell again. Dammit.

He paced about the apartment, sat on the balcony, tried to focus on the mountains in the dying light. When he couldn't drift into the sense of peace they usually gave him, he got up, brought out a sack of pretzels and flopped into a patio chair again. He swallowed at least a third of the Coke in one long draw, gagging on the sweetness of it. "Got to get soda water or something," he muttered, staring at the red and white can. My teeth'll rot right out of my head in six months if I drink half as much of this as I drink—drank—beer.

The front door opened and Paul came in. He kicked off his shoes and threw himself on the sofa.

"God, I'm ready for a vacation," he groaned, letting his feet hang over the armrest.

Danny laughed vindictively, turning in his chair to look through the screen door. "Welcome to the nine-to-five world, little brother."

Paul glared at him. "I had no idea selling shoes could be so exhausting. I had a man come in today who's been in almost every day since I started. He finally decided he wanted a shoe that's been on display the whole time. That very shoe, since all the others in that size had been sold. So I looked all over creation for the mate, and do you think I could find it?"

Danny shook his head grandly.

"Of course not. He wasn't satisfied I'd really tried, so I spent another twenty minutes in the stacks and shoving shoes around on every single display. And when I'd finally convinced him it I wasn't going to find it, he stalked off, saying, "Who steals *one* shoe? If you're too lazy to look for it, I guess you miss a sale. Your manager will be interested in your attitude.' Just what I need. The manager's already sure I don't care whether the store makes a profit. I've seen him watching me. He'd like any excuse to get rid of me."

Danny got up and grinned down at him from the door. Aha, he thought, the perfect moment. He slid the screen open and stepped in. "Well, put that aside. This ought to energize you. Looks like you get to see Emma again."

Paul sat up and squinted at him from under a furrowed brow. "Don't even tell me about it. I know that tone of voice. You've engineered something."

Danny spread innocence all over his face. "Now, little brother, would I do a thing like that?"

Paul gave him a mock glare. "If that were the least example of your idiocy, we'd all be better off."

"Well, I like that! I had nothing to do with arranging a meeting with your heartthrob."

Paul turned serious. "Don't call her that. So what is this meeting?"

"Nothing much. Really. A reporter called me, not the other way around. It's just a little interview with a small paper that no one ever heard of."

Paul flopped down again. "Absolutely not."

"It's some little local rag out of Chicago."

"No."

"Emma's going to be there."

"No. What paper?"

"*The Popular Probe.*"

"Never heard of it."

"See? So what harm can it do?"

"Sounds like one of those dirt rags to me. What does Emma have to do with it?"

"The reporter wants to do an interview with both candidates. Over dinner."

"No. Much as I'd like to see her again, I know this can lead to no good. I couldn't answer a single question about your party. Besides, once something's in the paper it's completely out of our control. It might get back to the parish in New Orleans. I told you my parishioners can't ever know about this." He poked his finger accusingly through the air at Danny. "Ever since you did this to me, the fantasy of actually ending up in the White House, by some horrible fluke, keeps hitting me in the face, and when it does, that's the first thing that springs to mind after the adrenaline subsides. It would be a nightmare for all those people."

"Yeah, I know that's a consideration." Danny heaved an exaggerated, resigned sigh and started toward the kitchen. "Still, it'd be a shame not to see Emma again when there's no chance in this world your ex-penitents will ever know."

"I can't run that risk."

Danny turned, enjoying the clinch. "You *did* make a bargain with me. Remember?"

Paul balled his fist at his side and his jaw worked itself into a display of muscle. "I remember. But that was when you promised I'd never be anything but an unknown name at the bottom of the ballot. The answer is a resounding no."

CHAPTER TWELVE

Standing at a lopsided school music stand that served as podium, Emma faced the tribal council. Behind her the last speaker, one of several who had spoken in favor of Earl Rides' proposal, returned to his seat. Her mouth dried up in the face hostile stares coming from four members of the council and the audience she sensed glaring at her back. This would not make her popular, certainly not enhance her practice, but someone had to bring out the risks they all wanted to ignore.

The seven members of the council sat at two scarred, wobbly tables. Behind and above them, a crudely painted buffalo head adorned about fifty square feet of the school's lunchroom wall. The smell of old school pizza oozed from the painted cinderblocks.

Tommy Suazo, the tribal chairman, sat in the middle with his legs squeezed between the legs of the two tables. His single long braid made a gray stripe down the front of his orange plaid shirt. A leather thong held the hair in place and the silver eagle on the end of it rested on the table. He regarded it with the same ponderous contemplation he exercised in making tribal decisions.

To his left sat Earl, his nephew, dressed in his shiny black leather vest and a blue and gray plaid shirt. His jet black hair was drawn flat over the top of his head, emphasizing his beakish nose.

To Tommy's right sat Leona Lewis, the school's only Achappassi administrator, looking gaunt and tired, her short graying hair hanging in bangs that needed cutting.

Emma took a deep breath. "I'd like to thank you for this opportunity to speak about the casino project," she began. "I've heard the arguments of the other speakers, and I recognize the economic impact casinos can have, but we need to look at the negative possibilities, too. For example, I'm afraid we're too remote to draw crowds. Why would any white gamblers or tourists come so far, when Deadwood is right on the interstate and already has a name everyone recognizes?"

"It's a little thing called advertising," sneered Earl.

"Perhaps some would come," she conceded, "though I can't imagine there would be many or that they would come a second time. And I believe the income that casinos generate should not be our only consideration. Do we know who's actually doing the gambling in tribal casinos?" She paused to let the question hang in the air for a second. "Are the gamblers tribal members? If so, the income is simply flowing into their pockets and out again. Has that enriched their lives in any way or has it just added another addiction?"

"What does it matter?" asked Earl. "If they're poor to begin with, they'll just stay poor. But those who know how to handle the money will spend it wisely, for example, to send their children to better schools or colleges."

Leona leaned forward and glared at him. "Thanks for the slap in the face, Earl."

Emma waited for Earl to apologize. When he didn't, she looked at the council members whose children attended the reservation school. "Do those of you who have the money send your children to other schools where their heritage is ignored? Does anyone here want to do that?" She looked around at the audience and back at Tommy. "And there's the problem of alcohol."

Before she could continue, the aging David Niwot raised his hand as if in school. A hunting guide who'd never found any other kind of work and wore his hunting gear year round, he was sitting next to Leona. "We can regulate that ourselves. We can forbid the sale of alcohol altogether, if we choose to."

"Of course we could," answered Emma. "But can you imagine a casino without a bar? Or would you sell whiskey to whites in the casinos and not to Indians? If we choose to ban alcohol, we might as well forget the whole idea. What has happened to the rate of alcoholism on reservations with gambling? And what of the crime rate?"

"We have our own tribal police. That's what we hire them for," snapped Earl, rolling his eyes toward the ceiling. "What do you...?"

Tommy raised his hand and held it vaguely in the air for a minute. "Just a minute, Earl," he said in his slow way. "Emma, do *you* know for sure that alcoholism and crime have been problems in other tribes as a *result of gambling?*"

"I'd like to study those problems more specifically, but I've seen some others I haven't mentioned yet." She waited for Tommy to ask about them.

He nodded, but it was difficult to know whether he wanted her to go on or was agreeing that alcoholism and crime needed further study.

Emma went on. "When you sent me to Santa Fe for the land rights conference last winter I visited three of the New Mexico pueblos, the Isabela, the Santa Clara, and the San Juanito."

She heard a few people behind her move to the front, and she moved the podium to the side to include them in the discussion.

"Of course, the pueblos are tourist attractions anyway, which we aren't, so the people make a certain amount of money selling their crafts during festivals and what not. That at least ensures that the old arts survive. And even a little of the old way of life. If you discount the church, the old adobe pueblos still look the way they did before the Spaniards came. In their way, the Isabela and Santa Clara get by, and even if they don't make the impression of great prosperity, you have the feeling that the people respect the old ways and live by them as far as they can in the modern world. But more important, you can see they respect themselves."

Earl leaned back in his chair and let his hands hang to the sides. He looked bored to the point of senselessness.

Tommy never took his eyes from Emma, but he put his hand behind Earl's shoulder and shoved him forward. He nodded at Emma.

Watching Earl seethe with impatience and frustration, Emma barely controlled the smile that was twitching at her lips. "The San Juanito pueblo is another story. It's right on the road outside of Santa Fe and seems to have gone over completely to gambling. The pueblo is all neon and glitz and traffic. I just couldn't stand seeing the glitter plastered onto adobe. It made me sad, not only because the old has been plastered over, but because the pueblo has adopted the most crass aspect of the white world to support itself."

"The old ways are dying," said Tommy, fingering his eagle sadly. The older members of the council nodded.

Earl jumped up, and his chair banged against the wall. "The old ways are not dying, Tommy," he shouted.

The audience and the council members gasped.

Earl turned red, sat down, and worked his face till a semblance of calm returned to it. "I apologize, uncle, but the old ways have been dead for a century," he said with forced patience. "And what we're facing now is not how to keep them alive, but what *new* ways work best for our future as a tribe."

"I don't believe a casino will do that," said Emma. "There has to be a way to keep our heritage alive while accepting the best parts of the culture that ran us over. And gambling is surely not the best part. I've heard of reservations in Arizona and New Mexico that have become self-sustaining without bringing in casinos. I think we need to find out how they did it."

Leona Lewis ran her hands through her hair, but the bangs flopped back into place. "I think Emma's given us a lot to think about. At the very least, we ought to know how the people are affected when the gamblers come. I'm ashamed to admit it, but I'm tempted by the thought of an income I don't have to work for. I don't know if I want to pass that on to my grandchildren."

Earl leaned forward to look at her past Tommy. "Did you ever use a food stamp or go to the BIA clinic? That's the same thing as unearned income."

Many in the audience nodded and grunted their agreement.

"Of course," said Leona, "but I can't say it made me feel good about myself. And besides, I don't think I want my grandchildren to grow up with the idea that drinking and gambling are part of Indian life." She addressed the audience. "Is that how you want yours to grow up?"

Those who were fathers and mothers looked away, and no one answered Leona's question.

Tommy gazed toward the back of the room, but Emma knew he was gauging the will of the tribe from those present and wouldn't treat it lightly. He leaned back with his head down for a minute, his hands and the end of his braid in his lap.

He sat upright again slowly and propped both elbows on the table. "Emma, if we postpone this decision, can you go to some of the reservations you were talking about and get information for us? Get answers to the questions you raised?"

"I can get you statistics a lot faster. I would have gone to the library in Casper and used their computer to get statistics on crime rates, accidents involving drunk driving, and so forth; but I was gone for four days. I can still get the numbers for you."

Tommy waved his hand slowly, canceling her suggestion. "I don't put much store in statistics. I put my store in people." He turned toward both ends of the table and addressed the whole room. "It would be wise to get some first-hand information, wouldn't it?"

Five of the council members nodded, and Emma heard some assenting grunts from the audience."

"So can you go to the other reservations?"

"Only if the tribe can pay me for the work, Tommy. My practice has come to a standstill, and I just can't afford the trip."

Earl was up again instantly. "Well, then, send me, too. She doesn't want the casino no matter what. I'll pay my own way. She'll come back with nothing but the answers she's looking for."

Tommy shifted in his chair to stare up at him with his mild eyes then faced Emma again.

As soon as he did, Earl threw up his hands in frustration.

Leona glared up at Earl. "I've known Emma all her life," she said and then looked back at the audience, "just like the rest of you. If there's one thing in her we can respect, it's her honesty."

The vote of confidence touched Emma. "Thanks, Leona."

Tommy looked at Leona. She flipped through some pages in a school binder and said, "We can free up about $100 a day. I'm sorry, Emma. It's all we can do."

"I'll manage on that. I'll sleep in the truck if I have to."

"Well, that's settled, then," said Tommy. "Now, what's next? Frank Three Crow, did you want to report on the action against the Texans?"

Emma went back to her seat and tried to stare Earl down. But his eyes were full of accusation and ancient blood lust, and she looked away.

CHAPTER THIRTEEN

P aul lay on Danny's sofa waiting for the national news and
wondering when the sound of tinkling communion bells
would stop haunting him. He tried to focus on something else,
but the only thing that came to mind was a pair of deep black
eyes that shone like a Light in the Lodge. They only caused him
more malaise, and he wished she'd get out of his mind.

His hand reached for the remote to surf the channels for
the next few minutes but fell on a folded sheaf of papers. He
picked it up and got a sudden but very small twinge of conscience. He'd forgotten the promise to read the Earth Rights
Party platform, and that was at least a week ago. Hardly worth
the trouble now, since he'd told Danny definitely to turn down
the interview.

He glanced at his watch, read the first few lines, and stifled a
yawn. The news would be more entertaining. By the end of the
first page, his head came up off the pillow. By the end of page
two, he was sitting on the edge of the sofa with his mouth open
in shock; page three, pacing the living room floor and slapping

his thigh with the stapled pages at the end of every paragraph. He'd barely started the last page when Danny came in.

Paul put his hand up in a "halt" gesture, and read quickly to the bottom. He looked up, aghast, shaking the platform at Danny's face. "You know what you've done?" he shouted. "You've made me the champion of the lunatic fringe. Have you ever actually read this thing?"

Danny stepped forward without a trace of shame. "Of course I've read it. I even helped frame a few of the planks. And keep your voice down."

Paul's ire rose like a rocket. "I will *not* keep my voice down," he yelled. "You mean you support the idea of placing a cap on the number of children per family?"

Danny slipped out of his suit jacket and hung it over the back of a dining chair. "Well, that or a graduated offspring surtax— the more children you produce, the more you use government services, the more you pay in taxes. We could have gone a step further, you know. In China they've been limiting families for years. They finally realized they could no longer afford to feed an uncontrolled population. 'Course, I know that's a novel thought for someone who just escaped the church."

Paul stared at him until he could draw a breath. "Well, what about this: phasing wood out of the construction of new homes?"

"There are other materials on the market..."

Paul flipped through the pages, ripping them from the staples. "The enforcing of two no-drive days per person per week, the banning of the internal combustion engine by the year 2025, the development of a sustainable non-growth economy, government regulation of all underground water, the restriction of news media to the airwaves and computers?" he shouted, jabbing the offensive subsections. "Saving trees, no doubt. What about books? Are you going to ban those, too?"

"Listen, I know all that must sound pretty radical..."

"**Radical?**" screamed Paul. "Raising taxes to develop ways to clean up the air is radical. These are the psychotic meanderings of...of...some idiot from Pluto."

"Listen, didn't you see the time frame for...?"

Paul grabbed him by the shoulder and spoke now with his jaw clenched. "Just tell me one thing. You did call that reporter and cancel the interview, didn't you?"

"Well, not yet, but..."

"*No buts.* Dammit, Danny, do it this minute."

"Look, Paul, let me give you some of the literature of the Population Connection. When you see what over-population is really doing to the world, these things don't seem as crazy as our racing hell-bent to self-destruction. Read up on it before you condemn it. Will you at least do that?"

"On one condition. Take that damned telephone in hand this second and cancel the interview. There's no way I'm going to have my name connected with this raving lunacy."

"Just a minute, bud. You made a bargain..."

"I don't give a damn about the bargain right now. You can drink yourself into the next world, but I am not doing this interview."

"All right, all right."

"Now."

Three minutes later Danny joined Paul on the balcony. "I left a message. I told her you'd declined the interview in no uncertain terms."

Paul put his hands on the railing and leaned heavily against them, his head down. "Are you still on the wagon?"

"Yeah."

"You sure? Because I will take any excuse at all to take my name off that ballot. I should have put my foot down the minute you told me about this insanity."

"Paul, calm down. Nothing's going to happen, I swear it. Come on, let's go get something to eat. I know a great Chinese place right over there on South Broadway."

When they returned from dinner, there was a message from Caitlin Pascoe on Danny's answering machine. "Hey, gentleman-bug, you can't back out on me now. You said you'd call back if your brother wouldn't do the interview, and you didn't call. I've already booked a flight and a room. And my editor's down my back about a deadline. You leave me in the lurch on this, I could lose my job. You don't have to do anything about lining up Miss Light in the Lodge. I called her myself, and she's agreed to meet me at the Hampstead Inn by six o'clock. She's going through on her way down to some Indian reservation. Don't let me down. Call me at the Hampstead around five on the eleventh so we can plan a place to meet. That's p.m., gentleman-bug."

The voice had lost the yielding tropical tang of a ripe mango and taken on the bite of a green persimmon.

"Great, just great," shouted Paul. "Damn, I should have read your raving-mad document earlier." He strode into the bedroom pulling at his hair with both hands.

CHAPTER FOURTEEN

Danny followed Paul into *Chez Toi* on Cherry Creek's Third
Avenue, shopping haven for Denver's elite. He brushed
a fleck from the shoulder of Paul's sport coat. Inwardly, he
grinned with satisfaction. Whatever there was between Paul and
Emma, he'd just nudge it along.

The hostess slinked forward. Skinny to the point of
emaciation, she was a slash of black from her hair to her
floor-swishing hem. Her smile showed unnaturally white
teeth emphasized by black-cherry lipstick. "You have a reservation?" she purred.

"Yes," said Paul.

"Greer," said Danny. "We're being met. Can you show my
brother to our table while I watch for the ladies from the bar?"

Paul looked at him sharply.

"No problem, I promise," said Danny. "It makes a better impression if someone greets them right away."

Paul hesitated. "Why don't we both wait?"

Annoyed now, Danny lowered his voice. "Paul, trust me. I admit this is harder than I thought, but I'm keeping my end of the bargain. And I could order a drink at the table just as easily."

Paul stepped back, palms out. "You're right. Actually, I don't know why I'm worried when I'm dying for you to fall off the wagon so I can fall off the ballot. Go right ahead. Order several. Strong ones." The hostess turned to lead the way. Paul followed the hostess, who undulated through the tables like a vertical worm. Seated, Paul looked around and began to perspire. He'd never been in one of these bistros with glittery silverware on white linen, rows of sparkling wine goblets, and fresh flowers surrounding the candle. Maybe a lawyer could afford this, but a single dinner would wipe out a shoe clerk's pay check. He reached for the oversized menu, knocking the white napkin-swan from his plate to his lap.

Hoping he looked casual, he perused the lists. The prices of the exotic *hors d'oeurves* alone suggested their spices were imported from a distant galaxy. He laid the menu back on the corner of the table and looked toward the entrance, sneaking glances at nearby tables. The white-gloved waiter was just delivering a tiny sorbet sculpture floating on a lake of pale green sauce crisscrossed by a filigree of refined colors.

Danny sat where he could watch the entrance. He'd just received his club soda when Emma and another woman walked in. He leaped up to waylay them before the hostess reappeared. "Emma," he called.

She turned, and the tiniest breath of disappointment flitted across her face.

"My brother's already at the table. Why don't you go fill him in on the latest from Gordy while I buy Caitlin a drink? You *are*

Caitlin, aren't you?" He smiled at the other woman without actually looking at her.

"Yes," she said, turning eagerly toward the bar.

The hostess wisped up and Emma followed her.

Danny steered Caitlin to his place at the bar. "What would you like?" He looked at her for the first time. She was wearing a light flower print dress and a very sheer matching jacket. She had the beauty of mixed races, curly black hair, a beautiful tan skin, and slightly almond-shaped brown eyes that stared back with breathtaking boldness. She was barely out of her teens. Close off that avenue right now, he thought. Beer-breath playboy I may be, Emma, but I'm not a cradle robber.

"What're you having?" she asked.

Danny balled both fists under the bar and tried not to hear the soft ripeness that had returned to her voice. "I'm sticking pretty close to club soda, but you order anything you like." He waved at the bartender.

"I'll have a margarita. Isn't that a specialty of this part of the country?"

"You're absolutely right. Best in the West." He ordered the drink and gave her his full attention

"So, Paul,..." she started.

"Oh, no, I'm Danny. And I do apologize for my rudeness the first time we spoke. It wasn't meant for you."

Her interest faded, but she smiled. "Ah, yes, the gentle-man-bug. Well, shall we join them? We can have the drink sent to the table."

"If you don't mind, let's give them a few minutes so they can get caught up. Politics, you understand."

A voice broke into Paul's apprehension. "Hi."

He looked up. Emma's smile radiated from beneath soft black waves at her temples and a mass of braids on top of her head. She was wearing white pants and a sleeveless pale turquoise blouse with an open neckline. A stylized silver bear hung from a slender silver chain into the dip between her collar bones. It might as well have been a grizzly whacking him in the chest.

She shifted her weight and leaned toward him. "Hello? May I join you?"

Paul leaped up, barely catching the back of his chair before it crashed into the diner behind him, and helped her into her seat.

"I like your bre...bear," he said, sitting down again.

"Thanks, it was a gift from a silversmith when I visited the Taos pueblo last year," she said, watching the variable, elongated S that was the disappearing hostess.

"Have you ever understood this thing people have about black clothes?" she asked. "They always look to me like holes in the day's happiness."

Paul laughed aloud. "To me, they look like all the nuns of my youth. Only skinnier. Emma, I'm glad to see you again."

She looked at him warmly. "Thanks. A little unexpected, huh? You think the fates are involved in this?"

Paul opened his mouth and closed it again. Was that a lead? Was this flirting? He hoped he wasn't blushing.

She touched his arm. "Just joking. No fates. Your brother's shenanigans, more likely." Grinning, she lifted her face to indicate Danny still at the bar in awkward conversation with Caitlin. "We're supposed to be getting caught up on party business." She wiggled two fingers on each hand to indicate quotation marks.

"You mean you think he's playing matchmaker?"

She nodded. "Well, he can play all he wants. We know where we stand, don't we?"

"Of course." Paul sat back in his chair and tried to look indifferent. "Would you like to look at the menu?" He offered his and knocked her napkin-swan onto her bread plate.

She took her own menu from the corner of the table and leaned back to give herself room to open it.

He followed the movement of her eyes through the *hors d'oeurves* and *entrées* and watched them shift to the price list.

She paled and looked up at him, embarrassed. "Paul, I'm terribly sorry, but I can't eat here. I'm on such a tight per diem I can't afford even the cheapest appetizer on this menu."

"To tell the truth, I was just wondering what I could cut out of my budget to pay for this, but now that I think of it, we should just stick Danny for the whole bill. After all, he's the one who got both of us into this situation, and the restaurant was his suggestion, too."

Emma laughed with the tumbling breath of a rushing brook. "Great idea! Worthy of the best politician. You sure you don't want to be president?"

"Don't even say it!"

They grinned at each other in amiable conspiracy and set the menus aside to wait for the others.

Then his tongue tied itself into a knot and left a silence hanging in the air. A really long silence.

Emma looked around at the other tables and stared at the waiter's gloves. She looked at her lap.

Paul searched his early high school memories for a conversation opener and nearly blurted out "How's school going?" Instead, he said, "How's your law practice going?"

"Still struggling. I hope it'll pick up again when I get back."

"Where are you going?"

"To visit the Mesa Utes near Mesa Verde, several pueblos in New Mexico, and a couple of tribes in Arizona." She looked at him for a minute before continuing. "I'm doing some fact-finding about casinos."

Paul relaxed a little. "They're spreading all over the country, aren't they?"

"Like cancer."

"A couple of weeks ago Danny took me up to Glory Hole, an old mining town in the mountains. He was telling me about the changes in the valley since gambling took over there."

Emma sat forward with both elbows on the table. "Do you know of any specific problems?" She reached into her purse and pulled out a note pad and a pen.

"In Glory Hole? He said property taxes skyrocketed so high a lot of the generations-old families had to sell out and leave. I think all the local hotels and restaurants went under."

Emma was writing furiously. "Anything else?"

"Well, this is the second time that men have plundered the valley. The old gold miners left it ugly. The new ones will leave it devastated. For example, they carved a shelf out of the side of a mountain for a dirt parking lot and did no erosion control. There are already deep channels in the mountain from runoff. The Victorian houses are literally overshadowed by huge hotels and casinos. I've never seen such devastation to a natural or historical setting. It made even *me* sad, and I'd never been there before, so I had no basis for comparison. The gambling interests managed to move in there against the vote of the townspeople, but I don't remember the details. And there's the drunk driving. But you should talk to Danny about it. He knows more than I do."

"I'll ask him." She put away the pad and pen. "And how's the shoe business?"

Paul grinned at her. "Well, my co-workers in *men's* shoes are gay as two sweet little wood sprites, and the one who's my immediate supervisor is fifteen years my junior, but it's not bad."

Emma gave him her rushing water laugh again. "And how's it going otherwise? Are you feeling comfortable yet as a..."

"Normal person?"

She nodded, smiling. "Actually, I was trying to think of the word for a person not in the church. I didn't want to say *heretic*."

Even with Danny he hadn't talked about feeling cut loose over a black hole, wanting to grab back at the security of the church. He looked at Emma's eyes. There was nothing in them but compassionate interest. "I still have flashbacks that..."

"Hurt?"

Paul looked down at the closed menu. "I don't know. They shake me up. I have a long way to go. But slowly I'm coming to the conclusion that I made the right decision." The sound of the confessional door slamming on Laurel's revelation jarred him, and he pressed his thumb into the burn scar. "Even if the timing was precipitate." He looked up and smiled. "Thanks for asking, Emma."

She leaned closer, and Paul smelled her for the first time, breathing in the freshness of an October day. It was the smell of nature and honesty, and it beset him instantly with yearning to lean closer and breathe at the source.

She cocked her head to her right. "What was it like, being a priest?"

Paul leaned into what felt like a lush but invisible meadow, wishing he could just absorb her smell. But she'd asked a question, and the answer demanded concentration. "In the beginning, when I was still all faith and ideals, I believed I was working for God and people. Later, I felt God had gotten shoved somewhere behind the altar and the church was the real power. Like any political machine, its real interest was self-perpetuation."

"You think that's the reason for its adamant stand on birth-control?"

"In some indirect way, yes. Of course, the popes think they're speaking with the voice of God, but I can't make myself believe any god would demand unwanted children when so many are born into poverty, hunger, violence."

"Not to mention being born into a world that won't be able to support even the wanted children much longer."

"That sounds like Danny's talk."

She nodded.

"I see," he said. The next question slipped out on its own, running right over a skip in his heart beat: "Does that mean you'd never want to have children?"

A hand moved the chair opposite him and Paul looked up, startled. Danny smiled as he seated the reporter, and Paul realized he'd heard the last question. He'd assume the relationship was proceeding apace. Paul grinned at Emma, but somewhere inside an insistent flutter nagged at him. His introduction to Caitlin almost escaped his notice.

"So here's the plan, if everybody's in agreement," said Danny when he'd settled in the chair opposite Paul. "We'll do the interview at the apartment after we eat. Paul, you take Emma in her car, and Caitlin can go with me. They came together and neither of them knows the way."

Emma looked at Paul and smiled into her lap.

"But it's so simp...Sure," said Paul.

"Well, it's all settled." Danny took up his menu with the manner of a CEO who's just ironed out the last minor wrinkle of a benevolent takeover. "What looks good?" he asked.

Caitlin glanced through the menu and blanched. "Uh... just so everyone knows," she said, blushing now, "I'm not here on an expense account or anything, so..."

"No problem," said Danny.

"I haven't had lobster in a long time," said Paul. "But I'm torn between that and the filet mignon." He glanced at Emma.

"Does anybody know what this New Zealand cervena is?" she asked with a perfectly straight face. "And I'm so hungry. The shrimp appetizer sounds good. So kind of you to pick up the tab, Danny."

"Oh, yes," said Caitlin, looking up from the menu.

Danny coughed. "Another thought—I guess if we're going to be doing an interview afterwards, we'd better dispense with the wines. Clear heads and all that."

"Right," came a chorus of three.

After the waiter had taken their orders, Caitlin looked each of them in the face and said, "It's so interesting to meet people who go in strange—well, other directions."

"And we don't even have horns or anything," Emma snapped back, smiling sarcastically.

"Oh, no, I didn't mean...damn, I'm really getting off on the wrong foot."

"Not at all," said Paul. "I'm sure you meant that as a compliment."

"I did, really. I meant *strange* in the eyes of old stick-in-the-muds," Caitlin said, looking pleadingly at Emma.

"Of course," said Emma. "Pardon my reaction. I don't know why I took offense."

"Anyway," Caitlin continued, "I guess this is the year to be in a splinter party."

The others waited.

"I mean, with the mud-slinging that's going on in the major camps."

Danny laid his menu back on the table. "Yeah, I heard the other day that Joseph Landsdon had a homosexual affair while he was at Oxford in the sixties."

Caitlin laughed. "I heard that. Hard to imagine that conservative old twit making out with..." Her face flushed to a burnished copper.

Emma cut her laugh short. "Sorry. It was the image... He can't possibly win the election. Who'd vote for that cold fish?"

"I sure wouldn't," said Caitlin. "And of course, he responded by accusing Carrington of participating in communist rallies a million years ago while he was with the Peace Corps in Ethiopia. My editor said the whole country is so fed up with both parties that a third party might even stand a chance. So maybe you'll get elected."

Emma glanced at Paul and smiled. "We don't have any illusions," she said, "although winning would be good. At this point, we just want to see that our word gets out."

Caitlin nodded. "Then you two were probably nailing down your brief to the Supreme Court while Danny and I were at the bar."

"What brief?" asked the others in unison.

"Didn't you hear it on the news this afternoon?"

"I was on my way to your motel," said Emma.

"I was in the shower," explained Danny

A shot of nerves started in the bottom of Paul's stomach and flew to the roots of his hair. "I was on the way home from the store."

"The Supreme Court granted the Revisionist Party's appeal for an injunction barring nationally televised debates until it decides whether all parties, even the smallest, should be allowed to participate. The major parties are sending in briefs to press for a negative vote. Next week's debate has been canceled. The president sent a letter to the justices asking for a prompt decision."

Paul's mouth went dry. He picked up his glass of water, but his hand shook so badly the ice rattled. He set it down and stared at Danny.

Emma laid her hand briefly on Paul's arm and said, "Yes, we certainly will write our own brief. But tell us about your paper, Caitlin. What city does it serve?"

"We're published in Chicago, and we're still a young paper. We focus on the controversial and the bizarre..."

"I knew it was a dirt rag," muttered Paul.

"Well, we don't publish anything like aliens getting nuns pregnant. I thought an article on the splinter candidates that no one has ever heard of...well, I, the thing is, I'm just starting out and someday I'll get on with a standard paper."

"So what kind of article are you planning to write?" asked Emma.

"Why don't we leave that for the interview?" suggested Danny.

Emma looked at him and nodded. "What's your paper's circulation?"

"About a thousand, but growing. Most of our readers are in the Chicago area, but we do sell some in a number of other states.

"Louisiana?" whispered Paul.

"I really don't know. Probably not. That's pretty far away."

Paul relaxed a little. The remainder of the dinner passed in bursts of tense conversation. Paul hardly spoke, nervous not only about the interview, but whatever lay beyond. A murky future loomed at him like a semi-truck bearing down on an armadillo paralyzed in its headlights.

CHAPTER FIFTEEN

While Danny started the coffee maker in his tiny kitchen, Paul seated Caitlin and Emma at the glass-topped table, wishing he'd driven right to Alaska in August. Trekking across collapsing glaciers would have been a lot safer than putting himself in Danny's hands.

I'll let Emma do most of the talking, he thought. If she and Danny take all the questions and I keep my mouth shut, maybe Caitlin will forget about me.

When Danny set coffee mugs and spoons on the table and joined them, Caitlin laid a small black tape recorder on the glass and pressed the record button.

Paul saw Emma wipe her hands against her pants legs under the table. Yee gods, she's tangled up in knots, too, he thought. His heart started an annoying thump. He balled his fists but released them again, realizing that the reporter could see through the glass, too.

"Well, let's get started, shall we?" said Caitlin, her eyes on Paul. "Perhaps you'd like to tell me first about the party itself. What, exactly, are the Earth Rights Party's goals?"

Paul swallowed nervously and waited for Danny or Emma to spring into the gap, hoping the reporter would think he was formulating an answer. On the other hand, if either of them mentioned the offspring surtax or the banning of paper for use by the media, Caitlin would... It was a thought he dared not pursue. She was still staring at Paul, expecting his answer.

Danny came to his rescue. "I guess either Emma or I should field that one. We've been in since its founding."

Caitlin turned her head to him but kept her eyes on Paul. "Which was in...?"

"1992," said Danny. "Enough Americans were embarrassed by our performance at the environmental summit in Brazil to coalesce into a movement. Not to mention the government's failure to protect such things as the wetlands that might have saved New Orleans."

Caitlin finally turned to Danny. "So what does it stand for?"

Danny looked at Emma. "You want to take this one?"

Emma intertwined her fingers on the edge of the table. "Ready for the big speech?" she asked.

Caitlin checked the revolving tape, nodded, and fixed on Paul again, expecting the speech to come from him.

"No matter where you go in the world," Emma said, leaning forward with her back perfectly straight, "you see the same thing. The earth is being raped and plundered to feed and house and clothe an exploding population. Here at home you see it in the stupefying array of consumer goods and the endless construction going on everywhere. Enormous homes built for one millionaire tycoon after another, big enough to house an entire third world village but occupied by families of three or four people."

Caitlin stared at her. "But they have the right..."

Emma put up a hand to stop her. "Of course. No one questions their *right* to build whatever they want, but that's another matter. Maybe we're trying to educate them to scale down their *expression* of the right. The energy it takes to run those houses would make life comfortable in any number of smaller homes for the poor. "

Paul sensed a gap in her logic, but he was too mesmerized by Emma's speech to identify it. Her voice had taken on an intensity he'd never heard anywhere, even in the most resounding sermons.

Caitlin, less mesmerized, sat back, cocked her head to the right, and pounced on the flaw. "This is beginning to sound like my mother telling me to eat my broccoli because there are a lot of starving children in Africa."

Emma nodded. Her eyes held Caitlin's like an electric current. "I know. I'm not saying that the energy not consumed by more modest homes necessarily ends up in those of the poor. Or that it should be donated to the poor. What I am saying is that any unused energy leaves that much more for the future. In America, our blatant consumption of resources says we don't care about the rest of the world, or more importantly, about the future of the race, don't you think?"

"I guess..." said Caitlin, but she still looked skeptical.

Emma shifted even closer to the edge of her chair. "In countries that can least afford it, people multiply geometrically and demand help when famine hits. And those countries are generally dominated by rigid or fanatical religions that forbid birth control. So poverty in third world countries, and even in our own, far outpaces the acquisition of comforts, and the more comfort we manage to provide, even the most basic, the more we violate the earth to do it."

Paul lowered his tense shoulders. Caitlin's focus was entirely on Emma now.

Caitlin wrinkled her brow. "Could you be a little more specific?"

Emma relaxed enough to put her hands in her lap. "I'm sorry, I'm getting on my soapbox. If you'd ever been to India, for example, or Turkey, or Vietnam, you'd understand. Masses of people living on the very edge of existence. So the long-term goals of the Earth Rights Party are to get population, depletion of natural resources, destruction of the environment, and worldwide economics back to a point where the earth can sustain the human race indefinitely."

Wide-eyed, Caitlin turned to Paul. "You realize you're trying to buck massive global trends, don't you?"

Paul's mouth turned to ash instantly. He nodded so slightly he feared the movement looked like a tic.

"Think about it," said Emma, but the words were more plea than command and shifted the reporter's focus again. "If we don't back-pedal in our consumption, we'll destroy the planet we depend on and create a life that's unspeakably miserable for the last few generations. There will be wars over water, over food, over simple space. Try to imagine paying more for drinking water than for rent, living in a tiny cubicle with several other people, never leaving it without a gas mask because the air is unbreathable, never seeing a sky that's blue because it's obscured by the brown smog. And maybe worst of all, try to imagine never being able to get away from all the people. No more tracts of wilderness, no more wild animals, no more escaping the crush of civilization."

She shuddered.

Paul stopped breathing. Danny stared.

Emma shook her head in short jerks. "Danny, could I have a glass of water?"

Danny stepped into the kitchen.

Caitlin said, "You're really passionate about this, aren't you?"

Passion, Paul echoed in his head. Passionate about the earth. Suddenly a young man in a brand new cassock, full of zeal and ideal, turned to face the world. He looked across the bitter disillusionment of the years at the glowing face of Emma and wanted to cry.

Danny set the water on the table and she sipped it.

"Have you ever actually been to all those places you mentioned?" asked Caitlin.

"Yes, though I spent more time in India than the others."

"You did?" cried Paul without thinking.

Emma laughed. "Actually, yes, when I was in law school. I went to UCLA on a BIA grant, that's Bureau of Indian Affairs, and all the courses I took had to be approved. Late in my junior year, I saw this course entitled 'Indian Studies,' and without giving it much thought, I sent it in for approval. By the time I realized they meant *India*, the approval had already come through and I figured I might as well go. So I ended up spending six months in Calcutta."

"Calcutta?" gasped Caitlin.

"That's supposed to be the cesspool of the world," added Danny.

"What was India like?" asked Paul.

Emma raised her eyebrows, took a deep breath, and focused her eyes far away from Danny's apartment. "Filthy. Shabby. Hordes of dirty people. Castes, from the Brahmins to the Untouchables, born to a station pre-ordained by their actions in previous lives. And except for the lowest castes, somehow content with the station, struggling to make the next life better by good behavior in this one.

"So there's always hope," said Caitlin.

Hope, thought Paul. What all religions should be about. Not power and self-perpetuation. Not saints and gods. Not candles and collections. Hope. It was a minute before he could concentrate on the interview again.

Caitlin checked the tape and then asked, "Could you tell us more about your time Calcutta?"

"I studied Indian culture, but the city itself is more interesting than anything I did there. Calcutta has an infrastructure for perhaps a million people, but no one knows how many actually live there. More than ten million, in any case. They come from the countryside looking for work. People live on the streets. They sleep, cook, eat, defecate, give birth and die on the streets." Emma's eyes saddened and her head tilted a little. "But for me, the worst part was the mothers holding their limp, skinny babies, begging on the streets, looking at you with eyes grown huge with hunger. And the gaping black eyes of the babies, staring without seeing." Emma's eyes closed, her brows knit, and she seemed to stop breathing.

Paul's hand came up to touch her shoulder, but she shuddered and he simply said, "Emma, are you all right?"

She looked at him, shook her head a little, as if to dispel the harrowing image, and then smiled wanly. "But the people were invariably helpful and friendly, warm and ready to laugh. I really like Indians." She grinned at him.

He smiled back. "Actually, I do, too." He felt his face go hot and wished Danny were out on the balcony and Caitlin didn't exist.

"Wow, I'm impressed," said Caitlin. "You really have a way of making people see things through your eyes. Did you go to the other places, too?"

"The program I was on offered a side trip to Vietnam during an Indian holiday. I used my own money to pay for it. Then, on the return trip, we had the option to stop in Istanbul. I had to borrow some money for that, but it was worth it. There were a lot of poor people there, too, crowded into a city that can't house them, just like Saigon and Calcutta. They live under bridges, in the cloverleaves of their few super highways. But the worst was India."

"So your big thing is overpopulation, then. What, specifically, does the Party want to do to alleviate the problem of overpopulation and overuse of resources?" Caitlin looked at all three faces and stopped on Paul's.

Paul waited for Danny or Emma to say something. When neither did, he swallowed hard, fearing to mention a single party goal. "The platform contains some proposals that would...uh... have to be...uh...predicated on a great deal of education."

"Such as...?" asked Caitlin.

Danny took up the conversation as he brought in the coffee pot and a bag of sugar cookies. "Allotment of foreign aid contingent on the distribution and enforcement of birth control measures. Eventual elimination of the internal combustion engine in order to clean up the air and hopefully repair the holes in the ozone layer."

Emma continued. "Gradual shift from a growth economy to a sustaining economy. Domestic laws to encourage reduction of our own population. And as Paul said, a lot of education, especially for us Americans, the most spoiled people of all. People have to learn willingness to make sacrifices. And, of course, the leaders must set the first and best examples."

"Such as those of your people?"

"I beg your pardon?"

"Indians...oops, there I go again. Native Americans."

Emma took a swallow of water but kept her eyes on Caitlin, her brow furrowed. When she set her glass back on the table, she opened her mouth but closed it again without answering.

Caitlin looked at Paul for help.

Paul squirmed, not sure whether Emma was insulted or simply considering what to say.

Caitlin wiped her hands on her skirt. "I mean...sort of...going back to the old ways?"

Emma nodded. "Aha. Sure. Of course, we'd have to send all the people whose ancestors weren't here before 1500 back where they came from."

Paul's mouth fell open. He heard Danny suck in a short breath.

"You're kidding!" cried Caitlin.

Emma laughed and leaned into the imitation black leather of the back rest. "Of course I was kidding. There's a limit to how far we can go. Can you just see us living in teepees and holding rain dances in the middle of a crumbling Los Angeles freeway?"

The others laughed.

"That's a great picture," said Caitlin.

"Thanks, but don't you dare print any of that about sending people back."

"What if I put it in a paragraph about your sense of humor?"

"Not even that. What I meant about the old ways was accepting the concept that the Earth is *literally* our mother and we can't go on ravaging her indefinitely."

"How about coffee for everybody?" asked Danny, pointing at the glass pot.

Emma shook her head and sipped her water.

No one else responded.

"Cokes?"

Again, no one answered.

Danny returned to the kitchen. "Well, if nobody minds, I think I'll pour myself a Coke." He put a little stress on the last word and turned back to smile at Emma. She was still looking at Caitlin.

"Would you say your trip to India was what got you interested in joining the party?" Caitlin asked.

"No, it just made me realize how desperately we need to change things. The party wasn't formed for several years."

"And how about you Paul? I've heard from Emma. And Danny, who's not even running. But you've hardly said a word. What got you into the party?"

Paul tried to ignore the feeling she was tightening a tourniquet around his chest. "My brother."

"Danny?"

"Er, yes. My own interest in politics has been more...uh...academic than active."

"So what is your background?" Caitlin's lovely brow knit suddenly. "And why are you running for president?"

Paul dried his hands on the sides of his pants, the glass tabletop forgotten. He glanced at Emma. She smiled back non-commitally.

Danny stood in the doorway of the narrow kitchen as if paralyzed, his Coke can frozen above his glass of ice.

Caitlin squinted suspiciously at all three of them.

Paul reached out and turned off the tape recorder.

"Hey," she protested.

Paul kept his hand over the recorder. "You have to promise me you won't print this."

"What? Are you going to tell me you just got out of jail or something?"

"No, of course not. But I have to have your word you won't print it."

"I can't promise that." Caitlin sat up and her young face turned proud and determined. "I'm a journalist. I have to print what's necessary for the public to know."

"Look, a lot of people could be very upset."

Caitlin stared at him and waited, her face resolute.

She wasn't going to budge, realized Paul. He could lie. Not exactly lie. Tell her he'd been a high school teacher. Which was true. He glanced at Danny standing in the kitchen doorway, his face betraying nothing.

The word *ethical* echoed in Paul's head, as it had in the office of Lord and Taylor's. He removed his hand from the recorder and said, "Okay, I'm going to rely on your sense of humanity, Caitlin, which I hope overrides your need to inform the public. Until a month ago I was a Catholic priest."

Caitlin's mouth fell open and she threw herself against the back of her chair. "That is absolutely the last thing I thought you'd tell me. It's perfect. It's page one stuff. It's the scoop of a lifetime. There's no way I'm not going to print it."

"Listen, Caitlin," said Danny, "put yourself in Paul's place for a minute if you can. He's been a priest. That doesn't just mean ringing bells and tossing holy water around. It means that people with gut-wrenching problems spill those guts out to you every few weeks, tell you their darkest secrets in the knowledge that you can never divulge them. Then you walk out on them and say you're not a priest any more. But that doesn't erase your memory. You'd make hundreds of people very uneasy."

Caitlin shook her head. "So why are you running in a national election if you don't want people to know about you? It doesn't make sense."

"I know..." Paul started.

"It was my fault," Danny interrupted. "I nominated him without thinking about the consequences. He wasn't even there. By the time he knew about it, the slate and the platform had already gone to press, and I promised him nothing would come of it, no speech; no notoriety; and guaranteed, no White House."

The reporter's mouth gaped open again.

"Caitlin, I'm asking you as a human being, don't do this to those people. You can say anything else about me you want, within reason. Just not that. Not even after the election's over."

"I can't promise that. You don't know what you're asking. An ex-priest who's accidentally running for president—it's too good to keep."

"Caitlin, please," begged Paul. "Look, we're a splinter party most people have never even heard of. If you print this, it'll blow everything out of proportion. It'd be a sensation for the sake of sensation. That's not the kind of reporter you want to be, is it?"

"No, but..." Her face contorted with indecision. "I'll have to talk it over with my editor."

"No, Caitlin," Emma said quietly, reaching across the table to place a hand on her arm. "You have to decide on your own. You already know what your editor would say."

Caitlin reached for the tape recorder. She sat up straight and said, "I'll think about it. I'll let you know in a day or two."

CHAPTER SIXTEEN

A man and a woman approached Paul at the cash register, and at first he thought they were together, mismatched though they were—she tall and lanky, he of minimum height and maximum girth. He was hauling a black garbage sack with great angular bulges. The woman gave Paul a short, serious nod, turned on her heels, and walked off.

Before Paul had a chance to wonder at the signal, the man began a tirade about a pair of scuffed brown loafers that he grabbed from the sack and slapped onto the counter. Great, Paul thought, an irate customer just when Roberson's finally considering me for full time. He glanced around to see if the manager was nearby.

Within a few minutes, Paul was leaning forward with his hands propped on either side of the cash register. "Sir," he breathed out, "there's no need to shout. A year is a long time to keep a pair of shoes and then expect to have your money refunded because they pinch the toes."

The florid customer leaned from the other side, shifting a good mass of his belly onto the counter and his face close enough for Paul to see leftover sleep-sand around his small green eyes. "I don't care how long it's been," the customer yelled, attracting attention from every nearby department. "I paid good money for these shoes and I expect you to stand by them. I'll get my doctor to swear they're causing bunions on both feet and slap you with a big law suit. And I'll see to it you're sued personally," he squinted at Paul's name tag, "...Mr. Paul Greed, for added pain and anguish."

Paul glanced in the direction of the stacks, where Toby had gone to phone Roberson's office.

"Sir, I didn't sell you these shoes, neither of the other salesmen remembers you, and you don't have your sales receipt..."

Shaking one of the shoes in Paul's face, the customer shouted, "I don't give a damn who sold them to me, it was this store... never mind, I'm going to get the manager."

Toby emerged at a run from the stacks and handed him a tiny white note.

"That won't be necessary, sir," Paul said, hissing more than he intended. He forced himself to add, "The manager has already given his approval for the refund..." he read the scrap of paper, "...in the amount of $95.57."

"What? I know I paid over a hundred dollars for these shoes."

"Our records show they sold for $87.50 plus tax. I can only refund our price. Assuming you didn't buy them on sale."

The customer hesitated only a fraction of a second, slammed his hand down on the counter again, turned to his left, and exhaled sharply. "Just give me the goddamned money."

Paul counted out the refund and watched the man lumber off down the aisle dragging the lumpy bag. In a minute the sound of hostile shouting rang across the racks and shelves from luggage.

Please, no more scenes like that before Roberson makes up his mind, Paul prayed by habit. And no more horrors today. He took the loafers into the stacks behind the display area, rested his elbow on a tall pile of shoe boxes and put his forehead on his arm. The pile collapsed and shoes scattered through the aisle. He turned, leaned against the shelves, balled his fists, and growled.

Larry Westley, his young supervisor, prissed in and stopped at the entrance with his hands on his hips.

Paul sighed. "I know. I'll get them back in the right boxes. I'm sorry. That guy just got to me."

"You don't need to tell me." Larry rolled his eyes and shifted his weight gracefully to the other hip. "I heard the whole thing. Come on, I'll help you. Toby's still on the floor. He'll call if he's suddenly overwhelmed with customers."

They stacked the shoe boxes in several smaller piles and Paul returned to the cash register. The shouting had stopped, and Harlan, the store detective in his flapping trench coat, was leading the man toward the escalator with the sack between them.

Paul glanced across at the wallets and briefcases, wishing he could escape the offensive smell of leather from both departments. Then he realized something was wrong. The woman who'd given him the strange nod was standing behind the display stand of wallets. In fact, now that Paul thought about it, he'd seen her out of the corner of his eyes during the entire altercation. She was wiry and taut, exceptionally tall and cadaverously thin, with a tense, wary face. Her brassy red-orange hair looked like a giant Afro-helmet.

"Larry," he said, pointing with his chin across the aisle, "see that woman over there in leather goods? Did you notice her before? She came in the same time as the man returning the shoes."

Larry pursed his lips in elegant disapproval. "No, but I was on break. Dikey looking, huh? Where d'you suppose she got that vest, for goodness' sake? The Salvation Army?"

Toby tittered. "Damnation Army, maybe. I noticed her, too, Paul. Can you imagine trying to run your fingers through that hairdo? Heavens! Looks like she barely escaped getting electrocuted in a Georgia prison."

"Well, that would explain why she looks like she's wired to about 20,000 volts," said Larry, sniggering. He and Toby shared a moment of mirthful superiority. "Anyway, keep your eyes on her, Paul. If she does anything suspicious, call Harlan."

"You'd think she'd go away now that she knows we're looking at her, wouldn't you?" asked Paul.

Instead, the woman's bony chin jutted another half-inch from her defiant face and her red-going-to-gray hair seemed to stand a little higher.

Skinny as a string bean, Paul thought, and she really does look wired. A strung-bean. He laughed to himself in spite of a twinge of shame. Eee-gods, it's contagious, he thought, and moved a little away from the sprites.

He went out for lunch to get away from the store and the odor of leather for a while. He bought a cannelloni from the Italian café and took it to the sunken, carpeted area that served as a meeting place for shoppers. Something nagged in his peripheral vision while he ate, and when he looked, the strung-bean was there again, behind a potted palm, leaning against a column, looking directly at him and then scanning the crowd.

Stunned, he stopped chewing and lost all taste of tomato sauce and cheese. She'd followed him. What on earth was she doing? Was she a private eye the church had sent? How had they tracked him down?

Back in Lord and Taylor's, Paul stationed himself behind the cash register and looked across at the wallets. She wasn't there.

In a spate of relief, he went over her appearance again in case he had to describe her to the police. As soon as he had a chance, he would ask the saleslady in leather goods whether anything was missing.

When he turned to answer a customer's question, a small movement caught his eye near the exit to the mall's second floor. The strung-bean was back, behind the rack of silk shirts, looking bored and shifting from one foot to the other. Maybe the store had hired her to watch him. But why? His cash register had always balanced.

By the time Paul's shift was over, she had worked her way around to the sport coats on the other side of the shoe department, where she stood like a discarded dummy leaning against a mirror. When he left the store, he watched behind him, expecting her skinny face to appear above the crowd or in the car following him, but she disappeared.

He spent the evening looking at apartments. As soon as the full time job came through, he could think about getting out of Danny's hair—and out of Danny's field of activity, where he'd begun to feel like the last atom in a chain reaction.

When he stepped off the mall escalator for his late shift the next day, he saw the woman immediately, pacing the entrance, consternation emanating from all parts of her gangly body. Her face went slack with relief when she spotted him. She obligingly stationed herself behind the wallets again.

Paul waited on a steady stream of customers, keeping an eye on her when he could. They'd told him in his training sessions to report anything odd, and she was definitely that. She distracted him so badly he had to void and redo two sales. By five-thirty he was angry. She had no right watching him like that.

He turned his back to the strung-bean and dialed the number for the house detective. "Harlan, this is Paul Greer in men's shoes. There's a woman who's been hanging around for a couple of days, and I...I don't know, there's just something about her. Could you come down and check her out?...Okay, I'll go up and talk to her when I see you."

Feeling a little like Judas, he waited till the burly detective stepped off the escalator, then left the cash register and walked over to the woman. She was leaning against the end of a display case with her elbow sprawled over the top, the side of her head resting on her hand. She'd drawn up one foot and was circling it in the air, a sure sign her feet hurt.

"Excuse me, but I've been noticing you since yesterday morning," said Paul. "Is there something you want?"

She ignored his question but came to attention, glanced at the fast approaching detective, leapt in his path and landed in a half crouch, her back to Paul.

Surprised, Harlan squinted as he moved through the sports coats. He grabbed his walkie-talkie and spoke into it. Only a few feet away now, he put his hand back in his coat. "I'm the..."

The woman sprang at Harlan like a panther. Harlan grunted when he hit the floor. She turned him and pinned him to the carpet, with her knee on his back, his arm twisted, his hand between his shoulder blades. He grunted and yelped in pain.

"Ah gotcha. Don't you go try anythang stupid," she shouted in a Mississippi twang as thick as swamp mud.

"What? Get off me this instant, you moron. I'm the store detective," yelled Harlan.

A small crowd gathered in the aisle.

Paul noticed Roberson running down the escalator, shoving shoppers aside. Great, just great. He reached for the woman's arm to pull her off.

"Does she have a gun?" squealed a small boy.

"A gun!" screamed a woman in a fur coat. She turned, flailed through the crowd, and ran for the exit.

"Gun!" yelled several others. They all plunged headlong for the floor or scattered among the displays.

Roberson stopped for a second, then ran toward them, ducked over, weaving in and out of displays.

"You awright, mistah Greeah?" asked the attacker, pressing the detective's arm harder but looking up at Paul.

"What?! Of course I'm all right. What on earth...?"

She loosened her grip and said, "Okay, bub, I'm going to let you on up now. Just don't you go tryin' any funny business, you heah?"

"I'm the store detective, for Christ's sake," shouted Harlan, struggling to his feet and snatching his badge from his inside pocket. "What in the hell do you think you're doing?"

"Protectin' him," she answered, jerking her head at Paul.

"What?!" cried Paul.

"What?!" cried Roberson, stepping out from behind the nearest shelves and fixing Paul with a look that sent pink slips darting through the light waves. The thinning black hair above his undertaker's face stood on end from his encounters with hanging clothes.

The woman shook her shoulders and straightened to look down on them all. "Look, I may not be the secret service or nothin', but Gordy hired me..."

Paul's mouth fell open and he focused on her instead of saying something to placate Roberson. "Somebody hired you to *protect* me?"

"I tole you. Gordy."

"Who in the hell is Gordy?" asked Paul, racking his brain for anyone named Gordy who would send a stalking calamity to protect him. He glanced at the heads peeping over the leather jackets. "I'm sorry, Mr. Roberson, Harlan, I'll straighten this out."

Harlan rubbed the back of his head and yanked at his skewed trench coat. "Uh-uh. The woman attacked me. I'm pressing charges."

Paul's adrenaline zinged up another notch. He couldn't let anyone ask her more questions. Too much would come out. "I'm sure it's just some malicious joke. Please, let me take care of it." He grabbed the woman's arm, ready to drag her toward his station.

Roberson pointed his finger in Paul's face. "We can't have scenes like this in the store, Greer. You gather up your things at the end of your shift."

Paul forced himself to grovel. "Please, sir, this is all a mistake. I assure you nothing like it will ever happen again."

Roberson narrowed his eyes to slits and opened his mouth.

The little boy who'd asked about the gun chirped up again. "Hey, that's not fair. He didn't do anything." He pointed at the strung bean. "She did."

Roberson seemed to notice the crowd now, all waiting to see whether he'd stick by the firing. He gave them an oily, thin smile; lowered his voice, and said, "Okay, Greer, but if you cause any other scenes around here, you're out. And don't even dream about full time. Come on, Harlan. Let it go."

Harlan huffed but said, "Yes, sir." He shoved his head toward the woman, his eyes up, his chin at the level of her flat chest. "I don't want to see you within a hundred yards of me again, you got that? If I do, I'll press charges for that attack." He turned back to Paul. "You better watch your step, Greer. I got my eyes on you, too."

Roberson waved his arms at the spectators like a farm wife herding chickens. "Look, folks, this was a mistake. It's all over. Please, go on about your business." He gave Paul one more meaningful look and strode away.

Harlan stood with his arms crossed, as if waiting to see Paul "straighten it all out."

Paul pulled the woman toward the shoes.

She dug in her heels. "This ain't no mistake and it ain't no joke. I told you twice already, Gordy *hired* me to take care of you. I'm Shirl Wainwright." She tried to jerk loose.

Paul grabbed her arm with both hands. "I haven't the faintest notion what you're talking about. Who is Gordy, for God's sake? Do you realize what you just cost me? I was supposed to go on full time soon. And you came within a hair of getting me fired outright."

She grabbed at the first sale table to halt their progress, knocking most of the shoes to the floor. "Gordy's mah cousin. Twice removed. You gotta know him. He's only the chairman of your own party, for crying out loud. He said there's enough money in the treasury to hire you some protection just like them big shots."

Paul glanced back at the aisle, wishing Harlan would vanish. "Keep your voice down, will you? Nobody here knows about this silly business, and if word gets around, I'll lose my job."

She worked her jaw for a few seconds before she said, "Well, that ain't no skin off *mah* nose. I'm just doin' what he tole me. I gotta have a job, too, you know."

Paul rolled his eyes and pulled her behind the cash register. "Given to you by your cousin. I don't suppose he mentioned nepotism, did he?"

Her eyes popped wide and she yanked her arm away. "All he said was 'protection.' He didn't say nothing about no funny stuff."

He stretched to his full height to get his eyes level with hers but gave it up. He'd have needed spike heels. "I don't care what he said. I don't need protection. No one even knows I exist, which is exactly the way I want it. So go back and protect Gordy if you like. As far as I'm concerned, your services are terminated."

She looked down with both hands on her hips. "You cain't fire me, 'cause you didn't hire me. I'm gonna keep watchin' you till *Gordy* calls me off, you heah?"

Paul grabbed the phone and shook the receiver in her face. "You'll be watching some pretty unattractive cops if you show up here again. Next time, I'll have the detective press charges and I'll press my own for harassment. Now get out of here before you get me fired."

She tried to snatch the receiver. "Lemme use the phone, then."

"Use your cell."

"Gordy didn' spring for no cell."

"Then use the pay phone just outside there in the mall." He slammed the receiver back on the phone and put his body between her and it.

She gave him a last glare and then her face softened a little. "Okay, I'm real sorry about your full-time job, but I'm doin' mah duty whether you like it or not," she said and stalked off toward the exit like a skeleton with a few joints too many.

"Jeez," muttered Paul. "I liked it better when I thought there was a god that might listen when I asked for no more horrors." What else could happen? The feel of hidden jaws chewing away at his life made his knees buckle.

CHAPTER SEVENTEEN

The telephone was ringing as Danny put his key in the lock. He opened his door and ran toward the bedroom, shrugging off his suit coat. He reached for the phone but hesitated. If this was Floyd after him again about the aquifers, when he'd had his number changed...

He shifted his voice a couple of intervals deeper and said, "Yeah?" into the receiver.

"Paul Greer?" asked a male voice with a familiar southern accent.

Danny rolled his eyes in relief. "No, this is his brother Danny."

"Oh, right, I guess we met in Clearwater. This is Gordy. I wanted to tell Paul about the paper. It came to national headquarters today."

Danny moved the receiver a few inches from his head and squinted at it. "What headquarters?"

Gordy huffed impatiently. "Okay, my post office box. Anyway, the article in the *Popular Probe* is sensa..."

"What?" yelled Danny. "She already printed that article? She said she'd call first, dammit."

"Don't worry. It's sensational. Well, sort of. Not too bad, considering he hasn't been all that cooperative."

"What's it say? Did she...?"

"Hey, I can't tie up my phone to read you the whole article. Get a copy of it. Tell him I sent copies to all the syndicated papers. Oh, and listen, tell him to leave the bodyguard be, okey doke? I guess they had quite a set-to in the store this afternoon."

"Bodyguard?" Danny echoed, feeling stupid. "Why would he call you about a bod...?" But the line was already dead. He dropped the phone on the bed and ran for the door, struggling back into his jacket. Only one newsstand carried the *Popular Probe*, and it was downtown.

The *Popular Probe* title marched across the top of the paper in red Gothic letters. A picture of an abominable snowman in a scene obviously put together from three photos took up about three quarters of the width directly below them. To the right of that were two short blurbs: "Yeti's cousin in the Cascades, p. 2" and "Meet the Unknowns: Bottom of the Ballot, P. 3."

Before he'd even bought the paper, Danny took one look at the array of pictures in Caitlin's article, gasped, and slapped the paper shut again. He checked to see whether anyone was near enough to read over his shoulders and opened it again.

The article spread over the upper half of page three, with the five photos at the top. Each of the candidates appeared possessed by multiple demons. In their company, Paul looked like a whacko with a mission, too. Where had Caitlin unearthed that old picture?

The shaking started again and he balled his fists around the edges of the paper.

Something nagged at him, something more than the line-up of fanatics. The other pictures showed at least the shoulders of the candidates. Paul's was cut off at the neck, but there was a clear curving black line around the bottom of it that any discerning reader would immediately recognize as the top of a Roman collar.

Now he forced himself to read the article.

Splinter Party Slates:
Anarchy or Theocracy?

Chicago, October 17

In keeping with its policy of delving past the obvious, the *Popular Probe* will bring you a series of articles on the candidates you never hear about until you receive your sample ballot. From the **COLD** (Coalition for Legalized Drugs) to the **ERP** (Earth Rights Party) to the **WOMN** (Women on the March Now), learn about the platforms and the candidates, beginning with the **ERP.**

The Earth Rights Party was founded in 1992 by Gordon Johnson of Florida, George Lone Tree of Oklahoma, Emma Light in the Lodge of Wyoming, and Raymond Holstead of California. It has grown geometrically since then to a total membership of just over 53,000 and is currently registered in all fifty states.

Danny skipped the paragraphs about the platform and found the sections describing the candidates.

The presidential candidate for the Earth Rights Party is Paul Thomas Greer, age 45. Born in New Orleans, Louisiana, Greer is a man of exceptionally religious background who seems embarrassed at the idea of running for president. A highly educated man with advanced degrees in history, he is currently employed as a shoe salesman in a Denver store, apparently while solving some personal crisis. He gives the impression of great sincerity and concern for people.

His running mate, Emma Light in the Lodge, from the Buffalo Creek Achappassi Reservation, Wyoming, has law degrees from the University of Wyoming and UCLA. She often represents her tribe, and this reporter has learned she is currently working to prevent the opening of a casino on the reservation, out of concern about the rate of alcoholism and entrenched poverty among Native Americans. Her main personal and professional thrust today, however, is environmental issues. By far the more impassioned and charismatic of the two candidates, Light in the Lodge can transport the listener into a doomsday view of miserable life on our dying planet in the not-so-distant future.

Given Greer's kindness and sincerity and Light in the Lodge's impassioned concern for "Mother Earth," the tiny, little-known Earth Rights Party may be a political force to watch as we pillage the last resources of "Mother Earth."

Staff Writer
Caitlin Pascoe

Danny paid for the paper and drove home, his nerves afire all the way. He threw himself on the sofa and concentrated on how to tell Paul. He tried not to think of the tavern right over there on University.

At ten on the dot, Paul banged the door open and stalked in ranting, oblivious of fanfare that announced the evening news on television. "Listen, brother, I am definitely removing my name as candidate. It was bad enough when I thought this was some stupid joke that would go unnoticed. But now it's gotten out of hand. Your idiotic game just cost me my full-time job. You'll never believe what happened today."

Danny breathed as deliberately as he could, knowing whatever happened in the store was one of the nicer events of Paul's day. "Something to do with a bodyguard? I didn't know he was going to go out and hire..."

Paul threw his windbreaker on a chair. "He didn't exactly 'go out' and hire one. He sent a cousin with the I.Q. of a dodo bird, the look of a deranged string bean, and the power of a black belt. I fired her. If she shows up tomorrow, I swear, I'll have her arrested. I can't afford to get fired over this lunacy. You call Gordy and back me out of this thing before it spins totally out of... Wait a minute. How'd you know about Shirl Bane-wright? He called here? What did he want?"

"He wants you to leave the bodyguard alone." Danny sat up straight and took a deep breath. "Uh...he also waxed pretty enthusiastic about Caitlin's article in the *Probe*. I got a copy of it. It's on the table."

"What's the matter with you?" asked Paul, looking closely for the first time. "You look like a..." Realization drained his face to an ashy pallor. He wheeled and snatched the paper from the table. He stared at the pictures of his competition and gasped, but before he could say a word, the television news commentator announced:

"In a stunning decision, the Supreme Court ruled only moments ago in the suit brought by the Revisionist Party against the media and the major parties. The Justices voted unanimously that under the equal-time law no national debate can be televised unless each party is represented by its presidential candidate. Further, they ruled that in order to qualify as a national party, any party must be on record with the election commission, field a candidate for the national ballot, and have registered members in all fifty states.

"Our staff is searching as we speak for the affected parties and their candidates to get their reactions. In the meantime, we go to our Washington sister station, WWAS, for reactions from political leaders and their opinions on the feasibility of actually scheduling a debate with the election only two and a half weeks away..."

Paul staggered backwards toward a chair, sat absently on its arm and landed on the floor.

Danny's blood drained from his face and flooded the pit of his stomach.

Paul rose to his knees. "Tell me this is a nightmare! Please, tell me that!"

Danny opened his mouth, but no assurance came forth.

Paul jumped up. "Well, that ties it. I'm out. You and your friends can keep the game going if you want, but count me out."

"We can't, Paul. Our literature is already printed..."

Paul waited, foreboding clawing at his innards. "And...?"

"Gordy already sent copies of the article to the syndicated papers."

Paul reeled and took up the article again. "My God, look at these goons. I'm such an idiot, I deserve to be in their company. I should've put my foot down in the very beginning. I'm out now, though."

"Read it. At least she didn't say anything about your being a priest."

Paul stared at him as if he'd morphed into a dense fog of idiocy. "What does that matter now? My name will be everywhere. You think those people at St. Simon's won't recognize this picture? Do you have any idea how that weighs on me? I actually thought that moron of a bodyguard was a detective sent by the parish."

"Why would...?"

"And aside from the parishioners, do you have any idea what you've done to me?" His next words came out slowly and individually, each one obviously painful. "I ran away, Danny, with nothing to run to. All I wanted was to find a new way to think and a new way to live. But now I'm living a nightmare and I can't even begin to focus on what I believe. I *need* to get out of this mess."

Danny's shaking intensified and all he could think of was something a lot stronger than beer. "So you're canceling our bar...?"

"Don't even say that word to me!" Paul shouted. "This has gone way beyond what you promised me, and you know it. The bargain's off." He waved an arm as if to sweep the very idea off the planet. "And I am not participating in any debate. You hear me? I *am not*. You tell Gordy to get someone else. You go. Emma. Gordy. Send Shirl Wainwright for all I care. But I am not going. Period." He righted the chair, sat at the glass table, and pulled his hair with both hands. "What am I going to do about all those people? Maybe I could write a letter and Father Morreaux could read it from the pulpit. No, that'd really throw them into panic, especially the ones who hadn't heard..."

Freed from the bargain and unable to control the shaking any more, Danny rose and started for the door.

"Go ahead," said Paul without looking up.

"I thought you just cancelled the bargain."

"I did. I told you you couldn't stop. So you go right ahead. You dragged me into hell, and I'm so angry I'd just as soon you went down with me."

Danny balled his fists and jammed them under his armpits, causing his shoulders to vibrate. "I *can* stop. I'll show you I can," he said through teeth clenched so tightly his jaws hurt. But even as he said it, he knew he needed to show himself he could stop even more than he owed it to his brother. He threw himself back on the sofa and tried to concentrate on the news. I can quit, he repeated several times. His head answered, *Oh, yeah?*

CHAPTER EIGHTEEN

Emma arranged her notes and folders on the scratched school lunchroom table, hoping she'd gathered enough information to block Earl's casino. Smiling at Tommy Suazo, who waited at a table under the buffalo head, she said, "Smells like cabbage in here today, doesn't it?"

He raised his head and sniffed. "Hmmm. You have a nice trip?" he asked in his unhurried way.

Emma nodded. "A bit hectic, a long, long drive, but I think it was worth it."

The door banged open and Earl Rides hurried in, followed by a gust of cold, north wind. It blew the eagle feather on its thong over the top of his black hat. He snatched the hat off, threw it on the table, and sprawled in the chair to Tommy's left with his feet sticking out from under the other side of the table. They sported a new pair of cowboy boots, shiny black leather with a red buffalo head tooled on the shin. "I hope this isn't going to take long," he grumbled. "I got other things to do."

"I thought you were the one who wanted to move on this casino thing as soon as possible," Tommy said. "That's why I called the meeting to hear Emma's report."

"Ha, we all know what she's going to say, don't we?"

The door flew open again and the wind shoved David Niwot into the lunchroom.

"Can't we get on with this?" asked Earl.

Tommy shrugged. "I guess it won't hurt to start. Leona's the only other one that can come anyway, and she said she'd be a few minutes late."

Emma's shoulders drooped. She wished she could wait for Leona. With so few present for a vote, she'd have to convince even Earl. She might as well tell the wind to go home. She sat straighter, picked up the first index card, and looked at the expectant faces.

"I visited the Mesa Utes in southern Colorado first and talked to some people who worked in the casino and voted for it, some who were gambling there, and some who voted against it to begin with. They all said there was a lot of money flowing into the machines, but almost all the gamblers were tribal members spending welfare money. The workers were glad of the jobs, but said the noise and the cigarette smoke in the casino were slowly driving them crazy. People who lived nearby said there were a lot more accidents, drunk driving, and domestic disputes since the casino opened. I suspect most of them voted against it."

Earl let his head drop backwards until he was looking at the ceiling. "My, what a surprise!"

Emma sighed. "Just so you know, Earl, I went out of my way to find people who could give me both pros and cons."

Earl sniffed. "I just bet you did."

Emma focused again on Tommy. "I couldn't find anyone who thought he was getting rich from the casino, but a few said the real estate bordering the reservation had risen in value. Unlike here, there are pockets of land privately owned by Indians on the reservation, and the pieces nearest the casino have been sold for liquor stores and gas stations. So somebody made a profit." She glanced at Earl. "No one seemed to know who it was, or to care much. In fact, I didn't find anyone who cared much about anything at all."

She waited for Earl's derision, but he simply eyed the acoustical tile overhead.

"A small amount of the property tax on the privately held land goes to the tribal schools, but most of it reverted to the county when the land was sold to outside interests. I have the specific figures from all the reservations." She got up and placed a folder in front of each of them.

"I visited the Isabela and the San Juanito pueblos again, one with and one without a casino. I didn't need to ask who most of the gamblers were at San Juanito. And the answers I got were mostly the same as before, except that one person admitted the casino is badly managed and losing thirty to fifty thousand dollars a month.

"At Isabela pueblo they had a vote two years ago about gambling. The people I talked to said they were sure the only reason why the issue was defeated was that it's mostly the elders who still actually live in the pueblo."

"You see," said Earl, "it's the young people who're willing to accept progress."

"One woman also said that those living in the pueblo were having a hard time making ends meet. The potters have to take their wares to Santa Fe and Taos except on their own feast days when a lot of tourists come to the pueblo. She was a potter herself, and I asked her what she thought of the San Juanito Pueblo when she passed it on the way to Taos. She said it made her sick.

She'd rather see her whole pueblo torn down and replaced by government barracks than see Isabela turn out the same way."

"Yeah, right," sneered Earl.

The door banged open. Leona stepped in and forced the door shut against the howling wind. She dropped a newspaper on the table and hung her jacket on her chair. She stood behind it and glared at Emma. "Why didn't you tell us this was going on, Emma?" she asked.

Earl snapped to attention.

Leona flipped through a couple of pages of the Cheyenne paper. "'Splinter Parties: Anarchy or Theocracy,'" she read. "It says here you're running for vice president. Is this true?"

"Yes."

Earl laughed. "Vice president of what?"

"The whole country, Earl, vice president of you, too," Emma answered, not bothering to conceal a sarcastic grin.

Earl's mouth fell open. Tommy and David stared.

"You're a free person, of course, but you might have told us this before we hired you," Leona continued. "There are some things in this article about the tribe that I'd just as soon not see in the national press. Why didn't you tell us?"

"I don't know, Leona, and I beg the council's pardon. But I did talk to a lot of people about the party. Remember I discussed it with you last winter? Anyway, the convention was in August, and when I came back, I got involved in this whole casino thing, and it didn't come up. It didn't seem, I don't know, like the two were related. The party's so small there's no chance of our being elected, though I admit I get annoyed if anyone else says that. I'm never actually going to be vice president. So you're safe from me as a political force, Earl."

All four council members still stared.

"Let me tell you about the platform then..."

Earl growled. "I don't have time to listen to a damned political platform."

"Well, let me just say the Earth Rights Party is the only one that should appeal to every one of us. Its aim is to stop the human race from ravaging Mother Earth. Or at least cut the destruction to a bearable limit. We, of all people, ought to support that."

"What we want to know is what that article says about us!" demanded Earl, reaching across Tommy for the paper.

Tommy slowly moved Earl's arm back into his own space and looked up at Leona. "Why don't you just read it aloud?"

Leona read through the article.

"You had no right to talk about the alcoholism or the casino," Earl exploded, "or any other internal affairs of the reservation!"

Aghast, Emma cried, "I didn't! I swear. There's information about Paul Greer in there that never came out in the interview, too. She must have done a lot of digging about us before she even came, because I never said anything about the casino, or Paul about where he was born."

"Actually, it says some pretty nice things about you," said David.

"Hmm...," Tommy started.

The others waited while he turned the eagle at the bottom of his braid over and over, staring at each side as if he'd never seen it before. "I guess if I wanted people to form an opinion about our tribe, that's as good a one as you could ask for," he continued. "But Earl's right about the alcohol thing. That had no business in the press. 'Course, if you didn't tell the reporter..."

Leona jumped into his pause. "Even so, we should have known about one of our own getting this much attention."

Emma tried not to squirm. She crossed her feet and clenched her hands on the table. "The reporter was from a Chicago-based paper with a very small circulation. I doubt the Cheyenne paper would have run it if the reservation were anywhere but Wyoming. So don't worry about national attention."

"That'd be something, wouldn't it?" mused David. "An Achappassi in the White House."

Emma laughed. "The vice president doesn't live in the White House, David. Come to think of it, I have no idea where he does live. Anyway, this thing is all an effort to get our message over to the people. Nice as it'd be to have the power to change things, we'll be content for now if we can make people aware of the urgency of the problem. We want to see people respect the Earth."

David leaned forward. "I think we ought to support her. We could get the Shoshones in on it, send flyers to all the tribes. It'd really put us on the map."

Tommy and Leona wrinkled their brows in thought. Leona opened her mouth, but Earl was quicker.

"Can we please get this thing over with?" he snapped, seething visibly and rolling a broken pencil between his hands.

Tommy turned and looked at him. Tommy even seemed to look slowly, as if along sagging light waves.

Emma picked at a hangnail and suppressed a grin at Earl's frustration.

Tommy turned back to her and asked. "What about the other reservations?"

"I spent several days at Many Sands in Arizona. It's a self-sustaining farming reservation irrigated with water they finally got from the USDA after a long legal battle. A number of white sympathizers helped with the lawsuit. The council at Many Sands showed me how they organize the people to work the fields and market the crops and keep the books. They guarantee a percentage to everyone who works a prescribed number of hours. They even allot a parcel to anyone who wants a small garden for his own household.

"Terrific," said Earl. "Sounds like a collective farm. We can all be communist farmers. Now *there's* progress for you."

"Let her finish, Earl," said Leona.

Emma sat straighter, and her voice took on a pleading quality. "No one there is getting rich at anyone else's expense..."

"No one's getting rich at all," muttered Earl.

"...no one gets paid for not working, and for the first time, I saw faces that reflected some pride and purpose. Please, Tommy, David, Leona, give this some thought when you vote on the casino."

"So you'd like to see us go into some kind of tribal venture?" asked Leona, shoving her gray bangs out of her eyes, the anger fading from her voice.

"It would make better sense than casino gambling." She shifted her eyes to Tommy. "Don't you think?"

He regarded the eagle fixedly. "What kind of venture did you have in mind?"

"It's not my place to direct the tribe, so I don't have anything specific in mind. It just seems to me we have enough possibilities here that either farming or ranching on a large scale could work. Maybe raising buffalo."

"Hmmmm," said Tommy. "Or maybe horses. A lot of us know pretty much about horses, and..."

The others waited while he ran his hand slowly down his braid.

Earl worked his jaw muscles.

Tommy looked dreamily up to the right and nodded. "And there's that wild herd up on Twin Circles Butte that could serve as a breeding pool. All we'd have to do is go up and catch them."

"There'd be more profit in buffalo," said Leona, her focus on Tommy now. "Buffalo meat is getting more popular all the time. We might get a few head from Yellowstone. The Park Service is always trying to thin that herd, keep them off neighboring ranches without killing them."

David, the guide, was suddenly alive. "Yeah, we could have buffalo hunts. Lots of people would come for that. I know those execs I take every year would like a change from antelope. Maybe the Park would even pay us something for taking the buffalo off their hands, or at least pay to transport 'em over here."

"Are you people crazy?!" shouted Earl, throwing himself against the back of the chair. "We don't even know how to *hunt* buffalo any more, much less raise them. Do you have any idea what kind of fence you have to build to contain a herd of buffalo?"

Tommy nodded in slow motion. "Yeah, but we could pay ourselves to build it. We could make good money from the meat and the hides. Anybody got any idea what a buffalo hide goes for these days?"

Earl hit his forehead with a tight fist. "Pay ourselves with what?" he demanded through clenched teeth.

"The oil well down on the southern end is still producing a little," said Leona.

"There's good water, good pasturage," added David. "That huge old meadow down on the highway'd be easy to fence off..."

Earl leapt up. His chair banged into the wall six feet behind him. "Now, just hang on. That's where the casino is going."

David was in full swing now and said at an almost normal pace, "Yeah, but if we get a good buffalo ranch going and breed up to some good horses, we could even have buffalo hunts on horseback! We wouldn't need a casino."

"Well, we're not going to vote on this tonight, anyway, 'cause Roy and Bernice aren't here," said Tommy. "Earl, how about if you look into the cost of getting a small herd of buffalo and building a fence for them around that whole pasture and buying hay to feed them in winter. Find out about the going price for hides and buffalo meat. You come up with honest information, just like Emma did. Then we can give this some thought and talk to the people about it."

Earl rolled his eyes and allowed himself to glare at Tommy, since none of the other council members was looking. "I'll get this information, because I know perfectly well it'll knock the whole stupid plan to hell and back. You can be sure I'm going to be talking, too. And I won't have one good thing to say about this cockamamie scheme of Emma's. Do you people have any idea how long it'd take to set up a ranch on the reservation? Years. And you couldn't get a dog food company to buy horseflesh bred from that string of nags up on the Butte." He retrieved his chair, slammed it against the table, and stomped out.

Another gust of cold wind rushed in and sent chills down four spines. It moaned around the corners of the building before howling away.

An hour later Emma closed her office and stepped outside. She stood for a few minutes in the last light, breathing in the cold air that swept the smell of approaching snow across the broken grasslands. It whipped her hair across her face. Not the howling, killer-wind, this was the wind she loved. It was like the breath of the Earth. It spoke of perfect freedom and distant lands.

She went around the building and started up the stairs. Just as she reached the landing outside her door, a black pick-up with a row of headlights across the top roared up and slid to a stop parallel to the front of the building, roiling up a cloud of dust that rushed east with the wind. The door slammed and Earl Rides strode around the corner. "You think you're gonna stop the casino, don't you, miss smart pants," he yelled up at her. "Well, think again. I'm gonna put it through no matter what you do. You just go ahead and get yourself elected—president, for all I care. Just remember, I *know* things."

A bolt of fear shot through Emma, but she turned it quickly into anger. "*I* know a couple of things now, too, Earl. I did a little research at county records when I got back. So interesting to see how one man can acquire such a large parcel of private land, which just happens to border the proposed casino site, and at such a price. How'd you manage that? I can't imagine Old Man Richards just gave it to you out of the goodness of his heart, not with his feelings about Indians. What'd you do, promise to tell him where Will was after all these years?"

Earl started up the stairs.

"You stop right there," she commanded. She walked down slowly until she stood on the bare ground and had to look up at him. She was shivering now in the cold wind.

He relaxed and shifted his weight to one foot with his arms crossed.

Emma pulled blowing hair from her face and hooked it behind her ear. "Come on, Earl. That was years ago, and we were too young and too scared to make intelligent decisions. Let it be, please. No good can come of dragging it into the open now, not to us and not to his parents. It certainly won't bring Will back."

A twinge of pain dimmed Earl's glare for a second. "I know that, dammit. But that doesn't mean I'm going to let you railroad me on this casino."

Emma forced a gentler tone into her voice. "Why is this so important, Earl? You own the only gas station on the reservation and make more money than anybody. And don't tell me it's for the tribe. I know you better than that. It's tied up with your speculation on Old Man Richards' land."

"I got debts. And that's all I'm going to tell you." He leaned so close his flapping eagle feather whipped her forehead. His eyes narrowed to black slits. "I'm telling you: get outta my way." He turned and strode back to his truck.

Emma looked after him, frowning. "I don't think I care to know about your debts," she said into the wind.

Before she reached the top of the steps, the telephone was ringing in her apartment.

"Hey, Emma, this is Gordy. How's it going out there?"

"Okay, I guess. We saw the article today, and my people weren't happy to see private tribal matters appear in the press. Did you tell the reporter about that?"

"Me? No, I didn't know about it myself until I read it. But don't worry. It only makes you look good. A real fighter. Say, tell me about this Paul Greer. You met him, didn't you?"

"Yeah."

"Now that's one weird bird. He called me a couple of hours ago ranting like a madman. You know what his problem is?"

Emma kicked off her shoes and slid her feet into old sheepskin slippers. "You know about as much as I do, Gordy. He practically begged the reporter not to print the fact that he was an ex-priest to spare the feelings of his former congregation. He's a very caring person. He just doesn't want to be president."

"Well, I wish his brother'd thought of that before this all came about."

"So do I." She moved the morning's tea cup from the table to the sink and ran water into it.

"Well, anyway, there's no way he can back out. I checked with a lawyer friend of mine. She said backing out now would be like breaking a contract. So we got him, whether either side likes it or not. I guess you heard about the debate."

"No, I just walked in the door."

"They've put it together for the evening before the election. In San Francisco. There's a cocktail party in the Regency Bay Hotel first..."

"The Regency Bay? Isn't that the one there was so much controversy about?"

"What controversy?"

Emma opened her small freezer to check the supper possibilities. "I don't remember exactly. It had to do with risky soil or something."

"So what? Anyway, there's also a big gala there afterwards, too, and all the candidates, including vice presidential, and their spouses are expected. So we want you to go out for the debate."

She took out the ice tray and a small casserole dish covered in foil. "What good will that do? The court ruled that the presidential candidate has to represent the party. I wouldn't even be allowed on the stage."

"I know, but Greer's a sorry candidate, and we'll pick up a lot of press just being there. I'd sure rather you field questions than this priest person."

Emma threw a couple of ice cubes into the glass of tea she'd made in the morning, not wanting to waste what was left of the teabag. "Sorry, Gordy, I just got back from a long trip, and I can't afford another one right now."

"Hey, we'll spring for gas and a motel. Might even go for an Eight, doesn't have to be a Six."

Emma thought about her empty desk downstairs and the single speech she was scheduled to give to the Cheyenne Sierra Club in a week. "Okay, send me $500 and I'll do it."

"You still at...wait, lemme look at my list...P.O. Box 43, Big Sleep, WY?"

"Yep."

"Okey doke. Signing off." His voice grew fainter, but she heard, "Jeez, what kind of name is Big Slee...?" The connection was gone.

"Maybe the same kind as Pen-sa-co-la," she drawled into the receiver.

Emma lifted the foil from the dish. Beneath it was such a mass of ice crystals she couldn't see the food under it. She shoved the dish into the microwave and set it for six and a half minutes. Earl's angry face tried to surface in her mind, but she put it aside and thought of Paul. The national limelight was going to trap him in its glare after all. If it weren't so horrifying to him, it'd be downright funny. She glanced at the microwave. Still five minutes and forty seconds. She could give him a quick call and see whether he'd chosen heart attack or nervous breakdown for his reaction to the news. She shuffled through the cards from Clearwater until she found Danny's new number. Her hand trembled slightly as she punched the numbers on the phone pad.

"Emma," Paul shouted, "am I glad to hear from you! I guess you heard about the article and the Supreme Court and all."

"Yeah, I got called on the carpet for some of the things she wrote. But this has to be a lot worse for you. I called to commiserate. You want some help with your presentation?" She took a sip of her tea and shivered as the wind whistled through a crack in the kitchen window.

"I'm not doing any presentation, Emma. I called Gordy this morning and told him in no uncertain terms that I was out. If I have to fake my death, I'll do it. So you can be the candidate, after all."

Emma stalled, not wanting to deliver more bad news. "What'd Gordy say?"

"He said he'd look into it. But I don't care what he sees when he 'looks into it.' I'm out."

She bit her bottom lip and hoped he was sitting down. "That may not be so simple, Paul."

"What do you mean? I'm a free agent."

"Of course. But Gordy meant he'd look into the legalities of it. You've been on the slate since the beginning. There's no time to convene again for another nomination. If the party chose to challenge you on this—mind you, I'm not saying it would, or that I would have any hand in the suit—but if it did, they could make a good case for breach of contract. We'd have a long process on our hands, and the debate would certainly arrive before any decision came down. You can ask Danny, but I think he'll tell you there's no precedent for such a case. And that means a long deliberation."

She could feel Paul's silent casting about for an out. His breathing came through in rough, irregular gasps.

"Did Gordy say anything about sending you money to make the trip?" she asked.

"He said something about not having to pay my way because the law required me to go anyway. Why?"

"Well, look, he wants me to go, too. What if we went together? He's sending me $500. We could spell each other and drive straight through both ways. We wouldn't have to waste money on motels, and we could both make it on party money. We can talk about the debate on the way."

There was another long silence. Emma's microwave beeped. She hooked the handset under her left ear and lifted the dish out. Frothy, melted lime sherbet bubbled in the bottom of it. She heaved a long sigh and set it in the sink.

"Paul?"

"I'm thinking. I guess thinking is not the most efficient way to run up your phone bill. You want me to call you back?"

"No, just say yes."

"Emma, you know...I...my parishioners..."

"Look, Paul, I don't think you have any choice. If you refuse, the debate can't be held at all, according to what I heard about the ruling. And that'd bring a whole lot more press down on you than just going to the debate and answering a couple of questions. Anyway, who do you think will get the most attention from the moderator?"

"The big guys."

"Of course. So the alternative is even worse. I'm afraid it's a simple yes or no."

Paul groaned softly. Then there was silence. Another groan. "Oh, my God. Yes. If I can arrange my work around it. On the way you can just find an insane asylum and drop me off."

Emma grinned. "Look at it this way—it's just your little bit for Mom Earth. And I promise I'll prep you for the debate."

"Don't bother. I'll sit on that stage like a sack of turnips. If anyone directs a single question at me, I'll make up sign language. Even the deaf'll think I'm speaking in tongues."

Emma laughed. "Your car or mine?"

"Mine's a little station wagon. I've got an egg crate mattress for it. If we get really tired, we can stretch out in the back."

"Okay, that's settled. The debate's on the evening of the fifth. When do you think we ought to leave Denver?"

"You have any idea how long a drive it is?"

"Maybe twenty, twenty-two hours."

"Let's allow twenty-four to be on the safe side. We'll leave here as soon as I get off on the fourth. That way, I can work Sunday and have Monday and Tuesday off. I'll try to get the late shift on Wednesday."

"Sounds good. I'll be at your place by four on the fourth. Bye, now."

"So long, Emma. Thanks for calling." He gulped audibly. "I'm looking forward to seeing you, if nothing else." Then the line was silent.

She was going to drive across half the continent with him. "Now, why did I do that?" she asked, dumping the sherbet down the drain. The crack in the window whistled at her.

CHAPTER NINETEEN

The drive west toward the interstate was awkward and mostly silent. From the wheel, Paul watched Emma out of the corner of his eye. She shed her gray down jacket and threw it into the back seat. Was she always so quiet, so self-contained, or was it her way of saying how indifferent she was to him? This was a mistake, he thought, signaling to pass a Wal-Mart truck. I should have my head examined, going on national television.

Annoyed with her silence and with his dry, knotted tongue, he asked himself, Why does this woman always crop up just when I think I've gotten her out of my mind? And what am I doing here when she thinks I'm a spineless ninny, anyway. Of course, it was her suggestion and I didn't have much other choice. Maybe she's attracted to me, too. Okay, this is a perfect opportunity to find out. No, it's an opportunity to get to know her better and find out I don't even like her. That'll take care of this idiotic infatuation. His heart responded to the suggestion with a silent, derisive laugh.

As they rose into the foothills, the first snowflakes hit the windshield. He glanced at Emma, clenched his jaw, and eased up on the gas. Within a few minutes, the road had shrunk to four gray tire tracks through dirty, packed snow.

"Have you had a lot of experience driving in snow?" he asked, relieved to find a reason to speak to her. He peered at the clouds that lay flat across the hilltops.

Emma blinked as if he'd dragged her back from a distant time. "What? Sorry Paul, I'm afraid my mind was on buffalo herds and fences—reservation business. Snow driving? Sure. But not much in the mountains. The reservation's out on the plains. You have snow tires on this car?"

"Retreads. On the back."

"Uh-huh. Well, I'd be glad to drive if want me to."

"I guess I can handle it a while."

The gray tracks disappeared under the packed snow. The car fish-tailed and righted itself.

Adrenaline shot to the ends of Paul's hair. "Okay, maybe I'll let you drive after all."

"Just pull over before the road gets worse."

"Right. How about the next exit?"

"Fine."

Yeah, just great. Another ninnyism.

"So you don't get much snow in New Orleans?" Emma asked when they'd changed places.

"Maybe once in ten years, and all it does is make the grass look like green whiskers on a white face. It never sticks on the streets. I've never even seen an icy road before, not even when I was in D.C." His voice was taut before he finished the sentence.

"Wise of you to let me drive, then. Most men I know would drive straight into a ditch before they'd let a woman take the wheel." She smiled. "We'll just take it easy and hope the other drivers don't skid into us." She looked at the hole where his radio had been. "Too bad you don't have a radio. We could check on the road report."

"Sorry. It was stolen right in front of the church. How long do you think it'll take to get through this? Or will we have snow all the way?"

Emma shrugged. "I've never driven this stretch of road before, but I doubt it. I checked the map. It shows a lot of ski areas up ahead, and if that's any indication, I think we'll be in snow for a hundred miles, at least."

"Good thing we left some extra time, then."

"Right."

"I guess I owe you thanks again. I'd never have made it driving without you."

Emma laughed. "There's no guarantee you'll make it driving *with* me. But relax. We don't have a problem till we have a problem."

The snow increased; flakes flew briefly as white streaks of motion in the headlights and then batted themselves flat against the windshield. The wipers swept them into two bars of slush and added rhythm to the silence.

Okay, Paul thought, she was talking. Keep it going. So, what's it like living on the reservation? he practiced. No, too personal. She's pretty sensitive about being Indian. He glanced at Emma, who seemed completely concentrated on the road. Her lovely profile brightened and dimmed in passing headlights. How did your trip to the other reservations go? No, the Indian thing again. What do you like to do? Who's your favorite...oh, for God's sake, cut it out, he thought. You sound like a driveling adolescent.

"So, what's it like living in New Orleans?" said Emma.

"Huh? Oh. Hot. Muggy. So hard after Katrina hit. So many people just lost in their lives."

"Did you stay during the hurricane?"

"No the church evacuated the residents of a nursing home, and I drove the school bus. We ended up in an old army base in northern Louisiana. The church was in a part of New Orleans that didn't take too much damage. One door blew off, but no flooding. Colorado's so different. Now that I've been here a few months, I see why everybody loves a dry climate. I'd hate to have to live on the coast again. Of course, I have yet to make it through my first winter in Colorado."

"It must have been awful, wearing all those black clothes in that heat."

"It was, especially on Saturdays. They didn't air condition the church except on Sundays. Big old barn of a building with a roof about fifty feet high. Then I had to sit in this little booth..."

The smell of the old damp varnish and dust was in his nose again, and doors banged open in memory. The tortured face of a woman whose emotional needs had defaulted to him swam in a miasma of human pain. His own guilt came back with the familiar smell of the confessional. All those people kneeling there when he'd bolted. They'd all seen him. It must have been the worst scandal in St. Simon's history.

And what of Laurel Broussard? Beautiful, desperate Laurel, who'd tried to follow him. What had become of her? She would surely have left her husband by now. To go where? She'd had family in Chicago. The thought made his heart thrash against his lungs. What if she'd been in Chicago when that article came out? He rubbed his thumb hard against the burn scar.

Emma glanced at his hands and up at his face. "You okay, Paul?"

"Yeah. Sorry. I just got a flashback, and whenever that happens, it makes me feel like there are two different people in here," he pointed at his head, "and I don't think either of them is me."

"I don't understand."

"I don't imagine you would, even if I could express it clearly. Your life has always been an arrow directed at one target, hasn't it?"

"What makes you say that?"

"Well, your passion about the earth. When I look at that in you, it makes me...I don't know, envious and sad."

"And you think my whole life has been taken up with that?" she asked, laughing. "I hate to disillusion you, but there's a lot about me you don't know."

Yes, thought Paul, an opening. "Would you care to tell me about it?"

She looked him in the eye. Her face, ghostly in the reflection of headlights on snow, softened before she turned away. "Some other time, maybe. Road conditions don't allow me to be much of a conversationalist right now."

Paul's heart flipped. "Of course. Don't mind me." The "some other time" made him smile into the deepening storm. "There's a hill coming up that Danny says is a real bear in winter. Floyd Hill. I remembered the name because he has this ex-friend named Floyd who keeps bugging him about something. And at the bottom of Floyd Hill is the turn off to Glory Hole, where the gambling is."

"Okay, thanks for the warning. We'll just take it in second gear."

At the top of Floyd Hill the snow thickened, and the road became slick as water on glass. "Hmm," said Emma, her voice shaky, "Forget second. I think I'll take this one in first."

"Uh, do you have half?" Paul leaned forward, his fingers dug into the edges of the seat.

"What?" She gave a shaky laugh. "Oh. Yeah, you'd think they'd build in an ice-gear, wouldn't you?"

After a long, tense stretch of precarious sliding and a couple of sharp curves at the bottom, she said, "Good thing you told me about that one." She strained forward. "You ever been in a white-out? Oops, silly question."

"What's that?"

"It's a blizzard so bad you can't see anything but white. Usually happens when the wind is blowing a lot harder than it is now. I was in one once in Wyoming. I couldn't even see the end of my car. It's pretty scary."

"Would you rate this as a white-out?" Paul peered out at the thick snow.

"No, I can still see the guard rails and taillights twenty or thirty feet ahead, but if it gets any worse, we'll have to stop until it lets up."

By Georgetown Emma suggested that they try to make it through the Eisenhower tunnel and then stop for a while in the first town for a late dinner.

"Sure, I'm all for that. We could stop for several days if you like."

Emma laughed her tumbling water laugh, and it made him feel like summer.

She glanced at him and said, "Sorry Paul. I know it isn't funny. You really hate this whole thing, don't you?"

"Of course I do. Try to put yourself in my place. How would you feel about it?"

"I can't even begin to put myself in your place, never having been a Catholic, much less a priest. You want to tell me about it? I can at least listen while I drive."

"Tell you about what?"

"Well, why did you become a priest in the first place?"

Paul stared absently out at the flying white streaks that muffled them away from the rest of the world, trying to recapture the months of adolescent agonizing over the decision; the conversations with his Jesuit uncle; and finally, at eighteen, his acquiescence to the idea that God had called him.

"Listen, I don't mean to pry into something that's painful or too personal," she said, touching his arm.

"No, it's not that. It's just hard to put into words for someone who's never been Catholic."

"Just tell me what you can and I'll try to understand."

"Well, take the attachment you have for Mother Earth and magnify it a thousand times. Then add a fear of sin that's been drilled into you since you were six..." He began to tick items off on his fingers. "...the pressure from nuns in school alarmed at the shortage of priests, and the need to pray for a brother you've idolized your whole life but who's gone off the deep end." Paul thought a minute. "A genuine desire to serve people and God. Idealism that knows no bounds. And a certain shyness where girls are concerned. Those are the Roman numerals on a long outline. It wasn't an easy decision, believe me."

"How long was it before you realized it was the wrong one?"

"Years. Or maybe I knew from the day of my ordination and just didn't tell myself."

"What changed?"

"Everything. My opinion of what the church was doing *to* people rather than *for* them—good people leading the simplest of lives a few steps ahead of poverty, but having a new baby every year or two."

"So you didn't agree with the ban on birth control?"

"No, among other things. The stand on divorce. Not that I'm in favor of divorce; at the very least I believe in trying every possible avenue to salvage a marriage, but there are circumstances when it isn't bearable any longer, and the people are trapped without hope." Laurel's face and a number of others floated in the snowflakes. "I saw a lot more pain than peace come out of church rules. Or maybe that was all I noticed, even though a lot of people find what they need in the church. And then there was the assumption of the evil nature of man. I got to where I couldn't teach sin to the little ones any more. Such innocent fac-es, capable of pure joy and pure love. It broke my heart to crush that and fill their heads up with guilt and fear. There were so many things. And the changes were so gradual I hardly noticed them. For years I'd wake up in the night feeling apprehensive and not know why."

"Did you ever miss having a family?"

"Every waking minute."

"So what was it that finally convinced you?"

Paul hesitated. "I can't talk about it, not specifically, but I want to be as open with you as I can without betraying a trust." He stopped and looked at her. Without seeing her intense eyes, he knew they were pulling him gently in, but he had no idea how to talk to a woman about his body's needs. He gathered in a great breath to rush through the hard part. "I guess they call it a burning libido. It finally pushed me over the edge, and when it did, the rest flashed into place in my head. After that, I did the cowardly thing. I ran. I'm not proud of running away."

"I understand that." Emma turned to him for a second. Something flowed between them, something on a plane com-pletely removed from the body's needs, but Paul had no idea what it was. It made him want to shelter her.

She focused on the road again. "Tell me about the rest of your family."

"There's just Danny now. My father, who was a good deal older than my mother, died of a heart attack not long after I was ordained. My mother died of cancer about five years ago."

"Wow, so you haven't been close to anyone but Danny for all that time?"

"Not even Danny. He'd been in Denver for several years when he came to New Orleans for the last funeral, and he had to leave again almost immediately. I didn't spend much time with him. After that, well, what can you say over the phone or e-mail? We barely kept up with each other until I showed up on his doorstep."

Emma raised her brows. "And he just took you in? That's pretty impressive."

"I wish you liked him better. He's a fine person. At the very least, he lives according to his beliefs, and they aren't all that bad. Of course, I'm furious with him for getting me into this jam, but I'm also deeply grateful for his kindness. And it feels good to have my brother back."

She smiled but kept her eyes on the road. "Actually, I do like him without a beer can in hand. But I see you as the better person."

Paul's heart lurched again and he looked over at her. She tucked a hair away in a motion so natural and graceful it was tiny ballet. A feminine motion. Female.

He clenched his hands in his lap to keep from grabbing his hair and pulling. What was it about women that drove men to distraction? What was it about Laurel, beautiful, tragic Laurel, who'd wanted him desperately, and whom he'd lusted after and then abandoned without a backward glance? What was it about Emma, who drew him like a moth to a bug zapper but still kept the distance of a will-o-the-wisp? Are we all doomed to want what we can't have?

"Emma..."

"So what do you think you'll do for the rest of your life? I'm sure selling shoes doesn't present much of a challenge."

Paul sighed silently in a mixture of frustration and relief. He had no idea what he might have babbled. "The rest of my life? You certainly know the big questions, don't you? I have no idea, but selling shoes is what I need while I sort things out. I still wake up with the apprehension. Or maybe it's just a frightening vacuum."

"Why?"

"Because I haven't figured out who I am, even if I finally got it straight who I'm not."

Emma's brow wrinkled, but she said nothing.

The wipers scraped out their rhythm. He tried again to explain.

"Who you are is never much of an issue to a practicing Catholic, since so much of your identification is tied up with the church. When you cut that loose, there's a lot of emptiness. You have no foundation to build on, and you have to start all over."

Still Emma said nothing, but the knit of her brow had changed from concentration on the road to an effort to understand.

They entered the Eisenhower Tunnel and both relaxed for the dry, lighted length of it. At the end, the yellow and blue flashing lights of a sanding truck appeared out of the white.

Emma smiled. "Wow, I think I'll just follow him down to— what's the next town? Can you see it on the road map?"

Paul held the map up. "Not without turning on the overhead light."

"Better not. I'll just follow him to the next exit."

"Listen, we hadn't counted on dinner in a resort area, and I hate to use up your money..."

Emma gave him a brief, warm smile. "Thanks, Paul, but remember it's not *my* money. It's the party's, and given the situation, I think you have as much right to it as I do. Probably more. Let's just use it judiciously till it runs out, and then we'll both be on our own. Okay?"

"Emma you..."

"What do you want to eat?"

"Anything." Paul sat back and gave up trying to tell her— what? What had he been about to blurt out? Something she clearly didn't want to hear. He sighed silently and said, "I'm not a fussy eater. If I can't have crawfish *etouffée*, I don't care what I eat."

Emma laughed. "What's *that* taste like?"

"Spicy, a little like lobster. You eat it with rice. When we get in the White House, I'll give the chefs the night off some evening and cook it for you."

Emma laughed again and Paul visualized deep, sparkling water in the sun.

"Now that's a safe invitation," she said. "Can you actually cook?"

"Gourmet. Specializing in Cajun."

"Wow, I'm sorry I'll never get to taste your cooking."

Paul clenched his hands. "That could be arranged. You have to go straight home when we get back?"

"I should." She laughed harshly. "You never know, there might even be some client banging on my door this very minute."

"Why are you having such a struggle? Certainly it's not because you're not a fine lawyer."

"I'm getting a lot of interference from somebody who desperately wants the casino to go through. He's blocking tribal affairs from reaching my office. And where I live, there's not much legal work that isn't a tribal affair."

"Can't you complain to someone? Isn't there some kind of authority?"

"Tribal council, and he's on it. Against his vote, they hired me to research the gambling issue. I suppose I could bring my problem before the whole council, and they'd probably slap his wrists, but I'm such an independent cuss. I always try to make my own way before..." She looked in his direction and her wrists flexed over the steering wheel. "Actually, since we're being all open and honest, there's more to it than that. We, well, we sort of have a history, this man and I."

"Can you..." Paul started.

A blast of wind buffeted the car into to the left lane as they emerged from the shelter of the mountainside into a valley. The white closed in around them until even the flashing lights of the sanding truck disappeared for a moment. Emma righted the car, followed the truck under a sign announcing the Silverthorne exit, and slid slowly to a stoplight. "I can make out a Denny's right here at the exit. Can you see anything else?" she asked.

"Not a thing. Denny's will be fine."

The restaurant was crowded with drivers waiting out the blizzard. Paul and Emma sat at the counter. Both poked at the snow in the tops of their shoes. Emma shivered and signaled the waiter for coffee.

She was close, closer than in the car, and Paul could smell her. It was not a perfume, just a sweet, open smell like a fall wind, mixed with the dampness of her pale blue wool sweater. Paul looked at the beads of melted snow and the few flakes still caught in her hair. "You look beautiful," he blurted. "I mean, you should see the snow in your hair."

Emma grinned at him. "You too. And thanks. I'll just go check it out."

She turned to get up and their knees collided. Paul put his hand on her arm to steady her, and she laid a hand on his shoulder. Their eyes met and held. His breath failed. He sensed her body under the wool, felt all of it with all of his, and knew that his face reddened. She squeezed his shoulder slightly and was gone.

Ten minutes later, absently eating his Denver omelet, Paul was acutely aware of her next to him. She hardly looked at him again, giving all of her intense concentration to her chicken sandwich. Everything was astir in him, his whole body vibrating, and he could not erase the image of touching her face, putting his arms around her. His hands tingling, he wanted to reject the thin hardness of his fork. His mouth wanted the secrets of her warm smile, not the stinging salsa of the omelet. The smell of coffee and over-sweet pies offended him, and he wanted nothing but to be back in the car with her, blizzard or not.

The rhythm of the wipers came back, and suddenly he felt their sweep shoving him aside, a splattered snowflake seeking peace in one direction but swept in the other by outside events and his feelings for Emma.

CHAPTER TWENTY

Danny shoved four Coke cans, a carton of orange juice, and a slightly moldy Emmenthaler cheese brick to the back of his refrigerator. He set two six-packs of Samuel Adams in the center of the top shelf, played the bottle caps like piano keys, and smacked Mr. Adams affectionately in the face with his index fingernail. "Just you wait," he crowed aloud. "Two more days till the election. Then we'll see how fast your little brown bottles can go from the ice box to the recycling bin." He left the kitchen whistling and rubbing his hands down his chest.

He looked down. Was it his imagination, or had the beer belly diminished? Huh. Think of that. Not that it had been all that bad before, but maybe he should ration himself after Tuesday so it didn't come...

The door buzzer surprised him, and for a second Floyd's veiled threat came to mind. He shook his head and went to the speaker. "Who is it?"

A woman's voice answered, soft and shaky. "Paul?"

Intrigued, he pushed the door release, dashed to the bedroom and changed out of his sweat suit into chinos and a long sleeved sport shirt, smiling at his body's profile in the mirror. That sly devil Paul hadn't even told him he'd met someone.

Her knock was so tentative he hardly heard it. Half expecting a still empty hallway, he opened the door.

He and the visitor stood on either side of the threshold, bewildered.

Deeply troubled blue eyes stared at him from under a mass of wavy blond hair netted with sparkling melted snow. Shivering in a thin navy windbreaker, she stood half turned toward the elevator, so nervous that red splotches covered her cheeks, her neck, and the V of skin bared by the open neck of a dusty rose sweater. Any more tense and she'd snap like a power line in an ice storm.

"Who're you?" they asked simultaneously.

He opened the door wider. "Please, come in. I'm Paul's brother, Danny," he said, not taking his eyes off her face. Beauty, pain, and honesty glowed through the splotches and hit him like a cement truck.

She looked past him into the apartment.

"Paul's not here," Danny explained, his tongue cumbersome as a sandbag. "He's gone to California for a couple of days."

"Oh." Her shoulders slumped. She leaned against the door frame and her knees gave way.

Startled, Danny caught her under the arm, pulled her up, and steered her into the room. "Can I help you, Miss...?"

She leaned onto a dining chair. "No, I'm so sorry to have bothered you. I shouldn't have come." Her breath caught. She closed her eyes and retreated into herself. "I knew this was the wrong thing to do," she mumbled. "Why couldn't I listen to my own better judgment?" She put her balled fists against her eyes and sobbed.

"Come on, sit down. Can I get you something to drink? A beer, a Coke..." He stepped into the bedroom and returned with a length of toilet paper in lieu of a tissue.

"Just a little water," she said, dabbing at her eyes and trying to regain control. "I get so thirsty up here."

Okay, not someone from the store, Danny mused, helping her slide out of the windbreaker. "So you're not from Denver?"

Freed from the jacket, her sweater fluffed into a cloud of angora.

She pulled at the hem. "New Orleans. I'm Laurel. Laurel Broussard. Maybe Paul told you about me."

"No, I'm afraid he didn't." Danny shied from the implications that came to mind.

She looked away. "Of course not. I don't know why I thought he would."

"You're a friend of Paul's?"

"Not exactly," she sighed. "A parishioner."

Danny's brain said, *Oh my god*, but his mouth said, "I see."

Her face went from splotchy to blazing red, and she bit her lower lip. "I wanted to look him up."

"As you were passing through town?" Danny asked, careful to avoid any hint of sarcasm. "Please, sit down."

She sat on the very edge of the sofa with her right foot forward, ready to bolt, glanced up at him, and turned redder still.

He hoped she saw understanding and kindness in his smile.

Her resolve collapsed, her back bent, and she drew the leg back. "No, I followed Paul here," she sobbed into her lap.

Danny sat, too, careful to leave her plenty of space. "I'm sorry, but I'm really confused. Paul's been here for months. I didn't know he'd written..."

"He didn't." She wiped at her face and blew her nose but said nothing. She covered her face again. "I can't talk about it."

Danny noticed her hands for the first time. Her skin was smooth and fine as living silk. He reached out and laid a hand on her soft sleeve. "It's all right, Laurel. No matter how bad you think this is, I've done worse. Nothing you could say would shock me."

"I can't talk to a perfect stranger, shouldn't talk to anyone at all about this. It's too stupid and shameful."

"And it'll never go anywhere but this room."

A minute passed. She shuddered and shook her head.

Danny waited, grappling with his own internal turmoil.

She kept her head in her hands and her first words were muffled. "I was in love with Paul at St. Simon's, or I thought I was, and when he left, I was devastated. After a couple of months, I kind of got over it." She folded her hands in her lap and rocked forward. "I told myself I'd let my emotions run away with me. But...other things got worse, and when I saw the newspaper article my uncle sent me from Chicago, and knew where Paul was, it was like a sign. Everything came crashing back. I just packed up my things and left."

"But how did you find him? Denver's a big city."

"The article said where he worked. I...well, I followed him here from the shopping center this afternoon. After he came into the building, I waited a few minutes. Then I came up to the lobby and put my finger on the button. I lost my nerve and didn't push it. I went back to the motel and paced, and then I finally just forced myself to come back. I'm such an idiot." She sighed and twisted the wet toilet paper. "Is it true he's running for president?"

"Yes, but..."

"Oh, God, I knew it."

"Don't worry about it. There's no chance he's actually going to *be* president."

"He really never said anything about me?"

"No. I'm sorry."

She stood up and stared absently into the reflection in the balcony door. Danny stared into it as well, aware of beautiful curves under the sweater and the dove-gray pants far too light for Denver's winter.

"I guess I knew he didn't love me, he just..." She bit off whatever she'd meant to say and turned to him, eyes wide. "Don't misunderstand, he never..."

Suddenly, Danny understood. Completely. Here was the cause of the lust Paul had alluded to in the beginning. And what a cause. Paul had run from Laurel. He'd wanted her, and obviously she was in love with him.

Danny struggled to keep an explosion of emotions from hurling him against the wall. Shock, envy, frustration. Celibate Paul had women chasing him all over the country. And Danny had—what? A sudden attraction so powerful he felt glued to this woman by Epoxy. And she wanted Paul.

She was still facing him, tense in the silence of his thought. She folded her arms across her chest and bent into them. "I'm so ashamed. And I'm really sorry. I won't take any more of your time." She headed for the chair where her jacket lay.

Danny pulled himself together. Steering Emma to Paul had been sacrifice enough. He couldn't let Laurel go, not without wedging at least a little of himself between her and Paul. Besides, she needed help, and he knew the years of pain and guilt that lay behind her tears, even if he didn't know the particulars. He stepped to her side and gently turned her to him. "I have the whole evening free, Laurel. And a sympathetic ear. You don't need to be embarrassed or to rush off to an empty, depressing motel room."

Laurel sniffed and pointed to the door, her face twisted in anguish.

"Look, it seems like you're in something of a bind here. What'll you do now? Wouldn't you at least like to figure that out before you go?"

The question seemed to surprise her. She sat down hard on the chair. "I hadn't thought beyond the point of seeing Paul again. Oh, God," she wailed, "what a stupid, adolescent thing I've done. I told myself that the whole way up here."

"Do you want to go home again?"

"No! It took me all these years to get up the guts to leave, when Paul kept telling me I'd be excommunicated. But I'm free now. Free of a man who couldn't love me and free of the church that chained me to him. At least that much became clear while I was driving up here. I'm never going back. I'll get a divorce now."

Danny smiled at her. "Good for you. At least that's a place to start. Now, could I offer you a late dinner? Just to compensate for my brother's absence?"

"Oh, I couldn't. I couldn't eat a thing. And I must look awful." She rubbed at her red eyes and ran a hand through her hair, plastering it together with the melted snow.

It looked scraggly, but Danny had never seen anything more beautiful. "Listen, one of my areas of expertise is home delivered pizza. We can stay here if you're embarrassed to go out, but you look beautiful, red nose and all. I'd be proud to be seen with you."

Laurel gave him a teary smile and sniffed. "Well, if we can eat here. I guess I should eat something. To tell the truth, I've been too nervous to eat all day. Sausage and mushrooms?"

"My very choice." Danny picked up the handset and pressed the speed dial for the pizza parlor. He was in big trouble now, he knew. This woman was already deep under his skin. She wasn't going to be one of those simply passing through his life. He knew it in his marrow, where she'd settled.

CHAPTER TWENTY ONE

Paul held the door for Emma as they left Denny's in Silverthorne, eager to be with her in the car again. This time, somehow, he'd let her know how he felt about her. Following her out into the last drifting flakes, he watched as she lifted her feet high, set them down straight in snow up to her calves, and pulled them out again, clumped with white.

"Hey, why don't let me go first so you won't have such deep snow to plow through?" he suggested above the rumble of trucks getting ready to roll.

"'Post holing' we call it," she answered over her shoulder. "Don't worry, the car's right over there."

"You want me to drive a while? You must be tired, having driven all the way down from...this is embarrassing. I don't even know where you live."

"Town called Big Sleep. And I'm okay. How 'bout if I drive till we run out of snow pack and you drive the wet road?"

He glanced at the column of semis already heading for the interstate. "Sounds good. Wet roads I can do with my eyes closed." He opened the car door for her.

She grinned up at him as she slid in. "I didn't hear that."

Sandwiched between a Safeway truck and a moving van, they joined the line of vehicles crawling up the ramp.

As soon as traffic thins out, he thought, I'll blurt it right out. The thought catapulted his heart rate. His hands went from cold to clammy.

Emma glanced at the car's clock. "Midnight."

Paul nodded. "We've already used up the extra time we allowed ourselves."

"No more long stops. Maybe you should get some sleep." She pulled into the left lane to crawl past the Safeway truck.

Vexed, he tried to find a reason to stay awake long enough to get his feelings off his chest. None came to mind, and he said, "I'm not sleepy in the least, but I guess I should try. You sure you don't mind?"

Emma shook her head.

Paul sighed. So much for blurting. She'd probably have driven straight off the road anyway. Better to wait till he was driving, but he would definitely tell her before they got to California. Paul tilted his backrest and leaned into the car door with his eyes closed. Within a minute, certain that sleep was out of the question, he opened them a slit and watched Emma. She was totally focused on driving, but her lips puckered into a silent whistle that calmed his anxiety about the road.

Ahead of them, the last tattered clouds drifted away from a three-quarter moon. He turned his head slightly and stared at the cliffs glittering with milky diamonds in the moonlight. Beautiful, cold, and dangerous, he thought, wondering whether he meant Emma or the snow.

When he opened his eyes again, the car was still and Emma was gone. He sat up and looked around. She was a few feet in front of the car, silhouetted against an orange ramp speed sign, jogging in tight circles and occasionally stretching to touch her toes. A sign at the bottom of the ramp pointed left to Avon.

Paul got out. Frigid air slapped his face, clearing the scraps of uneasy sleep from his head. A chain of goose bumps cycled up and down his spine.

Emma turned and jogged back to him on the wet ramp. "Bright moon, huh?" she asked.

Paul looked up. "Wow! I've never seen the features so clearly."

She jogged in place, breathing out, bobbing feathery mist that smelled of mint. "You get enough sleep?"

"Yes, and thanks for such a long stint at the wheel."

"It wasn't all that long. You've only been out about an hour and a half."

Paul rotated the shoulder that had been jammed against the door. "How many miles?"

"Not more than fifty. It was slow going."

He stuck out his arms and turned from side to side. "How long have we been stopped?"

"A couple of minutes. I needed to stretch. You want to walk away from the highway a little? There's a dirt road going off to the right. The moon's bright enough, but I have a flashlight if we need it."

Paul leapt at the invitation, and his heart leapt into high gear. If he was going to tell her, it'd be better to do it walking up a moonlit road than when either of them was driving. "Great idea. I'll put on my jacket."

They walked a few yards up the road. Paul watched the grace of her walk, vertical and balanced, as much in harmony with the earth as a willow tree perfectly rooted to it. He watched her hair flutter in a cold breeze, smelled the freshness of fall that came from her body. Now. "Emma, I..."

Emma stepped hard into a pothole. "Oof, that was deeper than I thought." She shook muddy water from her sport shoe. Her next step was unsteady.

Paul grabbed her arm.

"I'm not hurt," she said, and moved away from him a few feet. She stopped to wipe the shoe on a patch of snow at the side of the road.

They paced off another hundred yards or so.

She didn't ask what he'd been about to say.

Annoyed with himself as well as her, Paul said, "I'm awake now. Should we get on the road again?"

They walked back without a word.

Emma settled into the passenger seat.

"I've got the mattress rolled out in the back," said Paul.

Emma glanced back. "Why didn't you fold down both sides of the back seat?"

"The one behind you doesn't work anymore. But there's plenty of room for your legs there."

"I'll be fine right here." She raised her head toward the road. "You might come across a few patches of ice still, but traffic is lighter and I don't think you'll have any trouble if you watch the bridges." She spread her jacket on top of her and lowered the back rest.

Paul sneaked a glance at her. She certainly didn't have her eyes open a slit watching him. In a minute she turned and faced the door. He drove into the night with the painful realization that she wanted nothing to do with his feelings. The hell with laying them out for her. He'd drive all the way to central China first.

She seemed to run hot, well, tepid at least, and then cold. Was he only imagining warmth behind those intense eyes, or was it there, just not for him? What did he really feel, anyway? Was it only lust that would eventually fade to indifference?

He searched for answers from Avon to Glenwood Springs, where Emma slept through his filling the tank. He searched again to the state line, looking at the dark figure next to him from time to time.

An hour later, she sat up during a stretch of bumpy road and looked out. "Wow, this kind of reminds me of South Dakota's Badlands. Don't you just love this part of the country, where the geology's written all over the landscape? Every layer of rock a million years."

Grinning at her abruptness, Paul peered at the moonlit gray cliffs rising off the right side of the interstate, their horizontal layers outlined in snow. "I guess I would if I could see it better. Where I come from, the oldest visible thing is a huge, sweeping live oak tree. Do you always wake up in the very middle of a conversation?"

Emma laughed. "I don't know. There's never anyone there to talk to." She adjusted the seat, ran her fingers through her hair, fished a roll of breath mints out of her purse, and gave him one. "You ready to prepare for the debate?"

Paul slipped the mint to the side of his mouth. "Can I ask first whether you slept well?"

"I'm sorry, Paul. That *was* abrupt, wasn't it? Thanks, I did. You okay driving?"

"Sure. The road's been dry for quite a while."

"Where are we?"

"Fifty or sixty miles into Utah."

"What time is it?"

"About 4:30."

"Wow, we're going to be hard pressed to make it on time. Did you check out a route before we left?"

"I looked it over. I-70 doesn't go all the way through. We could clip up to Salt Lake and get on 80, but there's a pretty straight shot through Nevada. It joins 80 just before the California border and goes by a Lake Tahoe."

"Hmm. I'd go for the straight shot and find out about a route when we get closer. Tahoe's in the Sierras. If they got a load of snow, too, it might mean slow going again."

"*I* wouldn't mind in the least."

"I know. So let's get you ready for the debate."

Paul sighed. "Emma, let me ask you one thing first. Have you actually read the whole platform for the Earth Rights Party?"

"You could say that. I wrote it. Along with a couple of other people. I could recite it for you."

"So there's no point in asking whether you really believe all that stuff."

"Well, we may have gone overboard a bit about undamming the rivers, but otherwise..."

"And you think those plans could be pushed through Congress?"

There was such a long silence that Paul glanced at her. She put her hands out, palms up. "I wish I could give you an unqualified yes to that, because I believe so strongly that everything in the platform is absolutely necessary. But there's something about you that demands complete honesty from me. Must be the ex-priest thing."

Paul frowned. "Does that mean you'd lie to me if I'd never been a priest?"

"No, of course not. I just might not tell you everything." She laughed. "Besides, I never lie to my running mates. So I'm going to tell you what nobody else knows: my conviction hides a deep sense of hopelessness. People are too selfish to sacrifice their comforts and pleasures for generations that aren't even here yet." She sighed and stretched her neck before she went on. "But that doesn't mean I think we should do nothing, much less join the graspers and the destroyers and the polluters. Surely you agree with that much."

"Of course. But don't you think the Party's position is extreme?"

"I *know* it's extreme, but whenever people ask me that, I tell them about Marie Curie, who was called a fool for giving the discovery of radium freely to the world and not getting rich off it herself. You know what she answered?"

"No."

"She said something to the effect that there had to be people on her end of the extreme to balance out those on the other end. I think she was right. And besides that, I'm just plain stubborn. So I'm not likely to stop trying, even in the face of certain defeat."

Paul stared at her. If things were different between them, he'd tell her how amazing she was, but he only said, "I'd love to know where you get your strength."

She smiled and shrugged. "Okay, now about the debate. Let's assume that you'll be given a minute or so to present the Party's views at the beginning. You think you can do it with a straight face?"

His heart thudded at the thought of facing a television camera. "I'm sure you'll be embarrassed by my performance, but yes, if anyone asks me to, I can say what the *Party* stands for. But I'll tell you right now, if they ask me what *I* think, I'm not going to lie, not even for you, Emma, and you must know by now..." He caught himself.

Out of the corner of his eye he saw her look at him and fold her arms across her chest. A long silence hung in the car. "Know what?" she asked, in a voice that almost sounded defeated.

He looked out the window to his left and drew a great breath. Damn. Just when he'd decided there'd be no blurting. "That I'm attracted, no, to be honest, I have feelings for you."

For a minute he heard only the thrashing of his heart.

"Yes, I know."

His breath exploded out. "Well, that's finally out in the open. You don't have to respond to it, Emma. I know how things stand."

Her voice softened. "I doubt that." She stared out at the bleak landscape before she went on. "Look, Paul, I admit I'm attracted to you, too, but we both know this is a...it's not even really a relationship; it's little more than an acquaintanceship. And it's never going anywhere beyond a long drive to the coast. So I've been making myself avoid all the little steps people take to draw each other closer. Even if I were willing to get involved with a white man again, our two lives are so disparate that there's no point in trying to pursue a relationship. You know that."

Paul nodded, and the banging of doors echoed in his head, slamming shut this time.

She looked away from him, and her voice deepened. "Besides, you don't know me at all. And you wouldn't have the same feelings if you did."

"Are you taking bets on that?"

She didn't answer.

Paul frowned and asked quietly, "What are you hiding, Emma?"

She shook her head. "I can't tell you. I don't know whether I'd be telling you as a friend or a priest, even if I don't believe in priests."

"My having been a priest is in the way?" Paul's heart and his hopes slammed into a concrete wall. He'd put the church behind him. That much was clear. But if no one else could separate Paul the priest from Paul the man, there was no hope for any kind of normal life.

"Believe me, there's nothing priestly in my feelings for you, Emma," he said, hardly able to speak. "I'd like to be friends."

She watched him for so long he assumed she didn't know how to tell him she didn't want even that. He'd never felt so small.

"Friends, Paul," she said finally, and held her hand out to shake his. "And I mean that. But to go back to what you said—if I thought you'd lie about your beliefs or feelings, we wouldn't even be that."

Their hands met and held. He tried hard to control his reaction, to feel her touch as a mere hand, transmitting only her body's warmth. They smiled and let go.

Paul drove the gray band of highway that rushed into his headlights, vaguely aware of several mileage markers slipping by, trying to sort out his feelings. If this was love, or even the beginning of love, how did the non-priests of the world survive it? Was it always so hard to turn off positive feelings for another human being? Emotions that felt so right, even though he could not allow himself to have them?

Emma was right, of course. Coming from different places and cultures, they had no real relationship. So why was this such torture? Couldn't their worlds...? No, they couldn't, she'd made that clear enough.

He remembered something she'd said. "You were once involved with a white man, Emma? Did that not work out because of the difference in cultures?"

"That's all part of it—what I don't want to talk about." Her shoulders sagged. "Are you sure you want to hear the big dark secret of my past?" She said the words slowly, with no hint of lightheartedness.

"Well, you know mine," he said, smiling. "Only fair."

She thought about it. "I guess you *should* know. If we get a lot of notoriety from the debate and anybody digs into my past, it could come out. I'd hate for you to hear it from some other source."

She bent forward with her hands between her knees. "This is hard, Paul. I've never told anyone before." She took a deep breath. "The white man wasn't actually a man; he was just a boy. We were both too young to..."

Paul waited, but she sat frozen and tense. He sensed her backing away from something.

"His name was Will Richards. Will used to hang around the reservation every summer but lived the rest of the year with his mother in Memphis. His father—we always called him 'Old Man Richards'—owned a huge tract of land, hundreds of acres, bordering the reservation, but he didn't work it. He lived right in the middle of it, cut off from the rest of the world. He wrote books of some kind."

Her voice took on a bitter edge. "The only things we ever actually saw published were a few letters to the Cheyenne newspaper complaining about Indians. He was filthy rich, at least by our standards, mean-spirited, bigoted, and aloof." A nostalgic smile changed the voice again. "Will was his opposite, one of those white kids who have a kind of 'noble savage' view of Indians. His father hated that in him, but there was no use trying to keep him away from us because we were the only other kids around.

"Will loved the powwows and dances and feather bonnets and teepees when the rest of us thought of them as some kind of corny camping trip and called them 'Way, way *passé.*' All summer we used to do stuff together, from the time we were kids, he and Earl Rides and I."

"Who's Earl Rides?"

"Earl is the one who's trying to get the casino through." She waited while a noisy orange rental truck trailing a sailboat passed them.

Her hands were clamped tightly in her lap now. "The summer we were all fifteen, Will and I discovered we were in love. Looking back on it now, I know it was as much my rejection of life on the reservation as it was love, and rejection of my parents, who both drank too much to hold down jobs or make any kind of home for me."

Paul started to reach for her but remembered her shying from his touch in the moonlight. He put his hand back on the steering wheel.

"At that time I was living with Grams, my grandmother, and she was my legal guardian. I loved her a lot, but she resented whites more than any person I've ever known."

"So how did she take to Will?"

Emma shrugged. "I guess she was just used to him. I never told her I loved him because I wasn't willing to give him up. I thought he was my future. A few years down the road, of course, but my lovely future. I was naïve enough to believe an Indian girl could be at ease in white society, or that white society wouldn't reject her out of hand. I know better now, on both counts."

She paused, but before Paul could ask why she knew better, she continued. "Up to that summer, we'd all just been friends, never giving a thought to who was whose or who was anyone else's favorite. That year, though, Earl got it in his head that I was his. Maybe it was because he saw things shifting. And we *were* together a lot during the rest of the year. But I never loved him. I guess I did love Will. There's still a deep well of pain where he's concerned."

"Emma..."

"Don't stop me." She put both hands behind her neck, elbows forward, and breathed deeply. "This is the hard part. Late that summer, just before the Earth Cycle Powwow, I found out I was pregnant. I didn't dare tell anybody. My grandmother would have kicked me out. At least I thought she would. My mother would have beaten me raw, she was drinking so heavily at the time. She was always a mean drunk. And Will didn't want to tell his father, because Old Man Richards hated Indians, and Will was sure he'd withhold the money he'd promised for Will's college education. So we panicked." She clenched her fists in her lap again. It was a minute before she went on. "We found a place outside Gillette where I could get an abortion." She stopped again, her head drawn in, as if waiting for a blow to fall. When Paul said nothing, she went on. "I'm sure this is the last, most shocking thing you ever wanted to hear from me."

"You're wrong, Emma. After almost twenty years in the confessional, nothing shocks me anymore. And I'm only now beginning to understand the kinds of desperation that drive people. If this was part of what made you the person I...admire so much today, how could I condemn it? The last thing I'm ever going to do is judge you for some part of your distant past. And one thing I do know is that getting it out helps."

Her voice turned husky. "Thanks, Paul."

"So what did you do?"

"In the end, I had to get my grandmother's signature for the abortion, and she was furious. She probably wouldn't have signed for it if the child had been Indian. Earl didn't know about the pregnancy or the abortion, though it must have been obvious that Will and I were...doing things that didn't include him. In any case, he got surly and spiteful.

"Toward the end of August the tribe moved up to Twin Circles Butte for the powwow. It used to be held on the summer solstice as a celebration of the richness in the cycles of birth and death, but the weather was often terrible up on the Butte in June. Way back in the twenties some BIA official who was supervising the only road that's ever been built up the Butte suggested moving the powwow to later in the summer, when there wasn't as likely to be a huge thunderstorm."

"A butte is a kind of plateau, right?"

"Yes. This one is a huge old leftover lava pipe where the entire volcano eroded away, like Devil's Tower. A good part of the road was carved out of black rock. The Butte is very sheer but broad and the top is covered with grass. It's called Twin Circles, but it's really two parts of a single long mesa, rounded on both ends with a deep cleft on both sides right in the middle."

"Like a figure eight?"

"I suppose it would look like that from the air. The dance that is the highlight of the powwow starts on the western end of the western circle and winds slowly to the opposite end. The crossing from one circle to the other can be dangerous any time of year. The joint is narrow, just a few feet, and when the wind sweeps across the plains from the north and hits the mesa, it shoots up into the crevice and explodes out at incredible force.

"The powwow that year ended on a Sunday. Will and I gave Earl some excuse for not getting together on Monday and then hitchhiked up to Gillette for the abortion.

"They told me not to do anything strenuous for a few days, but on Tuesday, Earl insisted that I go back up to the Butte with him to get some things our families had left. I didn't want to explain anything to him, and I was feeling pretty good, at least physically, so I went. We ran into Will and he came with us.

"All of us were too young to drive, and the hike up that steep old road made me start bleeding again. I hid it until we'd picked up the things and started back across the windy mesa, but I was weak and nearly fainted as we crossed the joint. Then it all came out. Earl was furious. We were all shouting. Earl swung at Will. Will stepped back, and that's when the wind shot up out of the crevice."

She closed her eyes and rested her head on the back of the seat. Her voice dropped to a whisper. "It lifted him and then hurled him into the rocks at the base of the Butte." Her head lowered, as if to watch the falling path of her friend. "We just stood there with our mouths still open from the shouting, and the wind still howling up out of the crevice. Earl and I got on our stomachs and crawled to the edge. We couldn't even see Will's body. It had disappeared between the rocks, long, jumbled pipes of black rock. We screamed and screamed his name, but the wind grabbed our screams and shot them south. No sound came from below but the howling wind. We knew there was no chance he was still alive. One minute we were all there, squabbling over our little crisis. The next, Will, the best of us by far, was dead."

Her voice caught, and she struggled to finish. "A blast of wind just picked him up and dropped him off the earth."

Paul pulled to the side of the road. More than anything he could think of, he wanted to hold Emma away from her pain. "I'm so sorry, Emma," he said as the car rolled to a stop.

Emma put her hand out to silence him and wiped at her eyes. He reached for her.

She gently stopped his arms and waved for him to drive on. "That's not all," she whispered. "Let me get through this. If I don't, I'll never try again."

Paul put the back of his hand on her cheek and then pulled onto the road again.

"Everything I loved at fifteen and all my hopes for a bright future had flown off the cliff. I was so shocked, I think I might have jumped after him. But Earl grabbed my arm and dragged me away from the edge. We sat for a long time up there on the Butte, crying in the wind, both of us. And then Earl calmed down and said we'd get the blame if anyone found out, especially from Will's father. He made me promise not to say a word, or he'd tell everybody about the abortion. We'd just have to say we hadn't seen Will since the day of the powwow. And that's what we did. Of course, the body was never found because it was hidden by the rocks and no one but us knew he'd gone to the Butte. As far as I know, he's still listed as a missing person."

For a moment Emma stopped. She pulled her lips between her teeth and stared out her window, blinking hard.

Knowing his words would hardly help, Paul said, "So much pain for someone so young."

She turned back, surprised. "You think I would have cared less if I'd been older?"

"No, of course not. If you'd been older, it probably wouldn't have happened. I just meant—the young have so little in reserve to deal with grief, and given your life on the reservation, you probably had none at all."

Emma thought that over and nodded. "You might as well know the rest. I thought my life was over. I dropped out of school. My grandmother sent me to stay with some Shoshone friends of hers on the Wind River Reservation farther west, trying to guarantee that I'd never see Will again. The months passed, and again and again I thought I'd go to the police, or at least to his parents, but the longer it got, the more I was ashamed. And eventually it seemed a greater cruelty to drag it all back up again. So that's what I've been running from all my adult life, and what Earl thinks he can use against me if I continue to block the casino."

Paul knew there was part she hadn't told him, and that she needed to. He gripped the steering wheel with both hands to keep from stopping the car again and taking her in his arms. He asked gently, "If you want to get it all out, Emma, can you tell me how you felt about the abortion?"

She took in a series of ragged breaths, the prelude to a sob. "Horrible."

Paul waited.

"I knew it was the right thing to do. I didn't want to bring a child into my world of poverty and depression, but that didn't stop me from feeling guilty. Not a day has gone by since that I don't love and wonder about that baby. I don't even know whether it would have been a girl or a boy. I still feel guilty. I feel very guilty about Will, too, even though it was an accident, and I know the only thing we did wrong was keep our secret."

"What about Earl?"

Emma's breathing slowed and her voice calmed. "I hardly saw him for more than ten years, and when I went back to Big Sleep, we were like two wary strangers. With the Shoshones, where I didn't know anyone, I had a lot of time to think, and I decided if

I wanted to get out of the syndrome my parents were in, I had to get away from reservations altogether, and the only road out was school. As for Earl, he stayed put, learned to manipulate people, and in a few years began his rise to the tribal council. Whenever we meet, there's so much guilt and dead affection and fear between us, you'd need an ax to cut it."

"If you wanted to get away from the reservation so much, why did you move back there?"

"The little financial aid I got from the tribe was contingent on my working on the reservation for five years. But I would have gone back anyway. After I got out of those awful teenage years, I began to focus on something besides myself. I came back from lonely semesters at UCLA and began to see the plight of Indians in general, and my parents in particular, with more objective, maybe more forgiving, eyes. There's such a hole in their lives where self-respect ought to be. And they tried to fill it up with alcohol. My father still does.

"For a couple of years, I focused all my attention on the need to change that. Then some of my work sent me to the open pit copper mines in Utah and Arizona. I was horrified at the destruction—no—the rape of the earth. That horror, together with the memory of overpopulation in California, Turkey, India and Vietnam, plus a lot of reading, made me realize that helping Indians or anybody else is moot if the population destroys the planet we live on."

"And you learned to respect yourself in the process."

"Yes, I guess I did. Respect maybe. But I never liked myself again."

"You know, one of the things I learned as a priest was that even after I gave people absolution, they rarely forgave themselves. It made them miserable. Someday, Emma, you have to forgive yourself."

"I don't know whether that's possible."

Friends, thought Paul, wondering where he would find a place to put all the love that welled up and wanted to flow from his body through a simple touch to her face. His hands vibrated with longing, and he clenched the steering wheel until he feared he would wrest it from its housing.

CHAPTER TWENTY TWO

After giving Paul some ideas about the debate, Emma had drifted into sleep somewhere in the middle of California. Now she woke sitting nearly straight with her mouth open, dry as road dust. Instantly, she sensed him in the seat next to her and hoped he hadn't noticed her mouth hanging slack while she slept. She looked straight ahead, working her tongue to get the saliva flowing.

In the corner of her vision she saw the strange round scar on his hand stretch with his grip on the steering wheel, and the dark hairs of his arm below the white sleeve he'd shoved above his elbow. The car rounded a curve and the shadow of his arm moved onto her thigh, the tracery of hair making a soft fringe on her jeans.

A soft glow washed over her, followed by embarrassment. Driving through the night with him, she'd felt a kind of intimacy. She'd trusted him enough to sleep while he drove. But then she'd trusted him too much, telling him about Will and the baby.

Now, in the daylight, she wished she didn't have to look him in the face.

The temptation to let herself lean on his affection wouldn't go away. Admittedly, she felt somehow lighter with the secret out. And he hadn't condemned her. He'd wanted to comfort her in his arms. The thought heaved through her and flattened her defenses. Not even Grams had ever put her arms around her when she was hurt. No one but Will had ever tried to comfort her. Paul was a kind man, a man like she'd never known before. One she could really...no, that was a road she absolutely would not travel. It could never work.

She'd never go back to that kind of intimacy with him. She'd confine their conversations to the most superficial topics, keep her distance, and in the future concentrate on work for her tribe and the Earth.

To get her mind off him, she focused on the land passing by. A few miles away rose another ridge of the brown hills that separated California's fertile valleys. On both sides of the road, long rows of grapevines stretched away from the highway, their leaves brown and tired. Flimsy packing crates, faded drink cans, dusty plastic sacks, and fast food wrappers dotted the sparse, dry grass. She shook her head, angry with the litterers who had so little respect for the Earth.

Paul glanced at her when she moved.

Quickly, before he could bring up last night, she asked, "What's the first thing you'd do if you ever got to be president?"

He laughed. "You're awake? Right smack in the middle of a conversation again."

The easy warmth of his laugh made her smile. "Wow, you're right. Must be a habit I didn't even know I had." She stretched her legs and rolled her head to loosen her neck. "So what would you do?"

He turned to look at her. "Where on earth did that question come from?"

There was nothing in his face but affection. His warmth started to flow through her. She clenched her fists and propped up her defenses. "I don't know. Maybe the trash on the side of the road, but it's a stretch, I admit. Still, a good question that might come up in the debate."

"Well, it's a whopper. I've never given it a moment's thought. No, actually I have, but only in nightmares. Probably the first thing I'd do is have a heart attack. And if I survived that, I'd take four years' sick leave."

Emma ran her hands through her hair. "They don't give presidents sick leave. You'd have to take up golf."

"Very funny." Paul squinted in the sun as they rounded a curve.

She reached up and pulled her visor down at the same time he did. The road swung right again, and they flipped them back up simultaneously, grinning at each other.

Paul turned back to the road. "So what would be *your* first law?"

"Packaging."

"I beg your pardon?"

"Do you have any idea how much trash and garbage Americans create every year? Enough to make the Rockies look like mole-hills. And most of our *trash* is *packaging*. Ha! See? The litter did trigger the question. Think about it. Who do you know that recycles all that stuff?"

"Danny."

Emma laughed. "There may be a speck of decency in that guy after all. But seriously, it's the idea we could probably convince the public of the most easily. It'd be a start. In Germany they passed a law in 1991 that all packaging, even milk cartons and frozen food boxes, must be recyclable *and* recycled. They set up recycle bins all over their cities."

"You're kidding. The people actually accepted that as a law? In this country it's still pretty much voluntary."

"Unfortunately. Of course, the German program hasn't been without problems. I heard the amount of stuff to be recycled far outstrips the facilities, and they ship a lot of junk to someplace like Afghanistan, where it just stacks up and blows around the countryside. But surely it was a step in the right direction.

"Now, just imagine, if the law required manufacturers to package their goods in recyclable materials, the first thing they'd do is rush to minimize, and then they'd cut out all damaging dyes and chemicals. The packaging industry would have to develop materials that would hold flavor but could be recycled, there'd be new companies to melt down the old stuff to make new. We'd be forced to find ways to make it cost effective and at the same time create new jobs."

Paul stared at her. "You're absolutely right."

She laughed. "See? We're not so crazy." She looked out at the landscape again. "Where are we, anyway?"

"After we cross this ridge, I'd say about a hundred miles from San Francisco."

"Nearly four. We're not going to make it for the cocktail party, Paul. If we're not there, they might think we aren't coming at all."

Paul turned and gave her an absurd pumpkin-grin. "I guess they'd have to cancel the debate, since my presence is required."

Emma rolled her eyes and returned the grin. Dammit, he just kept drawing her back. "Well, the way things are going, we might be late for that, too. We made up some of the time through Nevada, but with the on-ramp to I-5 closed, it looks like we'll have to go over to San Jose and then up. You think we ought to call the hotel and get a message to the organizers that we're on the way so they can at least start on time?"

"Yeah, I guess we should."

"I don't suppose you have a cell phone."

"I have one in the glove compartment, an old one provided by the parish. I had the plan changed to my name, but I couldn't change companies because there was so much time left on the contract. Out here I doubt there's a signal. You can try it."

Emma fished the telephone number of the hotel out of her backpack and tried the phone. "Mm, you're right, practically no signal." The phone beeped. "I guess your battery is nearly dead, too."

"It's old, and the battery doesn't hold a charge very long. We need gas anyway. You call from a pay phone while I fill up. Then I think I'll organize a flat tire."

From the pay phone in the filling station, Emma waited for the hotel to answer. She watched Paul tuck a credit card receipt in his billfold and then start cleaning the windshield. What would it have felt like if she'd let him take her in his strong, gentle arms? His big man's arms with the dark hair, holding her... She'd barely slammed the door on that thought when the receptionist said, "Regency Bay Hotel."

As she hung up, she felt a vibration and a kind of yaw that started in her feet. She shook her head. No more endless drives like this. The constant sitting had played havoc with her equilibrium.

Half an hour later, as they were nearing the top of the range, Paul's nerves began to zing through his whole body. In another hour, his name would be all over the country and anyone with the intelligence of a garden slug would label him an idiot.

Emma put a hand on his arm. "Hey, you okay? You went all white."

Paul ground his jaw. "The only way I'm going to get through this is to keep reminding myself it'll all be over tomorrow."

"I hate to rub salt on your wound, but I'm kind of looking forward to it. Well, not for myself, but for the party's exposure." She looked down at her clothes. "Which reminds me, I can't show up in jeans for the debate much less the gala afterwards. I'll jump in the back and change into my dress. Then you can do the same."

Forcing himself to lighten up, Paul flapped his hand at her. "Oh, my goodness, I didn't even think to bring my dress!"

She poked him in the shoulder with her fist, unfastened her seat belt, and slithered over the seat.

The car seemed to lurch as she plopped onto the back seat.

Paul shook his head, wondering how someone so slender could make the whole car pitch. "I'd have been glad to stop for two seconds."

"Thanks anyway," she said. "Soon as I'm finished, you can change, too, if you want, and I'll drive the last stretch."

"Would it be okay if I stop before we do all the gymnastics? I'll leave the motor running."

"Oh, sure," she said, rummaging in her backpack. "Boy, what I wouldn't give for a shower. Before we leave, I'm going to spend at least half an hour in the restroom, and the other women can think whatever they like!"

Paul heard a zipper and the rustle of her jeans sliding down her legs. "I've been thinking about that, too," he said. "I dread facing the long drive again as soon as the debate is over."

"This was a dumb idea, I guess. We should have pressed Gordy for air fare for both of us."

Paul kept his eyes rigidly away from the mirror, forward, like in the confessional, trying to ignore the sound of her removing clothes. "Maybe. I'm sure the party ought to have money for a couple of plane tickets if it has enough to hire a bodyguard, even such a one as Shirl Wainwright."

"I thought you fired her."

The car pitched again and Paul wondered what she was doing back there. "I did, but she was still hanging around outside the store. I glimpsed her a couple of times at the door. She may even be following us for all I know, although if she was, I suspect we left her in the blizzard. Anyway, what I wanted to say was I wouldn't have missed this drive for all the plane rides in the world."

After a short pause and some silky rustling, she answered, "Actually, I wouldn't have either."

Her hand appeared, poised over his right shoulder. He took his left hand from the wheel to respond to her touch, but she withdrew hers without touching him.

Seconds later the car veered to the left and she grabbed his shirt. "Hey, keep your eyes on the road, will you?"

"I am. Stop bouncing around back there."

"I'm not...Paul, look out!"

On the other side of the road several boulders tumbled from the top of the embankment onto the road. Paul braked hard, but the rocks stayed on the other side. He'd have to watch for falling rocks...falling...when they shouldn't.

In front of him a milk truck was crawling up the hill. Its tank lurched suddenly as if a tire had blown. On Paul's right, a flock of sparrows lifted simultaneously from a leafless tree and flapped away.

"Oh my God! Emma. Hang on!"

Suddenly, the air filled with a deafening snarl, a sound like the gnashing of immense dry teeth. The road pitched, hurling Paul's side of the car up off the pavement. The car teetered and slammed back onto the road that was heaving and cracking. A wave of motion threw the car toward the end of the milk truck. He swerved to avoid it. Another pitch sent the back end of the car up and the front end onto the right shoulder. The right back fender struck a rock at the edge of the cliff. He heard Emma slam against the door as the rear end skewed around.

The car headed straight down a long, heaving slope, crashing through bushes and over rocks. Paul jammed both feet on the brake, but the car slid straight down the loose, pitching dirt. It bounced into and out of a dip, lurching to the right, and Paul's head hit the window on his left. He was barely conscious when the car came to a standstill between a boulder and a tree at the edge of a dry streambed. He forced himself to look back. "Emma," he whispered.

She lay crumpled on the back seat, motionless and silent.

The screech of tires came from above, followed by a crash.

Paul tried to focus in spite of the blackness that rushed in from the sides of his vision. He found the cell phone on the floor. The numbers were blurry, and he could only hope he dialed 911. The phone beeped the end of the battery, but a voice answered over a crackling connection.

"This is Paul Greer," he said. "Accident, someone badly hurt. I'm on..." He tried to think of the number of the highway, but the black was closing in now. "I'm near..." The muscles in his arm gave way and he dropped the phone. He tried to pick it up off the passenger seat.

His vision was already darkening when the earth rolled again, loosening a shower of brown leaves from the tree. Above them, the rock they had struck slid down the slope, bringing a small landslide that covered half the rear door.

Then silence rolled in as Paul sank under the blackness.

CHAPTER TWENTY THREE

D anny switched on the television as soon as he came into the apartment at five-forty. The set crackled its electronic awakening and the picture faded in. Expecting a couple of notes about the football game he'd missed while talking to Laurel last night, he wondered at the stricken face of a field reporter in a helicopter. Some accident on the interstate, probably. Without waiting to hear where, he muted the sound and went to the phone.

He hit the speed-dial for his favorite Chinese take-out and ordered hot and sour soup and sesame chicken, which Laurel would pick up on the way over. She'd be here by six and they'd watch the debate together. He forbade himself to speculate beyond that, much as he was looking forward to the soft blondness of her presence and the grace of her movement. He saw the lovely, tear stained face again, drawn by pain and shame. His chest expanded over a heart that warmed at the memory.

The lady was still too involved with Paul to focus on anything else for a while. He wasn't going to push her, but at least he could open a door for her to find him sooner or later.

He showered quickly, brushed his teeth, and examined his thinning hair and flattened stomach in the mirror. Okay, he crowed as he stepped back into the living room, Paul was a few years younger, but this trim and solidly mature form was nothing to sneer at. He switched on the sound and went to pour a glass of juice. "Tomorrow, tomorrow," he sang, smiling at the six packs in the refrigerator.

The words *earthquake in San Francisco* in Royce McClain's familiar voice penetrated his anticipation.

He froze. His glass crashed to the floor.

"...the Regency Bay Hotel, where the candidates of all the parties had gathered for the reception and debate. We have this report from Richard Hellmann, who had just taken off in the helicopter for the afternoon traffic report when the earthquake destroyed the station. He's transmitting to us via satellite and our affiliate in Stockton."

"Oh my God. Paul," whispered Danny. Stepping over glass shards, he rushed out of the kitchen, even though he could see the picture from the refrigerator. With his fist clenched at his mouth, he watched as the camera panned over a mass of broken concrete that ended in the water. The door buzzer sounded, but he remained rooted to the carpet in front of the television.

The camera shifted to the helicopter again. "The damage is so severe," the reporter said, "that the mind reels at the thought of the lives snuffed out beneath the rubble. No traffic is moving at all in this part of San Francisco. All major highways out of the city are closed, if not because of severe damage or broken bridges, then because of huge accidents. Those who can hear the emergency broadcasts have been warned to move far from any buildings if they're able, as after-shocks are expected to take nearly as great a toll. But, I tell you, Royce, it's hard to imagine anything as bad as what we can see from Copter 5."

Scenes of damage played across the screen: flames leaping from water where gas lines and water conduits had broken in the same place, cars twisted and piled together, frame houses skewed into jagged lumber, brick structures collapsed or cracked and lopsided.

"Has there been any attempt to approach the hotel, Richard?" Royce asked against this backdrop. "Does there appear to be any hope at all that there were survivors in the Regency Bay?"

"I'm afraid none at all, Royce. The Regency Bay was a hotel born in controversy." The field of concrete appeared on screen again. "Geologists protested its construction over concern about liquefaction in this reclaimed inlet in the event of a large scale earthquake. The builders assured the planning commission the hotel was as earthquake proof as anything ever built along the fault lines. It was masses of reinforced concrete, built in the shape a steep stadium, with 70% of its concrete in the foundation and back side and all its windows on the water side. It looks like the foundation simply tilted and pulled the rest over. There's no way to tell whether there were any survivors until after inspectors are allowed in, but I'm afraid everyone who was in the hotel died under that massive concrete wall."

Royce McClain's face paled. "Are you telling us that every single candidate in tomorrow's election is dead?"

"I heard they'd all assembled in the Golden Gate Room, which was on the top floor and is now under water. But our station in Stockton said the network received a message that both candidates of the..." He glanced down at a notepad and frowned in disbelief. "...Earth Rights Party had been delayed. They called about half an hour before the quake from sixty or seventy miles away, so it's known they weren't in the hotel. No one knows exactly where they were when it hit, and we haven't heard anything from them since. Word we're getting is that the San Andreas quake set off a number of other faults farther east, too, so they may have been in one of those. Information about that is sketchy so far." He glanced away from the camera and back. "My pilot is giving me a sign, Royce. The 'copter is needed for rescue operations on the Oakland Bridge."

"Just one more question, Richard. Is anyone looking for them?"

Hellmann answered from the turning helicopter. "I couldn't say, but given the number of dead and injured here, I assume every available helicopter is working rescue in the known quake zones."

The camera returned to the ashen face of Royce McClain. "Not only is the country shocked by the loss of life and the devastation in parts of San Francisco and scattered points along the San Andreas Fault, but we're now in a situation unprecedented in history. I can't even begin to guess how the demise of almost everyone running for president and vice president affects the election, with one presidential candidate possibly still alive. At this point I'm not even sure what governmental body has the authority to decide what should be done."

A knock on Danny's door was followed by Laurel's voice. "Danny? Are you there?"

He backed to open the door without taking his eyes off the television. She came in saying, "Have you heard...?"

He pointed at the television set. She sat down on the sofa and set the white sack on the floor. Half of it rested on her foot. He sat down next to her, and their hands found each other and clasped tightly. For more than an hour, the news of the earthquake went on. When there was a repetition of the scenes from the helicopter, he turned to her. She was ghostly pale.

His heart sank. Her face showed her attachment to Paul. Danny clenched his jaw and then assured her, "He didn't make it to the hotel."

Laurel's whole body loosened in relief. "He called? Oh, Danny, I'm so glad."

"No, he didn't call. All I know is what's been on the news so far. They were delayed driving out, probably because of the storm last night, and they called the station or the hotel from somewhere." His voice shook now. "They could still be dead. No one knows exactly where they were."

She bowed into herself and rocked forward. Her hand gripped his tighter. She looked down at their hands and blinked. Her fingers loosened and nearly let go, but then she put her other hand on his and kept rocking.

"Do you want to stay here?" he asked, ready to back off the invitation if she hesitated.

Her gray-blue eyes turned to him with gratitude. "Yes, please. I know it's an imposition, but I don't think I could take the wait alone."

"Nor I. It would mean a lot to me."

She smiled. "I owe you that much."

"You don't owe me anything at all." Danny squeezed her hand and they both sat back on the sofa, holding hard, facing the television set for the rest of the news.

It was another forty minutes before the broadcast returned to the local station and Danny felt he could breathe again.

Laurel sat forward and asked, "You said *'they* could still be dead,' Danny. Was there someone else with him? I thought I saw someone following him yesterday." Her face reddened. "Besides me. A tall, gawky woman with frizzy red hair."

"He's with the vice presidential candidate. An Indian woman from Wyoming. The party didn't give Paul any money for airfare, and she offered to drive out with him on the money the party'd given her. They were driving straight through, spelling each other at the wheel."

Laurel squinted and gave him a sidewise look. "The party gave her money to go and not him?"

He shrugged. "The party chairman has a strange logic." Danny started to say more and stopped. What should he say about Emma? If Paul and Emma never came back, there was no need to hurt Laurel. On the other hand, if they did come back, it might be better if she were prepared. And if she knew Paul was interested in someone else... He squeezed her hand and said, "I have to tell you, Laurel, I think they're pretty good friends."

Laurel bit her lips and looked away.

Now he damned his selfishness. "I'm sorry. I should've kept my mouth shut."

She gave a sigh that was half groan. "I wish I could say that doesn't affect me, but it hurts. I guess I needed to know, though."

His hands vibrated with the desire to stroke her face and pull her to him. Instead, he jumped up, brought the telephone from the bedroom, and laid it on the end table. He picked up the white sack of sesame chicken. "I just noticed the smell. Could you eat?"

Laurel shook her head.

He went to the kitchen, kicked the glass fragments aside, and put the sack next to the beer he'd gloated over an hour before, sure he'd soon be free of his promise to Paul. His throat caught. He slammed the refrigerator door and leaned against it, sobbing. Almost immediately, Laurel's hand touched his shoulder. He spun around and backed away from her. "Oh, God, if my brother's dead, it's my fault."

"Shhh, Danny, it was an earthquake."

"You just don't know," he said. And the whole story came out, his drunken nomination, his stupidity, and his wheedling.

"He made me bargain and I agreed to quit drinking till after the election, but..." He couldn't say it.

Slowly, she pulled the refrigerator open, saw the six packs and stared at him.

He saw a veil slide over the small trust she'd had in him. "I don't..." he started. No. No lies. "Yes," he groaned, "I still want the beer. If you weren't here, I'd be at those bottles this very minute."

"And that tells you he was right?" she asked quietly.

Danny leaned over his sink, bowed by guilt and acknowledgement. It was a long time before he could say, "Yes. He was right. I'm on the way to becoming an alcoholic."

She led him back to the sofa and set him down. She took off her shoes, climbed up next to him, and put her arms around him loosely. "He's not dead. We have to keep telling ourselves he's not dead."

"He was right and the whole thing's my fault. If I hadn't been drinking the night of the nominations..."

"I've only known you since yesterday, Danny, when you haven't been drinking. You've been wonderful to me."

"Ha, just wait. I'll find a way to screw things up for you, too."

She pulled his face toward her. "I know it's not my business, but if you're a screw-up when you drink and a wonderful man when you don't, doesn't it make sense he wanted you to quit?"

Danny nodded, but his heart was hopeless. Paul was dead, and only alcohol would ever drown his guilt.

Laurel shifted to face the television. "My father was an alcoholic," she said softly. "I'm glad Paul doesn't drink."

Of course. Why would this incredible woman attach herself to a drunk? Especially when she had Father Perfect as her ideal. Danny felt his hopes for winning her turn to ashes. She knew about drunks, and she'd been through one nightmare marriage already.

She breathed out a ragged sigh. "Anyway, it's not all your fault. The last thing he did as a priest was hear my confession, and I told him I loved him. It pushed him over the edge."

"He would have left anyway."

"Maybe, but I was the last straw, wasn't I?"

"He never said anything about a confession." Danny hesitated, afraid to ask the one question that needed answering. His voice lowered almost to a whisper. "Do you really love him?"

She looked at him with more pain than he'd ever seen in a human face. "I thought I did. I needed him. I don't want to love him."

Danny hesitated a long time and finally brought it out: "There's always me." He swallowed hard.

Her answer was an eternity in coming. She shook her head. "You've been so kind, Danny, and I admit I like you more than makes sense to me. But the six packs in there scare me too much, and what scares me even more is that I don't know how much of my attraction to you is connected with Paul."

Danny nodded. It had all gone wrong. He wanted to be free of his guilt about Paul and he wanted this woman, who was involved with Paul. Everything revolved around Paul. While Danny would fight anyone else to the death for Laurel, he'd done enough to Paul already. And even if he were willing to fight his brother for her, that wouldn't make her love him when it was her love he wanted. Nothing else would do.

He felt the pull of John Adams in every cell of his body. He jammed his teeth together so hard he could feel the roots protest. He would not let himself go back to the beer. That was the one thing he could do for them both. He shifted on the sofa so that his arms were around her, too, and they settled into the news, waiting, fearing, hoping.

CHAPTER TWENTY FOUR

P aul moved his head. A searing pain in his neck shot up over the top and slammed into his forehead. He grunted and tried to raise his hands to his head. His left shoulder screamed in protest. He opened his eyes and the dim form of a tree trunk slowly emerged from the fuzziness. Why was the tree so close to the car? Accident. Emma! He twisted to look in the back seat, and every muscle in his body jerked in agony.

Emma lay as she had when he'd last looked, crumpled against the door. The right side of her forehead was red around a large white lump that stretched the skin. The rest of her face was white as an altar cloth. Her legs bent at awkward angles with a pair of panty hose around one knee and the other ankle.

He snatched the cell phone up, ignoring the pain of motion, and tried again to reach help. The battery was dead.

Paul couldn't see whether Emma was breathing. Her backpack lay on top of her chest; and his suit, which had been hanging behind him, lay across that. The coat hanger was hooked into the neck of her sweater, exposing her slender chain with the little silver bear. A lump rose in his throat.

"Emma," he choked, "Emma."

He turned back to get out and saw his reflection in the rear view mirror. A streak of red ran from his temple into his collar, but the bleeding had stopped. He reached around with his right arm to open the door, but a rock was blocking it.

Slowly, he pulled himself into the passenger seat and got out. The fresh air cleared his head and eased the headache, but the shudder it sent down his spine reminded him he'd been very cold.

Emma. He had to get to Emma. He moved to try the back door and fell over, wrenching his left shoulder again. He was on the pile of dirt that had come down with them and covered the back end of the car. He looked in at Emma and saw that if he opened her door, she would fall out. He went around the front of the car, stumbling over rocks, and circled the boulder that had blocked him in. He opened the back door and knelt on the edge of the seat, fighting the blackness that wanted to wash over him again.

"Don't be dead, Emma, please. Oh, God, please don't let her be dead." He pulled the coat hanger out of her sweater and lifted the suit and the backpack. She didn't move. Her left arm was thrown across her chest at an impossible angle. He reached for her right arm, which hung between the seat and the door and touched the wrist, feeling for a pulse. It was faint, and her hand was icy. He felt her body just below the breast that hardly seemed to move. She was warm under the sweater she hadn't changed yet.

"Emma, Emma! Can you hear me? Wake up. I have to know what's wrong with you."

He rubbed her cold fingers. She moaned and tried to draw her legs up to her chest. Paul slid the panty hose down gently and allowed her to move as much as she could. He felt along both cold legs, looking for broken bones, and then tried her right arm. The left was either broken just below the shoulder or badly dislocated, but the other limbs seemed to be all right. He had no way to know about her neck or back.

"Emma!" he shouted. "Wake up and talk to me. I have to help you, and I don't know how badly you're hurt." He put his hand on her face and ran it over her hair. She raised her head. Her eyes opened but wouldn't focus.

"Can you sit up?" Paul shouted, desperate to penetrate her consciousness.

She raised her head again and started to sit up.

"Don't move if it hurts," he said, but she continued to try.

She moaned and her right arm grabbed for the left.

"I'll help you, Emma. I have to know whether I can move you." He reached around her and pulled on her right shoulder as she shoved herself up. "Do you have any other injuries? Anything I can't move?"

She didn't answer. Tears streamed out of her closed eyes.

He helped her sit up and shoved at her hips until she could lean comfortably against the door. "Hold your arm, Emma. I'm going to try to see if it's broken." He slid his hand gently up her arm. He couldn't feel any protrusions on the upper arm, but Emma groaned when his fingers moved close to her shoulder.

"Don't let go of your arm, Emma. I think your shoulder's dislocated. I'll make you a sling." He pulled his dress shirt from under the suit coat, tied its arms around her neck, twisted the tails and tied them around her chest with her hand sticking out. He took his belt from the pants and strapped her upper arm to her body.

Her closed eyes squinted in pain as he worked. By the time he finished, her head had lolled back.

"Emma?" Not even an eyelash fluttered, but her pulse was stronger now. He rolled up his dress pants for a pillow and let her head rest against the window. He covered her upper body with his wool suit coat and wrapped her down jacket around her bare legs.

By now his head hurt like a thumb under a hammer, his shoulder ached, and a new pain stabbed at his left hip. As much as he wanted to get her out and go for help, he couldn't carry her.

He slid out the door, his joints grinding. The sun was low, beaming up from the south. It would disappear over the higher west ridge within the hour, leaving them in darkness and dangerous cold. He had to get them out of here. He stepped into the dry stream bed for a better view of the road forty or fifty feet above him.

At the top of the grassy slope he could barely see the broken edge of the pavement. Earthquake. He remembered now. He scanned the incline for a safe spot to scramble up and flag someone down. Then the silence struck him. It was not the silence of sudden cessation of noise, nor a near silence against the distant hum of life. It was the still and lifeless silence of complete isolation. Why was there no traffic on the road? He had to get help for Emma but couldn't leave her as long as she was unconscious.

Paul scrambled up the yellowed grass next to the landslide and hauled himself onto the narrow shoulder. The damage before him shocked him so badly he lost his footing and slid several feet back down the slope. He pulled himself up again and made it to the pavement. At the point just above the landslide, the eastbound side of the road was now three feet higher than the westbound, which explained why it had simply thrown him down the ravine.

He looked in both directions. A hundred yards to his right, past a jigsaw pattern of cracks, the east lane met the west lane almost exactly, leaving two lanes that led to nowhere, and beyond that, just before the next curve, the road ended in a step up of five or six feet. The milk truck he'd nearly hit was there, glinting in the sun. To his left, a bridge over the ravine had collapsed.

His hopes for rescue vanished. No one was going to drive this road for a long time. He walked toward the truck to see if it was drivable, stepping over gaps and holding to the middle, hoping it was stable. A broken line of tire tracks stretched toward him from the back of the truck, the dotted lines of hell. Dried and rank milk whitened the pavement and disappeared into a jagged crack. The tank itself had opened at a mid-seam and the smell coming from the truck was already rancid. The cab had been crushed by the tank and lay flattened and bent over the rise in the road. Out of habit, Paul made the sign of the cross in the air for the dead driver, and turned back.

He couldn't remember any cars behind him or in front of the truck at the time of the accident, nor could he imagine any survivors in the terrible silence, but he scanned the area on both sides as far as he could. He found no other wrecks, but he did spot a place near the east end of the collapsed bridge where he might be able to get Emma up onto the road when she came to. Somehow, they'd just have to walk back to the last town, where they'd bought gas. It must be twenty miles away. He looked off in that direction, but the valley was hidden behind the hills.

He slid back down the slope and checked on her. She hadn't moved. He sat down on the rock by the driver's door, trying to ignore his hunger. He massaged his left shoulder and let the sun warm his limbs. Oh, God...the words came to his lips by habit.

His devastation when he'd thought Emma might be dead came back, and he saw himself kneeling on the seat, saying, "Please, God, don't let her be dead." Oh, yes, he'd wanted some being to have power over her death when he had none.

The smell of dry, dusty earth rose to his nose, so different from the dank confessional, from the church; and a long-stifled question flashed across his vision like lightening. Was there really a God at all? Or was God the antithesis of our helplessness in the face of death? Did we pray because we were desperate to prevent the death of someone we loved? Or didn't want to believe in our own death?

He looked up at the overhanging branches of the tree. They were dormant, brown against the blue, dead now; but they would green up again. Was there some being who controlled that? He'd always taught it, mouthed it. Suddenly all the suppressed doubts rose to challenge the priest standing in front of the class. Now he knew. There was no kindly grandfather in the sky, no one who laid an altering finger on the affairs of man. And no one who ordained what was good or evil. What had Danny said? You had to find your own ethic. Was it all just a matter of ethics or was there something more that he didn't grasp?

He glanced back through the window at Emma. She respected herself. She'd found her ethic on her own, without wasting time on doubts about heaven or hell. She knew her actions were right. And her certainty had nothing to do with any church. Any God. She knew where she fit in her view of life. What did she understand that he didn't? The love he'd been trying to suppress boiled to the surface.

What was good, then, if not what was dictated from above? The ache in his chest answered: *love* was good, the positive force. Only he wasn't allowed to have it. Not for her. Was it possible to love happily, indefinitely, without expectations? Could you put the hurt aside and keep the love without its turning to gall? Laurel Broussard's face swam in his vision, frustrated and bitter. The face of gall. He hoped she'd gotten a divorce.

He stared at the blue and for the first time knew it was only the universe, not heaven, and it was inexpressibly beautiful. He felt the last thread of the tie that had bound him to an afterlife unravel and slide into the dust of the ravine. The hardness of the rock shocked him suddenly, as if he had just been dropped to earth. He tried to lift his thoughts into the blue, but his mind's eye stayed on the man sitting on a rock in a minuscule cleft of earth, a man on a small planet with other men. Himself so small. So completely without significance. Living in the now, not the afterlife. What was it for, this microscopic speck of life? To make the world better, even if only by an iota, than it had been before his passage? To recognize the importance of now? Emma knew. Someday he would know.

He gazed at her again through the reflection of sky and man. He would love her whether she returned his love or not. He would do what good he could in the world, at least in the small circle in which he moved. Whatever life demanded, he would spend himself completely to accomplish it, and if there were a judging being anywhere out there, it could hardly ask more of a man. A tear fell from his left eye, and he knew it was for the final loss of the security of the church. The second tear was for the joy of seeking a new place to stand in the world, painful and tenuous though it might be.

He ran his thumb over the burn scar, and for the first time it was an annoyance, the scar of an act of cruelty, not of a child's failure. He'd find a plastic surgeon and have it removed as soon as he got back to Denver.

In the car, Emma stirred and moaned.

At last. They could go for help. Paul jumped off the rock and knelt by her door, smiling.

Her eyes opened. She looked around, confused, and rubbed at the bump on her forehead.

"You look better," he said. "I'm so glad. How do you feel?"

"Who are you?"

His heart stumbled over a beat. "Paul."

"Where am I?" She tried to sit up, but her eyes closed and she leaned back.

"We were in an accident, Emma. We're at the bottom of a small ravine, and I'm going to take care of you till we can get help."

"Who are you?"

"I'm Paul."

"What happened?"

"We had an accident. But we're both going to be okay."

"Where am I?"

"You're in California. We were on the way to San Francisco."

She stared at him with the intensity of a baby seeing something for the first time.

Paul's heart sank. She must have a severe concussion. He'd have to let her rest. His stomach growled into the silence.

Emma stared at his stomach. "Who are you?" she asked again.

"I'm Paul. I'm your friend Paul, and I'm going to take care of you, Emma. I know you're hungry, too. We have to get out of here.

She shoved her hips forward, moving toward him. "My arm hurts."

"You're going to be fine, Emma." He stroked her face and ran his hand over her tousled hair. "Do you have any aspirin with you?"

She stared.

"I'll look in your pack."

Paul found no medications in her things, and he knew he wasn't carrying any.

"Are you Paul?" She groaned and tried to sit up.

"Yes, hooray, you know me. Do you know who you are?"

"Emma." She stared blankly at his jacket and the down jacket that had fallen away. "Where am I?"

"You're in my car, Emma. We were in an accident on the way to San Francisco. Do you remember?"

"I have to get up."

"You just rest. You have a bad concussion."

"Where's the restroom?"

"Oh. Okay, let me help you up." He moved the jackets. "Watch your left arm."

"It hurts." She stared down at the shirt that bound her arm. "What happened?"

"Come on, we'll slide you out."

"Where's the restroom?"

"There's not one, Emma. I'll help you find a place and you call me when you need me again. Can you get your feet on the ground? Okay, stand up slowly. You're probably going to be pretty dizzy."

She took a step and began to tilt backwards. "Why am I so dizzy?"

Paul steadied her. "You hit your head, Emma."

"Where's the restroom?" She looked around and didn't seem to register the dry grasses, the rocks, the trees. She was actually looking for a door.

"It's over here. Come on, let me help you."

"Who are you?"

"Paul. Does it hurt to walk?"

"No. Some. What day is this?"

"Monday. At least I think it's still Monday. November sixth. We were on our way to the debate and there was an earthquake. Remember? Let's get you to the restroom and I'll show you the broken highway afterwards." He led her to a place where she could hang on to a tree and sit on the edge of a rock.

She stared blankly at the rock he was pointing to.

"This is the only restroom they have here, Emma. You go ahead, and call me when you need me." Paul walked away a few feet and faced the end of the ravine. A long time passed. "Emma, are you all right?"

"I can't find the toilet paper."

Paul slapped himself on the forehead. "I'll get you some." He ran to the car and returned with the roll of paper towels he kept for cleaning the windshield.

Emma shoved herself up from the rock and looked down at her bare legs. "I don't have any clothes on. Why don't I have any clothes on?"

"You were changing your clothes when the earthquake threw us off the road. Ready to put your jeans back on?"

"Yes."

He steered her back toward the car with his arm around her waist. He helped her into the jeans. "See up there, Emma? See the place where the pavement is all broken up? That's from the earthquake."

"I can't get the zipper up."

Paul ignored the tingle of desire in his hands as he buttoned the jeans and pulled the zipper up. "Do you remember yesterday, driving all the way from Colorado to be in the debate?"

"Where are we now?"

"About an hour out of San Francisco, I think." Paul knelt in front of her. "Here, give me a foot. Let's get your shoes and socks on."

She put her right foot on his knee and steadied herself with her hand on his left shoulder, setting off a wave of pain. "Are you Paul?"

He smiled up at her, frustrated, and tied her shoe. "I'm your friend Paul. Emma, I have to get help for us. Are you hurting anywhere besides your arm? Can you walk a bit?"

"I can walk. Where are we going?" She put the other foot up.

He pulled the other sock over her ankle and laced the shoe. "Let's walk up the valley a little bit. There's a place where we can get up to the road more easily. It's so steep here we'd have to crawl on all fours, and your shoulder is injured."

"It hurts."

"I know it does. We need to get you to a doctor. I want to see if you can walk a little bit on your own. Will you try that for me?" He stopped, made sure she was balanced before letting go, and backed up toward the tree. "Can you come to me?"

"Where are you going?"

"Just waiting for you. Walk toward me."

Emma stepped easily to him, and he beamed at her with relief. "You're doing fine. Are you still dizzy?"

She shook her head. "Was I dizzy?"

"Yes."

"Not now. We're in California?"

"Yes. Come on, now, let's look at that place so we can get you to a doctor." He steered her upstream in the sand. "If you get tired, tell me."

She walked with concentration. "I'm not tired. What day is this?"

"Monday. The day before election day."

"Whose election?"

"Ours. When the voters don't elect us president and vice president."

Emma laughed. It was a sound sweeter than angelic harmonies.

"I love you, Emma." Paul tried too late to cut the words off, and then he realized she would never remember them anyway. He said louder, "I love you." He spread his arms and sang, "I love you."

"Are you Paul?"

"I'm Paul in love with you."

"Are we going to California?"

"No, we're already in California. We're going to try to find a doctor for you."

"My shoulder hurts. I'm tired, Paul, it's getting black in here." She swayed against him. Paul held her, bending down to her slight frame with the awful vibration in his hands. "I love you, Emma, I love you from the core of my small new being. I swear to you, when we get out of this, I will measure up to all the things I admire in you."

"Are we going to San Francisco?"

"We were. We won't make it now. We have to find a telephone, Emma. You have to let your folks know you're all right, and I do, too. I have to call Danny."

"Who's Danny?"

Paul sighed. "My brother. Emma, do you know where you come from?"

"Big Sleep."

"Do you know where that is?"

"Do you have any food?" She gazed around at the brush and rocks in the sand. "I'm really hungry. I'm thirsty, too."

"I don't have so much as a pack of gum. That's why we need to get out of here. I'd go up and flag someone down, but there hasn't been a single car or truck by here since I've been conscious."

"Were you unconscious?"

"For a while. After the accident."

"Can we get some water soon?"

He stopped and held her by her right shoulder. "Emma, listen, I'm really worried. I know this is just a state road, but it seemed pretty well traveled when we started up yesterday. Now nothing is moving. I think it must have been a really bad earthquake, and no one is going to come any time soon to find us. We have to get out on our own. Do you understand that?"

"Are you hungry too?"

"Starving. Do you want to try walking again and see if we can get out?"

"Yes. Is there a restaurant there?"

"I hope so." They walked up the ravine again but didn't get far before she fell into him. With his arm around her waist, he dragged her back, laid her in the car, and spread the jackets over her.

Paul climbed onto the big rock again and watched her. Now he was worried she wasn't going to be able to walk out of the ravine at all, and he couldn't leave her without food or water when he didn't know how long it would take to come back with help.

He stared up at the sky again. It had turned golden in the waning sunlight. When she woke, he'd try again. He'd carry her if need be, until he found help.

CHAPTER TWENTY FIVE

At three in the morning, Danny passed seamlessly from fitful sleep to unforgotten and undiminished fear, his head at an awkward angle on the arm rest of his sofa. He turned toward the television, sending a wave of pain up his stiff neck. The set was on with the sound muted, replaying the same horror of the night before.

It switched to Royce McClain, still in the news room, gray of face and dark of eye.

Danny groped for the remote and found Laurel's arm across his waist. He looked down. She was curled into the deepest reaches of the sofa, her knees under his feet and her head between his ribs and the back cushions. He lifted her arm very slowly and tried to sit up without rolling onto the floor. He put a pillow under her head, took a blanket from the linen closet and spread it over her.

He upped the volume a little with the remote.

Royce McClain was introducing a mousy man, also exhausted, whose picture appeared on the split screen. "...Aaron Davidson, professor of constitutional law at Columbia University and our constitutional consultant. Aaron, can we possibly hold an election under these circumstances?"

"There are no regulations to cover this situation, Royce. If legitimate nominees are running..."

Everything in Danny went rigid except his thrashing heart. Had they found Paul?

"...the election must be held as scheduled. What the courts might do with the *results* if the major parties should choose to challenge them is another matter. Perhaps a special election would ensue."

Danny fought the impulse to shake the television set. "Is he alive?" he shouted and then looked back at Laurel.

Royce didn't answer his question. "It's pretty hard to imagine that anyone in the country will actually show up at the polls tomorrow—today—anyway. Would that constitute a non-election, so to speak, Aaron, if not a single voter turned up at the polls? Necessitate a new election?"

Aaron, his index finger capped by a rubber thimble, flipped to the front of the huge book on a desk and ran his middle finger slowly down the table of contents. He looked away from the camera with a pained expression. "I'm afraid that question isn't covered in the Constitution, either," he said. "And, of course, President Hartsell can't continue in office after two terms."

Laurel stirred and sat up, wide awake. "What's happened? Have they found Paul?"

Even tousled, she looked beautiful.

Before Danny could answer, a change in the tone of Royce McClain's voice called their attention back to the news.

The newsman had his finger to his earphone. "I'm just being told there's news of the missing candidates. We're going by satellite phone to Patterson, California. Who am I speaking to, please?"

"Mr. McClain, this is Arlo Waters from the Patterson Chamber of Commerce. All of our communications and emergency personnel are busy with the earthquake victims. I've been asked to inform you that we have evidence the presidential and possibly the vice-presidential candidate of the Earth Rights Party did at least survive the earthquake."

"Have they been found?" asked Royce.

"No. We're getting a helicopter in the air to search now."

"How do you know they survived?"

"Immediately after the quake one of our 911 dispatchers took a faint call. The speaker identified himself as Paul Greer. Either he wasn't able to give his location or the connection went dead, but he did say someone had been injured."

Laurel jumped up and stood beside Danny.

Royce McClain relaxed in his chair with his head lolling against the backrest, apparently unaware the camera was still on him, and asked in a tired voice, "Why is this only now coming to light?"

"The dispatcher had no way to respond to the call. She didn't know the location and couldn't raise the caller on dial-back if possible. She was flooded with calls. In fact, I think she's still at the switchboard. Only when someone mentioned Greer's name and the fact that he was a missing candidate did she make the connection."

Royce McClain faced the camera again, but before he could say anything, Danny's telephone rang.

Danny snatched it up. "Paul!"

"Danny? This is Gordy."

"What? I thought...Gordy, do you have any idea what time it is?"

"I guess you haven't heard from Paul."

"No, we've been up most of the night, but no one called."

"Well, Shirl followed them for a way, but she skidded off the road not far from Denver and lost them. Did you hear about the 911 call and the election going on as scheduled?"

"We just did."

"Well, listen, we got to be optimistic about this. We'll hear from them. In the meantime, we're starting a rigorous telephone campaign to get members out to the polls. We want you to start the Colorado network and get the voters out."

"Jesus, Gordy, my brother may be dead somewhere on a California highway. It's three o'clock in the morning, and you want me to start a phone campaign?"

"Now, don't go getting your liver all aquiver. I'm concerned about your brother, too. Not to mention Emma. I had no idea they were going to the debate together. He's got to keep us informed."

Danny made a futile effort to keep the sarcasm out of his voice. "Well, they wouldn't have been together if you hadn't been so tight with the treasury and paid *her* way but not *his*. They drove out to share expenses. Otherwise..." Before he'd finished his accusation, the truth dawned. "You may have saved their lives."

Gordy's voice came over pinched and snippy. "I certainly hope so. So, listen, as soon as you hear from Paul, give me a jingle. And get on the phone whenever it's light out that way, okey doke?"

Danny switched off the handset without saying good-bye.

Laurel shook her head. "I'm sorry, I couldn't help overhearing. What kind of jerk is that, anyway?"

"The over-gung-ho chairman of the Earth Rights Party."

"Any news before I woke up? Are they really going to hold the election?"

"Looks like nobody has the authority to call it off."

"Are you going to vote for Paul?"

"Not a chance. And I'm not doing any telephoning, either. Even if I didn't have to keep the line clear, I couldn't do that to him. I've messed things up enough."

He started to put his arm around her. "I'm glad you're here, Laurel."

She moved away and her smile was wan. "Me, too."

Of course, he thought. What on earth had made him think she'd welcome a hug? "Please, go lie down on my bed. I'll change the sheets for you." He started toward the bedroom.

"I'm wide awake now. I'd just like to freshen up."

"I'll put some things out for you if you want to stay."

She nodded. "I shouldn't impose, but I just don't think I could get through this alone."

"Then could I ask you to go out when it gets light and get something for breakfast? I'm afraid it's going to be a long wait, and I don't have a thing to offer you but the leftover Chinese."

"No matter, I doubt I'll be hungry after we ate so late. But I'd be glad to pick up some things. And I'd be glad to cook supper for you if we're still waiting."

"Gratefully accepted. You're a gem, Laurel. Whatever was the matter with that husband of yours?"

"Justin isn't a mean man. He just..." She blushed and lowered her head.

A light dawned in Danny's head. "Gay?"

She didn't answer.

"His loss." He gave her a little shove toward the bedroom. No wonder the woman pined for another man, even a priest. Well, he could still find a way to show her he was as good as an ex-priest any day. He turned back to the news.

CHAPTER TWENTY SIX

Paul woke feeling he'd just missed something urgent. Something that was his responsibility. He shoved himself away from the car door and glanced around at Emma, who was stretched out in the back with her head behind the driver's seat. It was too dark to see her clearly, but he could hear her even breathing. Still, something was wrong; he could feel it. He got out. And then he knew. The sound of a helicopter. Flying away.

He jumped back in and reached past the steering wheel for the headlight knob. The motion sent pain grinding into his shoulder joint. He shoved the knob in and out repeatedly to signal SOS. The last stutters of the rotors faded away.

"Damn," he cried, slapping the dashboard.

Behind him, Emma stirred. "What happened?" she asked, her voice shaky.

Paul banged his head on the dashboard as punishment. "There was a helicopter. I was sleeping and didn't hear it till too late. I shouldn't have gone to sleep."

"Are you Paul?"

"Paul the idiot." He turned to her. "Paul too stupid to stay awake."

"Why do you want to stay awake?"

Paul jumped out of the car again, talking to her as he ran around the car and stumbling over rocks and clumps of dry grass. "You have to get out, Emma, there's a helicopter and it has to be looking for survivors. We have to get out from under this tree and up on the highway. Get your flashlight."

Emma had already sat up and was shifting her hips toward him, her face scrunched in pain whenever the motion affected her left shoulder. "Flashlight?" She looked around her.

"It's in your backpack." Paul reached in and helped her out. He grabbed her backpack from the luggage space and held it out to her.

She stared at him blankly in the yawning silence of no helicopter.

"Flashlight," he prompted.

She reached in, felt around, and brought out a yellow flashlight.

Paul tried it, signaling three SOS flashes straight up. At the top of the ridge, the rising moon had begun to lighten the sky. "Okay, let's put everything we need in your pack, and we'll make it to the highway somehow."

He stuffed her pack with their belongings and shrugged into it, wincing at the weight on his left shoulder.

They picked their way down the streambed, Paul lighting the side often until he found the spot beyond the broken bridge where he thought he could get her up to the road.

He handed her the light. "Emma, you light the slope for me. I'll climb up first and leave the pack at the top, then I'll come back for you."

He started up the twenty-foot slope, looking for the largest rocks to step on and the most stable shrubs to cling to. It was difficult going on the loosened dirt, and the backpack upset his balance. Before he'd gone half way, the circle of light slid away. He started to remind Emma, but by now the moon had shafted into the ravine, lighting the slope. The last half of the slope was easier, and he made it to the top and shucked the pack. When he turned to go back down, Emma had already started up.

She was stepping from rock to rock, teetering when she had to grab from one shrub to the next with her only good arm.

Paul rushed down to her, riding a small landslide on his rear most of the way. "Emma, you were supposed to wait."

"I can do this."

He clamped his hand around her right arm. "I love you, Emma, but this is not the time for your 'I can do it myself' attitude. I'm helping you whether you like it or not."

She stared at him through squinted eyes. "You love me?"

Paul froze. She was more lucid now. He'd have to watch what he said. "Come on, here's a stable rock."

She put her foot on the rock he pointed to, and he scrambled in the dirt to find the next.

"Here, can you reach this one?"

She stretched her leg, but it wouldn't reach, and as she lowered it, she caught her foot on a clump of grass. She grabbed at Paul, but his feet were in loose dirt, and they both rolled back down the slope. She landed with her dislocated shoulder on his hip bone, cried out in pain, and went limp across him.

"Emma?"

She didn't answer.

Paul moved out from under her as gently as he could and laid her in the sand. Kneeling beside her, he brushed the dirt and dead leaves from her face and hair and bent to kiss her forehead. He stopped and swallowed hard. "I know. You don't want me to touch you."

Her breathing was all right, but her pulse was fast. She'd fainted in pain and he had to get her to a hospital. He looked up the slope. Where was the flash light?

He found it balanced on a small rock where she'd fallen. He scrambled up the slope again; ran up and down the road, looking for the most open place; and started signaling with the light pointed in the direction he thought the helicopter had taken.

He stood on the road for a long time, signaling in different directions. Finally, from the south, the rattle of rotors rewarded him. He pointed the flashlight in that direction and signaled. The beam was weaker now. The copter was far away, flying straight for him, but slowly, its own bright searchlight pointed at the ground ahead of it. The searchers would be watching the circle of light. Maybe the pilot...

The light on the helicopter went out, then on again three times. They'd seen him. Paul let out a shriek of joy and ran back to the back pack, still lying where he'd dropped it. He yelled down, "Emma, Emma, they're coming! They've seen us!"

She didn't answer.

Paul ran back and signaled again, and the helicopter was already nearly on him.

The copter flew back and forth over the road a few times, and Paul deduced the pilot was looking for a safe place to land. In the end, it hovered above him, battering his ears and hurling dust and leaves in his face. A stretcher basket appeared beside the runners, and then a man in a harness.

The stretcher bumped onto the road over a wide crack and Paul pulled it to his side. He pulled the man in the seat toward him, and watched him shed the straps.

The man shook his hand and shouted over the roar of the helicopter. "John Leeds, EMT. You Paul Greer?" he shouted above the roar of the copter.

Stunned, Paul took a step backwards. "How'd you know...?"

"Are you the injured party?"

"No. Yes, but there's someone else. She's at the bottom of the ravine." He pointed down the slope, where the downdraft roiled the loose dirt into swirling clouds.

Leeds walked over to the edge and looked where Paul shone the light. "She still alive?"

"Yes, but she's in a lot a pain."

Leeds studied the terrain. "We'll get her out. The chopper can hover higher to get above the trees and the ridge there. I hope the basket cable reaches her." He grabbed a bag from the basket, signaled the pilot to lower it over Emma, and started down the slope.

Paul followed him as the helicopter rose. When they reached Emma, he took her hand and called her name.

She opened her eyes and squeezed them shut against the flying dust. She groaned and raised her right hand to the injured shoulder.

"Ma'am," shouted the doctor, "I can't give you anything but a local anesthetic until after your head is X-rayed. Are you allergic to any medications?"

Emma shook her head.

Leeds checked her out first and then gave her a shot. Almost immediately she relaxed and smiled up at them.

The basket bumped onto the ground next to Paul. He and the paramedic stationed it next to her and Paul helped him lift her into it.

Paul gazed down at the accident site as the helicopter lifted him away. Everything looked so peaceful now, as if the raw contours of the earth and the ragged road had never been different. But the upheaval had changed everything. Now he knew he would always love Emma and she wouldn't return his love; he was free of his past and had no future. A dry ravine below him had been the birthplace of a human cipher.

He turned back to Emma, but her eyes were shut.

The paramedic had just gotten an IV going. He pressed a bottle of water into Paul's hand. "Let's look at you, Mr. Greer," he shouted above the din of the rotors.

"How'd you know...?" Paul started.

"They just told me to find you. Where are you hurt?"

"Same place, left shoulder."

The medic probed at the shoulder. "Don't think it's broken. You'll need some therapy. You want something for pain?"

Paul shook his head. He had so many questions to ask the man, but the noise made conversation impossible. And suddenly he was exhausted. He relaxed against the barely-cushioned seat and began to worry about how he was going to get his car out of the ravine.

In a few minutes, the pilot shouted back to them, "The hospital in Patterson is overloaded. I'm to take him to Modesto." The chopper veered to the left.

Paul wondered why, but he didn't care as long as someone would tend to Emma. He checked his watch and realized he'd missed the debate after all, and it wasn't even his fault. Well, at least that whole nightmare was over.

The pilot pointed down to the highway. An entire string of satellite vans was speeding in the same direction they were.

The helicopter landed on the roof of a hospital. Several others hovered nearby, as if waiting their turn, although it seemed to Paul that they must have been there first.

Paul had to help the paramedic lift the basket onto a gurney. "Why is there no one from the hospital out here?" he shouted.

"Too busy inside."

Paul grabbed the backpack and ran alongside Emma as Leeds rolled her past a row of gurneys waiting for the next helicopters.

In the corner of his vision, he noticed a line of flashing red and white lights that stretched for blocks away from the hospital. If there were sirens, they couldn't compete with the roar of the helicopter.

At the door to the top floor, a man stepped out of the shadows with a video camera aimed at them. A bright light went on, catching Paul, Emma, and the gurney in its beam.

Paul frowned in confusion and turned his face from the camera. Now he saw that Leeds was gray with exhaustion. "What's going on?" he asked as they passed through the automatic doors.

"Earthquake. The big one."

Paul stared around him. They were on the top floor of the hospital. It was after midnight. The floor was lined with people sitting or leaning against the wall, holding arms or legs against their pain, all dazed, some with dried blood over cuts or gashes, others moaning and crying. Most of them were wrapped in makeshift bandages or splints.

Leeds pushed the gurney past all of them and into X-ray.

Paul looked back down the hall. "Are all those people waiting to be X-rayed?"

"Most likely, but I wouldn't know. I just do the helicopter runs. You're going to be fine now." He turned to leave.

"Dr. Leeds, thank you."

Leeds raised a hand in acknowledgement as he ran back down the hall to the helicopter pad.

By the time Paul turned back to Emma, she'd already disappeared and he heard a voice in the next room say, "There's no more film." Emma's voice mumbled something. A doctor strode past him. In a few minutes he heard Emma cry out and then say, "It still hurts, but it feels right. Thank you." A soothing nurse's voice answered her.

The doctor strode past Paul again and stopped. "You dislocated, too?"

Automatically, Paul rubbed his left shoulder. "No, I…"

The doctor prodded at it and slapped him on the other one. "Get some therapy." And then he was gone.

An orderly with his black hair in a low pony tail and a silver Mexican eagle on a heavy chain wheeled Emma out, her arm now in a dark blue hospital sling. Paul's shirt and belt lay on top of her legs.

"Tonio," the orderly said by way of introduction.

Emma smiled up at Paul as he walked alongside the gurney. "Paul?"

"Hooray, Emma, you remember. How do you feel?"

"They gave me another pain killer, so I can't feel my shoulder at all. But the rest of me feels like a flea-ridden cave-woman. I smell like a road kill skunk, and my hair feels like I could plant things in it."

"I know what you mean. As soon as we get out of here, we'll find a place where we can shower."

Tonio didn't take them to an exit, but to a small windowless room that smelled of stale coffee. A dozen chairs were stacked on top of each other in the corners. There was a telephone on the wall above a mauve sofa, but no normal hospital-room equipment.

Tonio shoved the gurney against the far wall. "They hope to have a regular room for you in a few hours, but you'll be comfortable here for the time being. If you need a pain killer, send Mr. Greer to the nurses' station." He turned to Paul on the way out. "You're welcome to stay here, Mr. Greer."

"What? How'd you know…?" But the orderly was already out the door on the fly.

He turned to Emma, "I don't get it…"

"We were in a bad accident, weren't we?" she asked, rubbing at the bump on her forehead.

He leaned against the side of the gurney. "And a bad earthquake, I guess. Do you remember it?"

"I remember a lurch, and I remember thinking something was growling at us."

"That was probably the earthquake. I didn't know an earthquake was so loud, but I guess it would be, all that rock grinding away. Do you remember we were going to San Francisco for the election debate?"

"Not really. They said you took care of me after the accident. You saved my life." She turned her face toward him. "I don't know how to thank you."

He smiled down at her, his hands tingling with desire to touch her face. "No need. I'm just glad you're coming around now. Anyway, I doubt if I saved your life. You just have a concussion and a bum shoulder."

She pointed at the scab that had formed on his head. "You got hurt too, didn't you?"

"I got that and a bump on my left shoulder, but it's just bruised."

"Oh, Paul," she cried, tears welling and sliding down her temples into her hair, "and you must have moved me all over the place when you were hurting. I'm so sorry, I should have asked you..."

He laughed. "You couldn't even keep track of who I was, you were so out of it."

"I was?"

"You couldn't remember anything I told you."

"Like what?"

Like I love you more than life. The words surged up from his heart, but he clamped them in. "Like what day it was. And you kept looking for the restroom."

Emma laughed. "Down there in all the sand?" Then her face reddened.

Paul felt his face flush, too, and turned away.

"So we didn't make it to the debate," Emma said.

"Hey, you remember."

Her face reddened a little more. "Maybe I do remember a couple of things you told me." Then she grinned up at him. "I suppose you just drove into that ravine to avoid the debate."

"No, I conjured up the quake."

She laughed and then her face turned serious. "You look exhausted. Why don't you get on the gurney and I'll stretch out on the sofa."

Paul laughed. "Not likely. I'll watch to be sure you're all right, and when you go to sleep, I will, too."

"Go now." Emma closed her eyes and snored loudly. She smiled and put her warm hand on his arm. "I'm fine, really. I'll be asleep in five minutes, I promise. Please, take care of yourself now."

"Okay, I admit, I'm tired. But if you need anything, please wake me."

He started toward the sofa and noticed the phone again. "I'd better call Danny first. I'll call your folks, too, if you like."

The phone gave him a busy signal before he'd dialed anything. He tried dialing nine but got a message saying all circuits were busy. "Well, that's not going to work."

Emma looked at her watch. "It's the middle of the night there, anyway. They think we were in San Francisco, not in the earthquake. We'd just wake them up for nothing. Let's call them in the morning."

And so Paul lay down on the sofa and was asleep before his eyes were completely closed.

A metallic clank woke Paul. He opened his eyes and checked his watch. Nearly three. Another clank came from the gurney where Emma lay. The orderly was releasing one of the gurney brakes.

Paul jumped up.

Emma stirred and tried to sit up. "Where are you taking me?" Her speech was slurred. She shook her head, fighting sleep.

Tonio shoved the gurney away from the wall. "They've freed a room for you." He wheeled her into the hall.

Paul followed and stopped dead at the door. The hall was more crowded than before. "Are all these people waiting for treatment?"

"Sure," answered Tonio over his shoulder. "They're bringing the injured over from San Francisco. We haven't had a moment's break since five o'clock yesterday."

"The earthquake hit San Francisco, too?" asked Paul. "Emma, we should have kept trying to call."

Emma paled. Her eyes were clearer now. "You're right. We'll do it as soon...hey, wait a minute," she said to the orderly. "What do you mean 'they freed a room'? They moved somebody out? Why are you giving me a room if all these people need help? I don't need a room."

They passed an Oriental mother holding a little boy whose crying had subsided to weak sobs. He had a newspaper rolled around his thigh and tied with string to make a splint.

"Put him in the room," she said.

"Emma," said Paul, "you need to stay quiet till they can X-ray you."

"I can stay quiet anywhere," she said, reaching over the side to release the bar that held her in.

"Hey," said the orderly, "you can't do that. I have to take you to the room they assigned you to."

Emma grabbed the railing and shoved herself to the end of the gurney. She slid off and faced the orderly, swaying and holding on to the bar. "I'm not going to a room I don't need when all these people do."

Tonio reached for her, but Paul was faster.

"Emma, you're still full of pain killer. You can't just get up and leave."

"Maybe not, but I was fine where I was. The drug will wear off soon."

Tonio made a move to lift her back onto the gurney.

"No," she said.

Paul blocked his arm. "She's right. Neither of us will take a room that someone else needs more. Let it go, son."

The disturbance had roused some of the people lining the walls.

"But..." The orderly glanced toward the end of the hall.

Paul followed his glance and saw a man with a video camera aimed at them. Confused and unnerved, he turned back. He helped the Oriental woman get up from the floor and lay her son on the gurney. "Look, we're leaving. I'll take care of Miss Light in the Lodge. You get this child into the room, and tell your friend back there we're not interested in a video of a horrible experience."

He laid an arm around Emma's shoulders and led her toward the center of the hospital, where he hoped to find an elevator.

CHAPTER TWENTY SEVEN

Danny paced and paced and finally stopped in front of his balcony doors to watch for the dawn. Just as it tinged the newly snow-covered peaks a fragile gold-pink, he realized he'd heard Royce McClain mention the Earth Rights Party.

He rushed back to the television set.

Laurel looked in from the kitchen, where she was whisking eggs for scrambling.

"We're switching to our WPEN crew in Pensacola, Florida," said the exhausted Royce "where we now have Gordy Johnson, Earth Rights Party chairman."

Gordy appeared on the street of a trailer park. Behind him, a line of double-wides stretched to the vanishing point, flanked by golf carts. A tiny black microphone was clamped to his collar. He was holding a copy of the platform and fussing with the earphone, its wire trailing down his white golf shirt.

An off-camera reporter asked, "Mr. Johnson, did the candidates of your party leave any kind of driving plan with you? It would seem..."

Gordy straightened up, tangling his right arm in the wire and pulling the earphone out of his ear. "No, I'm afraid not," he said, struggling to right things and setting off a loud rustle of papers against the microphone.

A technician appeared, set him up again, and moved off camera.

"Actually, I thought Emma was going to fly. They didn't tell me they were driving out together."

The screen split and caught Royce with a surprised smirk. "I see. What can you tell us about Mr. Greer, then?"

Gordy's face reddened and he stared at some spot in space. "Well, not much, I'm afraid. I think you know the—ah—circumstances of the convention. I never personally laid an eye on Paul Greer."

Royce's eyebrows shot up. "You never even met the man who's running on your slate?"

"Well, you gotta understand, he was presented to us as the ideal candidate, and the vote just went his way."

Royce didn't bother to conceal an appalled shake of his venerable head. "I see. Mr. Johnson, would you quickly run down the main points in your party's platform?"

Gordy flipped over the title page of the platform, tearing it from the staple.

"Never mind," said Royce. "Our researchers have just handed me a copy."

"But don't you want me to...?"

Gordy disappeared, and Royce began reading the Roman numerals of the platform aloud, his eyes straying off camera after each heading, as if seeking the comfort of contact with reality.

Danny shuddered at the reporter's reaction. In McClain's mouth, the words sounded pompous and the platform fanatical.

Laurel was staring at the set with her mouth open. "That's really your platform?"

Danny joined her in the kitchen. "He just makes it sound insane. It's a platform projected into the future."Shaking her head, she finished whipping the eggs and poured them in his only frying pan. "Well, at least that ought to kill any chance Paul had of being elected."

Danny breathed in, trying to get the fresh smell of her, but all he got now was the dark aroma of coffee. "Thanks for making breakfa..."

Royce McClain's voice took on a new tone again as he said, "We have the first exit interviews of the election and take you now to Maine."

In Bangor, a young woman pushing a twin baby stroller smiled nervously into the camera. "I voted for Landsdon just in case they still find him alive," she said, "He's a good Christian, and what this country needs is good Christian values."

In Boston an elderly woman had voted for Paul. "Well, it's my duty to vote and we're pretty sure Greer survived. I know this'll get thrown out in court, but it'll be months before they can schedule a new election. In the meantime, *somebody* has to be president, and Hartsell has had his two terms."

In Providence a mailman had voted for Paul because he'd heard of the Earth Rights Party on the news for the first time and really liked what it stood for.

In Fort Bragg, a young Marine had voted for Landsdon. "I'm a Republican through and through," he said, "so I'm voting Republican no matter what. This is the first national election I ever got to vote in, and no stupid earthquake is going to take away my voting rights!" He saluted the interviewer, executed a military about face and marched off.

But by and large, most of those interviewed exiting the polls were members of the Earth Rights Party. They looked like a radical bunch, the sort that would chain themselves to old growth trees and blow up pipelines.

Danny's innards began to quiver.

The screen shifted again to an ill-lit scene in a hospital corridor.

Royce McClain's voice lost its ragged quality. "We have them on camera now! This comes to us from Modesto, California, where the rescued presidential and vice-presidential candidates have been taken for treatment of injuries."

Laurel grabbed his arm and pointed. "It's Paul. It's really Paul. He's alive, he's all right. Look, he's walking next to the stretcher."

Danny tried to let his joy and relief over Paul's rescue reign, but they shared his heart with jealousy.

He saw Emma getting off the gurney and Paul holding the orderly at bay. He watched, and knew the entire country watched, as Paul reached down to a Chinese woman and help her lift her injured son onto it.

An unfamiliar voice said over the video, "We understand Mr. Greer and Miss Light didn't want to be taken to a room that had been cleared for them when so many others needed it more. This was taken by a free-lance videographer, who watched them leave the floor. No one seems to know their whereabouts at the moment, but this certainly puts a new spin on the election."

"That's so like him, helping someone else first," said Laurel, and then she sighed heavily. "He really did look concerned about the vice president, didn't he? I mean, before he was distracted by the argument over the room."

Danny nodded.

There were tears of defeat in her voice when she continued. "Like he really cares about her."

Danny studied his fingernails. Out of the corner of his eye he saw her bite her lower lip.

She crossed her arms tightly across her chest, clearly trying to hold herself together. "I think I'll go on back to the motel now," she said after a pause, her voice barely above a whisper.

"I understand," he said. "But I hope you'll come back and fix me that jambalaya you promised me."

"Maybe. Can I call you later?"

Danny took a business card and wrote down his home and cell phone numbers on it. "Please do." When she'd left, he grabbed the pan of burned eggs and dropped it in the sink.

Paul and Emma found an elevator and headed for the front exit. They snaked through a mob of people in makeshift bandages and splints waiting at the triage center. Reflected in the glass covered bulletin boards on the wall, Paul saw media vans jamming the driveway. Several reporters stood around or leaned tiredly against their vehicles. Two stood at the door, looking in, obviously tired of waiting. On the inside, a fat security guard stood where the sliding doors joined.

Remembering the man with the video camera, Paul stopped before they stepped into the open space of the lobby. "Let's find another way out of here."

They turned to find Tonio shoving through the crowded hall toward them, a steely, gray-haired woman in tow.

"I'm Gertrude Cozens, chief administrator," she said when they caught up, breathing hard. She took Paul's left arm in an iron grip that fired up the pain in his shoulder. When he winced, she said, "Oh, I beg your pardon." She changed her grip to the other arm and steered them back through the crowd toward the oncology wing. "Ms. Light," she said, without loosening her clutch on Paul's arm, "we'll do as you ask and put the child in the room we cleared for you, but please, don't leave the hospital yet. We want your arm and skull X-rayed before you go. And none of your paperwork has been done. We rushed you through because we'd been asked to, but we do like to be thorough."

Paul stopped dead. "You'd been asked to? By whom? I don't understand."

She stared at him with her mouth open. "You mean you haven't heard?"

"We've been stranded in a ravine since the quake."

She let go of his arm and stepped back. "They're all dead, Mr. Greer."

Paul exchanged a glance with Emma as fear shot through him. "Who are all dead?"

"The other candidates. The hotel toppled in the quake. You're the only candidate running."

The fear whacked his knees from behind, and he barely caught himself in time to hold Emma up.

Tonio pointed toward the elevators, where the man with the video camera hovered near a hanging fern. "Why do you think all the media vans are out there? You'd better come back upstairs."

Paul felt pinioned now, a moth stuck to a collecting board before it was dead, struggling against a force beyond its reach or comprehension.

Emma took his hand and whispered to the administrator, "The election is cancelled, right?"

"That I don't know," she said. "I've been on duty since five, and you can see how chaotic it's been." She turned to Tonio with her brows raised.

Tonio shrugged. "Last I heard, they thought maybe the Supreme Court would cancel it."

Paul grabbed Tonio by the sleeve of his blue scrubs. "That's why you had someone in the hall taking a video of us, isn't it?"

Tonio hung his head. "That's just a friend of mine who free-lances..."

Paul pointed toward the man, but he'd disappeared. "You get that film, you hear me?" he demanded. "And keep him away from us."

Gertrude's face clouded in anger. "And report to my office before you leave your shift. Now, Mr. Greer, please go back and we'll make you as comfortable as we can in the waiting room. Our security has ordered the media to stay out of the building, but that's as far as we can go to protect you." She turned to Emma. "We really do need to X-ray you."

Paul hesitated. "Emma?"

She nodded.

Gertrude sagged with relief. "We'll send for you the minute the film arrives."

Emma leaned toward her. "No, I don't want any special treatment. Please, take care of the ones who're injured worse than I am."

Paul started to say something and then noticed the determined set of her chin. "She's right. Just have them get to her as soon as they can."

When they returned to the room, a freshly made gurney stood against the wall.

"I'll try the phone again," said Paul. When it didn't work, he went out to the nurse's station. "I can't get a connection on the phone in the waiting room," he said to the only nurse there, who was filling a hypodermic from a small bottle.

She put the bottle back into a metal cabinet and locked the door. "Don't even bother," she said. "We can hardly get inside lines. You won't get an outside line anywhere. They're completely tied up after the earthquake." She swished away from him, tapping the hypodermic with her fingernail to get the bubbles to the top.

Paul returned to the waiting room. Emma had stretched out on the sofa and appeared to be sleeping.

"Emma?"

She didn't move.

"I know you're pretending. Come on, let me sleep on the sofa."

No response.

"Okay, 'possum. You win." He climbed onto the gurney, and in a few minutes he was asleep, too.

At seven o'clock, Danny caught the change in the anchor's voice just as Laurel was putting bowls of steaming jambalaya on the table.

Royce McClain stared in disbelief at the pink foolscap that had just been laid in front of him. He looked askance at some person not on camera, and his eyes widened. "Current tabulation of our election results," he began with obvious reluctance, "show that the Earth Rights Party has carried every state on the eastern seaboard and through the central states by virtue of the electoral college. Early results from the Midwest and the Rocky Mountain states show that there, too, the Earth Rights Party is well on its way. A ground swell of votes cast for dead candidates in opposition to the radical party hasn't checked the wave of Earth Rights votes. Only California can turn the tide, and California..."

Growing paler by the minute, he looked absently into the camera. "Even if there were no earthquake to contend with in California, it's the state where 'radical' is normal. For the other states, I suppose there's some logic to this. Members of the Earth Rights Party *would* turn out to vote if they knew their candidate was still alive, while others were sure theirs had died in the quake...The majority of the votes cast is what..." He obviously didn't want to finish the thought.

He went back to the pink foolscap. "Current projections show that the Earth Rights Party..." his voice dropped to a whisper, "...could carry the election with a popular vote of approximately..." He stared at the source of the foolscap again, clearly hoping to have misread, "one hundred thirty-seven thousand, seven hundred? This can't happen. With millions of voters..." He touched the tiny speaker in his right ear. His mouth fell open. "We have just received word from the election commission that at current count candidate Paul Greer has carried all the Rocky Mountain States and unquestionably has the electoral college vote. Paul Greer, Earth Rights Party candidate, has, by simple default, been elected president of the United States."

Danny stared at the television, mouth agape. Laurel gasped and froze with a spoon poised over the rice. The pungent steam of her jambalaya wafted into the chandelier over the table.

Royce McClain lost his "objective reporter" calm, twisted in his seat, and practically shouted, "Get me one of those damned experts out here. This isn't possible! There's got to be a law..." Something blasted him from his little speaker, throwing his head to the right; he straightened up, listening, collected his cool, and then said, "Our coverage of the election now continues from our sister station in Chicago, where we introduce you to a newspaper reporter who interviewed Paul Greer in September, apparently one of the few people who even know him." Before the camera shifted to Chicago, he was out of his seat, yanking the speaker out of his ear and yelling, "Dammit, Frank, don't you ever shout into my ear like that again! I'll..."

Caitlin Pascoe appeared on camera outside a glass-front office with "Popular Probe" stenciled on the door. With her was Martha Warren, the stunning red-haired anchor woman from Chicago. Both looked exhausted.

"I'm speaking with Caitlin Pascoe of the *Popular Probe*, who, as you mentioned, Royce, interviewed Paul Greer for a series of articles on splinter parties and their candidates. What was your impression of him, Caitlin?"

Caitlin's face appeared to Danny as a memory, a dimly recollected prelude to a nightmare.

"He didn't strike me as a man with a mission," she said, "such as one might expect from a splinter party, but his running mate, Emma Light in the Lodge, certainly did. Greer is, however, an educated, intelligent man of great kindness and concern for people, as I indicated in my article."

Martha jerked the microphone back before Caitlin had finished. "Would you mind repeating that other name?"

"Light in the Lodge. She's an In...Native American from Wyoming. I forget what tribe."

Martha struggled to keep a straight face. "You mentioned that Greer's was an exceptionally religious background," she said when Caitlin was finished. "Could you elaborate on that?"

Caitlin stared off to her left. "Catholic."

Martha drew her perfect brows into perfect puzzlement. "There are many Catholics. Why would you call that exceptional?"

Caitlin was a long time in answering, her face torn with indecision. Martha repeated the question.

"Priest," said Caitlin, gripping her notebook to her chest.

Danny winced.

"Are you telling me the country has just elected an Indian woman to the vice-presidency and a Catholic *priest* to the presidency?!" The anchor-woman nearly dropped the microphone and quite forgot to hold it out to Caitlin for the answer.

Caitlin's answer came through muffled. "Ex-priest. Recent. He left the priesthood in August."

"This man came out of the priesthood, and the first thing he did was run for president?"

Danny felt Laurel at his side. She'd gone as pale as the blouse she was wearing.

Caitlin bit her lip. "If I remember correctly, his brother nominated him without his knowledge."

"Why?"

"I...I think it was some kind of joke."

Danny put his head in his hands. "Oh, my God."

Caitlin continued, "I know they never expected him to be elected."

Martha laughed aloud. "No, I don't imagine they did. Back to you, Royce."

The camera caught Royce shaking his head. A political expert was just taking the seat next to him. Royce collected himself and cast about for a question to put to the expert.

"Well, Professor Helding, would you care to comment on the situation before us?"

"In all truth, I haven't a scrap of wisdom for you, Royce. I've said for decades that the electoral college is a dinosaur. In the age of instant communication, we ought to do away with it, but it's still the law."

"What do you see as the options open to the major parties at this point?"

"I've no doubt they'll file injunctions, organize protests, and argue the issue before the Supreme Court. I'd expect all three within the next day or two."

"And their chances for success?"

Helding raised his brows and shrugged. "I do know there's no law that governs an election in the midst of this kind of crisis, but I couldn't begin to outguess the Supreme Court with its conservative make-up. It's a situation without precedent. If I didn't know better, and if this weren't happening against the backdrop of the tragedy in California, I'd say it was the hilarious product of a demented writer that had somehow found its way into the media, not unlike the Orson Welles fiasco some decades back. For now, I think we're all in the state of traumatized incredulity we've been in since the earthquake and the demise of the candidates."

"Traumatized incredulity," Danny echoed, staring at Laurel. The prelude was over. The nightmare was just beginning.

PART TWO

CHAPTER TWENTY EIGHT

After Emma was released in the afternoon, they borrowed scrubs from Tonio, left the hospital through a rear entrance, and walked for blocks towards the outskirts of Modesto, looking for a functional phone, a drugstore that still had pain killers, and a place to stay. All motels on the highway were already flashing "No Vacancy." They didn't pass a single drug store.

"I should have let them give me one more shot instead of a prescription," said Emma as they crossed a side street.

Out of the corner of his eye, Paul caught sight of a flaking motel sign half a block off the highway. "Come on, we'll try this," he said, putting his arm around her. As they neared the motel, however, he steered her away. "It looks like the kind of place they rent by the hour."

Emma grabbed his hand and pulled. "I don't care. I have to put ice on this or something."

They entered the office. A rolling fat man, totally bald, came in from an apartment that smelled of old cooking grease and cigar smoke. "Yeah, I still got a room," he mumbled before they even asked, keeping his head toward the television that was blaring news of the death count in San Francisco. He shoved a registration card toward them. Paul signed in and asked the price of two rooms.

The manager jerked his head around. "Two?" He looked at them suspiciously. "Well, I need you to fill out the second card." He leered at Emma and then stared at her rumpled clothes and the blue arm strap. "Oh, I guess you folks got caught in the biggie, huh?"

"Yes. Are there phones in the rooms?"

"Yeah, but lots o' luck. Although I did hear they were getting new routings going pretty soon. You want to make a long distance call, though, you gotta go through the office. You gotta feed the TV quarters, and we don't got cable. Don't get much call for it." He glanced at Emma's card. His hand jerked and he stared at her again. He looked at Paul's card and seemed to suck up all the air in the office in one gasp. "You're Paul Greer? Wait right here. Don't go away." He spun around, slammed the entire left side of his body into the doorjamb, and disappeared into the apartment.

"That doesn't bode well." said Paul.

"Nope."

The manager ballooned into the room again, an armload of clean sheets and towels covering his chest. "Right this way, Mr. Greer, I got two rooms right down here. My very best. You won't get none finer in town tonight, not here, not with all the injured being brought in and all. I'm sure you'll be perfectly comfortable. Anything you want, you just let me know. Anything at all."

He opened the door to room 7, ushered Emma in with a half smile, and then opened room 8, the end room. "Got windows on both sides here, the bathroom's bigger, got a tub as well as a shower and, just between me and you, the bed's better. Now, you just make yourself comfortable, and I'll make the bed fresh in both rooms."

"Do this one right now and I'll put the lady in here. She's in pain." Paul took his things out of the pack, left the manager bustling about the room and went next door. Emma was already lying down on top of the threadbare chenille bedspread. She smiled up at him.

"Can you wait a minute or two before you sleep?" he asked, setting his things on the end of the dresser. "He's putting fresh sheets on the other bed, and then you can go in there. As soon as he goes back to the office, we can try the phones. And then I'll see what I can scare up to eat if you'll be all right here by yourself."

"Fine, thanks, Paul. But you need to rest, too. Let's both shower after we call, and I'm sure that'll give me enough energy to go with you."

"All done here," the manager fairly sang coming in the door. "You go on over now, Miss—uh—Light the Lodge."

Paul helped her up and they went into room 8. Emma took in the thin, uneven curtains with the pull strings hanging to the floor, the cheap old knotty-pine wall paneling, and the sagging mattress. "Well, this one certainly is a cut above. A regular presidential suite."

Paul laughed. "I have a feeling neither of us will even notice tonight. Is an hour enough time for you to phone and take a bath?"

"Of course. Just knock whenever you're ready." She looked down at her sling. "I wish I weren't so lame. I'll be all right in the shower, but I'd really like to wash my hair. Not that I brought any shampoo with me for an overnight drive."

"I didn't either, but maybe I can help you with that later if you don't mind the motel soap. You look beautiful, though."

She answered with a little snort. "You're just having a delayed concussion."

Paul went back and instructed the manager to go straight to his switchboard. He forced himself to wait two full minutes and then dialed 0. A long time passed before the manager got the connection through.

"Paul?" Danny shouted over the wire.

"Yeah, it's me. I just wanted to let you know I'm all right."

"Oh, God, Paul, I'm so sorry. I really had no idea this would happen."

"Hey, take it easy. Nobody knows an earthquake is going to happen. We're okay. I just hit my shoulder and Emma has a concussion and a dislocation. It wasn't that bad. The car's at the bottom of a ravine, but we're going to be fine. She's probably talking to her folks right now, too. So, listen, could you call the store for me? I should have been there several hours ago. Talk to Ms. Wynne in personnel, I guess. Tell her I was in an accident and won't be in for a couple of days. I have no idea when, or even how, we might be able to get back. Things are pretty bad out here."

The line was silent. Paul looked at the receiver and thought of the inept manager at his switchboard. "Danny?"

"You don't know?"

"Know what?"

There was another long silence.

"Paul, are you sitting down?"

"Yeah."

"There's no one else running after the earthquake."

"I know, but I heard they were canceling the election."

"The court declined to do that. Even without the California results, you're in, Paul. You're president."

The receiver fell to the floor. Paul sat frozen, unable to breathe, his body jerking slightly, eyes wide and unblinking.

"Paul? Paul?" called a very small voice from the receiver.

CHAPTER TWENTY NINE

A knock at Paul's door barely touched the hearing receptors of his brain. He had no idea how long he'd been sitting on the edge of the sagging bed, trying to deny Danny's news. He shoved himself up and started toward the door but caught his foot in the telephone wire. The phone hit the thin carpet with a ding and the cracking of plastic. When he opened the door, there was nothing outside but the sole remaining empty parking space and a few yucca plants in the weeds. Another knock sounded from in the room. He turned and discovered a connecting door between the bed and the front wall.

Emma stepped in, pale and dazed. "Danny told you?"

Paul nodded.

She breathed in shallow gasps. "I never thought... This isn't funny, is it?"

He shook his head.

"The manager knew, didn't he?"

He nodded.

"Do you suppose he called the press?"

Nod.

"We're going to be swamped by reporters any minute."

Nod.

"I can't face them. There's going to be such a furor."

Shudder.

"Should we bathe, then go on and eat before they catch up with us? Maybe if we're gone, they'll give up."

Paul shook his head. "Go now."

"You okay?"

"No."

They hurried away from the motel but had hardly turned onto the highway before the first media van roared toward them. Paul stopped dead, not knowing whether to run back or head for the shadow of the next building. Emma grabbed him and pulled him to the sidewalk behind a bus bench. The van screeched around the corner.

"K-MOD ABC," she read on its side. "A national affiliate."

The crew jumped out and piled into the office.

Paul helped her up. "Come on."

"Right. Watch for a dark dive of a greasy spoon where they'd never think of looking for us."

Several blocks up the highway they came to the Immodesto Bar and Bare, a windowless, yellow-brick building with a flimsy red door flaked along the bottom. A bilious green neon sign hanging from the eaves announced "Eats Drinks Babes."

"You think they'd look for us here?" asked Emma.

"Never."

The miasma of stale beer and cigarette smoke in the dark shotgun space of the bar choked Paul like the smell of damp varnish—like a confessional. He stopped before the door closed and started to retreat. Emma pulled him forward.

The floor stuck to their shoes, letting go of each footstep with a *fft*. They passed the only other customer, a man sprawled over the bar with both arms on the glass-ringed surface, his head on his left arm while the right cradled his beer glass. They chose in a booth near the back, where they could watch the news on the television over the bar. The old picture of Paul from the *Popular Probe* stayed on the screen for a long time, but the sound didn't penetrate the grinding strip tease music from the side room.

Paul kept his face toward the wall while they ordered and ate hamburgers from red plastic baskets.

Emma shoved her basket away with her hamburger half eaten and the French fries drooping over the side. "I guess I didn't mean a greasy spoon *this* greasy."

Paul nodded but kept eating.

"Listen," she said, "let's wait till it's completely dark outside before we go back. If we're lucky, maybe we can climb in a bathroom window and avoid them."

Paul's daze had lifted a little by now, and he raised his eyebrows. "I thought you wanted all this."

Emma pulled her shoulders up, winced, and gave him a sheepish smile. "I just didn't expect it, and I never thought about being hounded by the press."

From a block away they saw the jam of media vehicles spilling out onto the highway. They slipped down the street before the motel, into the alley behind it, and along the unpainted cinderblock wall with its alternating air conditioners and frosted windows. Both their windows were painted shut.

"Come on, let's find a phone booth," said Emma.

"What for?"

"You'll see."

They found a phone on the poorly lighted side of a liquor store, and Emma thumbed through the yellow pages, bending close to the chained, tattered book. She dialed and a moment later said, "K-MOD? I just want to let you know that Paul Greer and Emma Light in the Lodge have been seen in a restaurant on,..." she looked up and down the street, "highway 132....No, I don't know the name, but I think it's pretty close to downtown.... Well, I imagine they went there to eat. That's what people usually do...You're very welcome." She hung up. "Let's go watch the fun," she said, grinning up at him.

They crossed the highway and stationed themselves behind some bushes. Within a minute the K-MOD reporter, whose van stood nearest rooms 7 and 8, jumped on the hood of his satellite van. He began shouting and waving at those farther back to get out of the way. The outermost vehicles roared out in reverse, waited, then screeched out onto the highway behind the K-MOD van. Soon there wasn't a soul near the motel but the fat manager, who stepped out of the office, put his hands on his ample hips, shook his head, and went back in.

"Don't turn on the lights," said Paul as they went in room 8.

"Don't even turn on the television."

"Well, I guess I should..." He turned toward their connecting door, but he felt like a yoyo at the bottom of a string with her presence pulling him back to the top. With his back still half turned to her, he looked back. "You said you wanted to wash your hair. Would you like me to help? There's a little light coming in from the alley."

Emma shook her head. She felt her hair. "Well, yes, would you mind very much?"

"Mind?" Paul repeated to keep from laughing aloud. "Not at all."

She bent over the sink and Paul leaned over her and poured warm water from a plastic cup over the beautiful, thick, black hair in his fingers. He lathered it with the little bar of soap on the sink. His thigh brushed her hip and she didn't pull away. He massaged her head, letting the sensuous warmth flow into the hands that had longed for such a touch.

"Mmm, that feels so good," Emma said. "It's so relaxing my knees'll probably give way."

"I'll catch you, Emma," he promised, stunned at a mushy quality his voice had never had before. He wished he could caress the strong, sinuous black hair forever. He rinsed with warm water, intending to lather it a second time, but Emma straightened up and handed him a towel.

Her eyes lifted to his and stopped his breathing. Her hair was a jumble of long black strands that hung wet onto her clothing. Water ran down her face and onto her sling.

He gathered up the hair, wrapped the towel around it, and rubbed, never taking his eyes from hers. She was so close, if he moved an inch, his body would touch her body. His arms would take her in and never let go.

She closed her eyes and leaned toward him but immediately drew in a sharp breath and glanced frantically toward the connecting door. She moved away. "I'm pretty sure this election will end up in court, Paul."

Paul blinked. She'd spun him to the bottom of the string again. Why had he let her draw him in? Idiot. "You really think so?"

"It has to come. You know what popular vote we got? Just over a hundred thirty-seven thousand. So don't worry too much about it. The major parties are going to challenge the results. My father told me so on the phone."

Paul forced himself to say, "I wish I could believe that, but after all that's happened, I expect the worst. Besides, there've been presidents elected by a small popular vote before."

"But so few out of millions? It's unthinkable. It may take forever to straighten it out."

"So what happens in the meantime?"

"I have no idea, but there's no chance the Supreme Court will let this election stand. At this point our first concern ought to be getting home."

"And joining the major parties in the challenge."

Emma laughed. "You never give up, do you? Maybe it's your destiny to be president."

"Don't even say it. I was just hanging on to the court idea."

She took a brush from her pack and tried to reach the left side of her head.

Paul waited.

After a couple of swipes, she growled in frustration. "This isn't going to work. Would you mind very much?"

Yoyo coming up again. He stifled a sigh and steered her to the one chair in the room. He tried to ignore the feel of the hair but soon found himself putting his hand on her head and following the brush down its beautiful black path. When he'd brushed her left side and started to move around her, she took the brush from him.

"Thanks, I can do..."

A heavy vehicle drove up and parked directly outside their window with its headlights on. Paul looked up, startled. A door slammed and a heavy fist knocked on the door of Paul's room. A voice said, "Go check with the office. They gotta come back sometime."

The illusory closeness he'd been able to steal from the moment vanished. He leaned to her and whispered, "Looks like I'd better get out of your room."

She hesitated before she nodded. She stood up in the light shafting through a slit between the curtains, her face torn with indecision. "I..." She shook her head slightly and put her hand on his arm. "I just want to say thank you, Paul. You're a true friend, and I'm glad you were with me."

Thoroughly confused, he left her standing in the shaft of light, the hairbrush at her side.

As soon as there was a wall between them, the word *president* crashed into his mind again, and he lay on the bed with his eyes wide open, desperately wishing he could turn back the clock and drive straight from New Orleans to the bottom of Baja.

Emma shoved the brush back in her pack without taking a single swipe at her hair. She'd let him get much too close, so close she'd nearly given in. And she'd hurt him. Again. Dammit. When he'd never been anything but kind to her.

She lay across the bed, desperate for sleep; but sleep was miles away, in the time before the accident, before Paul, who had "feelings" for her.

She rolled onto her right side and closed her eyes tight. It didn't help. She always slept on her left, and that shoulder was still sore. Besides, her bra felt like a harness, her sweater like a strait jacket; and she couldn't get out of them without Paul's help. She couldn't ask him. He was probably asleep anyway. No, he wasn't. He was in there lying on his bed, too, hurting and wanting her in spite of her push-pull behavior. He must be a fool to feel anything for her at all. No, he wasn't. He was a kind man who liked her in spite of herself. Maybe loved her.

She curled into a tight ball. She couldn't let herself love him. They'd both get hurt when it didn't work out. And there was no way it could work out. Never. Not Indian and white, not lawyer and shoe-salesman-priest, not fighter and peacemaker.

But at the bottom of her heart, where she kept the things she didn't tell herself, she knew she cared for him. It had taken every atom of her resolve to let him leave the room, and it'd been wrong. She did care. She'd have to get over him later, but right now, there wasn't so much as a picket of defense left between him and her.

Paul had no idea what time it was when a dim shadow fell across him and a hand slid into his.

"Paul?" she whispered in his ear. She knelt next to the bed.

"What's the matter, Emma?" He turned on his side, ready to leap up.

"Nothing's the matter. I'm so tired but I can't sleep. I've just been thinking and thinking. About this whole crazy business. And how much you've come to mean to me. I just want to apologize for the way I've behaved and show you..."

He put a finger of his free hand over her mouth. "I know where things stand, Emma. You don't have to show me anything."

"I know I don't have to. I *want* to. I've been such a jerk, but it's because I'm scared of you. No, of us. It can't work, and I don't dare let myself love you, but I do care." She put her forehead on their clasped hands and whispered, "You're such a good man. Do you think it's all right for 'just friends' to make love to each other?"

Desire shot through his body like a flash flood of adrenaline, closing his throat. He struggled to say, "In my entire life, I've never wanted anything the way I want to make love to you. I just don't think I can do it as a friend. And you don't owe me anything, Emma."

"I'm not talking about owing. I want to give you the only thing I have, even if just as a friend. And I'm afraid we may never have another chance. There's going to be a mob out there tomorrow, and we won't have another private moment for a very long time."

Paul's head screamed no and his heart cried yes even as his fingers moved for her face. "Are you sure your shoulder..."

Her index finger touched his lips and there was not a thing he could do but kiss it. He slipped from the bed and knelt with her.

"I'm sorry, I can't get out of my clothes," she whispered.

He kissed her still damp hair. "I'll have to take off your sling. Hold your arm."

He removed the straps and slid the hospital sling down her arm. He worked her sweater up on her right side, slipped it over her head, and then gently pulled it down her left arm. He unhooked her bra, fumbling with the unfamiliar hooks and fabric, fearful of hurting her. And then her upper body was bare before him, so soft in its lovely, female dimensions and so stunning it sent shock waves stronger than the earthquake through him.

He started to put the sling back on.

"Don't," she said. "I want it off. I'll be careful."

Her hand caressed his face, circled around his neck, and came back to rest over his heart. She kept it there, her eyes holding his, while he let his hands love her body. He traced her dark eyebrows, her straight nose and mouth. His hands found the wonderful hair again, the neck and back beneath it, the shoulders, the small depression under the silver bear, the rise of her breasts.

Without a word, they stood, helped each other with the remaining clothes, and touched with the full length of their bodies. His arms circled her. She melted against him and their lips met as he lifted her to the bed.

Her body. His body. Together. One body. How had he turned his back on this? He sobbed aloud for the lost years. She tightened herself around him as if pulling his very being into hers.

The wonder of it exploded in him, the complete power of feeling over mind or body. The most elementary and overwhelming of human emotions. The giving of oneness. And the key he'd always lacked to understanding life.

"Paul," she said a long time later. Her head lay on his chest to spare his shoulder.

He stroked the hair, still floating in the sheer wonder of touching her, of being in an entirely new dimension. "Hmm?"

"I'm scared to death."

He moved his head to stare at her. "You, too?"

"I dreamed of leading the world to respect for Mother Earth. But that's all it was, a dream. A really safe dream. I knew I'd never be elected to so much as the tribal council. Now that I have, I realize I couldn't lead a moth to light. I can't be vice president any more than you can be president."

Paul laughed. And then they were both laughing, shushing each other lest the media people hear, which made it worse. The bed shook until Emma said "Ow, don't make me laugh anymore." So he kissed her instead and their love-making was interrupted only occasionally by a giggle.

CHAPTER THIRTY

A heavy metal door slammed, and Paul's eyes flew open. His head leaden with unfinished sleep, he looked automatically for the cross on his wall and registered dingy paneling in the pre-dawn light. He blinked. Where was he? Slowly, overpowering memories rolled over him—the growl of pitching earth, his car crashing down the cliff, Emma hurt. The election. President. His heart flipped.

And finally he registered Emma. Naked. Close enough to feel her warmth and smell the motel soap in her hair. His body jerked with the impulse to jump and run. What had he done? He'd made love to a woman who'd never be anything more than his friend. He'd rejected the cross, the church, and made his commitment to life. And to her. A commitment she didn't want. But before the shock faded, the power of his love returned, and his conviction that both decisions were right.

Another door slammed. Emma's eyes flew open and swept the room, just as his had, seeking the familiar. She looked almost as disoriented as when she'd first wakened from the concussion, but when her eyes found his, they told him she knew exactly who he was.

He pulled her to him and held fast, acutely aware of her bare, warm skin against his chest, his legs.

She blushed and smiled.

More doors closed in the parking lot, followed by muffled voices.

"Oh, my God," he whispered.

"Shhh! What are we going to do?" she mouthed.

"You're asking me?! You're the politician."

Someone knocked tentatively on the door to room 8. "Mr. Greer?" a muffled voice suggested.

"Maybe he's in seven," said another.

Someone knocked at seven, loudly this time.

Paul kissed her and whispered, "I have to do *something*."

"Right. He's at your door." She started to get up, turned back, placed both hands on his face, and kissed him.

He opened his mouth to say he loved her but choked the words back.

She smiled, put her finger over his lips, and said, "I know." They kissed again.

A silhouetted shadow pressed against his window, elbows out, hands cupping the eyes. "Mr. Greer?" the voice repeated.

Indignant now, Paul shouted, "Move away from that window and give me an hour, please."

A whole chorus of voices now yelled, "Mr. Greer?" That was followed by a cacophony of questions as the chorus coalesced in front of the window.

"What are you going to tell them?" she asked.

"God, I don't know," he said, his heart pounding in earnest now. "What I really want to tell them is it's all a big mistake, and I'll join every effort to challenge the results, and I infinitely pre-fer being an obscure shoe salesman to being president, and..."

"Paul, there are three hundred million people out there who're going to get their first view of a man who *might* just end up briefly in the White House, mistake or no, including the ones who knew you in New Orleans. Even if the Party means nothing to you, be careful how you come across for their sake."

"I know. I haven't forgotten them." He swallowed hard and caressed her face. "Emma, I had a lot of time to think while we were in the ravine. I sorted some things out—what I believe, what I want to do with my life—and most of them are scary as hell, but I made a promise to you back there. I know you don't remember it. You weren't remembering things for more than a heartbeat. I swore I'd try to live up to all the things I admire in you—your honesty, your concern for things outside yourself, for people."

Her eyes filled. "Oh, Paul, don't you know it's what you've lived by all along? But what a kind thing to say."

"Not kind at all. I mean it. I promise you again, I'll do everything I can to make at least your life better, as your friend or—may the powers that be prevent it—as president. If this *is* my destiny, idiotic as it is, I'll put my heart and my back into it till the courts throw me out."

She smiled. "I already knew you would." She pulled him close and then jumped from the bed, picked up her clothes and sling, and tiptoed to room 8.

Paul showered and dressed in his rumpled, dirty clothes. He joined her for a moment in room 8 and they held each other for a last time.

"Wish me luck," he said.

"I do."

He ran a finger down her nose. "And the same to you, buddy."

"Thanks, we'll both need it."

"Emma, no matter what happens, I want you to know I'd go through this whole insane business all over again just for the joy of knowing you."

She smiled and put her hand on his cheek. "And the same to you, buddy."

Paul stepped back into room 7. "Lock this," he said, as he closed the door. He waited till he heard the lock turn and opened the door to the parking lot.

The reaction was immediate, loud, and unintelligible.

Before him stood a wall of reporters with microphones stuck in his face.

"Mr. Greer..." were the only words he understood.

Someone gave him a shove and a lift, and he found himself standing, badly balanced, on the stubby, sloping hood of the K-MOD van in front of his window. The reporters rushed to their cameramen and jumped on their vehicles to gain a better vantage point in the jammed parking lot. They scrambled for pencils and pads. A few bandaged people stepped out of other rooms. For a second there was an expectant silence.

He had no idea where to start. The cacophony rose again, and he put his hand out. It was shaking visibly. "I can only understand one question at a time," he said, mortified at the quaver in his voice.

A sea of waving hands swam before him. He pointed to a reporter in the back, smiling slightly as he recognized his old classroom ploy for keeping the front students quiet.

"Mr. Greer, is it true you're an ex-priest?"

"Yes."

"When did you leave the priesthood?"

"In August."

"Why?"

Paul hesitated, wishing he could simply say, "It's none of your business," but they would make it their business. "Philosophical differences," he said. A hand just in front of him shot up.

The speaker didn't wait to be recognized. "Do you really believe in the Earth Rights Party?"

"I believe...So many things need to be done...I realize the platform is..." He knew he was presenting himself as an idiot.

A woman standing in front of Room 4 with a cast around her right arm and a crutch under her left shouted, "I just heard that platform on the TV! You gotta be crazy."

The reporters ignored her. "Have you heard of the challenge to the election results that the other parties are preparing?"

"I only assumed there would be...," said Paul.

A reporter with the morose expression of a bereaved undertaker asked, "You mean you don't even know? By eight o'clock EST the Republicans and Democrats handed their challenge over to the Supreme Court, and the Court agreed to review the case immediately. What are you planning to do about it?"

Paul opened his mouth to say he was all in favor of it, but Emma's words echoed in his head. "It appears I've been duly elected for the time being, but I will abide by whatever the Court decides, of course."

A reporter standing on a station wagon at the back yelled, "You mean you don't even know there are already demonstrations against you in Washington?"

Paul felt his insides go empty. "No, but I can certainly understand that people would be upset..."

"Why were you not in San Francisco for the debate?"

"There was a snow..."

"Are you characteristically late for such important affairs?"

"No, I..."

"Mr. Greer, is Miss Light with you?"

"Her name is Miss Light in the Lodge, and I believe she's in room 8."

Several reporters checked the number of his room and exchanged wry, knowing grins.

"Mr. Greer, how do you feel about being elected?"

"I'm in a daze. You must know this was totally unexpected. I want to extend my sympathy to the families of those who died in the earthquake, and to the survivors."

A reporter near the back shouted, "Do you seriously think you can carry out the office of the president?" His sneering sarcasm was greeted with laughter.

Paul raised his right hand and his feet slipped off the van. He grabbed at the end of the hood, wrenching his shoulder. He climbed up again. The reporters laughed.

"Never mind," shouted the sarcastic one.

"If the election isn't invalidated..." Paul started to answer him anyway.

A short, chubby woman in a bright green pants suit cut him off. "You and Miss Light in the Lodge were seen in the Immodesto bar last night. What were you doing in a strip tease joint?"

"Eating."

The laughter rose again.

"Making up for lost skin, if you ask me," yelled a skeletal man in front of Room 2.

Paul felt himself blanch as the entire gathering hooted with laughter. "Sir, I assure..."

"And how did you get back here without being seen?"

"We walked."

Directly below him a man with gray hair and beard and no apparent cameraman actually raised his hand before saying, "Randall Post of the Sierra Club, Mr. Greer. Could we get back to the platform? The Sierra Club champions many of its issues..."

Paul felt a tiny breath of relief in the reporter's profession manner and his support.

"...however, we are concerned for the species that have now established themselves in the lakes if you put through legislation to undam rivers..."

"They're going to undam all the rivers?" shouted the chubby woman.

A howl of protest rose.

A skinny woman who reminded him of Shirl Wainwright yelled from the back, "That's ridiculous. No one's going to stand by and see that happen. This is a regular circus. Can we get Miss Light the Lodge out here so we can see what's in ring two?"

"Yes," said Emma, stepping out.

A great din followed. Someone lifted her onto the hood where Paul stood. He reached around to her good shoulder to steady her. Twenty cameras zoomed, and fifty pencils hit fifty notepads.

"Miss Lodge, what do you intend to do as the first Native American to hold executive office?"

"I intend to carry out its functions to the best of my ability."

The skeptic sneered. "Are you telling us you don't intend to take the country back for the Indians?"

Emma stared him down. "Are you telling me you'd be willing to give it?"

The other reporters laughed and wrote furiously.

"Sheesh," called a man with both his arms in casts. "Hand me the petition to have the election annulled! I'll sign it with my toes if I have to."

CHAPTER THIRTY ONE

Emma sat in the corporate plane that Learjet had sent to take them back to Denver. The soft beige leather at her back smelled of disdainful wealth sneering at the denim jacket she'd had on for five days. She frowned at the crystal goblets hanging over the brass-trimmed bar.

Sitting next to her, Paul sniffed the wine the pilot had given them before take-off and seemed perfectly at ease.

She squirmed in the excessive comfort. "Nice of Learjet, but this thing makes me fidgety."

Paul raised his brows at her before taking a sip of wine. "Why?"

"I can't reconcile this with tenements and hovels and homeless people with shopping carts. Too much luxury. I'm used to coach class and peanuts or long hours in my old truck."

He swished the wine in his mouth for a few seconds. "Great wine." He checked the plane's trappings. "I hardly noticed it. I've been surrounded by the gold and plush of the church for years while living in my own Spartan space. I never questioned it. I guess I should have."

Emma shuddered. "A shock to my...what? Democratic sensibilities, maybe. Or maybe I just feel the same way my old jacket feels against the leather—crude and shabby."

Paul started to answer her, but the pilot's voice came over the slight whine of the jet. "Mr. Greer, Miss Light in the Lodge, we're at cruising altitude now. You're welcome to go to the kitchen. You'll find a full course meal for you in the refrigerator and the warming oven. Please enjoy it."

Emma shook her head and realized Paul was doing the same.

"To tell the truth," he said, "I'm not really comfortable, either. Barely elected, and I'm already accepting corporate favors."

"Well, we did try to find somebody else who needed to get to Denver. And don't worry. It won't matter when the courts throw out the election."

He raised his glass, toasting the idea. "I'm counting on that. Anyway, at least we didn't have to take that long drive again."

She shifted to poke him with her right hand. "Hey, I thought you liked driving all over the country with me."

"I do, I do. It's just better without slings and weird concussion behavior and near death experiences. Right now I just want to get home. If I don't show up at work tomorrow, I'm sure they'll fire me. I'll be glad when things get back to normal and I have only Danny's shenanigans to contend with."

Emma felt a twinge at the thought of home, but she said, "Actually, I'll be glad to get back, too. Maybe I'll even get some work since I'm so famous. Are you going to tell Danny about... what happened in the motel?"

Paul's put his hand on her knee, his eyes glowing with leftover wonder. "No, of course not. But Danny's sharp. He'll know something came of his matchmaking."

Emma squeezed his hand, letting its heat flow through her. "Just let him guess. Come on. Let's go see what CEOs eat."

As she stepped to the galley, she felt him behind her like a warm blanket that didn't belong to her but she didn't want to give back. He wasn't like other men she'd known, who'd been more curious about an Indian than interested in her as a woman, and who'd left long before things got serious. Maybe Paul... No, no dream-catcher in the world would hold that solid gold fantasy.

When they met Danny on the tarmac at the Denver airport, he pulled Paul into a brotherly bear-hug, and Emma felt suddenly hollow. No one in Big Sleep would grab her and make her feel so important, so loved.

Danny shook hands with her. Before she could think about it, she smiled and hugged him loosely. Then he looked surprised, and she felt like a love-starved child begging for attention.

"Where are all the reporters?" asked Paul.

"Not allowed on the tarmac," said Danny. He ushered them to his car, which stood nearby with a special permit on the windshield. They followed a pilot car to the exit.

The minute they drove onto the airport exit, they passed a string of media vehicles parked in the emergency lane. As they passed the rearmost one, it pulled out, angering the drivers in front of it. They honked and jockeyed for position, creating such a snarl that Danny barely avoided being hit by a satellite van.

Emma looked past Paul out the back window as the media tangle sorted itself out and sped toward them. "Doesn't look like we'll avoid them this time."

Paul glanced back and shuddered. "Great. After yesterday's fiasco, they'll come at me with fangs bared." But he gave her one of those smiles that lasered right through her defenses.

As she turned back, she noticed that Danny caught Paul's smile in the mirror as well. He didn't give her a little triumphant leer, as she'd expect. Strange, but before she could wonder about that, he nodded at her blue sling.

"How badly are you hurt?" he asked.

"It's just dislocated," she said, surprised he'd asked.

"Well, you can't drive home like that," he said. "With Paul's car in California, there's only mine. If you can wait till Saturday, I'll drive behind the two of you and then Paul can ride back with me."

"No need," said Emma, aware of a difference. Danny was sober. And kind.

"Glad to do it," Danny said, smiling at her now. "But not till Saturday. I can't take tomorrow off after I took off all day Tuesday and Wednesday to watch for news of you guys."

"You did that?" asked Paul with a catch in his voice.

"Of course. I was scared to death."

Emma turned to glance at Paul in the back seat. He was looking so fondly at Danny that she felt a twinge of envy. What would it have been like to have a brother? What would it be like now without Paul? Empty. Drearier than Big Sleep had ever been.

Danny glanced at Paul in the mirror. "Listen, there's something I have to tell you..." he started.

Paul put both hands up to fend off any news. "Don't you dare. I can't deal with so much as shaving nick on top of everything else. Whatever new disaster it is, it'll just have to wait."

"I hope it doesn't involve me," said Emma. "I can't deal with anything else either."

"But..."

"No buts. You heard the lady. Right now let's concentrate on getting Emma home. She has to get back work, too." Paul checked his watch and tsked. "It's too late for me to call the store and ask..."

"Listen, Paul, Emma..." said Danny.

"Thanks for your offer, Danny, but I can drive myself," said Emma. "I'm sure they want Paul back at work as soon as possible. I'll be fine. I can steady the wheel with my left hand while I'm shifting. It won't strain my arm. I'll take it easy."

They reached the apartment and found a couple of cars with "press" signs in the windows blocking the entrance to the parking garage.

Danny had to park a block away, and by the time they approached the back entrance, the entire street was jammed with the vehicles that had trailed them from the airport. A swarm of reporters and cameramen with blinding lights raced across the little park toward them.

Emma lowered her head and covered her eyes to avoid the lights. Then she realized she'd appear more like a criminal being arrested than a vice-president elect. She glanced at Paul. He had his head down, too, but raised it at the same minute she did.

Microphones, lights, and a tangle of strident questions engulfed them. It was all they could do to keep moving toward the building.

"Please," cried Paul, pushing forward, "all we're doing is going home. There's nothing we can tell you now that you don't already know."

"Mr. Greer," came a voice more aggressive than the others, "what are you going to do about all the demonstrations against you?"

"Nothing," he shouted and elbowed a path through the mikes and lights. He shoved Emma through and hurried after her. Danny caught up with them when they entered the back door.

Emma walked down the fifth floor hall next to Paul, and Danny opened the door to let them in. In the middle of the floor stood a blond woman in a soft black sweater, a long strand of pearls, and gray pants. She was soft, beautiful, and elegant. Danny's girlfriend.

Behind her, Emma heard Paul take in a sharp breath. She turned.

Paul had stopped at the door. His eyes were nearly as wide open as his mouth, his face bloodless. He stood frozen with the backpack hanging from one elbow.

The blond clasped her hands tightly in front of her chest. "Hello, Fa...Paul."

Emma's nerves buzzed. The shaky scaffolding of her forbidden dreams collapsed. This wasn't Danny's girlfriend. She had come for Paul.

Danny stepped to the woman's side. "Emma, this is Laurel Broussard. Laurel, Emma Light in the Lodge."

The woman barely smiled and focused on Paul again.

"I...," she said, but nothing further came from her mouth.

"What are you...?" started Paul.

"Come on, Emma," said Danny, pointing to the bedroom and taking her right arm.

Emma yanked her arm away and stared at Paul. "Why didn't you tell me about...?" she started and stopped, horrified. She sounded like a hysterical shrew.

"I left him," Laurel whispered.

Paul's eyes popped wide. "For *me*? After I ran...?"

Danny tugged at Emma's arm again. "The phone's in here and we can call about a room for you."

Emma followed him blindly now. Paul was involved with another woman. She had to give back the warm blanket of his love, but she knew now she'd hurt forever without it.

Danny closed the door.

Paul stood for what seemed an eternity, staring at Laurel, while the muffled business of motel rooms was carried out exclusively by Danny's voice. Before him, Laurel's face crumbled from nervous anticipation to mortification and guilt.

Paul groped for words but had no idea what he could say that would make this situation right.

They stood without moving or saying a word until Danny returned with Emma.

Now all four stood in the strained, confused silence.

"I'll lead Emma to the motel," Danny finally managed to say. "I won't be back for at least an hour and a half."

"No," cried Paul, seeing Emma's stricken, bereaved face. He pointed an accusing finger at Danny. "I'm going, and I'll be back to talk to you as fast as a car can make it there and back."

"I tried to tell..." said Danny, but Paul's look cut him off.

Paul hoisted the pack onto his shoulder again and steered Emma into the hall, trying to formulate what he could say to her.

The elevator was still there.

"She's an ex-parishioner," he explained on the way down. "I'll tell you honestly, I felt a certain lust for her, but I swear, Emma, I never felt anything other than that, and certainly never did anything with her. I haven't the foggiest idea what she's doing here."

Emma's voice came flat and dead. "You don't owe me any explanation, Paul."

He moved in front of her and forced her to look at him.

She put a hand up before he could speak. "Don't say another word. I don't know what's going on, but I can't deal with it. Period. I knew this could never work."

The elevator stopped on three and an elderly woman with blue hair and a fluffy white poodle got on.

Frustrated, Paul tried to make her listen before she reached her pickup. She opened her door and simply shook her head.

He brought Danny's car so she could follow him. When they reached the motel, he parked, jumped out and ran to the pickup she was just parking.

He waited for her to get out. "Emma..."

She was more composed now, like an ice sculpture. Staring past him, she said, "Obviously there's something between you. The very air felt like nitro. But you don't owe me an explanation."

He grabbed her good shoulder. "I'm not talking about owing you anything. I care about you more than I can say, and I want you to know that with absolute certainty, regardless of how you feel about me. Look at me, Emma."

When her eyes reluctantly met his, he said, "I care about you. That's not going to change and it's not going away. And whether you like it or not, I do not care about anyone else in that way. Now you do with that knowledge whatever you want."

Emma's eyes held his for the longest moment Paul had ever known, and finally her face melted into simple sadness. "I'll put it in my peace pipe and we can smoke it together—as friends."

Paul shook his head and touched her cheek. It was wet.

She moved his hand away. "We have to back up, Paul. I made a big mistake in Modesto, and I'm truly sorry. I didn't want to hurt you. I had no idea there was someone else, and the woman threw me for a full knockout when I realized she wasn't Danny's friend. She made me realize *I'm* not part of your world regardless of whether *she* is or not."

Paul kicked the tire of her truck in frustration. "I wish I could explain...It wasn't just the lust thing. She was in my confessional every week for years, which means I can't tell you anything about her, ever. I can only say what went on in me, and I swear to you, I'll never lie to you about that."

She took a breath and her voice came out ragged. "It doesn't matter about her. I just can't deal with the hurt. Modesto didn't happen, Paul, and nothing like it will happen again. We probably won't see each other again, anyway."

Paul struggled. He wanted to badger her with his love till she relented, but he didn't want to torture her. In the end, he said,

"I don't feel right letting you drive home with your arm in a sling. I'd never forgive myself if anything else happened to you."

"I promise I'll take it easy."

"Will you call me the minute you get home?"

"I'll call you tomorrow night. If I stop somewhere to rest and get home late, you'll just worry. Besides, hopefully, you'll be at work."

"I doubt it. They're going to fire me after all this flap."

Emma grimaced. "I'll call you at nine, anyway."

"I guess I'll just have to be satisfied with that. What time is it now? Nearly eleven. Twenty-two hours." He touched her face again and before he knew it, she was in his arms, holding hard. Her body jerked with a sob, but he felt her stiffen and could sense her resolve rising from that source of strength he could never plumb. Her head moved back. She forced a smile and said, "It was one hell of a trip."

"That it was."

She pulled her pack from the truck and walked toward the office, each step a widening amputation in his heart.

She turned at the office door and called back, "Friends. But friends forever."

All through the ride back he saw her diminishing form against the lighted office doors and wished he'd run after her. Her last words echoed mockingly when he wanted so much more. Now she was out of his life, and it was Danny's fault, as usual. The thought made him so angry he felt knives and blunt objects in his hands, there to attack Danny with, and that made him furious. He'd never in his life felt the desire to do anyone harm, and now he wanted to bludgeon his own brother almost as much as he wanted to cry for the loss of Emma.

Well, at least Laurel would be gone by now and if he didn't attack Danny with a butcher knife, he'd scream at him for his sheer lack of sensitivity. He must surely have figured there was something awkward about Laurel's showing up out of the blue.

Miraculously, the press was gone and he walked right in the back entrance unmolested. When he reached the apartment, Laurel was sitting on the edge of the sofa with her face in her hands. Danny was nowhere.

She stood and wrung her hands. "I'm so sorry, Paul."

Paul closed the door and backed against it. He wanted to shriek, why in hell have you done this to me, but she was already so upset he feared he'd push her over the edge. He was still looking for words when she continued.

"Danny said he'd give you a message for me, but I had to do this in person." Her face blazed as she took a deep breath. "I had to see there was nothing in you that could ever belong to me. That's the only way I'll get over this. And I do see it. I apologize for embarrassing you."

"Laurel, you..."

"You don't have to say anything. I saw where things stand between you and Emma. I'm leaving now, and you don't ever have to see me again." She picked up the navy windbreaker that lay on the sofa.

Paul moved toward her, his anger shattered by her mortified honesty. All he could say was, "What's Danny's role in this?"

She wrinkled her brow as she shrugged into the jacket. "His role? None at all. He was stunned when I showed up. I followed you home from the store on Sunday, but you'd already left by the time I got up the courage to ring the doorbell. He was wonderful to me the whole time. And devastated when he feared you were dead. But we were both wrong to assume I could be here when you came. We didn't even think about Emma. Please apologize to her for me."

Paul stared, visualizing the worst that Danny could do. "What do you mean 'the whole time'? You've been with him since Sunday?"

"Most of the time. I only slept here Monday night, when the first news of the earthquake came through. We both fell asleep on the sofa. Why? Do you care?"

Paul backed away. "No. Yes. No. I...I just know my brother, and he's a...a lover of women."

She drew herself up. "Well, he's not my lover, but he's become my friend. Still, I'll stay out of your life now, don't worry." She opened the door.

"Laurel..."

She turned back.

He shook his head in quick jerks. "I didn't deal with this well."

"You were too shocked after everything else that's happened."

"That's no excuse. And I do wish you well. If Danny's your friend, I'm happy for you. Just don't let him hurt you. Give it time."

She cocked her head to the left and smiled sadly. "We all need time. Maybe someday we can be friends, too."

"I'd like that," said Paul as she closed the door. He went to bed intending to stay awake till Danny came in.

CHAPTER THIRTY TWO

The alarm buzzed into Paul's fitful sleep. He woke with the memory of Emma curled into his side and the smell of soap on her hair. He stared around him, disoriented by the familiarity of Danny's apartment when the only place he'd ever been completely alive was a shabby motel with her in his arms. She'd been his first tentative step into normal human life, and now that memory was all he'd have of her. Thanks to Danny.

Paul leaped off the sofa bed and stomped into the bedroom. Danny was already gone.

"Coward," he said aloud, heading for the shower and into the routine of a life that felt empty and meaningless now. Still, there was Lord and Taylor's to deal with, an apartment to find. Angry as he was at Danny, he couldn't be a parasite. He'd find an apartment, and if the store fired him, he'd find another job. At least now he had some experience to put on a resume.

He dressed and went out a side entrance into a blast of cold air, hoping to elude the press. Only two reporters accosted him, but their excited questions brought others rushing from front and back. He raised both hands and cried, "Please, I'm trying to get to work."

"Mr. Greer, what's your position on the growing water shortage in the West?"

"Mr. Greer, do you believe the demonstrations against you were orchestrated by the major parties?"

Paul pushed his way down the few steps. In his peripheral vision an orange ball of frizzy hair, glowing in the morning sun, bounced toward them above the fogged breath of the reporters. The ball hit the edge of the crowd and bounced off. The voice of Shirl Wainwright twanged through the barrage of questions like a mistuned cello. "Secret Service," she yelled, flashing around a small leather folder that might hold a badge. "You all get outta my way right now."

A few moved aside, but the innermost circle balked.

Shirl grabbed the shoulders of two and parted them like bifold doors. "You wanna get arrested?"

She reached into the circle, grabbed Paul by his still sore arm, and yanked him out. "Come on, Mr. President, I got yore car right down here."

He jerked his arm free. "I am not the president," he growled as they cleared the corner of the building, leaving the clutch of reporters to scatter to their vehicles. "And you're not Secret Service."

"I'm gonna be. Gordy promised me. There was some of them waitin' for you out front, but I'm the first one assigned to you, so you don' make no trouble for me, you hear? 'Sides, you wanna go back to fendin' those guys off on your own?"

Paul glanced back. "Okay, but you stay out of my way and do what I tell you, 'you hear?' They'll probably think I've been kidnapped."

She hustled him into the back seat of a two door Civic and screeched out of a parking place where the car had stood at right angles to the curb.

He didn't risk speaking to her again as she drove like a frenzied bat, darting into and out of spaces in traffic that were too small for the media vehicles. She lost them before they'd gone four blocks.

To get his mind off the imminent crash, Paul made a mental note to call the insurance company about his own car, sitting in a landslide a thousand miles away.

Car. Emma unconscious in it for hours and utterly conscious next to him in the motel. Emma's determination and quick humor and blue-black hair. Emma's face when Laurel had confronted them. Emma walking away from him. The memory froze his insides and he shivered violently.

"Sorry, Mr. President, the heater don't work," explained Shirl.

He nodded at her in the mirror. It *was* cold in the car. The first bitter cold of the winter bit through the wind breaker he'd bought in the fall, and he zipped it up. The snow, if it had fallen in Denver at all, had disappeared completely, leaving a mass of frigid air that he only now noticed. Maybe he should head right to the men's department and buy a jacket on employee discount before they fired him. A pair of thicker pants would have to be in this month's budget, too. He shivered from his hair to his toenails. Maybe they made full-body goose-down suits.

Blocks before Cherry Creek Mall they got mired in a traffic jam.

Paul leaned forward. "Let me out as soon as you get to the shopping center. I'll walk and you keep driving. Let them see you again so they'll follow you."

"But..."

"No buts, Shirl. If I'm the president, then I'm your boss. You do as I say."

She gave him a big smile in the mirror now, and it gave him the eerie feel of a giant weasel trying to look like a puppy.

He got out at First Avenue and loped the six blocks to Lord and Taylor's. Long before he reached it, he wrinkled his brow over the packed parking lot and the snarled traffic on First Avenue. He glanced down at his watch. At 8:30 the stores weren't even open yet. The lots had never been this full, even on Saturdays.

The mall was mobbed with people shoving toward Lord and Taylor's, the static of their collective chatter louder than the Musak. At the store's entrance, at least three hundred people, including several with television cameras or "**No Greer**" signs, milled in a tight knot, waiting for the doors to open. Paul backed through the crowd to the opposite side and looked up at the entrance on the second floor. It was equally crowded.

He left the building and went around to the loading dock, where he found several other employees waiting.

He stared at the cars jamming the no-parking zone behind the loading dock.

A woman in a down jacket over a long black skirt glanced at him and sucked in a sharp breath. "Hey, you're that Paul Greer that just got elected. How does it feel...?" Suddenly overcome by bashfulness, she turned red.

A clerk from leather goods opposite his station stepped backwards, saying, "Mr. President."

Paul gaped at them. It was nearly out of his mouth to reassure them they didn't need to worry about his ever being president, but he said instead, "Listen, I'm not the president now. I just work here, like you. Do me a favor and don't make a big deal out of that, okay?"

"Yeah, sure," said the woman. The others nodded and stared and moved away a little. An awkward silence followed.

Harlan, the house detective, opened the door and held it open till they'd all entered. He scowled as Paul went by. "Mrs. Wynne wants to see you immediately. Before you go on the floor." He ended with a smile that barely cleared being a sneer.

Ms. Wynne saw him through her office door and waved wildly for him to enter. She hung up the phone.

"I'm so sorry to have caused so much inconvenience, Ms. Wynne. I promise you, if you don't fire me, nothing like this will happen again."

"Fire you? Are you out of your mind? Have you seen what's going on out there? It's been like that since yesterday. We haven't seen so much business in the entire history of L&T. We're having to beg shoes from the other stores. Your co-workers are nearing exhaustion. Now get down there and prepare for the onslaught. Oh, and Roberson said to tell you he's putting you on full time. As of now."

Later Paul would think *onslaught* a pale word. Special guards struggled to keep demonstrators and media people out of the store, but as soon as the doors opened, a wave of shrieking bodies mobbed the shoe department. For a second he thought he saw Shirl carried along by the tide, but then they were on him. Larry and Toby paled and shoved Paul in front of them.

"He's here," screamed a California teeny-bopper voice, and the cry went through to the end of the mob. Soon it echoed up from the ground floor and then from the escalator on the other side of leather goods. By that time Paul feared for the stability of the cashier's station.

The first people, crushed by those behind them, leaned over the counter. Hands grabbed at him, frenzied faces swam before him, and Larry's and Toby's hands were on his back, pushing him forward to shield themselves. Paul raised his hand, and a hush swept back from the registers, back out the doors and down the escalator. He blinked and his head jerked in amazement.

At the edge of the mob a small group of middle-aged men began to chant, "No Greer, no Greer." The epitome of conservative Republicans to a man, they turned scarlet and fixed their eyes on the floor. When Harlan appeared to usher them out, they scattered in all directions, clearly glad their dabbling in activism was over.

Harlan turned to Paul and mouthed, "No Greer."

Paul turned to the first customer. "May I help you?" he asked the woman directly in front of him. She was wearing an old gray wool coat and looked as if she had spent her night in a refrigerator carton.

"You're the one who's going to be president. I'm DeeDee Wilbur, Mr. President, but my friends call me Dee. I was watching the news at Joe's Bar when they showed you helping that Chinese woman and I just thought that was so kind. I mean, her being Chinese and all. I'm so pleased to meet you. Now, can you tell me what you're going to do about...?"

"Ma'am, did you want to look at some shoes?"

"Oh, yes. I want to buy some from you."

"What kind?"

"Oh, I don't care. Any kind."

Behind him Toby said, "Just a minute." Paul felt one pair of hands let go of his back and shortly a pair of black patent leather shoes, size 14½ snaked into his hands from behind.

She beamed. "Those'll be just fine."

Paul looked at the box. "That'll be...ma'am are you sure you want these shoes?"

"Oh, yes."

"That'll be $128.95 plus tax, ma'am."

She blanched and reached into a pocket. She came out with a small wad of one-dollar bills, mixed with scraps of hamburger wrappers and a thin stack of restaurant napkins. She went through the motions of counting her few dollars.

"Oh, well, could I just get you to autograph this?"

Paul reached for the napkin she held out, but his glance fell on the crowd behind her. "Ma'am, I'm sorry, but I'm here to help customers find shoes. If I start autographing..."

"*I'll* take them," yelled a monstrously fat woman, shoving the street lady aside and plunking two hundred-dollar bills on the counter.

"Ma'am, did you want size 14½?"

"Yeah, sure, that's okay."

He rang up the sale and handed the woman the receipt, her change, and the shoes.

"Don't you have to sign the receipt?"

"No, Ma'am, that's not store policy."

She gave him a last look that clearly memorized every hair on his head and elbowed a broad and triumphant swath through the crowd.

Another pair of shoes appeared in his hands. He looked down and saw the scuffed brown loafers they'd taken back from the offensive customer after a full year. They were dusty and worn down at the heels. Paul looked at Larry.

"You'll see," Larry muttered, shrugging. "They're the very last thing in the stacks. We're supposed to get a whole truckload from the other stores today, but don't ask me what time."

"I'll take them," insisted a young man who looked like a lawyer or a dentist.

Paul said to Larry, "I don't even know what to charge him for these."

Larry shrugged again. "Charge him twenty dollars."

"I'm afraid these shoes are used, sir."

"Did you wear them?"

"No."

"Oh, well, twenty, you say?" He laid a fifty on the counter.

Paul made his change.

A man in a jogging suit leaned toward him.

"Larry, are you sure there's nothing left in the back?"

Larry and Toby nodded.

"I'm sorry, ladies and gentlemen, I don't think we can help you in shoes for a little while. If you'd care to come back later..."

"Can't you ring this up for me?" shouted a voice from the aisle separating leather goods from shoes. A belt whirled in the air, buckle outermost, and several of the taller customers ducked.

"Well, yes..."

Instantly the crowd surged in the direction of leather goods, shirts, and sport coats, and regrouped in front of Paul's register within seconds. From that moment until three hours after his shift ended, his work day was a blur. He sold articles he didn't even know Lord and Taylor carried, including some he was fairly sure came from Foley's and Neiman Marcus.

Not until the supper hour approached did the crowd thin, allowing him to leave the floor. He ran into Larry, who was hiding in the storeroom.

"Here," said Larry. "Elsie said to give you these." He handed Paul a stack of pink slips thicker than a Michener novel.

"Yow, how many times can one store fire you?" asked Paul.

"Those are phone messages."

"Oh, well, I'll look at them at home. Listen, Larry, I don't think this is fair, my having to ring up all the stuff while you and Toby do all the footwork. I'll ask Ms. Wynne if I can ring up a third of the sales under your employee number and a third under Toby's."

"That'd be great, thanks."

Paul slipped his windbreaker on with the collar up, sneaked out the loading bay doors, and headed toward the bus stop.

Shirl caught up with him before he'd gone three steps. "Geez, doggies, Mr. President, you look like I oughta carry you."

Paul stopped dead. "Don't you even..."

She pulled him forward, grinning. "Naw, don' you worry. That ain't in my job description."

Stretching across the back seat of her car, he wiggled his toes and rotated his feet to ease the ache. He pulled the telephone slips from his pocket and glanced through them as the car passed into pools of streetlight. They were from every Denver television channel, every major network, every syndicated newspaper, and every talk show he'd ever heard of. He would have stopped after the first few if he hadn't wanted to check for a message from Emma. He could hardly wait for her call. Maybe if he reassured her again...

CHAPTER THIRTY THREE

P aul lay on his side with his head propped on his right arm, staring out at the railing of Danny's balcony, a crossbar of the bed frame pressing his hip through the thin mattress. His mind churned with thoughts of Emma. Her short call last night had left him morose. She'd been distant, had hardly told him more than that she'd arrived safely. But the years in the confessional had trained him to hear what lay beneath voice tones, and he knew she was hurting. He wanted to hold her as he had in the parking lot, when she'd clung so hard.

His arms literally ached for her; he could still feel her mouth on his, hear her rich laugh. It was all too new, too stirring, too addictive. He tried to focus on getting his own apartment, one with a bed that wouldn't leave permanent dents in his hip bones. Instead he saw a sagging bed with her in it. He needed to call her, make her see he loved her. He glanced at his watch. Barely six, still too early.

The phone jangled the quiet morning, a loud ring from the bedroom, where Danny continued to snore, and a softer but higher pitched ring from the handset on the coffee table he'd shoved against the wall.

Paul threw off the blankets and jumped up, catching the hair on the back of his right leg in the folding mechanism of the bed for the fiftieth time. He stumbled to the phone, shivering and rubbing his calf.

"Emma!" he cried.

"Mr. Greer?" said a soft voice with a genteel Southern accent.

Now he wished he'd just let it ring and wake Danny, but that small revenge would stack up to Danny's thoughtlessness like a hangnail to an amputated arm.

"Yes?" he snapped in the voice he'd heard Danny use with telephone solicitors.

"This is Alice Winthrop, protocol advisor to President Hartsell."

Paul's eyes flew open and he jerked himself to attention.

"The President asked me to call and talk to you about the impending inauguration. He felt you probably had no idea what kind of preparation went into the ceremony itself much less the galas that follow in the evening. If I can be of assistance..."

"Ms. Winters, did you say?"

"Winthrop."

"Winthrop. Forgive me for being a little groggy; it's...uh...I just got up. I appreciate your calling, and please express my thanks to the President. As to an inauguration, I haven't given it a moment's thought. I'm sure you know the circumstances of the election and the challenge to it. So I don't think we really have to worry much about my being inaugurated."

"You may be right, Mr. Greer, but since we don't know for sure how things are going to turn out, it's probably best to be prepared. It's a great deal easier to cancel laid plans than to throw together a ceremony of that magnitude on a moment's notice."

Paul ran his hands into this hair and made a fist. The nightmare was nowhere near over. "You're right, of course. After the new election, the plans can be used in a pinch for the new president."

"No doubt."

"Well, what do you need from me?" Seeking calm, he moved around the bed to the sliding door and gazed out at the newly white peaks turning pink-gold in the first light.

"*I* don't need anything, actually. I'm President Hartsell's protocol advisor. Perhaps you've already thought of naming your own."

Paul laughed in spite of his best efforts to be serious. "I don't mean to sound flippant, Ms. Winthrop, but I can assure you nothing could've been further from my thoughts. Please excuse my ignorance, but how is your salary paid? By your party, the president, or the government?"

"The government."

"Well, would you consider staying on for the time being?"

"Certainly."

"I'm sure I'll be a great challenge to your talents. Your crowning achievement."

Ms. Winthrop laughed. "Then you don't remember Vice-president Baxter. Now, sir, the first thing to consider is the place for the swearing in."

"You mean there isn't some law that says it has to be done in front of the Capitol?"

"No, it's tradition, but not law. Occasionally it's been held inside the Capitol or in the White House for various reasons, usually inclement weather. January is not our finest month."

"Well, I can't think of a good reason to change it if we don't have to. I'm afraid if my election ever actually gets that far, the people are in for shock enough without uprooting the ceremony."

His bare legs and arms were beginning to chill. He moved from the glass door.

"Very well, we leave the swearing in at the Capitol. Now about the parade and the balls and fireworks..."

"Surely we can dispense with revelry, Ms. Winthrop, in view of the tragic deaths of the other candidates. I personally would not feel comfortable celebrating, even if I'd ever intentionally sought the office. I imagine the rest of the country will feel the same way, and certainly the major parties won't celebrate this."

Nothing came over the line but a stunned and palpably disapproving silence. Paul heard a swallowing noise and visualized her gagging on the unpalatable thought.

"Now here, we are definitely breaking with tradition," she choked out, "but I suppose you're right, sir."

Paul jammed the phone under his cheek, grabbed his pants, and failed to get his right leg in. "And maybe, Ms. Winthrop, it's time to bring a little sobriety back to the business of government, not to mention saving the taxpayers a hefty sum."

"Most of the gala events are privately funded, sir, largely by the president's party."

He sat on a dining chair and worked the pants up his bare legs. "Well, that settles it, then. I'm fairly sure the Earth Rights Party doesn't have a large treasury."

"All right, we'll spread the word that the inauguration will be a modest affair with no great revelry. However, if the party chairperson should wish to put on some kind of affair, an intimate dinner, perhaps, you can have him get in touch with me. Now, the next thing I'll need is a list from you and Ms. Lodge..."

"Her name is Light in the Lodge, Ms. Winthrop, a beautiful name, which I hope anyone who comes in contact with her will use without stumbling over it. It's important to me that no shadow of disparagement of her Indian background should ever reach her ears."

"Certainly. I'll be sure that wish is known, as well. Now, do you have any idea whom you'd like to invite to be on the grandstand with you?"

"Several hundred psychotherapists?"

"I beg your pardon?"

"Just joking. My brother. David Anthony Greer."

Ms. Winthrop repeated the name and then waited. "And?" she asked after a minute.

"Uh..." He hesitated, hoping this would sit well with Emma. "Laurel Broussard. I guess he'd like her to be there, though I'm not sure she can afford the trip."

"There are funds, Mr. Greer."

"Legal ones?"

"Well, yes, legal."

"All right. That's it, then. Just those two. And could you see to it that *he* gets a collapsing chair to sit on? He's the one who got me into this mess."

"Very small grandstand," she said, laughing as she wrote it down. "I must tell you, sir, it's also traditional to have former presidents, the speaker of the House, the Senate majority leader, and your future cabinet on the podium, along with their spouses. And higher ranking members of your party. Your campaign manager, others who helped get you elected. Of course, in this case..."

Paul tried to visualize the members of the Earth Rights Party. Danny and Emma were all right, but his conversations with that Gordy person didn't give him much confidence, not to mention the unshakable Shirl Wainwright. "Can I get back to you on that?"

"Of course. Do you have any idea about Ms. Light in the Lodge's guests?"

"None whatever."

"Well, I'll call her..."

"Who pays for the call?"

"I beg your pardon?"

"Forgive me, Ms. Winthrop. What I meant was that I can call her and call you back if this is running up your phone bill." Not to mention the good excuse to call Emma.

"Not at all. I'm calling from the White House, and believe me, the call won't mean a thing on the White House telephone bill."

Paul swallowed a surge of disappointment. "Oh. Well. Was there anything else?"

"Only about fifty million things, but this will do for the moment, especially since there's no ball to worry about. However, Mr. Hartsell did tell me to suggest you start giving some thought to a cabinet, staff, press secretary, security chief, et cetera." She paused and cleared her throat musically. "Your White House hostess, since you aren't married...I could...you know, the thousands of little decisions that have to be made during your term..."

Paul started to say Emma would serve as his hostess, but realized that was presuming too much and might look suspicious to the paparazzi. "I'll have to give that some thought, Ms. Winthrop."

"Naturally. Now, in the event you actually become president, you should probably plan to be in Washington by January first. The president said to call him at the White House if you need help, and he'll return your call as soon as possible. He'll help you in any way he can."

It was on the tip of Paul's tongue to say, "Ask if he'd mind changing his name to Paul Greer." Instead he said, "That's very kind of him. Please tell him I will definitely take him up on his offer if the Supreme Court puts me in the White House." He nearly choked over the last two words.

"You're not the only one whose teeth are chattering about that, sir. Both parties are determined not to let it happen. The decision should be handed down fairly soon. I don't know how you'd feel about it, but judging from this conversation, I'd say you might at least stand a chance of balancing the budget, and that wouldn't be so bad."

Paul laughed. "If you need any other information, please call."

"I'm sure we'll be talking often, Mr. Greer."

"Please, call me Paul."

"Certainly, Mr. Greer."

Paul stared at the handset for a second and then switched it off. He turned to find his brother giving him a mock glare from the bedroom door.

"I heard that about the collapsing chair," Danny said, running his hands up his black morning stubble and through his tousled hair. "Now I know what to watch out for." He tightened the tie on his maroon robe.

"Minimal revenge. I'm sorry she woke you up. No, I'm not. May you be wakened rudely every morning for the remainder of your natural life."

"If you're president, you can call me every morning. But only four years. I can't believe she didn't send you into a fit ranting and raving."

"I think I've gotten beyond that. Or maybe the absurdity is finally getting to me. She actually told me I should plan to be in Washington by January first. Right. Live at the Hilton for three weeks while they orient me to something far beyond my worst nightmares. I'm convinced this is going to be over as soon as someone pinches me."

"After that crack about the chair, I'd be happy to give it a try," Danny said, rinsing the coffee maker to start a new pot. "But seriously, the notoriety is about to drive even me bonkers. I had at least twenty phone calls yesterday from people who just wanted to find out if I was your father. And those were the ones my secretary couldn't screen out."

Paul laughed, folding the sofa bed back into itself. "Serves you right. I had customers all day who didn't want a thing but to touch me. I couldn't move without being mobbed. One woman even came behind the counter and did a bump and grind against my hips. Another one showed up with the bridal register so she could give her cousin a sterling silver butter knife ordered by the future president. I stood at that cash register till I thought my bladder would burst. I had no lunch. And at the end of the day, you should have seen the stack of telephone messages they handed me."

Danny rinsed out two cups. "Have you checked out the answering machine? I'm sure the tape is full."

"Great. This is all your fault, you know, plus the fact that Emma barely speaks to me now. We're still going to have a conversation about that, believe me."

Danny turned to face him. "No need, Paul. I apologize for everything. Especially Emma. I promise nothing bad will ever happen to you because of me again."

Paul laughed bitterly. "So what? You've already done the worst that can be done. I can't go on like this. I'd like to say I just want things to go back to normal, but I never even got a chance to find out what normal is. The press alone is driving me nuts."

"Why don't you grant an interview to one local television station on the condition that they share it simultaneously with all the others. That way it would be small enough for you to handle and maybe you could ask people to stay off your back until the election question is decided. After the decision they'll drop you like last week's *TV Guide*, anyway."

"We hope. But the interview is a good idea." He headed toward the bedroom.

Danny turned on the television to the six o'clock news.

"...who contacted the president-elect from the White House only minutes ago. Mr. Greer has already indicated the Spartan nature of his regime by declining to participate in any gala events to follow the inauguration. National opinion polls conducted yesterday show Mr. Greer's approval rating at three percent with a margin of error of four and a half percent. His approval is expected to plummet after this morning's news..."

Paul froze at the door. "*Now* I'm going to rant. Did you hear that?"

"Hey," Danny said, laughing. "If the polls were inaccurate, you could already be in the minus. I don't think I'd worry about plummeting."

"That's not what I meant. And this is not funny, Danny. I said I thought it inappropriate to celebrate in view of the terrible losses of the earthquake. I'm going to tell them a thing or two..."

"Listen, Paul, if you try to defend yourself against everything that's said about you while you're in the limelight, you'll spend your life on the defensive for nothing. People are going to believe what they want to believe."

Paul expelled a breath of disgust. "I can't wait till the Supreme Court straightens all this out."

He'd be free then and would find some way to see Emma, even if it meant moving to Wyoming.

CHAPTER THIRTY FOUR

J ules Blanchet of the *Denver News* evening paper and the lovely
Valerie Adamsson of Channel 5 sat facing Paul in the Denver
BCA studio. A make-up person applied the last brush of rouge
to Valerie's cheeks and smoothed her long auburn hair.

In his lap, Paul checked on the order of his index cards for
the third time, trying to keep his hands from shaking. He had
already asked them to confine themselves to two or three questions each and to allow him to say a few words at the end.

"Ready to roll," said the cameraman.

The little monitor next to the camera flicked and his eyes
moved involuntarily to it. He and Valerie were in the screen from
the chest up. She looked welcoming and friendly. Even at a glance,
Paul could tell he looked ill shaven and ill at ease and ill in every
other way.

"Welcome to Sunday Morning in Denver," said Valerie.
"We're honored to have with us this morning president-elect,
Paul Thomas Greer, who has asked us to arrange this small in-
terview for general media distribution."

The camera moved to focus on Paul alone, and he felt his face redden. His mouth dried to dust. He tried to smile. The corners of his mouth twitched.

"Mr. Greer, I think the whole country is now acquainted with the circumstances of your nomination and election. Your brother nominated you as a joke…"

Paul opened his mouth but nothing came out.

"Our sources say he was drunk at the time," said Jules.

"I wasn't there," Paul said, sounding like an adolescent whose voice was changing. "You'd have to ask him about it. Certainly, he didn't think things through."

Valerie summed up the circumstances of his election and continued, "You've asked us to keep the interview short…"

"Yes, I have to be at work at eleven."

"Mr. Blanchet and I have tried to formulate the questions we think the public most wants to ask. We're all aware that you were a priest until a few months ago. I think people are concerned that the Catholic Church will suddenly gain enormous influence in the government."

"Ms. Adamsson, whatever my personal religion or lack of it, I've always been convict…convinced that the wisest thing the founding fathers of our country did was separate church and state." Paul felt his face redden again and forced himself into the kind of concentration he had used in the pulpit. "For those who believe that Christianity or Islam or Judaism or Buddhism presents a code they want to live by, I say that's a plus in their lives. However, there are too many sects and too many intelligent people with their own code of ethics to expect harmony when they mingle in government, and our focus ought to be on our national problems, not on a religion."

"Are you saying you're opposed to prayer in public schools?" demanded Jules.

"I am. Even as a priest, I was opposed to forcing religion on anyone. In the first place, prayer is an entirely private matter and in my opinion can only be done in moments of personal serenity that can't be achieved in a minute's time or in a school setting. Second, if religion is important enough to a person, he will find the time for prayer without having it regulated by government. In the third place, the spirit of rebellion is so strong in American youth that the fastest way I can think of to turn children *away* from prayer is to mandate it."

"So I suppose you refused to lead students in prayer in the school where you taught?"

"Mr. Blanchet, I'm sure you know it was a religious school where the time for prayer was set aside, a great deal more time than a minute. I personally always tried to prepare my students for it with some relaxed withdrawal from the hectic atmosphere of the classroom."

Jules sat back in his chair and regarded Paul intently. He wants me on the defensive, Paul realized, suddenly dreading the rest of his questions.

"Well, then," continued Valerie, "tell us how you plan to implement the party's...shall we say...innovative platform?"

Paul flashed back on his first reading of the platform, pacing the apartment and slapping the poorly copied papers against his leg. He smiled in spite of his nerves. "The first time I read the platform, which was after the nomination, I admit to being astonished. Since then, I've become more informed of the severity of the crises that will face future generations. I've come to believe that action is not only desirable, it's imperative. I must tell you, I've been greatly influenced in this by Ms. Light in the Lodge. I wish she were here; she can speak far more eloquently and convincingly on this than I can. I'm sure I'd rely on her a great deal if I were ever in office. She's more experienced with this..."

"As a matter of fact," Mr. Blanchet goaded him, "you have no experience in politics at all, is that right?"

Paul swiveled toward him. Why has this man made himself my adversary, he wondered. "No, Mr. Blanchet, I have no experience in office. My study of history and law has been entirely academic. I'm sure you understand it was never my intention to run for any office. At this point, both the country and I have been catapulted into a situation that neither of us was prepared for."

Blanchet twisted his face into the inviting smile of an alligator. "So, in your inexperienced zeal, what will be your first attempt at legislation?"

Paul put his hand up pleadingly, realizing too late that he was still holding the index cards, and they fell away, half on his lap, the rest fluttering to the floor. "Oh, sorry... I don't know..." he tried to gather up the cards from his lap and realized how that would look on camera. More cards fell to the floor. "...Mr. Blanchard, I...excuse me..." he grabbed at the cards on the floor, scooped the others into his hands, and hit the edges on his knee to straighten them out. "...you know, it's been less than a week, and so much has happened, with the accident and all, and I just haven't given it a moment's thought."

"You haven't given a moment's thought to the fate of the entire country? Well, sir, do you seriously believe you're competent to run the government?"

"No..yes...I mean, I would do my best..."

"*Your...best?*" Mr. Blanchet sneered at him with the camera full on his face.

Valerie signaled the cameraman to move to her, and asked, "I believe our time is almost up, Mr. Greer. Perhaps you could answer one more question and then we'll give you the time you requested to say a few words of your own."

Paul looked at her and hoped his gratitude wasn't blatantly pathetic on the air.

"Why don't you tell us how you feel about having been elected?"

Paul exhaled loudly and searched the studio lights above for words to describe it. "I've never been run over by a fast-moving steam roller, Ms. Adamsson, but perhaps that's how it would feel."

Jules Blanchet snorted off camera.

Valerie gave him an appreciative smile. "Well, what other words did you have for the nation this morning?"

Paul looked down at the cards, now in hopeless disorder. The camera caught every line of his frown as he stuffed them between his thigh and the arm of the chair. He forced himself to look at the camera but could not hold his eyes there and looked at his hands. "I wanted to say...I had a sort of speech...but the cards...I guess I'm not coming over as an intelligent human being this morning. Look, everything's up in the air just now, and maybe there'll be a re-election. But if there's not, I'll do my very best to be worthy of the office. Also, I'd like to say, I'm an ordinary person. I have to make a living, pay my taxes, and struggle with life, just like everybody else.

"January is still a long time away, and I'd be very grateful to the media, and especially to the people of Denver, if I could just live normally until this is settled. So could you please just ignore me, at least until you know there's some real reason to follow me about?" Perfectly aware that he could not stop there, Paul searched for something more intelligent to add. He found nothing.

Valerie kept her eyes on him for a minute and then turned to the camera. "Thank you so much, Mr. Greer, for speaking with us this morning." The rustling of Mr. Blanchet detaching his microphone, leaping from his chair and exiting the studio off camera interfered with her words, and she frowned with her brow while her mouth smiled.

"Wrap up," said the cameraman.

She unclipped her microphone and pulled the studio mini-speaker out of her right ear. She got up to leave. Paul still sat there, staring at his hands.

She turned back to him. "That's it, Mr. Greer. Thank you so much for coming. Would you care to join me for coffee in the lounge?"

"Could you edit out all the stupid parts? Never mind. I know. There wouldn't be anything left of it."

"It wasn't all that bad. The beginning was pretty good. And you'll get used to the camera."

"It's not the camera I can't get used to."

"Mr. Greer, the next crew is waiting to get into the studio."

"Could you please call me Paul?"

"Of course. Mr. Greer, I understand you'll be looking for a press secretary..."

He stood up; the wire of the microphone clipped to his tie caught on something, he yanked at it, and the index cards flew in all directions.

CHAPTER THIRTY FIVE

On the first Friday evening he'd had off since starting at Lord and Taylor's, Paul stood in Danny's kitchen with shrimp, rice, Cajun spices, and the makings of a tossed salad crowding the small counter. For the moment, there was only silence in the apartment. Danny had gone to pick up Laurel and a loaf of French bread. The Secret Service agent on the balcony, bundled to the eyeballs and backed against the door for warmth, had refused to come in.

All Paul had to worry about was getting the gumbo right, and he felt at ease, almost like the early years in the rectory. He would savor this one peaceful evening before the Supreme Court decision, which was long overdue with the inauguration date only days away, and he would savor every minute of it. Afterwards, finally, it'd be over and he could decide what to do with his life. Maybe move to Wyoming...

He desperately wished Emma could eat with them. Even as he stirred the shrimp into his rice mixture, the feel of her stirred him, her slight body in his arms, delicate as a gardenia and strong as a wire cable. He felt her long black hair in his fingers again, and its smell overwhelmed the pungent spices.

They talked occasionally, and though he had the feeling she was often as reluctant to hang up as he was, she never spoke of her feelings nor gave him an opening to express his. She'd accepted the fact that Laurel was Danny's friend now, so why couldn't she let go and care for him? He ached to call her but didn't want to pester her to death with his love.

The door opened and Danny and Laurel came in laughing.

When the greetings and pleasantries were over, Paul said, "You're just in time to get the table set," and gave her a handful of Danny's mismatched silverware.

Grinning, Laurel turned the utensils around in her hand, as if looking for something. "You'd probably better give me a shovel for Danny. He's been raving about your cooking the whole way here. He drooled all over the steering wheel." She looked up at Danny affectionately.

Her cheerful banter as they set the table made Paul feel bereft of Emma, but it also showed him he was in the way. Here it was the middle of January. He should've been in his own apartment by now so Danny could grow into his love for Laurel, which was different from anything Paul had ever seen in him.

With his first bite, Danny rolled his head back and croaked like a contented alligator in the sun, his mouth too full to make intelligible sounds. He swallowed and added, "Lord, I'd forgotten how delicious Creole cooking can be. You did yourself proud, brother."

"I'm just annoyed I couldn't find any crawfish."

Paul relaxed more than he had in months, enjoying the unconstrained conversation, the easy comfort of people who belonged together. So normal for them, so unaccustomed for him. If Emma were here to make it complete...

They laughed over shared memories of New Orleans through supper. When they'd cleared away the dishes and offered a plate of gumbo to the Secret Service man, Paul said, "If I can use your car, I think I'll go to a movie."

"You can try it, but the streets are probably getting icy," said Danny. "It started snowing just about the time Laurel and I got home."

"Oh. Well, maybe I'll go down to the pool and swim for an hour or so."

"After that meal?" cried Danny. "You'd sink like a meteorite."

Laurel looked at him with her hands on her hips. "Is this on my account?"

"Only in the sense that I'd like to give you two a little space."

Laurel's face flushed. "You thought Danny and I were...?"

Danny put his arms around her shoulders. "Not that the desire isn't there."

She rested against him but spoke to Paul. "I know you must remember me as a love-starved narcissist, Paul. I did a lot of wrong things in New Orleans. Danny knows about them, too. But underneath all the desperation I was a decent person, I think."

Stricken, Paul stepped toward her. "Laurel! I never thought you weren't."

"Anyway, there's still something in me that believes in commitment, at least until there's some kind of... official permission to break it." She looked away from him. "Justin was only too happy to file for a divorce for us. When it's final, I'll feel like I can start over with my life."

"I'm glad, Laurel."

"And in the meantime," she said, "I'm about as happy as I've ever been." She smiled at Danny, and the room filled with their happiness and Paul's ache.

"And we don't want you to go downstairs and swim up and down some stupid pool, staring out at the snowflakes," she said to Paul. "We love having you around."

"Thanks." For a moment Paul allowed himself to imagine these two people gone from his life, leaving him alone with his yearning. His breath caught, and he had to force himself to say, "Actually, I've been thinking it's time for me to find my own apartment. I should have moved today."

"What?" cried Danny. "Why?"

Paul shrugged. "I've stayed too long already. This can't be all that great for you."

"So it's a little crowded. Anyway, I don't see any point in your moving till we know what the Supreme Court's decision will be."

Paul's heart lunged at his throat.

"Speaking of which, it's too bad Emma couldn't be with us tonight," said Danny.

"I've been thinking the same thing all evening."

"Why don't we call her? All of us," said Laurel.

"Oh, I don't know..."

"Hey, come on," said Danny.

"It's almost ten. You always watch the news."

"We'll do both." Danny reached for the remote and switched on Channel 5. Laurel put the telephone in his hand.

Though a picture of Senator Chavez faded onto the screen, Valerie Adamsson's voice came on instantly, giving the teasers for the news program to follow. "Coming up, Senator Chavez from Durango takes another spill from his motorcycle and breaks another bone. Stay tuned for that and the Arctic cold spell that's bearing down..." She put a finger to the ear-speaker and her eyes widened. "We have breaking news about the Supreme Court's decision regarding the election." She listened again. "We'll be right back." The station graphics and fanfare started.

Paul dialed Emma's number, his hands shaking so that he had to concentrate on each finger placement. Her line was busy. He clicked off the handset, and it rang in his hand.

"Paul," Emma's voice quavered, "Are you listening to the news?"

"Yes." His heart revved to full speed.

"Paul?"

"Yes?"

"I'm scared to death. I wish you were here."

"Me, too."

The fanfare was over. Valerie and her co-anchor came onto the screen. "Good evening, and welcome to Five News," she began. "The Supreme Court has just handed down its decision on the presidential election, and we'll be switching to our correspondent in Washington as soon as he's set up."

The other anchor appeared on screen. "In all the debate over the probable outcomes of the major parties' challenge to it, several scenarios have been discussed. Most people are convinced that the Court will rule the election invalid." The camera switched to interviews on the street.

"I think they gotta just start all over," said a man opening the back of a plumbing truck.

"For sure they need to get that nut out of there," said young woman in a business suit.

"Ye gods, get to the decision," yelled Paul. "Have they said what it was yet?" he said into the phone.

"No, I can't believe this. They went right to some oil well accident down by Casper."

"We take you now to Weston Sinclair in Washington."

Sinclair stood on the dark street in front of the Supreme Court Building with Chief Justice Stanley Ward at his side, still in his robe and dark around the eyes. "This action has been expected for days, Mr. Ward. What is the decision?

Ward took a breath before answering. "The court denied the motion of the major parties to declare the election invalid. The election stands."

Paul's knees gave out and he sank to the floor. "Oh, my God, Emma, we're in."

"Oh, my God." She repeated herself several times.

Sinclair wiped the shock from his face. "Sir, that is surely the one stance no one expected. Could you explain it?"

Ward looked into the camera. "The duty of the Supreme Court is to *interpret* the Constitution, not to *write* it. The election was legal and valid since there is no provision in the Constitution to cover the extraordinary circumstances surrounding it. We cannot rule on a law that doesn't exist."

"So you're saying two political nobodies will become the president and vice-president."

"I'm saying the Court had no other choice. We've been in session eighteen hours a day since receiving the challenge, and in the end, the decision was unanimous."

Emma whispered into the phone, "Paul, I can't do this."

"You?! You're a born leader. All I want to do is hide in a hole."

Channel 5 had switched to a network interview with a political expert from Georgetown University, Professor Steffen Humboldt, who looked as if he'd been dragged from his bed. "...Court has been moving away from the more active stance it assumed in the early nineties," he said, smoothing his thin gray hair, "and of course, the Republican-dominated Congress refused to approve any of the more liberal judges Hartsell nominated after Bush lined the bench with ultra-conservatives. There's nothing the parties can do at this point. There's no recourse above the Supreme Court. I imagine we'll see Greer sworn in and within a day or two there'll be impeachment proceedings against him, if they can find a trace of a scandal anywhere. For a change, we'll actually experience some bi-partisan effort."

"Emma, they want to impeach us already."

"Yes, it's on here now, too. What am I going to do, Paul? I can't leave my practice till they impeach us. I actually have two clients now."

The Secret Service man outside jumped and spoke into a cell phone. He shoved the door open, leapt in, and closed it again. "Mr. Greer, a new detail is on the way..."

The knock on the door came instantly and when Danny opened it, three more agents streamed in, looking to Paul like triplet executioners.

He jumped up and backed into the half frozen agent.

Laurel and Danny were shoved into the kitchen.

"Paul," cried Emma, "I've just been invaded."

"Me, too. God, I wish you were here. This is beginning to feel like death row."

One of the agents took him firmly by the shoulders. "Mr. Greer, we need you to hang up now and move away from the door. We also have some papers for you to sign."

"Emma, I have to go now. I'll call you back later."

"Please do, no matter what time," she said, and then the line went dead.

Throwing the phone on the sofa, he glared past the blank face of the Secret Service at Danny. Anger boiled to the surface. "Forget the collapsing chair I promised you," he said, scribbling his name on something that looked like a duty roster. "It's going to have dynamite under it, and I hope it blows you all the way to the North Pole for getting me into this mess." He grabbed his wind breaker and would have slammed the door behind him, only he was trailed by four agents.

CHAPTER THIRTY SIX

Sitting with his back to the Capitol, Paul stared at the lanky figure of Chief Justice Stanley Ward, whose short introductory speech for the inauguration appeared in extended bursts of breath-fog. Each puff formed a great vaporous circle, which Paul visualized with an N in front of it to match the "NO" hammering in his brain.

Next to him, Emma sat so rigid she could well be an ice sculpture.

Behind him sat several hundred people when he'd expected a dozen or so, but he dared not turn around to see who they were.

Far in front of him, a sparse crowd—fewer than the number on the grandstand—had gathered in the thin midday sunshine and near-zero cold. Several people carried placards, but from the distance between the stand and the barricades, he could read only one, stretched across several spectators. It said, "**This is absurd.**"

Paul shivered in the overcoat he'd bought before the move and fought the desire to hunch his back and cross his arms over his chest. The drive to the grandstand in the open car with President Hartsell had frozen him to the marrow, and his eyes still watered.

He tried to look at Emma without noticeably turning his head. She looked as dazed and detached as he felt. Her head moved slightly and she forced a weak smile. He felt a small pressure against his arm and returned it. They sat that way through the remainder of the introduction, like two first graders in the principal's office. Paul hoped no cameras registered the touching overcoat sleeves.

He heard the words of the speaker, but they hardly penetrated. Instead, behind the constant staccato of "No, no, no," in his head, he focused on his speech for the news conference he and Emma had called in lieu of an inaugural address—another breach of Ms. Winthrop's protocol. He ran his hand slowly over his chest, over the pocket where he'd put his index card notes. Flat. The cards weren't there. Panic slammed his wind pipe shut.

"...Mr. Paul Thomas Greer," said the speaker in tones louder than the rest of his speech. The bottom fell out of Paul's stomach and he forgot the cards. A thin applause sounded from the dignitaries behind him; not one spectator moved a finger. He stood up, fighting a buckling in his knees. Stiff-legged, he stepped over to the Chief Justice, who already held a Bible toward him, at waist height.

Paul swallowed, realizing that the inauguration could only proceed on the basis of a lie. He did not want to touch the Bible. It was no more than a book of parables to him now, a collection that had somehow gained the upper hand over Aesop's fables. He should say he no longer believed in the old book and swear on his own honor as a man, but he'd let things go too far to risk that now. Too many of his countrymen believed his word would be anchored to the book.

Squaring his shoulders for them, he laid his hand over the scrollwork of the word *Bible* on the cold black leather. He stared down at his lie. The old burn scar glowed and ached in the cold. He couldn't do this. He raised his hand until no part of it still touched the book but held it steady in a compromise he hoped not even the cameras would detect.

The Chief Justice inhaled sharply.

Paul swallowed again and waited. Then he realized that the Chief Justice was waiting for him in the eerie, frozen silence of the capital. He looked up.

Justice Ward stared at him quizzically. "Ready, sir?" he whispered.

Paul closed his ears to the screeching *no.* "Yes."

I, Paul Thomas Greer, do solemnly affirm that I will faith-
fully execute the Office of the President of the United
States, and will, to the best of my ability, preserve, protect
and defend the Constitution of the United States.

He stumbled over the word *execute* and had to take a deep breath before he could utter the word *President.* No applause followed. Forgetting Ms. Winthrop's instructions, he started back to the seat next to Emma. The Chief Justice caught his arm and directed him to the seat at the right of the podium. Ex-president Hartsell had somehow moved and now occupied the seat to the left. As he took his seat, Emma began her swearing in, her right hand on the book, the left extended and splayed, as if seeking a buttress.

Surrounded by gray-suited men so engrossed in their function as to be robotic, Paul left the grandstand and was swept into a black limousine. The door closed with officious firmness even before he settled into the seat. He squirmed around to see where Emma was. Through windows that dimmed the light to deep dusk both inside and out, he watched as more automatons, surrounding her like a moving wall, made a quick opening and deposited her into the next limo. He hadn't even thought to ask her what the vice president did after the inauguration. He hoped they would sweep her straight to the White House.

As the cavalcade moved away, he could see a long line of waiting limousines and suddenly asked himself, who *were* all those people on the grandstand?

"I assume you want to go to the White House, Mr. President," announced a voice from a speaker behind him.

Paul swallowed a surge of shock at being addressed as President. "I assume so, too. I already checked out of the hotel."

Having held on to his job as long as possible, Paul had been to the White House only twice before. He'd met with Hartsell for briefings on foreign and domestic issues. He'd tried to retain the overwhelming gush of information and names, but he hadn't overcome the awed state of a tourist who'd blundered into the inner sanctum.

During both sessions, Hartsell had been surrounded by secretaries, advisors, and factotums whose functions never became clear. Paul had never had a chance to ask the questions that rushed through his veins in a constant flow of adrenaline: Were you terrified when you started? Is it possible to grow into the job?

Now, except for the gray-suits, he was alone, walking weak-kneed down an unfamiliar hall that felt like a one-way route to the gallows.

Two marines stood on duty outside one of the doors. They snapped to attention on his approach, never glancing at him, their faces masks of impersonal duty-consciousness as he stepped between them into...an office he didn't recognize. He turned back, perplexed.

"This is your private office, sir," said one of the gray-suits. "The Oval Office is through there."

Paul thanked him and stepped across the carpet.

Then he was in the Oval Office. He closed the door and leaned against it, stifling the desire to rush back out. He'd never felt so out of place.

He stared at the small desk where he would have to organize the global business of government. And there were his index cards. Relief flowed through him, followed immediately by annoyance and embarrassment. Someone must have read through them to know what they were. There was no privacy any more. He snatched up the cards, slid them into his pocket, and turned back to the room.

For a few weeks, anyway, he would have to get used to this. Perhaps if he took his time and made himself familiar with the office, he would lose the feeling of illicit presence and gawking tourism.

Alternating strips of light and dark wood shone at the edges of the beautiful blue carpet, tapering toward the center. Was the whole floor inlaid in this manner? He kicked at the edge of the carpet where it wasn't pinned down by furniture. The design continued. He kicked the edge down again.

He peered at the two Chinese vases on either end of the mantelpiece and the portrait of George Washington above it. He passed another door, almost invisible, and a grandfather clock. Near the French doors that led out to the Colonnade and the dormant Rose Garden stood a table with a dark bronze sculpture, a man on a bucking horse. "Bronco Buster" said the little plaque on the side. He reached out to touch the original Remington but jerked his hand away and looked over his shoulder.

He reached the curved, south-facing bay window, drew the blue curtain aside, and looked out. In the distance, unreal in the cold haze and lit by slanting sunlight, the Washington Monument pricked the silver sky. Reality struck again, whacking the breath out of his chest.

How many presidents had pressed the carpet in exactly the same place? How many had reeled at the thought of such awful power in their weak and unprepared hands? No matter what he did, he would leave a mark on history.

A knock sounded from the reception area, but the door remained closed. "Yes? Come in," he called.

The door opened for Emma and closed again.

"Thank you, Norma..." said Emma. "Oh, too late."

"Is that her name? I'm glad at least *you* remembered."

"I didn't, I just read it on her badge."

They were standing almost as far apart as possible in the daunting room. Emma wore a black suit and a plain white blouse open at the neck. On her silver chain hung a tiny silver buffalo. The desire to be back in a sleazy motel in Modesto with her in his arms overwhelmed him. He moved toward her. She took a step, and they flew to each other. He felt her arms wrap tightly around him, gripped her harder, and closed his eyes to all else.

She whispered into his neck, "I told myself I wasn't going to do this."

The warmth and supple strength of her body eased his tangled nerves. "You have no idea how glad I am you did."

"Please don't read too much into it. I might have been able to control myself if I weren't absolutely petrified."

Chagrinned, he nodded. "If you weren't in this with me, I think I'd have myself committed." He relaxed his grip slightly and looked in her eyes. "I need you, Emma. Not just for my sanity and all the feeling I have for you. I need your help."

She put her head against his chest again and nodded. "I'm here," she said.

"You remember you once asked me what I'd do first if I were ever president?"

"Yes."

"Now I know. I'll order a secret tunnel built between your house and mine."

Emma managed a laugh. "You'd have to have the workers executed after every shift if you wanted to keep it secret. God, what a tongue-wagging place this is. This morning I heard the hotel maids talking about some senator's page who'd been in a room with a woman old enough to be his mother. They looked at me as if I were the latest grist for their mill."

Paul nodded, ignoring the desire to run his hands through her hair and down her face. "We've seen the last of privacy. By the time they finally get me impeached, I think I'll be ready for a long, solitary sojourn way back in the swamps of Louisiana."

"Don't even say that. If they impeach you, you know who'd be president."

"We could present ourselves at the conference as drooling idiots. Maybe they'd impeach us both."

"Perish the thought. You know who'd be president then?"

"Ye gods, that little strutting born-again."

Emma shuddered.

He put his hands on her shoulders. "All right, then, we'll go out there and do what good we can in the time they give us. You ready for this conference?"

This time, Emma's laugh sounded maniacal, and a moment passed before she could say, "Not even faintly. Remember, they've been hounding you for the last six weeks. Maybe the reservation was too remote for all but one Secret Service agent, and only a couple of tabloid reporters deigned to look me up. There hasn't been a camera trained on me since the week after Modesto. How do I look?"

They stepped apart.

"Beautiful. Scared."

"Well, I don't suppose all the Max Factor in the world is going to cover *that* blemish."

"What about me?"

Emma cocked her head. "You know, even though it's obvious you're terrified, your kindness still comes through. At least, I think I'm seeing it, not just remembering. You have a charismatic sincerity that everybody will see."

"I doubt that. I feel I've started the whole thing out with a lie, Emma."

"What do you mean?"

"The Bible. When Ward put it in front of me, I couldn't keep my hand on it, but I'm sure it looked as if I did. It was a lie."

"I wondered about that when he swore you in. It'll be our secret."

Paul nodded. "I take some comfort in the fact that if *I* don't believe in the Bible, there are many out there who think I'm bound by my words because of it. Sad."

"Well, you don't look like a liar." Emma cocked her head to assess him. "You know how presidents seldom look presidential? Somehow, they all seem to have faces you wouldn't trust if they were car salesmen? Well, yours fairly radiates honesty and intelligence, and the people will see that."

A knock sounded on the door she'd used.

Paul cupped her face in his hands. "Thanks. Coming from you, that means a lot." Then he moved away from her. "Yes, come in."

Norma poked her gray head in and said, "Five minutes, Mr. President."

"Right."

The door closed soundlessly.

"You know which door leads to the newsroom?"

Emma looked from one to the other. "Uh-uh."

"Well, let's try Norma's."

"Let me look at you."

Paul stood at attention. Emma brushed imaginary lint from his shoulders. He pushed imaginary hairs back from her temples.

"I'd like to..." he started, but he didn't have to finish. They held each other again and smoothed imaginary wrinkles from each other's clothing.

Paul drew a deep breath. The news conference would set the tone for his "presidency"—at least until they impeached him. His heart flopped against his ribs.

CHAPTER THIRTY SEVEN

Two gray-suits joined them as they entered the reception area, and Caitlin Pascoe fell into step at the head of a corridor, looking different from Paul's memory of her. She wore a plain business suit; she'd pulled her hair straight back and fixed it into a tight bun. The severity only emphasized her Eurasian beauty.

She was one of the few people Paul had needed to hire, since Hartsell's press secretary had left for reasons of health. Prompted by the memory of her tact in handling his background, he'd called her at the Chicago paper, stunning her beyond words.

"Mr. Gr...Mr. President," she started as they followed the gray-suits.

"Paul will be fine," he said. "I'm not used to that other word, either."

Emma pointed her chin at the gray-suit in front of her. "I guess he knows we're going to the press room," she whispered.

Paul shrugged. "I hope so."

Caitlin checked the lines of her clothing. "I had no idea what it felt like from this side of the media." Her voice wobbled under its soft richness. "I feel like I'm being ushered into a tank full of sharks."

The gray-suit stopped in front of a sliding door, opened it, and let Caitlin through to make the introduction. Paul could see a slice of her through the narrow slit. He moved closer. She announced herself as President Greer's press secretary. With her left hand she gripped the podium until the knuckles were white. With the other she wadded the fabric of her gray skirt into a tight ball.

"Ladies and gentlemen, the President and Vice President of the United States," she said. She stepped back, releasing the grip of both hands. A knotty wrinkle remained in the side of the skirt. The reporters stood.

Paul and Emma stepped in. A hundred cameras flashed and clicked and whirred. Paul stopped, blinded by the flashes, his concentration shredded. He stepped too far forward and ran into the podium, rattling the microphones. Several foreign correspondents gasped and yanked little speakers from their ears. He steadied the battery of mikes, keeping his head down, and laid his index cards in front of him. He breathed deeply, swallowed, and forced himself to look up at the faces and cameras.

"Ladies and gentlemen of the United States," he began, his tongue dry as a tablespoon of sand. He turned and drew Emma to his side. "...our fellow travelers through this startling moment of history, you're already aware of the unprecedented and tragic circumstances surrounding the recent election. That a man named Paul Greer would become president was a thought assuredly further from my mind than from yours. However, we are all in this together now, and Ms. Light in the Lodge and I called this press conference to introduce ourselves to you.

"What you will hear from us today is not the work of a speech writer trying to raise our approval ratings, since we do not expect your approval unless we earn it. We are people like you, cata-pulted into a position for which we feel, even now, unprepared." The last word evinced a change in the breathing of the pack of reporters, and he hardly felt Emma melt away from his side, leav-ing him the center of attention.

He looked up from his notes. The reporters were either scrib-bling on pads or staring at him, obviously composing in their heads. The television cameras at the back stared at him, a row of dark, accusing eyes. The pause disrupted the flow of his speech as well as his concentration. He had to glance at the next index card.

"Uh—I know many of you are concerned about the fact that I was a Catholic priest until August of last year." He summarized his reasons for leaving the church and outlined his belief in the wisdom of separation of church and state.

The room filled with an elongated, almost hostile silence. He flipped his top index card to the back, knocking his hand against a glass of water he hadn't noticed. A question flashed through his head—did the White House have any official tasters to test for poison? He took a sip. His hand was still shaking, but his voice steadied.

"By now most of you know my background—born in New Orleans, and educated largely by the Church in history and in-ternational affairs, for which training, by the way, I am extremely grateful. It will serve me well in the difficult months to come. Incredible as it is, I am, in fact, your president.

"This brings me to the second area of concern that you must all have—the aims of the Earth Rights Party. Before I read the platform, I thought of myself as environmentally friendly. I rode the bus whenever possible; I doused unnecessary lights; occa-sionally, I even preached recycling from the pulpit. I will con-fess to you that the first time I read the platform I was stunned. Everything in it seemed like the ravings of a lunatic. Since then, I've come to realize that the Earth is, quite literally, our home.

"None of us would lay waste to our home, no matter how humble, for fear of exposing ourselves, and more importantly, our children, to untold dangers. Yet we lay waste to the Earth, our ultimate home, as if we could simply pull up stakes and move on, as if there were no future generations who depend on us for their safety and well-being.

"We consume energy and resources at unprecedented rates not only because of burgeoning population, but because we Americans can afford to buy them. We build homes and commercial buildings of magnificent proportion and luxury—and waste. Our dismal performance at the Brazilian environmental summit and our abrogation of environmental treaties showed the world our unwillingness to be part of the global community or to sacrifice our convenience for the benefit of our descendants. We *must* change that. No other choice is open to us.

"The Earth Rights Party platform is radical, but at the very least, it gives us a series of goals to aim for. You can be sure that my administration will focus largely on the environment. Ms. Light in the Lodge and I are in agreement that the best example for the country must come from the White House. We hope the initiative will spread to Congress and from there to all of you.

"To further this end, I have asked Ms. Light in the Lodge to head a volunteer task force composed of homemakers, workers, teachers, scientists, industrialists, and economists from all parts of the country. It will concern itself with education on the environment; slowing the depletion of resources; a viable non-growth economy; and, above all, overpopulation. We will all be hearing a great deal more about this in the months to come.

"I hope I have addressed the issues that most concern you for the present. I wish to add only that I intend to carry out the duties of the office by working at it harder than I've ever worked at anything. As to rumors of impeachment, in all modesty, I believe the Congress will find it difficult to find a past scandal on which to base impeachment proceedings. As I understand it," he smiled into the cameras, "my clean record was the crux of my nomination to begin with. But *you* should have a choice. If you become dissatisfied with my performance, I am willing to resign at any time upon receiving a no-confidence vote from you through the House of Representatives. Thank you."

Another round of clicks and flashes punctuated the end of his speech, and reporters' hands waved frantically for attention.

"Please, hold your questions for now," he said. "I would like to introduce the vice president, Ms. Emma Light in the Lodge, for whose support and advice I am eternally grateful. As you get to know her, you will see, as I do, that the country is fortunate to have her." He turned and reached for her arm. She stepped forward with her usual grace, but he could feel the tension in her body. For a fleeting second he wondered whether the cameras would record the fact that he was senselessly, idiotically in love with her. He squeezed her arm before letting go and giving her room at the podium.

Emma smiled nervously in the direction of the cameras and began with her usual directness. "I would like to answer for all Americans the questions I've been asked most often since coming to Washington," she said. "Is my name really Light in the Lodge?"

The reporters responded with polite laughter.

"Yes, it's my real name. I was born into it on the Buffalo Creek Achappassi Reservation in Wyoming, a place of appalling poverty, unemployment, and hopelessness. In my early years, I hated the reservation and could not wait to leave it, but as I matured, I was able to view my people with more compassion. I turned to the study of law as means of helping them.

"No doubt my desire to help my people triggered the second question—what do I plan to do about the Indians? One of the less tactful reporters even phrased it: 'What are you gonna do about the fact that you're an Indian?' There is nothing I can do about that fact. There is nothing I *want* to do about the fact that I'm a *Native* American. I wear this skin and bear this name with pride.

"As to the plight of my people, I plan to do whatever is in my power as vice president to eliminate poverty and unemployment wherever they exist. For my reservation specifically, I will continue efforts begun months ago to help it become self-sustaining in ways that are consistent with our culture. There is no going back to the age of tepees and buffalo hunts for Native Americans, any more than the descendants of the pioneers can go back to covered wagons. But we can all learn to live in ways that are less destructive to our planet. If we fail to do that, the most abject poverty on earth will look like the good life to the last generations of man.

"I'd like to thank the president for appointing me to the task force. Of all the areas in which he might have asked me to serve, he's chosen the one closest to my heart."

Emma stopped and made a visible effort at composing herself before the next part of her speech.

Paul guessed she was about to say, and just as when she'd revealed it to him on the long drive west, he yearned to hold her tight enough to absorb the pain from her.

Her voice became strained and she lowered her eyes to the battery of microphones.

"Mr. Greer has indicated his confidence that his past will stand up to the scrutiny of the media. Mine is less likely to do so. To save the scandal mongers the trouble of research, I will tell you now that as a girl of fifteen I fell in love with a white boy and wanted to follow him away from the reservation when we grew up. I became pregnant, and in panic, we arranged for an abortion."

A woman in the last row leaped to her feet. "You're saying that a murderer is now the vice president of the United States!"

Emma blanched.

Paul rushed to the microphones and put his hand on Emma's back. "Whatever your personal opinion on the subject of abortion, madam, you will not address the vice president in that tone of voice, nor in those words. We may be new here, but we will have courtesy in this room." He stayed at Emma's side.

The press corps was riveted on Emma now. Not a pen touched paper, but every face radiated eagerness to trace this back to the smallest filament of its roots.

Emma stiffened her spine, ready to continue. Her voice wavered with emotion as she answered the reporter. "The abortion was legal. I will not speak to you of the toll it took on me then, and still does." She bowed her head and seemed to slip into the past.

Paul touched her back again.

She inhaled sharply. "Shortly after that, the boy was killed in an accident, and though I knew where and how he died, I was terrified to tell anyone, lest the whole story come out.

"In the weeks since the Supreme Court's decision to let the election stand, I've been in touch with both his parents and apologized for my indifference to their suffering all these years. I would like to make that apology public at this time." She blinked several times and swallowed.

She looked up, directly at the journalists. "To reporters, I would like to add one thing. Mr. Greer and I are friends and must be each other's best support in times that will be trying for both of us. We would appreciate it if the media would not draw baseless conclusions and drag our friendship through the mud." She looked directly at the cameras again. "Like him, I pledge to you my best efforts on your behalf and on behalf those still unborn who must breathe the air we leave behind. Thank you."

Immediately the hands went up again and a chorus of "Mr. President!" rose from the reporters.

Paul moved in front of the microphones and put out his arm to keep Emma with him. "Here it goes," he said under his breath. He nodded at a reporter in the first row.

"Mr. President, what do you intend to do about the continuing chaos in the Middle East?"

"I would feel more comfortable answering that question in a few days. As you know, I've asked all of Mr. Hartsell's cabinet and staff members to remain at their jobs for the time being so their experience will lend us continuity in government."

"Are you telling us you're not even going to appoint your own cabinet?" yelled a voice from somewhere in the middle.

Paul frowned. "Sir, courtesy dictates that you wait to be recognized." He nodded at a reporter in a back corner.

Grinning, the man stood. "Thank you, Mr. President. Actually, I have the same question."

Paul smiled. "Eventually, I may appoint others, but as a neophyte in politics, I know few people I could ask to serve now. Until I feel confident that my opinions are based on a sound understanding of all sides of domestic and foreign issues, I hope they will advise me, although, of course, I don't expect them to make executive decisions. I'll be meeting with them individually over the next few days."

"Mr. President, would you care to comment on the number of priests who've been accused of molesting children in the last ten years?"

"No, I wouldn't."

The rude reporter from before leaped to her feet again. "You're saying you don't care..."

Paul turned to the gray-suits who waited at the door behind him. "I'd like you to remove that woman, please."

They ushered her out the back while the remaining reporters sat utterly still. When the gray-suits returned, Paul nodded for the questions to continue.

"Mr. President, what will be the first bill you send to Congress?"

Paul nearly laughed aloud. "This is the one area in which I feel eminently qualified to act immediately. I will ask for an amendment to the Constitution to allow delay of an election that occurs at a time of crisis."

"Mr. President, what's the first bit of environmental legislation you'll send to Congress?"

Paul hesitated, at a loss. A stretch of California highway, just before the accident, flashed through his head, a place where boxes and plastic bags littered the roadside. "Packaging," he said, expecting a howling demand for explanation. Instead the reporters scribbled and went on to other topics.

When it was clear the important questions had been asked, Paul signaled the conference was over and took Emma's arm to step off the platform. As the door closed behind them, Emma leaned against the wall and nearly slid to her knees.

Paul helped her stand straight and struggled not to pull her into his arms.

She regarded him for a minute, her eyes filling with tears and emotion. "Thank you, Paul," she whispered.

"I know how hard that was. I wish you..." He felt the presence of the gray-suits, who were not deaf, though they waited like two tree stumps.

Emma swiped at a tear and stiffened again. "How do you think we did?"

"I have no idea." Paul looked up and addressed one of the gray-suits. "How do *you* think we did?"

"I beg your pardon, Mr. President?"

"Never mind."

"Yes, sir."

CHAPTER THIRTY EIGHT

The gray-suits delivered them to the West Colonnade and ushered them toward the White House proper. Intensely aware of Emma next to him, Paul shoved his hands into his pockets to keep from grabbing her hand. At least he'd have a couple of hours alone with her and then do his best to put her parents and Danny and Laurel at ease when they gathered for dinner.

A tall, ambassadorial gentleman with a full head of snow-white hair was waiting for them at the door to the House. He actually bowed. "Welcome to the White House, Mr. President," he said in a faint Southern accent without the drawl. "Welcome, Miss Light in the Lodge. I'm Maurice Rutherford, Chief Usher—that is, head of the White House domestic staff. It will be my pleasure to see that your stay in the House is not marred by problems with the daily routine. If you have any questions about how things work or where things are, feel free to call on me at any time."

Paul liked the man immediately. "Thank you, Mr. Rutherford. I'm sure you'll be hearing from me often. And from Ms. Light in the Lodge, too. She's agreed to serve as hostess for the White House."

Rutherford bowed and smiled in her direction and addressed his next question to them both. "Do you know where you'd like to have drinks served before dinner?" He joined them as they walked into the ground floor corridor with its massive vaulted ceiling.

"I have no idea," Paul answered.

"The first families often take them in the West Sitting Hall, which is less formal than some, sir, partially furnished with the families' own things. It's especially cheerful on a winter afternoon, but as the Hartsells' things have been moved out and yours haven't arrived yet, it looks a bit bare at the moment."

"Aha. Actually, all my 'things' *have* arrived, but put us wherever you think best."

"The East Sitting Hall is quite nice."

"That'll be fine."

He led them into the elevator and up to a broad hallway. From left to right, the hall glowed in yellow and creamy white, as did the rooms at either end. He deposited them in the East Sitting Hall and waited by the entrance.

They stopped just inside, awed.

"It looks like spring sunshine in here," said Emma.

A floor-to-ceiling arched window dominated most of the east wall, emphasized by drapes and a valance in rich yellow taffeta. The rings of frost outlining the windowpanes merely heightened the warmth radiated by the yellow. In front of the window stood an antique sofa in yellow damask, and two matching armchairs. Glowing lamps graced the antique sewing tables at either end. Before the sofa stood a table too high to be a coffee table, with a tall, colorful flower arrangement.

"Oh, Paul," said Emma. There was a catch in her throat. "I've only seen such elegance in movies. It's all so...everything matches."

Paul hardly heard her through a haze of unreality. He would never belong here. He turned to Rutherford, who was still standing at the entrance.

"Would you like anything else before drinks are served, Mr. President?"

The presidential reference slapped him back into reality. "No, thank you, Mr. Rutherford."

Rutherford seemed to vaporize, and a hush settled over them. They inched to the center of the room, staring at the cut-glass chandelier, the antique chairs and tables. Neither moved to sit down.

"Do you suppose we could go exploring while we wait for the others?" whispered Emma.

"I don't know. Maybe."

"If we didn't leave this floor?"

"I guess so. I live here now, don't I?"

"Right."

At four o'clock Rutherford ushered Mr. and Mrs. Light in the Lodge and Danny and Laurel into the East Sitting Hall and evaporated again.

The Light in the Lodges stunned Paul. He'd never seen two human beings so ravaged by life and could find almost nothing of Emma in them. Though Raymond had the thin nose and high cheekbones of Emma's face, there was a sunken, haggard quality about his entire person, like last year's scarecrow. Erlinda's face was round and flat. Paul chided himself for the impression of a thoroughly reamed, four-day-old grapefruit rind. Both faces reflected lives degraded by hopelessness and wasted on alcohol.

"I'm very happy to meet you," he said, shaking hands with them warmly. They were both trembling. They even looked out of place in the new clothes Emma must have bought them for the inauguration.

No one sat down.

Rutherford wheeled in a cart with an assortment of drinks and intricate *hors d'ouerves*. He stopped by an ornate chest of drawers to the right of the window, set the trays on the chest, and hovered, waiting for instructions.

Emma looked nervously from her father to the whiskey bottles.

Watching her, Paul said to Chief Usher, "I don't believe we care for anything but club soda. Would you leave that and take the rest back, please. And we'll serve ourselves."

"Very good, Mr. President. At what time would you like dinner served?"

"I don't know." Paul polled the others with his eyes but got no response.

They were all glancing around furtively, as if newly delivered into an alien world of undetermined hospitality. Even Danny was not himself.

Paul tried again. "Is seven all right?"

They nodded.

"Seven it is, then."

"Would you prefer the President's Dining Room or the Family Dining Room, sir?"

Paul shrugged. "I saw two dining rooms, but I don't know which is which."

"The Family Dining Room is larger and brighter. It's on the floor below us. The President's Dining Room is right down the hall, just before the West Sitting Hall, on your right." He gestured down the long yellow hall.

Paul peered down the hall. "That will be fine." When Rutherford disappeared, he suggested, "Why don't we all sit down?"

They distributed themselves like wounded animals seeking defensive hiding. Erlinda sat on one end of the Empire sofa, put her elbow on the high armrest, and took it down again quickly. She crossed her knees, uncrossed them, and laid her hands primly on her lap. Raymond lowered himself to the edge of one of the chairs, eyeing the spindly legs under him with distrust. Laurel and Emma settled opposite them. The only place left was the center of the sofa, behind the flowers.

"I guess we could move a couple of these," Paul said, taking a straight chair from the desk. Danny brought one from the other side, and they set them across from Erlinda and Laurel.

"Did everybody see the news conference?" Paul asked, leaning to the left and peering around the flowers to include Erlinda.

"Oh, yes," said Laurel. "Danny and I even watched it on two different channels so we could hear as many of those man-on-the-street reactions as we could."

The Light in the Lodges nodded.

"How do you think we did, Mr. Light in the Lodge?" asked Paul.

"Fine." He forced himself to smile and gazed across at the tray on the chest of drawers. Paul got up, put some ice in two crystal glasses, and filled them with soda water. Erlinda took hers and stared at the light playing in its beautifully beveled design.

"What did you think, Mama?" asked Emma.

"I thought so, too. Fine."

"You looked beautiful, Emma," added her father. He shifted on the chair and looked for a place to set his glass.

"What do you do for a living, Mr. Light in the Lodge?" asked Laurel.

"I sweep out the tribal building. In Big Sleep."

"I see. What about you, Mrs. Light in the Lodge?"

"You can call us Raymond and Erlinda. That's what we're used to."

"Thank you," said Laurel. "I hope you'll call us Danny and Laurel."

"And Paul."

Erlinda nodded. "I don't have no regular job. There ain't much work on the reservation. Sometimes I help with the commodities. Mostly I just used to drink." She adjusted the fabric of her navy dress to wrinkle less. "I quit now, though."

"Hey, me, too," said Danny, leaning toward her. "My brother made me quit after I got him nominated. You think I'll ever get over the hankering for a beer?"

She gave him a long hang-dog look. "No."

"Ouch!"

A weighty silence followed. Paul filled it with the sound of ice in the fine glasses. Laurel brought an empty goblet to the coffee table and pinged it on the side with a fingernail. It chimed a perfect A into the room. "Real crystal," she said. Everyone stared at the glass except Raymond, who was on the wrong side of the flowers.

"Danny, how did you two think we came across?" Emma asked.

"Pretty well, actually, once you got started," said Danny. "I wrote a few man-on-the-street impressions down." He glanced at Paul. "You want to hear them?"

"I'd rather be mauled by an alligator, but I guess I should."

Danny pulled a Motel 8 notepad from his coat pocket. "Okay. One said maybe you'd be better than a lot of politicians because you didn't owe anybody anything. They caught one woman right outside St. Simon's who said you had no right to do this to them. But another said you'd been a great priest and a really kind man. She was sure you'd make a great president and lead the country back to God."

Paul leaned against the backrest of his chair shook his head. "It feels like a million years since that assumption might have been reasonable."

Danny glanced around at the alien setting. "You've come a long way." He went back to his list. "A mailman in New York said give you a try for a few weeks and if you don't do a good job, kick you out. A retiree in Oregon said he's not giving up his gas-guzzling Winnebago, no matter what you legislate. A yuppie wife in Dallas said they paid good money for their house, which was a sizable mansion in the background, and anyway it had double glass in the windows, so it didn't use nearly as much energy as you seem to think."

Laurel took up the roll call. "A cab driver in Chicago said, 'Was that what it was? I thought it was some kind of funeral.' A regular Adonis on a beach in California said three cheers for surfing because it didn't use any fossil fuel. A woman protesting outside an abortion clinic in Cincinnati...oh, we don't really need that one."

Emma jerked herself upright. "She said what?"

Laurel gave her an apologetic smile. "She just called you something they beeped out. A Mafia-looking type in Las Vegas said you try to take out the gambling Meccas in the desert and you'd have him to contend with. A park ranger at the Everglades was glad you'd won because you'd do something about the habitat for the alligators. A minister in Birmingham said you were the Anti-Christ and ought to be crucified for having that good Christian reporter thrown out."

Paul and Emma shook their heads.

Danny put his pad back in his pocket. "Actually, I thought it was great to have that woman removed. Showed some presidential spunk. And other than that, you came across as very sincere and honest. Both of you."

Paul smiled weakly. "Thanks."

The conversation ground to a halt. Emma looked at her watch. "Why don't we take them on the little tour?"

They all stood up instantly.

At ten of six, when they returned from their venture to the floor below, another servant was waiting at the door to the East

Sitting Hall. "Would you care to watch the evening news, Mr. President?"

Paul looked at the others. They all regarded him with a you're-the-president expression. "Yes, I guess so." He looked about for the television set. The servant left and returned with a large set on a rolling cabinet.

Royce McClain faded onto the screen, standing near the White House fence. Wearing a lamb's wool hat against the cold, he stood straight and exuded his usual pompous intelligence.

Paul fought the impulse to look out the window to see whether the anchor was reporting live.

Royce took a breath of biting air, coughed, and began. "One can only wonder what it must feel like to be the man in residence here now," he said, his breath streaming away to his right in frozen puffs. "Surely no president has ever been as ill-prepared for office as this one, and probably none ever served for as short a time as Paul Greer will. CBA has it from a reliable source that already leaders of both major parties plan to meet to discuss impeachment proceedings against him."

Paul sighed impatiently. Didn't the country already assume that? His concentration slid away from the reporter, replaced by annoyance. Okay, let them start. He'd do everything he could in the meantime to seek peace and put the country on a path toward healing the earth. How long did a fast-track impeachment take? Was it like a dishonorable discharge from the military? Would he find another job?

And what of Emma? Here at least, he'd see her often. If they kicked her out, too, she'd go back to Wyoming. Could he work in Wyoming? Would she even want him to?

The President's Dining Room sparkled like the inside of a jewelry box. Light from the cut glass chandelier, the fire in the fireplace, and a dozen candles already burning on the table reflected off the many glasses and the gold tableware.

The group entered silently and stood at the door in a tight phalanx.

Wallpaper depicting scenes from the American Revolution against the twilight blue of an evening sky covered the walls; the draperies on the two windows were dark blue, and the lighter blue curtains under them were drawn. The table setting was breathtaking in beauty and intimidating in formality. From each plate a very regal gold eagle glared into the room, surrounded by a broad blue border and a gold rim. Four crystal goblets and a broad array of gold utensils flanked each place.

Emma prodded her parents. "Come on, let's sit down." Raymond and Erlinda stayed close together as they made their way to the far side of the table. Laurel and Danny sat down on the near side, and Emma and Paul took the places at either end.

"It's beautiful," Laurel whispered to Raymond over the low arrangement of delphiniums and baby's breath.

He nodded, staring at the tiny fork on the left end of his setting.

Rutherford and a butler materialized, pushing carts covered with silver domes. The servant plugged in several food warmers and left. Rutherford circled the table, apparently checking the settings, glanced at Raymond, and stopped at Paul's seat. "I beg your pardon, Mr. President." He picked up the smallest fork in his gloved hand and held it closer to the light. "Is that a spot on this shrimp cocktail fork?" he asked. "No. I was mistaken. Have the staff set things correctly? Cocktail, salad, fish, dinner, dessert." He laid a supervisory finger on each in turn and switched to the knives. "Butter, fish, meat, yes, it all seems to be in the order of service." He moved toward the trays.

"Does the Chief Usher normally serve dinner, Mr. Rutherford?" asked Paul.

"Oh, no, sir, but on the first night, I thought things might be a bit...unfamiliar. I wanted to make sure everything was satisfactory."

"Well, we certainly appreciate your taking the extra time." Paul felt a rush of embarrassed gratitude. "This is truly kind of you, Mr. Rutherford."

Rutherford smiled at him with real warmth. "Not at all, Mr. President."

"Is dinner always this formal?"

"Not necessarily, sir. This is the kitchen staff's way of welcoming you and your guests." He bowed in the direction of the Light in the Lodges. "They wanted your first dinner to be...memorable. Your meals can be as formal or informal as you wish."

Paul laughed. "This dinner would have been memorable if they'd served us bread and water, but please tell them how..." He searched for a word large enough.

"...perfectly delighted we all are," Emma finished for him.

"Yes, really, this is so lovely," said Laurel.

The others nodded, and Erlinda even smiled at Rutherford.

"They'll be pleased to hear it. Shall I start, sir?"

"Yes, thank you."

Through the soup, salad, and fish course, conversation proceeded haltingly about the reactions of the major party potentates to the news conference. When Rutherford wasn't announcing a course, he stood to the side, apparently deaf as a floor lamp.

"Roast capon with macadamia nut stuffing," he said after he'd removed the mahi-mahi plates.

Raymond and Erlinda stared at the tiny birds resting on a bed of saffron rice, outlined with fresh asparagus and decorated with a cherry tomato in a cluster of dill weed.

Danny looked across at Emma's parents. "Yipes, what'd they do? 'Honey, I Shrunk the Turkey!' Ha, ha..."

Paul, Emma, and Laurel tried to join his laughter. Raymond and Erlinda and Rutherford simply stared.

Paul realized comfort was never going to be a component of White House living. Still, it wouldn't last long, and then he'd sound Emma out about moving to Wyoming.

Paul stood on the drive watching the blacker-than-night limousines pull onto the street, taking Danny and Laurel to Dulles and Emma and her parents to her house. Before he could formulate a good image of himself sneaking off with them, a shadow joined his in the trapezoid of light thrown out of the entrance, followed by the voice of Rutherford. "Will you be retiring now, Mr. President? I'd be happy to show you to the president's bedroom."

Paul sighed as the cars disappeared. He turned to the entrance that yawned at him like a black hole despite its light. "Yes, thank you Mr. Rutherford."

"It would be entirely appropriate for you to call me Maurice, Mr. President."

"Right. And I don't suppose..."

"Sir?"

"Never mind. How about if we settle on Rutherford?"

"That will be fine, sir."

"Tell me, Rutherford, is it always this... terrifying?"

"I can't say, sir. I came to the White House just after the last inauguration. But I imagine it must be different if you've set your sights on getting here. You'll get used to it in time, sir."

"Fifty years, maybe. Do you suppose they'll give me fifty days?"

"I wouldn't know, sir."

"You're the soul of tact, Rutherford."

"Thank you, sir."

Rutherford led him to the room opposite the President's Dining Room.

Paul stopped at the door and stared in at the canopied bed, the deep blue watered silk wall paper, the sofas and chairs of the sitting area.

"This is it?" he cried. "I thought this was just for show. It's huge."

"If there's anything not to your liking, sir, it will be changed."

Paul laughed. "I won't change much, Rutherford. We'd no sooner get a carpet rolled up or a new bucket of paint on the wall than they'd have me out on the street again. Actually, there's one thing, though, if it's not too much work. Could you have them get rid of the canopy on the bed? It blocks the lamplight, and I always read before I go to sleep."

Rutherford turned toward the door. "I'll send for..."

"Not now. Tomorrow will be fine."

"It'll be done, sir. Your closet is here." He opened a door and switched on a light.

The walk-in closet was larger than Paul's room in the rectory at St. Simon's. Above the built-in chest of drawers hung the five other dress shirts and one other suit that he owned.

"The bathroom is there," said Rutherford. He pointed toward the opposite side of the room. "What time will you be wanting breakfast, sir?"

Paul shrugged. "Around seven? Where is it served?"

"Anywhere you want."

"Across the hall will be fine. Please tell them I'm happy with cereal and coffee. And milk for the cereal."

"Any particular brand?"

"Coffee?"

"Both."

"No. And Rutherford, they can keep the private dinners very simple, as well. Whatever's in season will be fine."

"Very good, sir. Is there anything you especially don't like?"

"Eggplant."

"Eggplant. Will there be anything else, sir?"

"No, thank you, Rutherford, I've kept you far too long, I'm sure. And thank you again for the extra consideration this evening." He stuck his hand out to shake Rutherford's.

Rutherford was already bowing and brought his hand up at the last minute, surprised by the gesture. "You're most welcome, sir."

He closed the door soundlessly and Paul was alone in the huge bedroom. He stood in the center of the floor, staring around him. After a few minutes he forced himself to the bathroom to brush his teeth. He went to the closet, hung up his suit, looked in vain for a laundry basket, and shoved his shirt, socks, and underwear in a bottom drawer. He took them out, folded them, and put them back. In his shorts, he rushed to turn off the light, and then groped his way to the bed, wondering how long it would be before the entire world knew the ex-priest slept in his shorts. How would a president go about buying pajamas and a bathrobe? Especially a president who was almost broke.

He lay under the plain coverlet and down quilt with his hands under his head, listening to the faint sounds that penetrated the bulletproof glass of his windows. He had never been so alone.

Somewhere a car honked. The muffled, distant sound carried him out to the streets of Washington, D.C., and expanded in all directions until his mind encircled the earth and knew the life that pulsed everywhere on its solid surfaces. Billions of pieces of life, with his little scrap of it isolated from them all by a title, a single word. Life that could be influenced or destroyed by his decisions, starting tomorrow. He turned on his side and pulled the pillow over his ear.

CHAPTER THIRTY NINE

Across the Potomac, a private meeting of congressional leaders was getting underway, hosted by Clive Jaubert, Speaker of the House. As he seated his guests around his free-form glass coffee table, he realized the *D.C. Scene* still lay there. His anger flared. Flaming liberal rag with its article on the front page characterizing him as "a strutting five-foot-six Elephant with the attitude of God and the manner and vocabulary of a sophomore class president." He whisked it under his chair before his guests could focus on it. They'd just love to take that and run with it. Morons. He'd need every ounce of his patience to deal with them.

He sat forward in his wing back chair and felt the warmth of the fireplace on his face. "Well, gentlemen," he drawled, "we can cut the TV crap here and get down to the business of how to get Greer out of there. I know perfectly well you all don't want him any more than we do."

"Of course not," said Axel Blomster, House Minority Whip in the booming voice that had gotten him elected for five terms, "but it isn't going to be that easy."

Clive raised his hand with the palm up. "So let's get together on this and when we've got him out, we can go back to the old comfortable partisan squabbling. I don't know what you think will be so hard." He leaned back to ease the constriction of his belt and wiped the stone of his huge LSU class ring on his slacks.

Axel rested his aging and completely bald head on the chair. "Even I could see the way he'd appeal to some people." He stared ponderously at the ceiling and appeared to drift away from the conversation.

"You're right," said Elijah Jackson, eight-term Congressman from Fort Worth, Texas, and unofficial but acknowledged leader of the Blacks in both Houses. "Every person in this country will see himself in this man...the storybook babe in the woods who sets everything to rights through his very innocence."

"Isn't there some way we can get him on this innocence thing?" asked Joe Giordano, Senate Majority Whip from New Jersey.

"Not likely," responded Al Skinner. Nominally he was Jaubert's assistant. In fact, it was the ties with his former position that made him valuable—FBI section chief of Southern states. "We researched it all. There's no hanky-panky with little boys, no pilfering of the poor box, no communion-wine alcoholism, not even internal church infractions that we can find. He had a grand total $11,472 and change in his savings when he bolted, and all of it from his small salary. The man really is squeaky clean."

The others greeted the news with a thoughtful silence under raised eyebrows, except Axel, who hadn't returned from his contemplation of the ceiling. Clive twisted the class ring round and round his puffy little finger.

"Listen, I don't know what you're in such a flap about," said Elijah. "You Republicans still control both houses. That Earth party took its few seats from us, not you."

Axel transitioned directly from his reverie to his oratory persona. "It occurs to me that this'd be a good time to hike taxes against the deficit. The election year's over and those earth fanatics would get the blame when the next one rolls around."

Clive's groan was audible despite his effort at patience.

Elijah recrossed his long legs and said, "Axel, the topic at hand is Greer." He returned his focus to the others. "He doesn't come to the office dirty, like so many of us. Maybe he can even do some good. At the very least, if he does a bad job, he's already said he'd quit if the people demand a vote of no-confidence."

Clive allowed himself a snort of derision. "You know how 'the people' are. They'll sit around on their fat duffs waiting to see what happens next, and before you know it, Paulie Boy will be giving his first State of the Union speech. No, thanks. The man's not even God-fearing, for Christ's sakes."

Elijah rolled his eyes. "'Godfearing' has nothing to do with it, and you know it. It's your rider in the Parks funding bill. Hartsell never did sign that, did he?"

Clive stifled a twitch of surprise. He'd assumed no one would even bother to read into the bill far enough to discover the rider, which meant everything to his future career. "No, and there's too much pending in it. I got Sun Gas and Ex-oil on my back like Sumo wrestlers, not to mention lobbyists for the whole state of Nevada."

Elijah's brows shot up. "You running with that breed?"

Clive's heart did a flop. Nevada lobbyists were widely known for gambling and organized crime connections, and he shouldn't have let that slip. He hurried to add, "Look, people need water, and I need those western aquifers freed for private drilling. I don't care if Greer *was* from my state. I want him out of there before he even discovers my item in that bill."

"Maybe if we got up a bi-partisan committee we could persuade him to resign," suggested Joe.

"Okay, so let's consider what will happen if he resigns," said Elijah.

The obvious struck them, and four of the five faces sagged.

"Emma Light in the Lodge would become president," whispered Al.

Elijah laughed and slapped his knee. "Ha, put that in your cuds and chew a while!"

Clive gave him a withering glare and turned to Al. "Did you look into the woman's past?"

Al nodded. "A regular up-by-her-own-boot-straps story. Practically beats Lincoln. And what she said about the accident is apparently true. At least the part about contacting the boy's parents. However, there's the possibility a third person was involved in the story some way."

Clive smiled and twisted the ring. "That's an angle..."

"She sounds like a good woman to me," protested Elijah. "What do you want to wreck her for when Greer's what you're after? Anyway, since she confessed her own part in it and didn't mention anyone else, you'd only do yourselves more harm than good if you go after that business."

"Okay, you're right. We focus on Greer," said Clive, but he gave Al the very slight raise of the eyebrow that meant "keep this in mind."

"What about this 'friendship' with Greer?" asked Joe. "Didn't I read somewhere that the motel where they stayed after the earthquake had connecting doors?"

Elijah stood up. "Where do you buy your newspapers, Joe, the local porn shop? This is getting too dirty for me and it goes way beyond my sense of fairness."

"Me, too," said Axel with uncharacteristic focus. He set his whiskey glass on the coffee table.

Elijah gave Clive his you-know-I-mean-business expression. "If I hear any 'friendship' mud flying around the Hill, I don't ever want to find out it was a result of this meeting. Let them dig their own graves, for God's sake. They're scared spitless. They haven't a clue how things get done in Washington. They'll do themselves more harm than we ever could, and when the time comes, *Mr.* Jaubert, maybe *this* time around the Republicans will finally nominate you."

Clive let the sarcasm slide right off his thick political hide. "Come on, now, sit down, Elijah. Joe was just thinking aloud, I'm sure. And you're right. We'll do nothing for the present. But at the first blunder, I'm going to be ready to pounce with the full force of my party and my position."

"Right," said Joe.

Elijah and Axel sat down again on the edges of their chairs.

Clive twisted his ring in the other direction. "So we give him a few weeks to screw up royally and demand his resignation. Once he's out, we can easily find a reason to impeach the woman. You saw her, she's much the more radical of the two, and the people aren't going to sit still for it if she sends us bills that make them sacrifice their hard-earned comforts. They'll demand an impeachment."

"My, my, think of that," said Elijah. "And then who gets to be president?"

Clive only smiled back, but he felt the mantle of the presidency slip over his shoulders and knew it was only a matter of time now. A short time.

CHAPTER FORTY ONE

Paul woke at 4:14 with a start. His dream of a searing iron in the shape of a big white house crushing the breath from his chest faded into a quilt that was too hot. He threw off the covers and stood up, catching his face in the canopy. It took a second to realize where he was. He opened the curtains, then turned and paced in the dim light.

He should go down to the Oval Office now and read up on the members of the cabinet, but he had no idea where the information might be stored, nor even whether he could enter the west wing in the middle of the night. Shouldn't he have a key or something?

At five of seven he opened the door and was surprised to see a vaguely familiar man rise from a chair on the opposite wall, a man so nondescript Paul assumed he was a gray-suit.

"Good morning, Mr. President," he said. "I'm Ed Petersen, your Chief of Staff."

Surprised, Paul looked more carefully and realized Petersen was a man of extraordinary force of will. "Well, good morning, Ed. Do you always join me for breakfast?"

"Oh, no, sir. I've already eaten. I'm here to help you get things started. It's my job to ease the way for you."

"I see. Well, I have a cabinet meeting at ten and I need a run-down on the members, pictures if possible, a little information about their backgrounds, and what their current concerns are."

"I can come up with that," said Ed.

"Fine. Can I have at least an hour to go over it?"

"Certainly, sir."

"Just let me eat first. I'd hate to keep the kitchen staff waiting."

Paul stepped into the dining room and ate his cereal from a bowl surely intended for flaming cherries jubilee or *sorbet du roi*. Afterwards, he followed Ed, noting the way and vaguely hoping it was Ed's habit to head where he needed to go. And then he nearly laughed aloud at himself, the most powerful leader in the world who'd done nothing so far but follow other people around.

Norma showed Emma into the oval office at 8:00.

Paul jumped up from the sofa where he'd taken the report on the cabinet members. When she'd settled opposite him with the pages he'd already read, he asked. "How was it in the vice president's house?"

Emma shuddered. "The walk-in closet is bigger than the trailer I grew up in. I felt..." she searched for words, "like a mangy coyote trapped in some hallowed art museum. I kept waiting for guards to tell me the museum was no place for the likes of me."

Paul laughed. "I felt the same way. Remember that bedroom, the one across from the dining room? That's actually where I sleep. I guess I thought at the end of a day of pomp and circumstance I could escape to a room as spare as the one in the rectory. I'd give a lot to be your coyote. They'd throw me out and I could go back to hunting mice where I belong."

She laughed. "Anyway, you can forget about building that tunnel. The vice president's house is miles from here. It's in the middle of a naval something-or-other. An observatory, I think." She held up the report. "What's all this?"

"Information about the cabinet members and their concerns. I'd like you to go over it with me, steer me in the right direction if I forget who's who. Would you mind?"

They shared a grimace and settled into the reading.

Ed knocked and entered a few minutes before ten. After greeting Emma, he said, "I thought I'd see if you have any questions before the cabinet meeting."

"I'm as well prepared as I'm going to get. Emma quizzed me like an old pro. Actually, I do have one question. Where is the cabinet room?"

"Just follow me, sir."

The assembled members greeted him with a chorus of "Good morning, Mr. President," and stepped to their seats without haste, several of them smiling at the floor as they went.

Well, Paul thought, maybe he could gain a little respect if he ran the meeting well. When they were settled, he began, "First, I want to thank you all sincerely for staying on." He cleared his throat to get the slight tremor out of his voice. "I have no doubt the next few months will be very trying for you. If you reach the point where you wish to resign the cabinet, I'll certainly understand. I'd only ask that you make several recommendations for a successor. Since I'm new here, everyone in your areas of expertise is unknown to me.

"Next, I'd like to get acquainted with each of you a little, and at the end of my part of the meeting, I hope you'll mention any concerns that I don't touch upon."

Stephen Harlowe, Secretary of State, straightened his back and tapped the edges of papers in front of him to align them more perfectly.

Paul looked around. "Now, let's see, the matter that demands our immediate attention is the devastation in California, especially since the government has done little so far to aid the victims. I'd like to hear from Housing and Urban Development. Ms. Sanchez..."

Harlowe's shoulders slumped ever so slightly.

Rita Sanchez, formerly a whirlwind of Latino activism who had broadened her sphere of interest only slightly on entering civil service twenty years before, jolted forward. "Yes," she snapped. A diminutive woman with fire and anger in her eyes, she leaned around Secretary Harlowe, glaring at him in the process.

He returned her stare but leaned into his backrest to clear her view of the president.

Paul glanced at his notes. "You're from California, I believe."

"Yes. Which is where I should be right now."

"Of course. I'll schedule you for my first meeting, Ms. Sanchez, so that you can fly right back. Did you lose anyone in the earthquake?"

Rita was taken aback. She swallowed a lump of brimstone before answering. "No, but I have two uncles who live in the area of Los Angeles that was hardest hit. One uncle's house is a total loss, the other barely still livable, and both families are living there now."

Paul sensed she somehow blamed him. "I'm really sorry to hear that."

Another lump of brimstone. "Thank you, sir."

The other cabinet members murmured their sympathy.

"And your own home?" asked Paul.

"We hardly felt the earthquake at all. We live in El Centro, on the eastern edge of the Imperial Valley east of San Diego. Not far from the Mexican border." She glared defiantly around the table.

Other cabinet members showed no interest in the border and were already taking on the look of a bored civics class. Paul switched to the urgent question. "I wanted to ask you, Ms. Sanchez, although I know this is basically a state issue, where your department stands on the debate about rebuilding cities as they were or requiring a safety zone of several miles in either direction on known fault lines."

"You want me to answer that right now? I can tell you..."

Paul raised a hand, palm out. "No, that's all right. I'd just like you to bring as much information as you can to our private meeting." He turned to look her squarely in the eyes. "Both sides of the argument. And a geologist acquainted with the area. Perhaps a congressman and a senator from California. Could you manage that by this afternoon?"

Secretary Sanchez reined herself in, and her voice lost some of its defensive edge. "The geologist will be a challenge, sir, but I'll do my best. If I can leave now..."

The room waited while she snatched her things from the table, slapped them in a black briefcase, and hurried out.

Paul looked for the next person on his list. "Mrs. Kendall, you're the Secretary of Education."

Harlowe drew in a breath of shock. Several members smiled into their laps or sat up in interest.

Mrs. Kendall beamed and let her eyes rest for only a second on Harlowe as they moved to Paul. "Yes, sir." Her face was a study in serenity and steel.

Paul had the impression that if he could see into her lap, there'd be a crochet hook bobbing along a pile of lavender angora interlaced with stout fishing line.

"I believe your staff has been working on raising the general skills of American high school students to match those of European and Japanese students and..." he glanced at the notes

Ed had given him, "...on expanding the role of vocational training for students not interested in college."

"Yes, sir," said the little woman who looked like everybody's grandmother.

"You can count on my support, especially in vocational training. When we meet privately, I'd be interested in whatever statistics you have, including the skills of students from different kinds of secondary schools in Europe, not just those that are strictly academic."

"Yes, sir!"

"Would Thurs...oh, I have a secretary for that—I think her name's Lee-Anna. I'll have her get in touch with you. I'm looking forward to sharing views with another old school teacher."

"Thank you, Mr. President." Sitting back in her chair, Mrs. Kendall gave him a look that was reflective but sharp.

The next person he'd planned to interview was the Secretary of the Interior, but Paul sensed the dudgeon of Harlowe, Harvard alumnus, Bostonian and elitist by birth, and a man of such secure social eminence that he was the gracious and capable emissary to the most exalted or the most primitive societies.

Paul decided to get right to State before Harlowe's bruised ego discolored his face. "Now, Mr. Harlowe, I think I'm actually more or less current on the trouble spots you're dealing with these days, being a modest student of international affairs myself. So if you'd just bring along all the fine print and the spy dope," Paul said with a small grin, "we can work from there."

Stephen Harlowe's eyes widened, along with all the others'.

Paul glanced around in the silence. "Intelligence reports" he hastened to correct himself. "Of course, there are so many potential dangers to our national interests, I'd better have Lee-Anna schedule you a little more time."

Not even faintly mollified, Harlowe sat back and glared past Commerce at the blue and gold draperies.

Several members bit their lips to keep from laughing.

The thin veneer of respect Paul had felt after the other interviews evaporated, and he tried to restore it. He polled the remaining cabinet members for matters of concern and adjourned the meeting shortly before noon, knowing the meeting had been a borderline disaster.

As he walked back to the Oval Office with Ed and Emma, he asked, "Ed, do you know how it works for lunch around here?"

"Lunch is waiting for you in the House, sir."

"Well, I figured that, but will it be all right if you and Emma join me?"

"Any time, sir. They always cook for several just in case."

"Well, then please stay, if you can. And Emma?" He turned to her.

"That'll be fine, thank you. I told my folks I wouldn't be able to meet them for lunch, but I'd try for dinner." She laughed. "I offered to take them to the airport in my Toyota, but they've fallen in love with the limousine. Still, I'd like to go with them."

"Mr. President, I took the liberty of having my assistant put pending legislation on your desk. There are several bills that Hartsell didn't sign, and you might wish to read them."

"Thanks. I guess that's on the afternoon's agenda after Ms. Sanchez. Could you have a second copy made for Emma?"

"Already done, sir."

Paul stopped and smiled at him. "You know, I've been feeling guilty about the incredible number of people who work directly for me. What is it, upwards of a hundred? But if I cut any positions, I think yours is one I'll keep."

"Thank you, sir. Mr. President, I got a call today from the Secret Service. Apparently a..." Ed glanced at a slip of paper he pulled from a pocket "...Shirley Wainwright is claiming to be your bodyguard and demands to be on your Secret Service team."

"Oh, my God. I'd completely forgotten her."

"She's the one you called the strung bean?" asked Emma.

"In a malicious moment that I regret." He turned to Ed. "Can you just tell them to send her packing?"

"Well, yes, but a Gordon Johnson called, too, very officially, as chairman of your party. He wants this appointment as a 'presidential plum.'"

Paul frowned.

"You can do what you want, sir, but the president makes a lot of appointments, and since you've kept most of the cabinet and staff from before, I doubt anyone would raise an eyebrow if you hired her."

"Surely she'd have to undergo rigorous training. That ought to knock her out of the running."

"That, a civil service test, and security clearance. But that's the odd thing. Apparently she just went in and breezed right through the first two. All she's waiting for is clearance."

Paul stared at him and looked at Emma. She shrugged.

He grinned at her. "Well, if that comes through, put her on Emma."

"Yes, sir."

"Thanks a lot," said Emma.

"Do they get guns, Ed?"

"Of course."

"Have them give her a pop-gun. The woman's definitely trigger-happy."

CHAPTER FORTY TWO

P aul moved a chair and sat facing the fireplace of the Oval
Office as the meeting about the earthquake began. For the
first time since taking the oath yesterday, he felt a spark of hope.
This was important. If he did nothing else during the time he'd
have, he wanted to help the victims get back on their feet. The
government was moving too slowly in releasing disaster aid, and
anger and frustration were pouring out of California faster than
money was flowing in. These people would help him get things
rolling.

At the near end of the red and gold striped sofa to his left
sat Brent Howards, a blond young representative from San
Francisco, also an Earth Rights member. At the other sat Kevin
Nguyen, geologist flown in from the Colorado School of Mines,
still breathless from his rushed trip. Facing Paul, Rita Sanchez
and Emma sat on chairs at the other end of the coffee table.
Erskine Brooks, the long tenured, very conservative Republican
senator, took the other sofa, next to Ed Petersen.

"Please accept my sympathy for the tragedy in your state, Mr. Brooks, Mr. Howards," Paul began.

Brent murmured his thanks, but Brooks' strident voice drowned him out. "Thank you, Mr. President. I didn't suffer any family losses, being from Sacramento, but there isn't a person in California who doesn't feel the aftermath of the earthquake deeply."

"I'm sure there's no one in the whole country who doesn't mourn with you. Were you spared, too?" Paul asked Howards.

The slender, fair-haired congressman bit his bottom lip and his eyes misted over. He caught Brooks' disapproving glance and reddened. "I lost my...partner and the bookstore we owned together, and most of my friends," he said.

"Mr. Howards, I'm very sorry," said Paul. "If this meeting is too painful to you, we could ask another representative..."

Rita Sanchez glared at the ceiling and drummed a thumb on the armrest of her chair.

"No, please, sir," said Howards. "There aren't any others here now, anyway. They're all busy at home. I know this is only my first term, and we're not even sure how many people I represent, but I want to be in on this. It's only thing I have now. I'll try not to impede the discussion."

"Don't worry about that. Were you in San Francisco at the time of the quake?" Paul said, catching Ed's subtle glance his watch.

"No, sir. I'd gone to Boise several days before on a family emergency."

Out of the corner of his eye, Paul noted Brooks' obvious distaste for Brent and Emma's look of sympathy. Maybe we can befriend this young man, he thought, and went to the next person, the Vietnamese geologist, whose air of cowed amazement was familiar enough to give Paul a moment's comfort. "Thank you for joining us, Mr....would you mind if I ask you to pronounce your last name for me? I've seen it so often and never quite figured it out."

From staring around the room, Kevin Nguyen jerked to attention. "If you say it like the word *win*, you're about as close as you can get without sneezing, sir."

"Mr. 'Win,'" repeated Paul. The others echoed him.

Paul smiled. "What a nice coincidence that your name has such a positive ring in English. Mr. Nguyen, can you give us any information as to the state of the San Andreas Fault, whether you can predict how soon the Fault might shift again and at what magnitude?"

Kevin Nguyen unrolled a large map of the Pacific minus the water. "As you probably know, sir, the fault line is the edge of the Pacific Plate, which crosses the entire ocean, from below New Zealand to northern California."

Paul stared at the rift in amazement. "I had no idea it was that long."

"Over 10,000 miles." Nguyen anchored the corners of the map on the table. "There was a lot of movement all along the eastern edge of the Plate this time, shifting in a number of stress points with varying degrees of damage. It was the first time since we've been keeping records that there was so much activity along the entire rim, so we're not sure what it means. The San Andreas quake set off a couple of sympathetic breaks and opened new faults in California. I'm sure the damage to the road you were on was one of them.

"But the damage wasn't limited to our end of the Fault. The South Sea Islands suffered severely." He looked up to see whether Paul wished more information. "Tahiti, Bora Bora,..."

Ed cleared his throat. "Sir, you wanted to get to the bills..."

Paul sighed. "Mr. Nguyen, much as it would interest me personally to hear about the whole quake, I guess we'd better limit the discussion to California, then."

The geologist flushed. "Sorry, sir. By far the worst hit was San Francisco."

"Yes, we know that from the news reports," said Ed.

Paul raised a hand at Ed to keep him from dominating the discussion. "I'll take it from here, Ed." He turned back to Nguyen. "I think what I need from you now is an assessment of what we can expect in the near and the long term future along the Fault."

"I wish it were that simple, sir. We need a great deal of time to study the quake areas and the entire fault line," said Nguyen, "but our best information to date indicates that a new area of extreme stress developed just here." His finger traced a stretch of the rift off the coast of northern Baja California. "We just don't know at this point how long it will take for that to let go, nor how far-reaching the effects will be. Depending on its strength, it could trigger a tsunami that would devastate Baja California and a large part of our southern coastline. The Plate isn't going to stop moving, sir, and I have to tell you, the San Andreas Fault is a question mark."

"And how long do you think the study will take?"

"Eight to ten years, sir, maybe longer."

The news hit the others and they simultaneously fell into the backrests of their seats.

"We can't wait ten years to decide what to do about rebuilding!" cried Rita. "Our offices have been flooded every day for weeks with demands for disaster aid."

"Even the homeless are demanding to go back in," added Howards.

"But surely we don't want to spend disaster money to create another disaster," said Paul. He could see Emma squirming in her chair and remembered the radical platform she'd helped write. He asked quickly, "Wasn't the Regency Bay where the candidates died built according to all the latest quake-proof designs?

Didn't several others that were supposed to withstand a nine point quake suffer enough damage to cause loss of life? If they failed, we don't dare rebuild until we have more information and better methods. That certainly speaks for the safety zone, at least for the next several years."

"If you require a buffer zone on either side of the fault," said Rita, "you'll eliminate a large stretch of the coast. How can we compensate people for the loss of that property?"

Emma was squirming in her chair, her face reflecting the zealous dedication she evinced only when she talked of saving the earth. She opened her mouth, but fearing something radical, Paul headed her off. "Haven't the insurance companies taken care of that?"

Brooks shook his head. "Very few homeowners in California actually had earthquake insurance. It's just too expensive. Nevertheless, most of the California companies are going broke. And no others are going to underwrite earthquake insurance in the future."

Emma jumped in before Paul could respond. "The Earth Rights Party would be in favor of the buffer zone, with the possibility of turning the coastal section of it into a national park with educational facilities on earthquakes and geology, a wildlife preserve, and own-risk use."

Her words stopped the discussion like a concrete wall. Rita Sanchez tsked and quickly cleared her throat.

Erskine Brooks blinked and stared. In a minute, he said, "With all due respect, Miss Light in the Lodge, can you imagine the uproar if you tried to do something like that on the East Coast?" He waited a second to let that sink in. "You have no idea how determined the survivors are to build their lives right where they were before. Broken as the land is, it belongs to them. I can envision a zone in which the own-risk factor might be required, or some more creative insurance program. But there's no way the people are going to give up the coast. Nor will those who are temporarily sheltering the homeless sit still for the urbanization of the interior, even if we could develop it. Do you realize how much of the produce you put on your table comes from those valleys?"

Paul gave Emma a look that he hoped said, "Please," and returned to Brooks. "So you would not distribute disaster aid on the condition of relocation?"

"Where on earth would you relocate them?" asked Rita. "Can you think of a state willing to accept a couple of million Californians?"

Paul suppressed his annoyance with her manner. "Not one, but perhaps several, where the economy is depressed. What about the high-tech companies that were damaged? Could they be convinced to relocate? Most states are delighted to receive clean industries."

"Not if they include the entire work force, they're not. They only want new jobs," snapped Rita.

"So your advice is to release money and allow the reconstruction of California to go uncontrolled?"

"We just can't do that," said Emma. "You and I saw the wounded and the homeless."

Paul turned to Howards and snatched the conversation back before she could continue. "What do you think, Mr. Howards?"

"I don't know, sir, but maybe it would be possible to release disaster aid to the people now on the one condition that it not be used in the quake zone until the prognosis is clearer. By that time, I think a lot would have relocated on their own. Of course, that still leaves the problem of what to do with the coastline." He glanced at Erskine Brooks and blushed.

"Are you in touch with the governor's office, Mr. Brooks?" asked Paul.

"Often."

"How is the state government leaning in this?"

"It's wrestling with the same dilemma. I don't think I've heard anything like Howards' proposal, though." He regarded Brent with a more neutral expression, but there was a slyness in it, as well.

"Would you say it was appropriate to try to encourage the state government on one side or the other?"

Rita snorted. "The federal government's influence is already built in, in the form of disaster aid."

Paul sat back, disappointed, and stared at the map. Nothing was going to be settled at this meeting. He turned to his Chief of Staff. "Ed, see if you can clear Friday's schedule and I'll fly out to survey the damage myself."

"I'll just check with Lee-Anna." Ed left the room briefly and returned with the word that Lee-Anna could juggle his appointments. The meeting broke up by four.

Rita, Ed, Nguyen, and Erskine left immediately, but Emma stopped Brent Howards to express her sympathy. When Paul asked him to join them the next evening for dinner, he accepted, flushing with wide-eyed gratitude.

Perhaps he could be a friend, thought Paul. He hadn't had a real friend since high school.

Now if only he knew a way to get a muzzle on Emma without hurting her feelings or squelching her best ideas.

CHAPTER FORTY THREE

Paul read through pending legislation, looking up occasionally to revel in the wonder of Emma's presence on the sofa opposite him, engrossed in the bills. At six-thirty, when his eyes went bleary, he got up, stretched, and groaned. "I can't read another word. Who on earth do you suppose formulates this stuff?"

Emma sniffed and threw her copy on the table. "Someone with an M.A. in legalese and a Ph.D. in obfuscation."

Paul laughed. "I desperately need some exercise. Join me for a walk before dinner?"

"Sure, thanks."

They put on their coats and stepped out onto the south lawn with their collars turned up against the damp, bitter air. The frosted grass crackled under their feet.

Behind them a thickly bundled gray-suit spoke into a walkie-talkie, and within a few seconds several more appeared in their gray parkas and imposed themselves discreetly between Paul and Emma and the distant fence.

The gawky Shirl loped out from the Colonnade with them, dressed in regulation gray, her hair red as a bull's eye. With her long arms angled out, fingers splayed, she backed up to Emma, invading her personal space.

"Howdy, Mr. President," she twanged, barely turning her head in his direction. "Ms. Light in the Lodge, Ahm Shirl, yore personal bodyguard. You don' need to be 'fraid of one single thang."

Emma backed away and stared up at her huge red dot of a hair-target. "Well, I'm just glad you're so much taller than I. You think you could stop the bullets just as well from a little farther away?"

Shirl's head snapped from left to right and back, casing the lawn. "Yore the boss, ma'am," she allowed in a voice heavy with reluctance. "You tell me when it's far enough, okay?" She took a step, stopped, and looked back.

"A couple of yards will be fine," said Emma. She gave Paul a mock glare and added under her breath, "I may have to impeach you myself for this."

When Shirl was suitably placed, Emma said, "Did you catch Jaubert's item in the parks bill?"

"The one freeing aquifers for private drilling?"

"Uh-huh. Pretty sneaky, to slip a thing like that in a parks funding bill, don't you think?"

Paul shoved his hands deeper into his pockets and hunched his shoulders against the cold. "Yeah. 'Course, being from Louisiana, too, I know his ties to the companies trying to move into water drilling now that the oil reserves are dwindling. I suspect he needs them for campaign funding."

"No doubt, but the subject is much more important than that."

"Of course. Even I know water is going to be *the* crucial issue for the rest of this century, probably the millennium."

"Paul, I did a lot of water rights research on the reservation, so I know a little about this. The most important thing about aquifers is that it takes thousands of years for them to regenerate."

Paul stopped dead, completely unaware of the cold now.

The gray suits stopped and faced the fence. Shirl's arms twitched.

He stared down at her. "Then this isn't a political issue at all. It's a survival issue. You're sure? When they're empty, they're gone for good?"

"For all practical and modern purposes, yes. And they're the earth's last source of clean, drinkable water. They overlap state and national boundaries. If I remember the maps, the aquifer he wants extends far into southern California, so if a company drills in Nevada, it might well be draining water from under the Imperial Valley. Or to give you a more global example, the only large aquifer in Israel is half under the Gaza strip. And letting water rights fall into private hands means it can simply be sold to the highest bidder."

"With Jaubert's friends angling for a monopoly." He took her arm and walked on. "Aren't there any laws already in place to control the aquifers?"

"Some. The problem is that each state has a different set of regulations, as well as each country."

"Okay, not only do I nix Jaubert's bill; we're not going to let this rest. We'll get information and send a bill to Congress. We'll ask for a uniform code and rigorous water conservation."

"Great idea. I should have thought to put that in the party platform."

"Too bad about the parks funding. I liked the rest of the bill. They'll just have to resubmit it minus the riders. After I finished the parks bill, I went back over the others a lot more carefully. I'll have to ask Ed what the procedure is for returning something and telling them to redo it without all the garbage. Do I just mark up the copy I have or is there some form with paragraph and subsection numbers on it that I fill out? And who do I send it to? Through the mail or by courier, or do I jog over there with it?"

Emma laughed, letting out breath fog that glowed against the lights of the House. "Ed probably just spirits it off to the right place. Are you going to sign all the others?"

"Most. I need to get more information on the welfare bill first. I thought they just overhauled the welfare system. How did you feel about that one, by the way?"

"I'd like to see it require classes in birth control and parenting for mothers and fathers of children on welfare, and maybe zero or reduced aid payments for the second child born into welfare. I don't want to preach, but I can tell you how I feel about welfare in general, if you're interested."

"You know I am."

"It saps the spirit out of you. I've seen enough of it to know. A pretty large percentage of the Indian population is on welfare."

"Is that really welfare? I thought the tribes had some special claims on financial support."

"Both, really. Way back then, when the government obligated itself to take care of us 'as long as the grass grows,' tribes all over the plains believed that meant space to hunt, a protected supply of buffalo, opportunities to trade—basically, life as it had always been, only maybe more confined."

Paul shuddered. "Not exactly what it meant to the white man, was it?"

Emma laughed harshly. "To him it meant a dump for second rate goods, surplus food, cast-off clothing. These days it means welfare and the worst kind of degradation: food stamps, dependence, lousy housing on land where no sane person would choose to live, depression...well, you saw my folks. They look pretty typical of our tribe, if you subtract the fine clothes for the inauguration." As she said that, she pulled her coat closer around her.

Paul looked down at her but saw the face of her father, a face in which the light of the human spirit had long since dimmed. He put his hand on her cheek and looked around, half expecting a flashbulb to blind him from the nearest bush. "I don't want to interrupt you," he said, "but you're freezing. And I am, too. Let's go on to dinner and continue this over a hot cup of coffee."

"I'm for that. God, this damp air goes right through you, doesn't it?"

"I've got icicles in my bone marrow."

They carried their coffee to the cheerful yellow of the East Sitting Hall and settled in two of the antique chairs in front of the fireplace.

Emma took off her shoes and held her feet toward the flames.

Paul watched the small, vulnerable action and wondered which would get him thrown out of the White House first—her radical ideas or his love for her. "You know, of course, what kind of reaction we'd get if we proposed your welfare ideas to Congress."

"We'd be labeled as child-haters by some, but if there's a howl of protest, they can always try for that no-confidence vote."

"You want to be president?"

She turned from her enjoyment of the fire and grinned. "Ha. They wouldn't leave me in office three days. They'd find something."

"You really think I should send the bill back with those proposals in it?"

"I don't know. Do you believe in them?"

"What if we expanded the job training program and raised the support for the first child so that it's less likely to grow up in poverty, but cut off payments for further babies born into welfare?"

Emma cocked her head and thought about it. "You know, I just grasped the concept of 'tempered steel.' That's a great idea. Maybe if a child is the product of rape there ought to be an exception."

"Okay. I bet it'd save the taxpayer a bundle in the long run. Who do you suppose could give us the statistics and dollar figures on that?"

"Ed. He knows everything."

"Right." Paul smiled at her. "Could we talk about something else? My brain is fried."

"Gladly!"

Paul got up, set his empty cup on the sideboard, and sat down on the floor in front of her. Tentatively, he took her foot and started rubbing to warm it. When she didn't jerk it away, he dared to rub right up to her ankle. "Do you remember not long after we started out for California you asked me what it was like growing up in New Orleans?"

Emma smiled and nodded.

"At that very moment I had just discarded the idea of asking what it was like growing up on the reservation. I thought you might resent it."

"I might have, at the time."

Her intense eyes warmed him where the coffee hadn't reached.

Paul tried to douse the spark of hope that shot through him, but her eyes said she cared, whether her mouth said so or not. She'd hugged him before the press conference. It wasn't Modesto, but... He kept talking to drown the ache in his body to be one with her again. "And now?"

"I'll be glad to tell you anything you want to know."

"So what was it like? You lived in a trailer park?"

Emma laughed harshly. "I don't think you'd call it a park. A trailer, yes, squatting with a few others in the broken, rolling grasslands. My grandmother's trailer, mostly, which was even smaller than my parents'. I slept on a sofa so short my head hit one arm rest and my feet the other." She grinned. "I think that's why I never got any taller. Wind howling around the corners night and day, nearly tearing the door out of your hands every time you opened it.

"The wind spooked the secret service men who came out after the Supreme Court decision, by the way. After a while they just drove down from Gillette, checked on my continued existence, and sat in their cars outside my office. Till it started snowing. Then they came in and took up the chairs in my little waiting room."

"Why didn't they stay on the reservation?"

Emma snorted out her bitter laugh again. "I guess you think there's a nice Best Western right across the street or something. There's nothing there, Paul. Not one thing that's pleasant or comfortable or fine. There's only the bleak, littered land and the howling air." She looked down and bit her lip. "That's one of the reasons I didn't want you to drive me back after the accident. I didn't want you to see where I lived."

"Emma, I..." He rose and knelt at the side of her chair.

"I know, Paul." She took his hand, smiled weakly into his eyes for a moment, and looked around the cheerful, elegant sitting hall. "Would you sit in this chair with me? Maybe feeling you next to me can get my mind off this fancy room where I don't belong."

They stood, and Paul held her close, lowered his head to her ear, and whispered, "I love you, Emma."

Emma sobbed and tightened her arms. He lifted her face and kissed her, trying to erase her memories of poverty and hopelessness. He picked her up and settled in the chair with her curled in his lap. He stroked her hair, kissed the top of her head, kissed her lips again.

She melted into him for a moment but stiffened and drew away. "I'm sorry, Paul," she whispered. "We can't...I didn't mean..."

He kissed her again and put a finger over her lips. "You care, too, Emma. You don't say so, but I know. And don't apologize for your fear. I understand," he said, raising her tear-channeled face. He drew a difficult breath to cool his passion. He had to get his mind off her body. "Tell me more, please, I want to know everything about you. Your mother mentioned 'commodities.' What does that mean?"

"Part of the 'taking care.' Commodities are surplus goods distributed once a month on a reservation: huge bricks of cheese, canned meat—I wish I had a dollar for every can of Spam I've eaten—canned fruit juices, dried beans, lentils, raisins, prunes..." She laughed. "Oh, God, the prunes. When I was about nine, the October commodity was prunes. Earl and I went trick-or-treating with a couple of other kids, and when we got back to his trailer and looked in our pillow cases, all we'd gotten was prunes. Not one other thing." She laughed again, and Paul laughed with her, but when she continued, there was grief in her voice. "Some of them were wrapped in waxed paper tied with orange ribbon, most were just loose against the cloth, and the only other thing in there was lint.

"We were sitting cross-legged in a circle. We just looked at each other. No one said a word. We got up and left. I dumped mine out somewhere between Earl's trailer and my grand-mother's, and the rest of the way I worried about whether the prunes had left brown stains on the cloth." She breathed out suddenly. "I never realized before how much that hurt."

Paul wiped two tears from her cheeks. "Did the people actu-ally eat all that stuff?"

"A lot of it. I doubt any family ever finished those huge old cheese bricks before they bled their fat and dried up, though." She puffed out a small laugh. "Not to mention the flour. Every person is entitled to ten pounds of flour per month. So a family of five gets fifty pounds."

Paul's eyes popped wide. "What on earth can you do with six hundred pounds of flour in a year?"

"I know what my father did with it. He'd hitch-hike up to the poorer section of Gillette and sell it. A lot of the drinkers did. He and my mother used to fight over it because he always drank the money up before he got home."

"Were holidays always like that Hallowe'en?"

"Christmases were worse. Our leaders tried to emphasize the Indian ways then, criticize the glittery commercialism that was all over TV, but that didn't help a child who desperately wanted a bike or a doll."

"So you were torn between two cultures."

"I don't think there are many Indians who aren't in a permanent state of identity crisis. We want to hold on to the old values of simplicity and respect for earth and elders while enjoying the comforts and freedom of the modern age. The dilemma hits most of us when we reach puberty and try to be our own persons. We don't know who we are when our old world has been trampled to death and the new one rejects us."

"God, Emma, I wish I could say something to help you. I've encountered pain this raw before, but never in an entire people. Tell me what I can do."

She looked in his eyes now, and it was a minute before she said, "Just be my kind heart in a white world."

"Always."

Her tears welled again. "I don't believe in always."

Paul kissed her on the forehead. "When I look at you, I know there is always."

CHAPTER FORTY FOUR

Paul waited in the Green Room for Brent Howards and Emma to arrive. He tried writing a note to Danny, but his mind returned to the young, unhappy representative. Obviously gay, Brent reminded him of the young people he'd counseled from the confessional without an inkling of their real plight. They'd been shredded by guilt over their sexuality but unable to change it.

Now, from Emma, whom he could no more stop loving than he could will his heart to stop beating, he'd learned so much about being human. If he could befriend this young man, it wouldn't help any of the others, but...

He rubbed his thumb over the burn scar on his hand. It reminded him of his failure as a priest more than of the vicious boy who'd put it there. Paul sighed. All he could do was balance his mistakes with what good he could do in this House.

Rutherford announced Brent, and Emma trailed him by a few steps.

After greeting them, he waved his hand to indicate the Green Room. "I decided to welcome you in here. It's less intimidating than other rooms in the House."

Brent looked around uncomfortably, as if hoping for other guests. "It's very kind of you to have me, Mr. President."

"Not at all. It's my pleasure."

"Our pleasure," added Emma. "Paul, why don't we take him on 'the tour'?"

They showed him the House and ended in the President's dining room, where Paul had ordered a simple buffet.

"This is beautiful, Mr. President," said Brent, staring around at the glowing candles and silverware. "It looks like fireflies in a blue grotto."

Emma drew in a sharp breath. "What a beautiful description, Brent. I bet you write poetry, don't you?"

Brent flushed but didn't answer. When they'd all served themselves salad, he sat on the very edge of his chair and glanced toward the door.

Paul poured iced tea into Brent's glass.

"Thank you, Mr. President."

Paul leaned toward him. "I'd like it a lot better if you'd call me Paul."

Brent stopped with his napkin in mid-air. "Oh, sir, I don't think I..."

"You'd be doing me a favor. You have no idea how isolating this job is."

"Well, if I can help, sir..."

"Not 'sir,' just Paul."

Brent hunched his slender frame a little more. "Okay."

"And I'm Emma."

"Yes, ma'am, uh, Emma."

All three poked at their salads while a strained moment passed.

Paul searched in vain for a conversation starter.

Emma stepped into the gaping silence. "I think I remember a Brent Howards on the list of new Earth Rights members at the convention last summer. Was that you?"

"Actually, I was at the convention," said Brent, "but I'm sure you wouldn't remember me. I didn't talk to other people much."

"Why did you join the Earth Rights Party?" asked Paul.

"I really believe in what it's trying to do." Brent turned red and lowered his head. In a minute, still staring into his lap, he took a deep, ragged breath. "I know you think I belong in the Gay Rights Party, but there's still something in me that doesn't want to...come out. It would kill my folks."

The ravaged admission struck Paul in the stomach. He put a hand on Brent's arm and said gently, "Look around you, Brent. We have sitting at a table in the White House: an Indian, and ex-priest, and a homosexual. Each of us is...I don't know, an oddball in a world that would just as soon not have to deal with us."

Emma reached out, though the table was too wide for her to touch him. "You're among friends here."

Brent glanced at Emma, still apprehensive.

Paul felt the entire tangle of the young man's guilt and need, love and shame. He softened his eyes into what he hoped was an expression of complete acceptance. "Look at me, Brent."

Brent looked and shifted his eyes back to the table. He shoved a small circle of ripe olive around on his salad plate and left it in the dark blue rim. "I'm an ex-Catholic, too. I used to confess my attraction to other men, and the priests always told me it was a sin."

"I'm sorry to say I told enough young people the same thing," said Paul. "At the time I even believed it. Now, I simply see human beings trying to cope with a part of their humanity they didn't ask for." He smiled at Emma. "I've learned it's not possible to shut down love for another person on command, and certainly not on someone else's command."

Brent looked at him now, for a long time. He took a deep breath that seemed to lighten his burden of fear and self-doubt. "Thank you." He straightened his shoulders and changed the subject. "I really liked what you said at the first press conference, Mr...Paul. And the simple inauguration. It was a lot more appropriate than all the hoop-la they usually have. And you too, Emma, and I liked what you said at the convention, and I was really upset after the quake when you were missing. I didn't have any idea I'd ever be here talking to you. This is so amazing, isn't it?"

Emma and Paul looked at each other and laughed aloud.

"*Amazing* is a skinny little word for it," said Paul. "But tell us how you came to be elected."

Brent speared a slice of tomato and a spinach leaf. "My partner nominated me and we had a good laugh about it afterwards. When the election came, I was with my family because my mother had just been diagnosed with cancer. I didn't even think about going back to San Francisco before the election. I never expected to be elected, anyway. After the Supreme Court decision I called the governor and asked what I should do. He was amazed. No one but local party members had ever heard of me, but since I was the only survivor, he said I should get on to Washington. They were too busy with the earthquake to worry about a representative for a city that hardly even existed anymore." Brent flushed. "Oh, I'm sorry, I'm just going on and on. I haven't had anyone to talk to for months..."

Paul smiled. "It's okay, Brent. It's why you're here."

"You had a bookstore in San Francisco?" asked Emma.

"A combination bookstore and coffee shop. With my partner. It was really nice. You could sit in the window of the shop, read the paper or a book, or just look out at the boats on the bay. We both love to read." His voice faltered. "I don't know what happened to him. Whether he was at home or the shop. I just keep seeing him crushed under stone. We had a sweet Chinese girl working for us, too. I don't know what happened to her. And all the books." He bit his lip. "I'm sorry to burden you with this. I couldn't say much about it at home because my folks didn't know. I don't have any friends here. So I've kept every bit of this to myself."

Paul shoved his salad plate aside and searched for a less painful subject. "Brent, how do you think most people feel about the rebuilding of California?"

Brent shook his head. "Personally, I could never live there again. You could rebuild San Francisco with every Victorian curlicue in place, and every cable of the Golden Gate, and I couldn't go back. In spite of what Mr. Brooks says, I know there are a lot of people who feel the same way, and a lot who are just too scared."

As they got up to help themselves to braised beef in wine sauce, Paul asked, "Would you be willing to serve with Mr. Brooks as a liaison from the White House?"

Brent blinked in surprise, spooning fresh green beans onto his plate. "I don't think he'd want me, Paul, but if you ask me to, I'll do it."

"I'm sorry to ask you to go back, but I need your voice in the discussions. Hear the survivors out, and meet with insurance companies, builders, and the state government to work out a plan for helping people get back on their feet while encouraging them to move away from the fault line."

"You'd trust me with a thing like that? I don't have any experience."

"No, but you have their interests in your heart, Brent. Argue the hurting side for them. I think Erskine Brooks can handle the practical side."

Brent swallowed hard with nothing in his mouth. "Thank you, Paul."

Paul and Emma walked Brent down to the Grand Entrance and watched him drive off in his Honda.

From a van outside the gate, a video camera recorded his exit and then focused on Paul's smile as he turned to Emma.

Emma's limousine pulled up and Shirl Wainwright unfolded from it like a skeleton on steroids. She opened the door for Emma.

Emma smiled and waved her back. "I'm going to stay a little while longer."

"Yes, ma'am," twanged Shirl with a knowing grin.

"You think Shirl's discreet?" whispered Paul, taking Emma's arm as they went back up the steps.

Emma glanced back and smiled. "I sure hope so. Whatever Shirl is, she's it to the core and will be it till the buffalo roam again."

Paul laughed. "You were wonderful with Brent, by the way. Did you notice his face when he left?"

"He looked different because you gave him back his sense of purpose," Emma said.

The camera kept rolling until Rutherford closed the door.

CHAPTER FORTY FIVE

I n his Capitol office, Clive Jaubert leaned back in his soft leather chair, feeling smug as a full alligator. He tossed Paul's welfare proposal across the Louisiana cypress desk toward Elijah Jackson, who was just lowering his lanky frame into a straight chair.

"Well, seems as how you were right, 'Lijah," Clive said, tilting his chair back with his hands behind his head and swinging his feet for the exercise his doctor demanded. "They're gonna do themselves in real fast."

The black senator glanced through the highlighted lines and his eyebrows shot up to make room for his bulging eyes. "My God! Zero payments for more than one child born into welfare. Birth control class...for mothers *and* fa..." Elijah stared at the paper for several more seconds, his mind obviously racing.

Jaubert smiled and twisted the LSU class ring around his little finger, wondering vaguely why this comforting old habit had begun to hurt. The smooth metal pulled more and more at his skin these days.

Elijah tossed the papers back across the desk. "Well, I wondered how long it'd take him to commit political suicide. What else has he sent over?"

"The proposal to change election laws so this kind of crisis won't happen again."

Elijah laughed. "That'll get a unanimous vote in both Houses. He'll make history."

"'Course, the wording needs to be changed. Doesn't sound like constitutional language at all." Jaubert's voice rose in annoyance. "He signed everything else but nixed the welfare and the parks bills."

Elijah raised his brows, and a spiteful smile played at the corners of his lips. "So he gave you a double-bladed sword—sliced you off with one edge and himself on the other."

"So much for his savvy as a politician. He actually sent me a personal note saying if I wanted the aquifers privatized, I'd have to pass it through Congress in the normal way, with the usual EPA studies."

Elijah gave him a sarcastic smile. "That'll please your constituents."

"Look, this is an important issue. The aquifer feeding Las Vegas is giving inconsistent performance, which means it's emptying fast. It's a relatively small aquifer, but the whole state of Nevada is undercut by a loose network known as the Basin and Something-or-other Aquifer. They want to tap into it in hundreds of places and run pipelines to Vegas and any place else that wants to buy water."

"They? Meaning Sun-Oil? Now why does that name ring such a loud Jaubert bell?"

Jaubert's neck tensed. In his lap, his hands arched with the fingertips together, and he visualized Elijah's black neck between them, but he controlled his face. This sorry Texan swung too many votes to let him lean to the other side. "Look, everybody knows the there's not that much oil left to drill, and the oil men want to move their equipment into water exploration. They've got Las Vegas and Reno and all the other Nevada towns backing them."

Elijah's humor evaporated. "Meaning the gambling interests would own the water rights in practically the whole state of Nevada and could sell it to the highest bidder?"

Jaubert swatted away Jackson's alarm with a wave of the hand. "Of course, like any other commodity. It's the American way. But Greer said he's working on his own bill regarding aquifers. Probably limit them to old fashioned hand-pumps for God's sake."

Jaubert didn't like the ponderous frown he was getting back now. He slapped his knees and his feet hit his deep moss green carpet. "Anyway, we don't need to worry about that. He's so far off on this welfare thing, he'll be out in no time. You ready to get Giordano and Blomster together to call on the good President?"

Elijah shook his head in a tight arc to catch up to the change of subject. "Well, I haven't met him yet, so why not? If I don't, I may never get the chance. Looks like this is going to be the shortest presidency in history."

"What's this, Friday? I heard he was going to California today. I'll set it up for Monday. That vice-president ought to be back from Chile by then, too."

Minutes after Elijah left, Jaubert's secretary ushered Al Skinner into the office. Skinner was grinning.

"You're looking about like I feel this morning," said Jaubert.

"Wait'll you hear what I got. Greer had dinner in the White House with Brent Howards again, you know, that new little congressman from California. This time they were alone."

"So?"

"His girlfriend wasn't even there."

"Howards has a girlfriend in Washington?"

"Howards doesn't have *any* girlfriends. I meant the Indian."

"So you think they had a lover's quarrel?"

"Howards and Greer?"

"Jesus, Al, Greer and the Indian."

"Look, Clive, maybe you haven't met Howards yet. You don't even have to meet him. All you have to do is see him. He's a flaming faggot, for God's sake."

Jaubert jolted forward with his eyes straining their sockets. "Are you telling me Greer's using the White House for tête-à-têtes with a homo? Greer's a queer?"

"No, he's not, but..."

"But it can look... Listen, Al, keep this under your hat and document it in the future. Pictures of Howards at the House, his whole background, whatever else you can get, just in case. But I don't think we're going to need it; the guy's already totaled his administration against the brick wall of welfare."

Jaubert walked Skinner to the door, asked his secretary to hold appointments for five minutes, and stood smiling blindly at the Washington Monument. On the steps of the Capitol just below his office he saw his own inauguration, far less funereal than the recent one. This was much easier than he'd calculated. Wise old bird after all, Elijah Jackson.

CHAPTER FORTY SIX

Paul shook Clive Jaubert's hand and then Elijah Jackson's, Joe Giordano's, and Axel Blomster's as Jaubert introduced them. Everyone greeted Emma and Ed Petersen, and they settled themselves around the coffee table in the Oval Office.

"We'll get right to the point, Mr. President," said Jaubert with only a hint of sarcasm on the last word.

Paul's eyes swept over them all and stopped for a second on Elijah, whose face radiated the dignity that Jaubert's lacked. "May I say first that I'm very glad to meet you all, especially you, Mr. Jaubert, being from the same home state. I already knew a lot about you."

Jaubert gave him a feral stare and twisted his ring. "To start with, it's this welfare bill."

"Aha, well, Ms. Light in the Lodge and I figured that'd get a rise out of somebody. Ed, did you bring copies of the figures your people worked up?"

"Got them right here," said Ed, handing them around the table.

"All right," said Paul, "our figures show that even if we raise the welfare payments for the first child so that it needn't grow up in poverty..."

"What?" cried Elijah. "You didn't tell me about that part of the bill, Clive."

Clive shrugged. "You got your own copy of it."

"You're right, and I was certainly remiss in assuming the parts you marked were the only salient changes in it. I beg your pardon for the interruption, Mr. President."

"No matter. Now, here's our thinking on this. If we begin educating people to their responsibilities, implement the classes within the next year, and in three years stop aid payments to dependent children with the second child, we'll save the taxpayers..." Paul flipped to the last page of his report, "about eight hundred million dollars a year within a decade."

Emma, whose eyes were darkened with exhaustion, leaned forward, and said, "We'll alleviate poverty, reduce crime rates and population, and give poor children a brighter future than they've ever had. Please, don't dismiss this until you've asked yourself whether it's more humane than the welfare we're currently paying."

"Humane?" shrieked Jaubert. "You call this humane? It's nothing but government regulation of the family. It's a pie-in-the-sky solution to a problem that's been around since...since there *was* a sky. Just what do you intend to do with the children who are born by accident into poor families?"

"First of all," said Paul, "the birth control classes will go a long way toward eliminating unwanted children. And we'll encourage welfare mothers who have second and third children to give them up for adoption. Allow visitation rights if need be, but people must be responsible for the lives they bring into the world."

"This bill is against the family," shouted Jaubert, "it's against the church, it's against God and...and..."

"Re-election?" asked Emma. She sucked in a breath and squinted at Paul with an "oops-I-did-it-again" look.

Jaubert sputtered and flecks of foam appeared at the corners of his mouth. Elijah laughed aloud. Ed bit his lips to keep from following suit. Paul tried to frown at Emma but couldn't help smiling.

"I guarantee you this bill isn't going anywhere in *my* Congress," Jaubert said, slapping his briefcase shut.

"*Your* congress?" asked Paul, stunned.

Jaubert grabbed his belongings and stalked off. "You're a hell of a lot dumber that I thought, you and your...sq..." he shouted, slamming the door behind him.

For a moment there was shocked silence, finally broken by Elijah. "Mr. President, I do apologize for my colleague. I won't make any excuses for that performance. Let me just say, I can't vote for this bill, but I believe you're approaching your presidency with more thought than I would've expected under the circumstances. We came here today as a bi-partisan effort to get you to resign. And actually, for your own sake," he nodded in the direction Jaubert had gone, "I'd still advise you to do that before this gets heated up."

Paul swallowed to steady his voice. "I'm sure you know I agreed to resign when the people direct you to pass a vote of no-confidence. I will do that, but they should have a chance to hear about my very first program."

Elijah laughed. "Oh, don't worry about that. Jaubert's out there on his cell phone, calling for a press conference within the next ten seconds. I can't speak for Joe or Axel, but I personally can't wait to see what happens next."

"I can't support it either, Mr. President," boomed Axel, "though I come from a largely Protestant state with a hard-working middle class and though I personally believe in putting people back to work and encouraging responsibility. It's just too radical. You won't get much support from the Deep South, either, nor from largely Catholic states for obvious reasons."

"Thank you, Mr. Blomster. And you, Mr. Giordano? New Jersey, isn't it? Will your people go for it?"

Giordano glanced at the door that still seemed to vibrate with Jaubert's anger. "About half, maybe. I can't say whether I'll vote for it or not."

When the three congressmen had left, Ed began gathering the papers he'd distributed earlier.

"That didn't go over well, did it, Ed?" asked Paul.

Ed shrugged. "It sure polarized Jaubert."

Emma clasped her hands at her waist. "Paul, it was my fault. I apologize for that bit about re-election. It just popped out before I knew it was coming."

Paul hesitated, looking for words to caution her about her directness without hurting her feelings.

She raised her hands, palms out. "I know. It wasn't my place to say anything at all. I promise I'll lash my tongue to my teeth."

Paul grinned. "Actually, I think he would have been our enemy no matter what."

Ed looked up at him. "If I may be so bold, sir, Clive Jaubert *is* a formidable enemy. He has more power than anyone in Washington, even you, given your circumstances, and he can make or break you. If you have any thought of re-election in four years..."

"I haven't, but I'm appalled by the confidence he has in his control over Congress."

Ed looked him straight in the eye. "It's not misplaced, and he has his eyes on the Oval Office. He would've gotten the nomination if Carrington hadn't upstaged him in the New Hampshire primary. They say when the Court made you president, Jaubert needed a rabies shot."

"Well, the thought of his presidency would almost be enough to make me run again. Emma, you definitely hit him where he lives. Maybe he'll support me just to keep you out of office."

Ed laughed. "Never. You can be sure, if he manages to oust you, he'll already have a plan in place for her. I have to tell you, sir, I don't think Jaubert is above using anything he can get his hands on. Or rather someone else's hands. *His* are always white as fresh snow."

"Well, that's a game he can just play by himself. May I ask you something, Ed?" asked Paul. "How do you feel about this proposal? Would you vote for it?"

"Actually, I would, sir,"

Paul grinned at him. "Call your congressman, would you?"

Ed smiled back. "If you really want this bill, I'd advise you to get to the press as soon as possible and lay your reasoning out clearly so people who support it can let their congressmen know."

Paul barely kept himself from groaning. "God, I hate getting in front of those cameras. Still, tell Caitlin to call a press conference."

Ed slipped out.

Paul turned to Emma. "You look exhausted. You only got back a couple of hours ago. How was it in Chile?" he asked.

"Interesting. Would you believe Shirl speaks fluent Spanish in the most atrocious twang? Actually, I'm getting to where I kind of like her. She'd leap into the jaws of a shark for me. And it's nice to have another woman along on a state trip." Emma shook her head. "I guess we're not the only country where affairs of state are largely a matter of staging—where to stand, when to rise. But even with all the theatrics, the funeral was sparsely attended, and very few people turned out to see the procession."

"Really? For a dead president?"

"It made me wonder what would happen if either of us died."

Paul laughed. "They'd dispense with the procession and stick us in a tomb for unknown administrations. Listen, why don't you go home and get some rest?"

"I'm still vibrating from the long plane ride, but I must look more tired than I feel. It'll catch up with me in a couple of hours. I didn't get to see you after the tour of the earthquake area. What was that like?"

Paul steered her to one of the sofas. "Emma, it was awful, much worse that I imagined. I know it's all been in the news constantly since November, but you have to see it for yourself to have any idea of the devastation. We flew from about eighty miles north of San Francisco all the way to the Mexican border. San Francisco is very nearly a ghost town, even though most of the buildings are still standing, waiting to be inspected."

"That's so sad, Paul. Our finest city."

"Coit Tower is a pile of rubble. There are huge gaps in the Golden Gate and the Bay Bridges. Houses shattered. At the bottom of hills huge piles of vehicles; a few had exploded and set nearby buildings on fire." Paul swallowed with difficulty. "It's like looking down on the framework of people's lives, only the people are gone, probably dead.

"Bridges and roads for twenty miles on either side of the fault line will have to be inspected thoroughly. If you and I had been twenty miles closer to the Fault, we'd have been killed.

"By forty miles south of San Francisco, the damage diminished to almost nothing and then picked up again in various places all along the Fault. Here and there, even months after the quake, I could see people crawling over the rubble, or standing and scratching their heads as if they couldn't find their addresses, or trying to lift walls or roofs. And in almost every spot flat enough for a helicopter, there were still crews in contamination gear looking for the dead."

"Did you make up your mind about the safety zone yet?"

"I still want to talk to Howards and Brooks, but separately. They're getting back this afternoon. Do you think you could get a rest and join Brent and me for supper? He's turning into a real friend, and he seems a little less lost."

Emma put her hand up and stroked his face. "Paul, I..."

"You don't think I should befriend him?"

"It's not that. I...I just hope there aren't too many stray dogs in Washington." She bit her lips and the words came haltingly. "I'm learning so much from you, Paul. I've been scrapping with the world all my life. I've never been able to reach out to another person because I always expected a slap in the face. Knowing you has put a...I don't know, a kind of warmth in me."

Paul took her hand and kissed the fingertips. "Thank you for saying that. Emma, I want to make love to you."

Emma's neck tensed and she drew her hand away. "I'm so scared of that, Paul. Anyway, they must've passed a law against making love in the Oval Office after the Clinton debacle."

Paul's eyes traced the hallowed curves of his office. "Whether they did or not, I guess it just wouldn't be politic. Emma, seriously, I don't want to push you, but trust me—I'll love you with my last breath."

She gazed into this eyes a long time and then leaned her forehead against his chest. "I know you love me. What the future holds is another matter, and there's no way our two lives can ever mesh. But for our four years—or four days..." She nodded her head against his chest. "You have a bed in that mansion of yours?"

Heated anticipation shot right through him. "A huge, lonely one."

"Do you have an after-dinner opening?"

"What's this, Monday? I'll ask Lee-Anna what my bed schedule looks like."

CHAPTER FORTY SEVEN

P aul laid aside the book he was reading in bed and reached for his private telephone. He dialed Danny's number for the tenth time in three days. This time he got a tinny female voice that told him the number had been disconnected. He stared at the receiver, tried information and was told the new number was unlisted. He turned the phone off and it rang in his hand.

"Hey, li'l brother," boomed Danny's voice above the clatter and hum of a restaurant.

Paul jerked himself upright. "Danny, I've been trying to get you for days. What's with the unlisted number? Is that guy still harassing you?"

"Floyd? No, not now. But le's talk about that later. How's it going, Mr. Pres? Tell me what they don't say on TV every day. Why's Jaubert so hot to wreck you? He always looks like he's gonna die o' aplexy—apoplexy—right in front of the camera."

Paul's whole body pumped acid anger at the slur of Danny's speech. He slammed his fist into the mattress and cursed its softness. "Dammit, Danny, you've been drinking."

"Hey, jus' a couple. I'm drinkin' a strong cup of coffee right now. See?" He slurped. "Damn. Hot. Listen, I'm fine. Just need a minute to think straight. Talk 'bout you first, then I'll tell you wha's goin' on. And then you can scream at me. Promise." He slurped again.

Paul strangled the receiver, but he knew he wasn't going to get anything till Danny was ready. He spoke quickly. "I'm getting mixed reviews on the welfare proposal. All radical. They light up the whole congressional e-mail with demands for sainthood or crucifixion."

"They gonna impeach you?"

Paul shrugged. "Ed Petersen says Jaubert doesn't dare call the no-confidence vote at this point for fear of pushing the fence-sitters over to my side. Now tell me..."

Danny interrupted, pronouncing his words carefully. "So what else is going on in your neck of the jungle? Come on, I haven' talked to you in a long time. How's Emma?"

"Fine, now..."

"There's a lot of talk about how much time she spen's at the Whi' House."

"I'm going to ignore rumors. Come on, Danny, tell me what's going on."

Danny slurped. "You hear the coffee? They say you've been blowing the hell out of protocol. Wanting to fly commercial jets. No more Air Force One. Recycling water in the fountains. Turning off lights on the White House grounds."

Paul ground his teeth. "My travel staff nearly had a fit over the commercial jets, and the press corps, too. You have no idea how many media people travel on Air Force One. Either we start charging for the flights, or we all fly commercial, at least for domestic flights. Emma and I promised, after all, that the best examples would come from us. We can't back down. What do you think?"

"Me? I'm not the president."

Paul sighed. "Yeah, well I wouldn't be either, if... Never mind. How's Laurel?"

Danny sounded nearly sober now. "She drove back to New Orleans to sign the divorce papers and bring up the rest of her things. I miss her, Paul. I had no idea how much of my life she'd filled up."

"Do you have any vacation coming up when she gets back? Maybe we could all get together here. We could have evenings together, anyway. I know Emma'd like that, too."

Danny hesitated. "Well, listen, Paul, you might not want to have me around in the future."

"What do you mean?"

"You mentioned Floyd, the guy who wanted me to revive an appeal to the EPA for oil companies to drill into local aquifers. He was in with some shady people who bought up the land above it. They thought they were going to make a killing on selling water all over the southwest."

"I think we put a stop to that, at least for the time being. I vetoed the bill allowing it. And I'm working on a new bill to regulate water."

"I heard that, but don't count on passing it. These are a new bunch, Paul. They're geared to the electronic age and absolutely ruthless. They can access computer files everywhere, police records, credit ratings, military strategies. They're dangerous people. They're hired by the gambling interest and the oil companies, who both need the water for survival."

"How do you know all this?"

"First, they sent Floyd to my office with a demand to go to the governor and use my influence as your brother to get an executive order rescinding the EPA's decision. Floyd begged me and he looked like hell, so I was sure he'd been given some kind of ultimatum. I refused, of course, and I haven't seen him since. I'd be surprised if he's still breathing, Paul."

Paul jumped up, grabbed his robe and struggled into it with his free hand. "Are you telling me you think he's been murdered?"

"I'm just saying there's nothing so low they wouldn't stoop to it and come away unscathed. Yesterday some executive type with the air of Machiavelli came into my office without an appointment. Sent my secretary scurrying with little more than a quiet word. He handed me a copy of my arrest record in Chicago, but it'd been altered to show I'd been convicted of pushing heroin, not that I'd pleaded no contest to minimal possession of pot. This guy, Paul, he hardly said a word. He just laid the papers on my desk and sat there smirking, letting me draw my own conclusions."

"Good God, Danny." Paul was pacing now. He headed for the door, feeling the need for more room, but stopped at the thought of the gray-suits who'd hear the conversation.

"Wait. That's not all. He laid a picture of Laurel on top of it. A full face picture taken the day before she left for New Orleans. And one of both of us when I saw her off. I'm scared for her, Paul. She's so far away, and I can't protect her. If anything happened to Laurel, I think...I don't know what I'd do. I could go to the press with the other story and cancel its effect, the way Emma did with the abortion, but I'm afraid that'd put Laurel in even greater danger."

"Don't do that yet. Let me see if I can get to the bottom of this from here. Do you have any idea who this man was?"

"None. But finding him wouldn't do a thing for us. He's nothing more than a messenger, believe me. Riding up-scale shotgun for powerful people."

"I'm going to get the FBI on it. I'll have them get Laurel and take her to a safe place."

"Thanks, Paul. Be careful who you trust. And don't let them keep any records at all."

"Danny, get out of Denver until I get to the bottom of this."

"Don't worry about me. If things get too hot, I'll vanish for a while."

"No, not 'if things get too hot.' Do it now, please."

"Right, and what'll I live on?"

"You can have my salary. All of it. I hardly get to spend..."

"Not an option. But I'll take care of myself. Promise. So if you don't hear from me, don't worry."

Paul tugged at his hair. "Don't worry? I'm already turning gray. I can't believe you made me blither on about my trivia with this hanging over your head."

"Well, I just figured this would be the whole conversation if I'd mentioned it first. And I really did want to hear about you."

"You're damn right it would have been. Don't ever do anything like this again, you hear me? This line is open to you any time, day or night. I'm leaving instructions that a call from you should interrupt anything I'm doing. Now give me your new number. No, better not, in case this line is tapped."

"I doubt the White House is, but I'll get it to you some other way. Thanks, Paul."

"Danny..."

"Yeah?"

The anger rolled through him again and Paul ground out, "Get...off...the...booze. I'm still holding you to your promise. Remember? The deal was no more drinking till this nightmare is *over.* But if you won't keep your promise to me, think of Laurel."

"I haven't forgotten, brother. And this was my only lapse, I swear. I'm just so worried about Laurel. And I'm way beyond promises now. I know what I have to do, and I'll do it for myself, not for her and not for you. It has to be that way."

"I'm glad you realize that."

"Yeah, well, let me add this: you get Laurel to a safe place and I swear on our mother's good heart I've just had my last drink."

"Consider it done." Paul paused a few seconds. "Danny, I..."

"I know. Me, too."

CHAPTER FORTY EIGHT

Late the next morning Paul stood at the window of the Blue Room, gazing at the Washington Monument with its point hidden in low, dark clouds. He saw it an image of himself, standing pathetically straight with his head stuck into matters too dense to penetrate and too heavy to hold. For a second, he half expected to see the Monument buckle.

Six months ago to the day he'd run from the church and crashed headlong into an institution far more intimidating. He'd wanted a time of peace to figure out how to live and had gotten chaos and Emma. Well, a small part of Emma. But even that small part balanced him, gave him the strength to stand and clear a place for benevolence in a greedy world. He pointed a finger at the Monument. "Buck up," he whispered.

He leaned his head against the window pane. What he wanted to do after a night of sleepless worry was go out, walk among the budding cherry trees, and figure out how to help Danny; but he had at least four more appointments before lunch.

The Vietnamese premier, who'd come to broaden trade relations, had just left, having delivered a lecture on recent Vietnamese history. He'd started with the aggression of the Americans and ended with the cowardice of the Americans. The middle he'd filled with the atrocities of the Americans.

Surrounded by blue opulence, Paul forced himself to rehash the garrulous Mr. Binh's view of America. How much truth was in his opinion? Did America try to drag the rest of the world around by the neck, like some worthless but possibly trainable dog?

Rutherford came in. "Excuse me, sir, Brent Howards is here. Mr. Petersen took the liberty of sending him over because you're about half an hour behind."

"That's fine. Tell me, Rutherford, have you learned a diplomatic way to shut someone up when you can't get a word in edgewise?"

"No, sir, I'm afraid not."

Paul sighed. "If *you* haven't, I guess it can't be done. Well, show Mr. Howards in, please."

When they'd shaken hands, Paul said, "Brent, I need to get out of here. Can we walk a little before it rains?"

Brent grinned. "They let you do that?"

"Well, after a fashion. They'll be discreetly visible."

"Doesn't that make you uncomfortable?"

"Very. I've never gotten over the feeling the person they're guarding is over there somewhere, and *I'm* the intruder. Tell me how things went in California."

Brent followed him out and down the stairs. "It was a mixed bag, sir...Paul. It looks like the legislature might accept the suggestion that disaster money not be used to rebuild within five miles of the fault line until it's been studied. And they're working on a compromise making the zone permanent on both sides, with a further own-risk building zone of ten, but it's getting a lot of resistance from the people. On those sections of the coast not included in the zone, no buildings will be of more than one story. Displaced property owners will be given first option on land that reverted to the state because no heirs could be found, and the state is working with insurance companies on other compensations. It's going to take years, and a lot of people are already unhappy, but I think this is the best the state can do."

Paul held the door for him. "That's a good compromise, Brent. You must have spent hours going back and forth between victims, insurance, and bureaucrats. I'm proud of you."

"Thanks," Brent said as he hesitated at the edge of the lawn, eyeing the gray-suits. "You sure we can step on the grass?"

Paul laughed. "If we get arrested, I'll pardon us both." He steered him toward the fountain. "What are they going to do about San Francisco?"

"I don't know yet. There was talk of rebuilding it exactly the way it was but farther up the coast, and somebody suggested building a scale model as a museum, but the loss seems to be too great for anyone to deal with right now." His voice had sunk to a whisper.

Paul shook his head. "This isn't easy for you to talk about, Brent. It must have been that much more difficult to do. Maybe I shouldn't have sent you." He stopped and put his hand on Brent's arm.

Brent walked on, as if trying to escape the topic. "It's just San Francisco. All those wonderful old buildings, the Tower, the Wharf, the cable cars. The people..."

"I'll take you off the job."

"No, really, Paul, I want to do this." There was still hesitation in his voice.

"Something else is bothering you. What are you holding back?"

Brent looked down at the grass still wet from yesterday's rain. "It's not that important."

"I'd like to know."

"Well, if I can tell you this in confidence..."

Paul laughed aloud with the memory of the thousands of confidential confessions he'd heard. "Is there any other way?"

"It's Erskine Brooks. He suggested my idea to the governor as if it were his. I mean about the disaster money. Which is okay, except that most of the time he treated me like...well, a nobody. I don't know whether he doesn't like gays or whether he just thought I was too young to count. He's probably insulted that you didn't ask *him* to report yet."

"God, you're right. There's probably some unwritten protocol about who gets called first—venerable senators or junior congressmen." He waved absently at the tourists calling to him from outside the fence. A mounted policeman shouted at several who were trying to stick their cameras through the wrought iron fence. "I'm never going to get this politicking straight."

"Well, you're still here, at least. They haven't installed Emma in the White House yet. How's she doing?"

"She'll be glad to know you're back. She's finally got her group together to study alternative economy. They're meeting at the vice president's house. She told me never to call it 'her' house."

"You think they can actually come up with something?"

"I hope so. I ought to send you over there. You have good ideas."

Brent turned to him with the look of an adoring son. "I'll go anywhere you send me, Paul."

A bolt of blinding envy for every man who'd ever had a son struck him, and Paul had to collect himself before he could answer. "Feel like taking on Clive Jaubert?"

Brent stared at him and nearly tripped into the tulip bed around the fountain.

Paul grabbed at his arm as he righted himself.

"Make that almost anywhere," said Brent, dragging his shoe in the grass to remove a clod of mud. "If I came within fifty feet of him, he'd get a lynching going."

"Well, there is something else you can do for me. It doesn't involve Jaubert directly, and I need someone I can trust absolutely. A friend of my brother's may be in some danger over this drilling bill, and I want to protect her. Could I ask you to go to New Orleans and convince her to go to a safe place? I'd ask the FBI, but I've been thinking that over, and I'm afraid of outsiders hacking the records they keep. You wouldn't be able to write anything down or put anything in a computer."

"No problem. Where do you want me to take her? And what if she won't go? Or doesn't trust me?"

"If she doesn't trust you, tell her...the man who wishes he'd done better by her in the church wants to make up for his failings. The question is where to take her."

"I could ask my sister in Detroit to take her in for a little while. She's good, Paul, she's the only one in my family who knows about me and doesn't care."

"No, but thanks for the offer, Brent. We couldn't ask her to take in a perfect stranger, especially when danger might follow. And I don't know how long this is going to drag on. Or whether Laurel has money to live on."

"Maybe she already has a place. Why don't you let me play it by ear when I find her?"

A few lazy drops of rain hit his face and Paul looked up at the heavy clouds. "Bring her here, Brent. It's the safest place I can think of, and we can figure out what to do once she's safe. I shouldn't ask you to do this at all. You must have enough work to do here without adding this to your plate."

"I'll check on things coming up in the next few days so I can be on the floor to vote if need be. Since I don't have any real constituency at the moment, the only other thing I do is answer calls from quake survivors."

"Thanks, Brent. I owe you one. Personally." He put a hand on the young man's shoulder with a fondness he hadn't felt for anyone for years. Was this what it felt like to have a son?

Thunder rolled across the sky from the other side of the Capitol.

Brent glanced down at Paul's hand and his face reddened. "No, you don't. You said this didn't have to do with Jaubert *directly*. You think he's involved some way?"

They headed back through the wet grass, keeping a greater distance than before.

Paul stuck his hand in his pocket. "I don't have any proof, but I'd be surprised if he weren't. I guess you heard he killed the welfare bill."

"Yeah, but only by twenty-eight votes. I was amazed. When you stop to think that basically the whole Congress is your opposition, that was a razor thin margin. The packaging bill looks pretty close. And you did get the election crisis bill passed."

Paul laughed. "Unanimously. Which may just be a reflection of my popularity."

"Oh, come on. It was a necessary bill. And anyway, your approval rating is going up."

Paul sniffed. "The last I heard it was all the way up to 14%. Actually, I think it'd drop if Clive'd just shut up. All that posturing and exhorting the people to demand the no-confidence vote."

"He sure gets people's backs up, doesn't he?"

"Either that or the religious right is swinging back a little toward tolerance."

"That'd be nice."

They reached the House just as the first bolt of lightning flashed through the gloom.

On the street behind them, a photographer with a huge zoom lens glanced toward the policeman on horseback, packed his gear quickly, and hurried away.

CHAPTER FIFTY

P aul and Emma waited under the Colonnade through the last few words of Caitlin's introduction and stepped toward the podium set up in the Rose Garden. Paul glanced up at clouds gathering for storms. The speeches they were about to make would cause a lot more thunder.

He felt Emma's support from beyond the small space between them and wished he could close it forever. She'd changed toward him through the spring and early summer; she gave more of herself now, came to him happily whenever they had a private moment. He knew she cared, but she never said the words he longed to hear.

Behind the media audience, the television cameras glared at him with their little red eyes, just waiting for him to stumble over his words. He forced himself to look in their direction.

"Before Ms. Light in the Lodge speaks," he began, his heart running like a jackhammer, "I'd like to ask the cameramen to pan around the White House lawn."

The reporters squinted at each other, looking for explanation, and then watched the panning of the cameras over the perfect green lawn and the roses in full bloom.

"It's beautiful, isn't it?" he asked. "Maintained by a diligent staff—and a huge amount of water, little of which falls from the sky. Now let us visualize it as it may be by the end of our lifetimes, the grass and roses gone and the entire expanse covered with flagstone because there's no more water to keep it green."

A few reporters and one camera turned back toward the roses.

Paul let that sink in and spoke into the cameras, moving his eyes to each one. "Now, think of your own lawn, gone to dust. That could be the least of your worries. Visualize a world in which bathing means one tub of water shared by the family." Paul paused and scanned the wrinkled brows of the reporters, who clearly wondered where he was going with this. He went back to the cameras and said slowly, "Visualize a world in which you must ration your child's drinking water." He paused again. "Now ask yourself whether you could give up a little of your desire for the lushest of lawns and the most exotic of flowers so that your grandchildren don't inherit the world you imagined.

"Very shortly I will submit to Congress a bill that I hope will slow our progress toward that horror. The bill is designed to protect our last sources of clean water by giving the government control of all aquifers within the fifty states to prevent interstate and international disputes over water rights. It will put a stop to indiscriminate drilling into our aquifers for profit."

Most of the reporters looked bored now. A few were staring back, aghast.

"I see some of you realize the vast implications of this bill. Government regulation or our most basic necessity. I can only compare my submission of this bill to my work as a teacher. I never made a rule for a class until I saw a student or a situation getting out of hand and the rule became necessary. *This* rule is necessary. We know that most aquifers need hundreds or thousands of years to regenerate when they've been emptied. If we don't control them, we'll leave dire need for our grandchildren. And I'm not speaking metaphorically. Two generations, if we continue to use water at the present rate. We must learn to live with the constraints of overpopulation. We cannot allow water to be wasted. For example, if we choose to live in the desert, we cannot try to turn it into an oasis by watering the sand. We must allow it to be desert."

Jules Blanchet was on his feet with the hostile air he'd had since the television interview in Denver. "Mr. President, you're telling us you want the government to take over state water supplies. That's unconstitutional."

No longer cowed by him, Paul said calmly, "Mr. Blanchet, you will wait to be recognized or you'll be removed." He nodded to the gray-suits and a couple of them moved toward Blanchet.

Blanchet sat down, red of face but with the smile of a gambler who knows he's holding the aces.

Paul stared him down and then continued. "The aquifers are a national issue because they overlap our state and national borders." He returned to the cameras. "I know most of us don't trust government any more, and often with good reason, but if you're uncomfortable with the idea of government regulation of water, ask yourself how comfortable you'd be with corporate control of water prices. Perhaps this bill won't make *anyone's* life *easier*, but it is an essential step toward making *future life possible*. So I am now asking for the support of the thinking public. We've established a web-site which outlines the bills and shows a map of our aquifers and our hydrologists' best estimate of the remaining water in them, as well as how long each will need to regenerate. Please visit the site, which will be advertised everywhere in the next few days. Please look at the aquifer in your area and ask yourself where your water will come from when there's none left below you. Let us acknowledge our responsibility to the earth we live on and the generations that follow us. Please, write or phone your representatives in Congress and ask that the bill be passed as soon as possible. Thank you very much for the time it takes to do this, and I'd like to say a special thank you to those who are already doing their part in conserving water.

"Now, ladies and gentlemen of the press, could you please hold your questions? I've asked Ms. Light in the Lodge to give you an update on her committee studying the feasibility of a non-growth based economy." He turned the podium over to Emma.

Emma stepped past him, barely brushing his hand with hers. "Thank you, Mr. President," she said, then turned to face the reporters. She leaned into the podium with one foot on the cross beam at the bottom. "I believe you already have the list of committee members and their areas of expertise. I hope you will publish them with my sincere thanks for their continued efforts to find solutions to a problem of extreme complexity and far-reaching consequences. And I'd like to say a special thank you to Mr. Elijah Jackson, my co-chair on the committee."

Paul watched Jules Blanchet while Emma began. Okay, he was obnoxious, but why so adversarial? Could he be connected somehow with Jaubert? No, he was a reporter, surely just a loathsome but neutral observer.

Emma spoke into the cameras. "Until the mid-twentieth century, we considered our economy healthy if population and industry grew. They made a neat and seemingly harmless parallel. We know now, however, that we *must* reverse the trend of population. We all feel the crunch of over-building; we resent the smell of automobile exhaust in our clogged streets, lament the disappearance of our forests and grasslands, even our deserts. We are heading for a crisis in water and energy supplies that can only be averted by population reduction."

Paul checked the reporters. They gave the impression of one big knitted brow, creased in disbelief.

Emma didn't falter. "The question before the committee is how to reduce the population without destroying our economy and creating vast unemployment. Once the population reaches a sustainable level, the law of supply and demand will be functional again. In the meantime, manufacturers will have to scale back on production for the gradually reduced market. We hope to have recommendations ready by the end of the year. Again, I'd like to thank the members publicly for their hard work and their creative ideas. And thank you, Mr. President."

Before she stepped from the podium two dozen hands were in the air.

Paul recognized a stout woman toward the back.

"Mr. President, all this talk of water conservation—do you seriously believe you can force Americans to conserve enough to make a difference?" she asked against the first roll of distant thunder.

"Can I get you to do it?"

The reporter flushed as every other head in the room turned to her. "Well, yes, but..."

"Thank you, I'll count on that." Paul smiled at her and nodded at another reporter.

Grinning, the White House correspondent from CBA asked, "Miss Light in the Lodge, what areas is your committee studying to bolster the changing economy?"

Emma moved back to the podium and answered without consulting her notes. "Foremost among them is job retraining, new uses of recycled materials, and alternative energy sources. But our own economy is only part of a global problem. We're examining strategies to aid developing nations cope with famine and disease; ways to encourage population control; and education about our place in the world community."

A reporter from the *Wall Street Journal* stood. "How are you going to finance the retraining programs you're talking about?"

Emma shoved her notes aside. "I can't speak for the committee about that yet, but one thing occurs to me personally that I can give you as an example. Every year our government subsidizes tobacco farmers. When cigarette manufacturers were hit by suits demanding compensation for health care to smokers, they expanded their advertising campaigns all over the world to balance the losses at home. Now, I don't know about you, but I do not want my taxes used to export and advertise a known addictive carcinogen. My suggestion in this case would be to use the subsidy to retrain farmers and cigarette makers to produce materials that build healthy bodies, not destroy them."

A short, thoughtful silence passed before the next hand went up, and it was Blanchet's. Paul had no choice but to recognize him.

"Mr. President," Blanchet began, his voice sharp with spite, "our sources have come across a police report from Chicago. It shows that your brother David Anthony Greer was convicted of pushing heroin."

Paul's mouth fell open. How on earth...?

A clamor of voices rose, mixed in timing, but all asking, "Is this true, Mr. President?"

Stifling the desire to set the gray-suits on Blanchet, Paul bent toward the microphone, and spoke deliberately to prevent stammering in anger. "My brother has never been convicted of anything. He was a teenager and did the same kind of experimenting that many teenagers do. He made mistakes. We all make mistakes. He was arrested for possession of marijuana and I believe he pleaded no-contest. You would have to check that with him. I can tell you that my brother is now a respected attorney who works with the EPA and Population Connection."

Blanchet waved a thin document above his head. "So how do you explain this conviction record?"

Danny's words of warning came back. These were a new breed of thugs, and their power had metastasized even to the press. Paul realized there was a connection between Blanchet and the aquifer bill after all. Blanchet could ruin him and everything he was trying to do, could render him helpless if he didn't strike back.

Paul narrowed his eyes and leaned forward. "Mr. Blanchet, I would be as interested to know how it came to be in your possession. The record was apparently altered by people opposed to the aquifer bill. I won't say more about them until I have all the facts and have assured the safety of innocent people who've been dragged into this. But I can assure you that anyone caught using bribery or blackmail to influence government officials will be prosecuted."

Blanchet sat down, but his eyes pinioned Paul in a vindictive glare for the remainder of the press conference.

CHAPTER FIFTY ONE

P aul sat in the East Sitting Hall with half his concentration on the latest report from the FBI on Ex-Oil and the other half on the hall. It'd been a whole week since he'd seen Emma, and he couldn't wait to have her at his side again. When he heard the elevator, he jumped up and met her at the entrance to the Hall.

Emma gave him a brief hug, trudged in, and dropped her purse on a chair. "Ugh," she sighed, "everything they say about D.C. in August is true. What a sticky, smelly heat."

"How's your father, Emma?" Paul asked, noting the dark circles under her eyes.

"Give me the dry heat in Wyom..."

Why was she dodging his question? He laid a hand on her shoulder. "*How's* your *father*, Emma?"

She turned away from him and swallowed hard. "He won't live much longer."

"Oh, Emma, I'm so sorry."

"He's back at home, but the detox didn't do much good. He'll never stop drinking and the whites of his eyes are already yellow."

"His liver."

Emma lowered her head. Her hair slid up her back and sagged into her collar.

Paul lifted her face gently. "Do you know how long he has?"

She moved her head from his hand and pulled her hair forward, where it fell over her breast in random black curves. "I couldn't make myself ask. I know I'll dread the sound of the phone, but I couldn't keep thinking of my father gone by Christmas, or Thanksgiving, or whenever."

"Do you want to go back? I'll manage here."

"No, thanks. It's not just the work here. Pop's scared. If I go back, he'll know he's dying."

"You want some iced tea?" he asked while he sought a less depressing subject for her.

She shook her head.

"So, how are things on the reservation?"

Her shoulders sagged. "Oh, Paul, nothing ever really changes. The tribal council voted down the casino over Earl's bitter objections in favor of raising buffalo for hides and meat. They got the Parks Service to deliver two dozen animals on the first of June, so in February they started building the fence around the land Earl had wanted for the casino. They were paying the workers with money from the one oil well we own. But half the workers drank up their money and didn't show up again." She sat down heavily on the edge of the desk chair. "Those who did set the fence posts too shallow. As the money ran out, they bought fencing that was too weak, and when the buffalos arrived, it didn't take them a month to discover the weak places and disappear. A few of the old cows with calves stayed in the enclosure, and somebody shored up the fence. I think they have about seven animals now."

Paul put his hand on her shoulder.

Emma turned her head away from his hand, stood, and moved toward the door.

"I feel so bad about it," she said with her back to him. "I know the casino would have failed, too, but I feel this is my fault. I was the one who suggested raising animals as a tribal venture, and I think they were influenced by the fact that I was going to be vice president. I should have let them listen to Earl."

Paul hardly heard the last part. What was going on? Why had she changed so much during the week she'd spent at home? She was holding back the way she'd done when he'd first met her. "You did the best you could, Emma. You can't make things that have been wrong for a century right in a year."

"I know. But I wanted this to work, and all it did was assure Earl's influence. He's already after me for some kind of funding to get rid of the animals and build the casino."

"Do you think a shot of cash from a casino might set the tribe off in a better direction?"

Emma sniffed in contempt. "No, I think it'd create another addiction to ravage the tribe." She let out a huge sigh. "I don't want to talk about it anymore. Tell me about Washington."

Paul hesitated, anxious to keep her on the subject until she'd worked through her feelings and come back to him, but he knew if she wouldn't look at him, she certainly wouldn't talk. "Have you heard the news today?"

She shook her head.

"The packaging bill passed."

She spun around. "What? You're kidding."

"Nope. Several Republican senators turned at the last minute under pressure from home, and the vote was 53-47. Clive Jaubert frothed at the mouth over 'the triumph of the absurd.'"

She smiled for the first time since she'd come in. "Paul, I'm so glad. It *is* your triumph, and the Party's, too."

Her smile rippled through him, a wave of hope. "The final version sets full compliance a little later than we hoped, five years instead of three; but we're on the way."

Emma stepped toward him.

Paul raised his arms to take her in, comfort her, and feel her supple strength against his chest.

She took his hand and shook it with both of hers. "Congratulations, Paul. Now tell me what else is going on. Have you heard from Danny?"

Paul shook his head, but his heart followed the nosedive of his stomach. He could hardly focus on her words.

"It's been months," she said with a frown. "Was it May when he came and got Laurel?"

"April." He forced himself to concentrate. "I tell myself they're safe, but I keep seeing them crushed in a car somewhere. Or at the bottom of a river."

Emma rested both elbows on the back of a chair, placing it between them. "No, Paul. If anything had happened to them, you'd have heard by now. The gambling thugs wouldn't kill them. They'd take them hostage maybe, but they'd have made demands if they had. Laurel and Danny have to be alive. And safe."

"I hope you're right, though the thugs might well kill them and assume I'd get the message."

"Anything new on the people behind this?"

"Nothing. The FBI is doing its best, but every time they come across any kind of lead and try to research it, they hit a block. We've got the best computer wizards in the government on it. In the meantime, they keep watching Sun Gas, Ex-Oil, and the gambling moguls, following anyone who seems even faintly suspicious. One of the executives of Sun Gas called a D.C. area number the other day, but he actually had a scrambler on. We suspect he called Al Skinner, though the number's listed to someone else."

She straightened up but stayed behind the chair. "Who's Al Skinner?"

"He's Jaubert's assistant. Ed Petersen says he's former FBI with a lot of connections and experience on their computers." Paul moved a step closer. "Jaubert himself came to see me this morning. The aquifer bill is making some progress in committee, and he's scared. He looked like a frightened dumpling. You're not going to believe this. He offered to reintroduce the welfare bill in the next session if I'd rescind the aquifer one."

"That slime. What'd you tell him?"

He took another step. "That I believed absolutely in the merit and necessity of both bills and would do everything in my power to get them through. The EPA has taken a strong stand for the aquifers. And I told him I was planning to send the welfare bill back next year anyway. Elijah Jackson has decided he can support it with the changes, and maybe he'll swing enough votes to get it through."

Emma nodded. "Elijah's been pretty positive about you lately. If we just had him in the Party, we could really get somewhere."

Paul smiled thinly. "Let's get him drunk and sign him up. Danny can nominate *him* next time around."

Grinning at him, she stepped from behind the chair. "Well, I'd better get to the vice president's house. I badly need a hot shower and a rest. The economy committee meets early tomorrow." She reached for her purse.

Paul took her arm, afraid if she left, the rift would never close. "Emma, is something wrong? Something other than your father?"

"I...I just have a lot on my mind right now, okay?" She looked toward the door.

"Anything you want to talk about?"

Gently, she pulled her arm away and stepped toward the hall. "No."

"You know there's nothing I wouldn't do for you."

"Yes."

Paul walked her down to the entrance.

Shirl was waiting in the little hybrid sedan Emma insisted in using instead of the gas-guzzling limousine. There were no other gray-suits around.

Paul grabbed her arm just as she started to climb into the sedan. "Emma, where are the escort cars, the other gray-suits?"

She turned back. "Oh, Paul, I just hate having all those people guarding me. I feel so cluttered. I can't breathe."

"I don't care. You're the vice president. You can't take this kind of risk."

"Don't worry, I think Shirl has them hiding in the bushes. She won't let anything happen to me." Without giving him a chance to protest further, she jumped in.

Paul watched the sedan leave the grounds. No gray suits materialized out of the bushes to follow her, but he forgot about them as the emptiness descended on him again. She was gone from him in more than body. What had happened in Wyoming? Was it Earl? He turned back to the White House and felt its symbolic weight crush his alien presence. Without Emma he was so alone here, a speck on the center of the infinity symbol with time and space looped away from him on all sides, encompassing nothing.

CHAPTER FIFTY TWO

On a late-October Saturday, Al Skinner tossed his wind-breaker on a chair in an office above a seedy strip mall near Alexandria. It suited him admirably—shabby enough with its scratched desk and ancient file cabinets to preclude interest if anyone broke in, and rented untraceably, the funding for it an obscure item under "travel" in Jaubert's expense account. He'd altered the telephone records to show it connected several streets away, under a false name. The office allowed him to work the darker aspects of his job while keeping his office in D.C. innocent as a convent.

Skinner rubbed his hands together as he sat down at the desk. Yep, when Jaubert was president, he'd pay back big time. Skinner's three B's lit his imagination: Bimini, beaches, and bikinis. He smiled at the sun-splashed daydream. If he could just get that sanctimonious blob in office. Soon. Before Jaubert's puppeteers got any more desperate. A frown trailed his smile. This was getting darker than he'd anticipated before the Court put that bleeding-heart Earth-nut in office.

The telephone rang on the dot of seven. He reached under the desk and switched on the scrambler he'd listed as lost when he left the FBI.

Krieger's voice came through with its throaty New Orleans accent, but Skinner noted a whine he hadn't heard before.

After a minute's listening, he blew out a breath between clenched teeth and said, "Jeez, Krieger, how many times you gonna ask me the same question? No, I haven't found them....I know it's been months, dammit. Don't blame me. Your guys were supposed to be watching her every move. I told you you shoulda let the Nevada guys handle that....No, I haven't figured out who took her away....Even my New Orleans connections don't do me any good when I'm pissing in the dark, you know. She didn't leave a paper trail, didn't use a credit card...."

He listened for several minutes, rolling his eyes toward the water-stained ceiling. "*Forget about* the brother. Your guy already blew that possibility months ago when he showed his hand at that press conference. You need to get a muzzle on him....Yeah? You got someone lined up in Chicago to swear to that?...Well, drop it then. You heard what Greer said when Blanchet brought it up. You go after the brother now, and you're gonna look doubly suspicious....good....Jaubert? You kidding? That fat toad only works the sunny side of things. He makes sure he keeps his Mister-Second-Coming face clean and shiny....I'm telling you, he won't. He doesn't even want to know what we do. And he doesn't care, as long as no one connects anything to him. But listen, *I'm* beginning to care. This just gets deeper and dirtier every time I talk to you."

Skinner's eyes popped wide and his hands began to shake. "They're gonna do what?" He jumped up and paced as far as the cord would reach. "Uh-uh. No way. You know how that woman's guarded? You'll never get away with it....I don't care how 'capable' your guys are. You back off, you hear me? It's *not* just politics any more. That's high treason." A tremor rattled his stomach and spread to his vocal chords. Jesus, Krieger wasn't controlling those people any more. They were controlling him. And they didn't care shit about the holier-than-God appearance that politicians treasured. "Listen, I'm not getting involved in anything that's going to end in murder, and nine times out of ten kidnapping does....I don't trust those guys to draw the line between...Damn you, don't threaten me. I know too much, and if I go down, you and the others go down with me." He slammed down the phone, grabbed his jacket, and was just reaching for the door when the phone rang again.

He turned and squinted at it. No one else was supposed to call. A wrong number. Or that stupid Krieger again.

He strode back and yanked the receiver to his ear. "Dammit, Kr..."

Skinner listened for several minutes and sat down hard. The blood drained from his face, his organs turned to sludge, and he hung up without another word. He spun the chair around and stared out at the hill behind the mall, covered with bare, scraggly bushes and littered with WalMart sacks. How the hell did they know? It was years ago, and he'd hidden that grave so deep in the swamp not even the alligators would find it. His shoulders sagged. Turning again to his desk, he raised the false bottom of the middle drawer and slowly drew out a manila envelope. He opened it and slid out the enlarged photos. Paul Greer stood in front of the White House with his hand on Brent Howards' arm. His face was full of affection.

CHAPTER FIFTY THREE

Paul was still shaving when he heard a knock at the bedroom door and Rutherford's muffled voice called, "Mr. President?" He threw on his shirt and opened the door.

Rutherford's face was red.

Paul stepped back, astonished. "Rutherford? What's going on? I've never seen you flustered."

Rutherford handed him a newspaper. "I'm sorry to bother you so early, sir, but I thought you might want to see this right away."

Paul took the folded paper, trying to read the problem in Rutherford's eyes, but Rutherford reached in and pulled the door shut. Paul opened the paper, the November first edition of *We See D.C.*, the nationally syndicated rag that focused on Washington. The headline read:

HOMO HANKY-PANKY IN THE HOUSE?

A large color picture followed the title—Paul and Brent on the south lawn. Paul had his hand on Brent's arm and was looking at him with affection. A caption appeared under the picture, but no article accompanied it. The caption read:

President Greer with California representative Brent Howards on the south lawn of the White House. Howards, who arrived at his post under similar bizarre circumstances as Greer, is a member of the same radical fringe party and a known homosexual.

Paul staggered backwards, staring at the offensive paper in shock. How dare they do this? Brent would be devastated. He'd tried so hard to spare his family embarrassment.

Paul twisted the paper and threw it at the door. It left a gray smudge on the white paint. He yanked his clothes on, grabbed the paper, and ran to the Oval Office. The office staff wasn't at work yet. He tore through his desk looking for a list of representatives' home phone numbers. Surely the president had one. He paced, ranted, slapped his hand down on his desk, and paced again.

The minute he heard Norma's voice in the outer office, he banged the door open and demanded to have Clive Jaubert on the phone immediately, no matter where he was. "And get me the FBI," he said.

He stood behind his desk, watching his phone. When the connection came through, he punched the flashing button and yelled into the receiver, "Jaubert, this is Paul Greer. I want you in this office in fifteen minutes." He slammed down the phone and paced again.

When Norma showed Jaubert in half an hour later, Paul said, "Norma, show the FBI chief in the minute he arrives. And get Ed Petersen in here. I want a witness."

He turned to Jaubert, whose unshaven face drained above his poorly knotted tie. "Sit down."

When Jaubert hesitated, trying to draw his round body into a wall of defiance, Paul shouted, "I said *sit down.*"

Jaubert plopped onto the sofa.

Ed came in carrying his own copy of the paper.

Paul shoved the wrinkled paper under Jaubert's nose. "What do you know about this?"

Jaubert grabbed the paper, flattened it on his knees, and read the headline. His face turned ashen as he went from the picture to the caption. He looked up at Paul.

"I..." He looked from one to the other.

Overwhelmed by the fact that Jaubert's cronies were destroying Brent to get at him, Paul wanted to slap his face. He balled both hands into fists, struggling not to lower himself to that level, and growled, "Do you have any idea what you've done to that young man's life?"

Jaubert shoved the paper at Paul, as if he could reject the blame. "Listen, you, I didn't make him a flaming..."

Ignoring the paper, Paul bent close to Jaubert's face. "Don't you dare say..."

The door opened and Wes Schmidt, head of the FBI came in. Ed offered him his copy of the paper, but Schmidt shook his head and glared down at Jaubert.

Still stuck with the paper in hand, Jaubert threw it on the sofa. "I don't know why you think I had anything to do with this," he yelled.

Paul stood over him. "Well, let me explain how I made the connection." He bent back a finger for each item: "This just happens to appear the day the aquifer bill reaches your committee. Your constituents are rabidly opposed to the bill. Ergo, you have a vested interest in stopping it. My brother and his friend are in hiding because they've been threatened by people in the employ of *your* constituents, who've allied themselves with gambling interests. And don't forget, I'm from Louisiana, too. I remember the dirt that appeared about everyone who ever ran against you, so I wouldn't put it past you to plant something like this."

Jaubert edged away from the paper. "I had nothing to do with it. All I did was what any senator *is supposed* to do for their constituents. I can't help it if Louisiana's full of oil companies."

Schmidt leaned toward him. "We have recorded conversations between Al Skinner your man Krieger as well as between Skinner and a known 'troubleshooter' of the gambling cartel."

Paul looked sharply at Schmidt. The recordings were muddled by the scrambler on a phone they weren't even sure was Skinner's.

Jaubert took a gasping breath but tried to revive his spunk. "So what? They need the aquifers, too. It was strictly politics, you can ask Al. He'll swear to it."

"Al won't be able to do that," said Wes.

"What do you mean?"

"He's dead."

Jaubert's entire body shuddered like a Jello mold. "What?!"

Paul's head jerked, too, as did Ed's.

Schmidt kept his eyes on Jaubert. "His office was ransacked late last night. Very professional job. No prints, no leads whatsoever. Whoever you're playing with, Jaubert, you'd better watch your own back."

"I had nothing to do with any of this."

Schmidt regarded him neutrally. "Are you sure your 'constituency' will see things the same way?"

Jaubert's mouth gaped with disbelief. "They can't touch me. I'm the Speaker of the House, for God's sake."

"Maybe not for long," said Paul.

"My record's clean. You can't prove a thing." He started to get up.

Paul stepped closer, invading the space Jaubert needed to stand.

"Implications can be made," said Ed. "Something like this filthy one." He held the paper in Jaubert's face.

"No," said Paul. "There'll be no implications. We're going to get to the facts. You hear me, Jaubert?"

"I'm telling you, I didn't know about that. Not really. It was Al."

"Al is dead because he was working for you," said Paul.

"Al was a scumball."

Paul nodded. "Which is why he worked for you. To do your scumwork. Don't think your 'clean record' is anything more than a veil of gauze, Jaubert. There's not a person in Washington who doesn't know you for a self-serving bas..."

Jaubert jumped up, his stomach shoving Paul. "How dare..."

Paul stood his ground and swatted at the air an inch from Jaubert's nose. "Get this sorry waste of human flesh out of my sight."

Schmidt grabbed Jaubert under the arm and towed him to the door.

When they were gone, Ed faced Paul. "You have to use this opportunity, sir," he said. "You'll never have a better chance to get Jaubert out of your hair. All you have to do is pressure him a little more, and he'll resign."

Paul stared blindly at him, fighting the temptation. He shook his head. "No. Speaker of the House or not, Jaubert is only a pawn and I doubt he even realizes it. I want the facts. The oil companies and the gambling dons have some kind of hold on him. I want to know what it is, and I want them. If the facts warrant his impeachment, fine, and I will personally bring criminal charges."

Ed shook his head in resignation and left.

Paul sat down hard on the nearest chair, put his elbows on his knees and his head in his hands, his stomach burning. He'd never felt the glittery, oily lure of power as he had standing over Jaubert. He'd never felt so dirty.

Nearly as dirty as Jaubert, who'd thrown poor Brent to the sharks.

CHAPTER FIFTY FOUR

Hearing the elevator doors slide open, Paul looked up from the Thanksgiving edition of the *Washington Post* and called, "Come on in, Brent."

Brent joined him in the East Sitting Hall. Melting snow glistened on his sandy hair and the shoulders of his coat, but the gold glow of the room's lighting did little to brighten the depression on his ashy face.

Paul showed him to a chair near the fireplace. "Did you get to see your folks before you came back from the coast?"

"I was still in Sacramento when the picture appeared." His face turned grayer. "I spent the last two weeks in Boise, but in a motel. They wouldn't let me stay at home."

Paul's chest wrenched in pain for the fine young man. "That bad?"

Brent nodded. "I should've known when my father hung up on me right after the picture came out. I should've stayed away. When he finally did speak to me, he berated me about doing this to my mother when she's so sick, and she berated me about doing it to him when I know how he hates gays. I tried to explain..."

"I'm so sorry. I feel this is my fault."

The phone rang before Brent could protest.

When Paul hung up, he said, "Emma's coming up. She sounds pretty upset, too. I hope it's not her father."

He left Brent staring at the floor and went to the elevator to meet her.

The door opened and she stood without moving, staring at the floor, lost in some other world.

Paul took her hand and guided her out.

She looked up and her face, so much like her father's, showed the despair that had sagged the proud lines of his face.

Paul knew immediately that Raymond Light in the Lodge was dead. He took her in his arms, and for the first time in weeks she clung to him.

He kissed her forehead. "I'm so sorry, Emma. When do you have to leave?"

"Not till tomorrow morning. Air Force Two needs daylight to land on that little Casper runway."

"Can I come? I want to be with you."

She looked at him for a long minute and seemed to come to a painful decision. "Yes, please. It's such a waste, taking both planes, but I...want you...I think it's a good idea."

"Can you stay for a few minutes? Brent's here."

He kept his arm around her shoulder as they walked into the Sitting Hall, trying to focus on comforting her when he was about to explode with the feel of her body next to him.

"Hi, Brent," she said, smiling weakly.

Brent stood and hugged her. "Your father? I'm so sorry, Emma."

Paul brought another chair and they sat down.

"Thank you." Emma bit her lip and straightened her shoulders. "Did you get to see your mother? How is she?"

"Real sick. She's on a fourth round of chemo." He slumped in his chair and stared into memory. "She used to have such beautiful hair. Thick chestnut hair that fell down her back. It's dead. What you can see of it under the scarf." He drew himself back to the present and looked up at Emma. "I was just telling Paul they both really blasted me for being gay. I tried to explain it to them. My mother wouldn't have cared if my father hadn't been so angry. He just wouldn't listen. And I was so lame. I wanted to tell him I might've turned out differently if he'd ever loved me." He balled his fists and looked into a corner, biting his lower lip. "I never set out to be gay. Nobody does. It's too hard."

"You really think he never loved you?" asked Emma.

Brent nodded. "If he did, he hid it behind his own toughness. Maybe that was my fault. He always thought I was too soft." Brent sighed. "He hardly even spoke to me. I just wanted him to say, 'It's okay, you're still my son.' He didn't have to say he loved me."

"Brent," said Paul, "sometimes when a man is vicious about homosexuality, it's because he isn't sure of his own masculinity."

Brent stared at him. "I knew that, but I never thought of him in that light before. Maybe. It doesn't matter now anyway. I can't go home again. Ever."

"He'll come around, son," said Paul.

At the word *son* Brent looked at him and closed his eyes.

"They both will," Paul continued. "Give them time to get over the shock."

Brent shook his head. "I don't think my mother has much time."

Emma stood and put her hand on his shoulder. Brent laid his cheek on it.

"It's an awful thing when our parents are negative examples for us," she said.

"You sure seem to have coped with it better than I did," said Brent.

"I don't know how you can say that." Emma bent down to look in his eyes. "You made your way to San Francisco and found your own success and happiness with your partner. I just kept scrapping with the world and failing."

Brent took her free hand. "I'm sorry. I'm monopolizing the conversation when you've lost your father altogether, Emma. Is there anything I can do for you?"

"No, but thanks, Brent. I know the offer comes from the heart."

Paul added his hand to Brent's other shoulder and put his arm around Emma.

Brent sobbed. "My mother's going to die and I won't be there. And he won't let me go to the funeral."

"What's the prognosis on her cancer?" asked Paul.

"They won't tell me. I know she's gotten worse since that picture was in the paper. It's my fault."

"It most certainly is not," said Paul, and Emma's protest was lost to his louder voice. "You did everything you could to spare your parents for years; you allowed their opinions to control your life."

"It wasn't *your* hand on *Paul's* arm in the picture," added Emma, "and it wasn't you who took it."

"We've traced that back," said Paul. "The photographer was hired by Al Skinner, of course, and there's no doubt Jaubert at least knew about it."

All three turned eagerly to another topic.

"How's the investigation coming?" asked Emma.

"They've found the man who threatened Danny. A man named Leonard Freeman. Danny's secretary identified him. He has no record, but he'd been a body guard for Ralph Krieger of Sun Gas in the early nineties. Wes Schmitt is having him tailed blatantly in hopes of pressuring him into making a mistake. We've got a tap on Krieger's phones. We'll get them, Brent, no matter how long it takes. I promise you that."

"Thanks, Paul. Well, I'd better get going."

"Brent," cried Emma, "there is something you can do for me. Come with me tomorrow. I'd like for you to be there."

"Of course I'll come."

"Wait," said Paul, disappointed. "If I go, too, and the paparazzi are there, it might make the situation worse. You want me to stay here?"

Emma thought about it. "No, what if Brent goes with me and we let them take pictures with his arm around me or something, and then later with both of us next to him?"

Paul relaxed. "That's a wonderful idea."

Brent smiled wanly at them. "We can try that, but it doesn't matter anymore. The damage is already done. You two are...well, I just don't have anybody else here. It means a lot. Thank you."

"There's nothing to thank," they said simultaneously.

Paul shook them both gently. "And don't let me hear either of you talking of failure again. Look at you Brent. You're doing such good work with the rebuilding of California. I'm proud of you. And you, Emma, look at the aquifer bill that was your idea. And your work with the economy committee. I'm proud of you, too, and you should both be happy with yourselves."

Brent took a deep breath with his teeth clenched and his chin puckered. He raised his hand in farewell and hurried to the elevator.

When Brent had disappeared into the elevator, Emma kept her back to Paul, her head down. "You're such a dear man, Paul." She took a breath as if to speak again and then said nothing.

Paul put a hand on her shoulder. "Then why have things changed between us, Emma? You haven't been the same since you got back a month ago. I know you were worried about your father and all, but... well, I miss you."

She moved away from him and balled her fists at her side. "Maybe you'll see tomorrow. When I went back, I...touched my roots again. They're not your roots, Paul, and they draw at me the way roots sap the moisture from the soil. I may have failed my tribe with the buffalo idea, but there's still so much to do. This is all going to end in three years and we have to go back to our lives."

"Doesn't it count that we love...well, I love you and you care about me?"

Her arms went around her chest and she drew her shoulders in. "It counts more than I can say. You've given me so much. I do care, you know that, even if I don't say so. If I shut you out, it's because...I guess because I want the pain of parting sooner rather than later, when it'll only be worse." Her voice went hoarse. "I care from a deep place in me where I'm just a woman, no, not even that, from a place where I'm just a human being. I'll always care, Paul."

"Oh, God, Emma, I love you so much."

She turned to him, breathing hard and trying to resist her emotions, and flew into his arms.

"Just don't talk to me about the future, please, Paul. We don't have a future. Not toge..."

They kissed until they could hardly stand. He picked her up and carried her into the Queen's Bedroom off the Sitting Room because his own was too far down the hall.

CHAPTER FIFTY FIVE

Paul stood outside the House Chamber, his knees shaking and his teeth clenched to keep them from clattering. A year ago he'd stood outside this building in a daze, repeating words both familiar and terrifying. A year in Washington and he could count his friends on his fingers, even if he amputated a few. But his enemies—those were legion. They were all in the Chamber, daring him to justify his existence to the entire world. Could he justify it, even to himself? He'd tell the world what he'd accomplished, and it wouldn't sound like much.

Emma appeared at his side. "Knock 'em dead," she whispered. She squeezed his hand and stepped into the Chamber to preside over the joint session.

A gray little man walked past him into the chamber, and yelled in a strident voice, "Ladies and Gentlemen, the President of the United States."

In a second's flash he saw ex-President Hartsell enter the room for his last State of the Union Address, all smiles, pressed from both sides by representatives who stretched out their hands for him to shake. Paul wiped his palms on his pants, squared his shoulders, and stepped through the door.

Polite applause greeted him. Other than the gray-suits, nothing filled the space of the aisle. No hands reached for his, but Elijah Jackson and a few others who'd been invited to sit in the front rows kept the applause going.

At the bottom of the aisle he turned left, as he'd rehearsed it with Ed. Now a few hands reached for him and he shook them without recognizing the owners. The steps appeared before him, and his leaden legs dragged one foot after another up them. And then he stood in front of every representative; every senator; every news medium in the entire world; and Brent, Danny and Elijah in the front row, still standing and clapping.

With his savings depleted a few weeks ago, Danny had returned to his practice. He'd called from a friend's cabin in the Cascades, and Paul had put him under the watch of Secret Service. Laurel was still hiding there.

Paul felt Emma, cheering him from the top of the dais, and Jaubert, sneering. He looked at the pitcher of water and the glass on the podium. The glass was empty. Why hadn't someone filled it? He knew if he tried to he'd spill the water.

Against his better judgment, he'd left his index cards aside and tried to get used to the teleprompter. He looked up at it.

"My fellow Americans," he read, slurring the last syllable of *Americans*, "I appear before you this evening with the same degree of amazement as a year ago and only slightly less trepidation. For all that, the year has been good to me, and I think, to the country. We have..." He looked away from the prompter and sought out Danny and Brent. They both smiled, encouraging him to go on. He could feel Jaubert's eyes boring into the back of his head, full of hostility and anticipation of his every mistake. Though Jaubert had lost a great deal of weight and his face often looked like gray ravioli, he'd lost none of his influence in Congress and never shrank from showing his contempt.

Paul took a deep breath and extemporized. "No, before I talk about what *has* happened, I would like, perhaps as a reflection of my own astonishment, to mention a few things that have *not* happened since I first forced myself to step into the Oval Office: the American economy has not fallen flat on its face..."

The hundreds of people jamming the chamber burst into laughter.

Paul looked up, stunned, and then he was laughing with them. "I suffered neither heart attack nor nervous breakdown, neither impeachment nor no-confidence. We were not plunged into global warfare, though we had close scrapes with the civil war in Saudi Arabia and the sinking of the Greenpeace ship by the North Korean whalers. And most of all, we were not thrown into civil war ourselves. Given the crisis that accompanied the election, the uncertainty that followed, and the general resistance to my presidency, I think we can all take heart in the knowledge that we are, after all, a nation of strength, resilience, and tolerance. With these things in mind, I feel it was a pretty good year."

He glanced at the teleprompter again. "We achieved a little, and I speak for Ms. Light in the Lodge as well, without whose support and endless work I could not have accomplished anything at all."

He backed away from the podium and turned to raise a hand toward Emma.

His three-man cheering section rose to clap for her. The rest applauded lightly.

Disappointed with the response, Paul continued. "We passed the election crisis bill. We passed the packaging bill, and though the deadline for full compliance is still years away, many manufacturers have already simplified their packaging. Far from losing money, they're showing greater profits."

He summarized the effect that the recycling had already had and looked directly at the shared-feed camera. "I wish I could look each of you in the eyes, as I used to be able to do from the pulpit, to thank you for your efforts. Now we need to work toward eight or even ten percent reduction this year and fifty percent within five years. I know you will accept the challenge as you did when I first asked your support for the bill. Again, I thank each one of you for taking the trouble to do this for our children.

"But the passage of two small bills is still a meager achievement for a year's worth of living in the White House."

Jaubert let out a small but derisive snort.

Irked, Paul ignored him. "We failed to pass the welfare bill that would have eased poverty everywhere while taking a step toward reducing population. Within the week I will resubmit that bill, slightly modified. I believe we now have nearly enough votes assured for passage, but I would ask for your support again if you believe in its benefits, no, its necessity."

Behind him a paper rustled. No doubt Jaubert was taking notes for his censure of the speech later.

"I will also submit a bill asking for an increase in fines for improper disposal of polluting or hazardous waste, with the revenue to be used as incentives for major cities to expand their rapid transit systems while lowering fares for the sake of easing traffic congestion and air pollution. Part of it will also fund research into more viable alternatives to the internal combustion engine. The aim is to phase it out altogether by the end of the next decade."

Paul heard Jaubert's gasp behind him, then a loud rustle followed by a squeak of his chair, and everyone in the audience shifted focus to the Speaker of the House.

The oil companies would be on Jaubert's back again, Paul thought. For a second he saw Jaubert cowering in the Oval Office and regretted he hadn't followed Ed's advice about squeezing him until he resigned.

In the House, many heads leaned toward each other. The room filled with the white noise of whispering.

Wishing he had his own papers to riffle, Paul peered at the teleprompter and tried to pull the audience back.

"In April, Miss Light in the Lodge and her committee, which includes homemakers, industrialists, day laborers, bankers, clergy, statisticians, and many others, will appear before you with their recommendations for easing our economy through a period of population reduction. I can't tell you how many hours they've volunteered for this difficult and challenging task. I've seen the preliminary report, and I've been delighted with the creative ideas in it."

Paul paused before he turned to the most negative topic in his speech. "My greatest disappointment in this year has been the fact that my aquifer bill is held up in committee when it's clear that a majority of citizens favor it."

Behind him, Jaubert fell into a fit of coughing.

Paul grabbed the glass, filled it, whirled around to hand it to the Speaker, and whispered through clenched teeth, "Shut up, Jaubert. Don't try me."

He glanced at Emma, who was glaring at Jaubert with eyes glittering like sparks from a blowtorch, and returned to the microphone. Rattled and furious, he said, "Something appears to be choking Mr. Jaubert's committee, as well." Danny's laugh rang through the chamber, followed by a titter from the Democratic side of the floor.

"Although it's clear to the general populace what the aquifers represent, perhaps it isn't clear enough to the committee or to the corporations that want to control our water. We all know there's abundant water on the earth, but four fifths of it is in our oceans. Sea water *can* be desalinized, of course. We just don't know what the removal of large amounts of water from the seas will do to aquatic life, not to mention our climate or the balance of the global ecosystem. We do know that the water in our aquifers is clean and drinkable. We also know they need hundreds if not thousands of years to replenish themselves. Water is not just an issue of our immediate needs. It's a critical issue for all the generations that follow us." He took the time to let his eyes rest for a second on the camera. "Please, continue to exert pressure on Congress to avert the takeover of our water supplies by corporations."

He paused before his last paragraph. "We are headed in a new direction, my fellow Americans. The changes are long overdue, but I'm optimistic enough to believe we will make the sacrifices necessary to assure that our passage through time does not leave a ravaged earth and dire existence for our great, great grandchildren. Thank you."

For a moment silence greeted him as the audience, barely settled into the evening's speech, asked inaudibly but obviously, "That's *it*?"

Paul missed the small business of collecting his index cards. He caught Jaubert's belittling smile as he turned in the wrong direction and turned back toward the stairs.

"Bravo!" yelled Danny, leaping from his seat and clapping loudly. Brent joined him, and Emma was clapping enthusiastically. The rest of the representatives and senators applauded politely.

Justify himself to the world? Ha. It had been a dismal failure. Paul kept his back straight as he walked up the aisle, but in his mind he was bowed over the empty space where his confidence had been.

CHAPTER FIFTY SIX

Emma waited on the dais in the elegant East Room for Paul to finish his introduction, her legs unsteady, her breathing short and difficult. This was the most important thing she'd ever done, and she was terrified. It could mean the difference between healing and killing the Earth. If she presented the bills badly, she would fail not only herself, but the committee volunteers, who were sitting behind her. She'd fail Mother Earth.

She glanced around the room with its gold draperies, its delicate decorations, and cut glass chandeliers. For a second she tried to imagine Abigail Adams supervising the hanging of the presidential wash in this room two centuries ago. Her eyes fell on the life-sized portrait of George Washington, her historical father. It stared right back, urging her to lead the country in the right direction; and her mouth, already dry, turned to steel wool.

The red eyes of the cameras radiated hostility. Why didn't they make those lights green? Didn't they mean the cameras were "going"? She tried to swallow but made a whining grunt that she hoped didn't carry as far as the microphone.

Paul turned to her.

She stepped to the podium and took a sip of water. "Ladies and gentlemen of the press, thank you for coming," she began, horrified at the quake in her voice. She looked into the bank of TV cameras. "And thank you to all my fellow Americans who take the time to watch this broadcast.

"As you know, the tri-partisan committee on non-growth economy has been meeting for the better part of a year, and I would like to thank them personally at this time." She called them forward, shook their hands, and asked them to stand on the podium with her. She introduced Elijah Jackson last and thanked him for co-chairing the committee. Feeling them at her back, she began her speech, a little calmer now.

"President Greer has approved the recommendations of this committee and will send them to Congress tomorrow as a series of bills entitled Transitional Economic Measures. We would like to outline the bills for you today, explain where the funding for the proposals will come from, and ask you to consider carefully how this will affect you, your children, and your descendants for centuries to come."

The reporters were still and attentive. This was going better than she'd hoped.

"Bill one concerns education on the subjects of over-population and the environment. The committee is unanimous in its opinion that Americans are reasonable people, who, when shown that one path leads to disaster, will choose a better one, even if the disaster lies further in the future than they may live to see. Over the next few years you will hear much about what life on earth will be like if we don't control our population. We're sure that, sufficiently informed, Americans will voluntarily limit their families. It should never be necessary to mandate the number of children a family can have or to pass penalty taxes for large families."

Now the reporters were attentive but hardly still. Hands went up.

Emma ignored them and looked at the cameras. "We believe you'll be willing to sacrifice a part of your pleasure or comfort to assure that we will not be remembered as the generation who knew...but...did...not...care." She paused and tried to look each reporter in the eye before returning to her notes.

They were staring back through a forest of raised arms.

"The funding for the educational program will be provided by savings from the welfare program which President Greer re-submitted to Congress last month and which is expected to pass."

"Madam Vice President," cried a voice from the front row.

It was the mellow bass of Royce McClain, who normally an-chored the CBA news. Why had they sent him instead of the usual correspondent?

She refused to let him dominate her, but he made her hands sweat and her breath shorten. "There will be time for questions later," she said without looking at him. Out of the corner of her eye she saw him fold his arms across his chest and lower his head. He reminded her not so much of a chastised child but a buffalo about to charge. The other arms came down.

She cleared her throat. "The second bill regards housing. Rather than continuing to build at the present rate, which will eventually leave a reduced populace with more buildings than it needs, we are proposing incentives for families and businesses to remodel existing buildings.

"As the demand for new construction diminishes, we must accommodate construction and lumber workers in the econ-omy, which is bill three. We propose to retrain construction workers in salvage and remodeling, with special emphasis on energy efficiency and pleasing surroundings." She looked up from her notes.

The reporters were squirming, impatient and radiating negative astonishment.

Her hands began shaking, and she grabbed the podium to steady them. "I should insert here that there's a great deal of retraining included in the bills, all of which is voluntary as to specialty. The retraining provided in bill three will be funded by savings from welfare."

She realized suddenly she'd written this speech for the reporters when she needed to talk directly to the people. Why hadn't she started the way Paul had begun his speech in the Rose Garden? She wiped her hands on her skirt and kept her eyes on the cameras, dismally aware of how pedantic she sounded. She started the next bill on replacing slums with green space, but her mind was racing forward.

She forced herself to extemporize. "Sections of the green belt will be leased for private gardens. If you've lived in apartments all your life, imagine having your own small plot where you can pick tomatoes from your vine or peaches from your own tree."

Nothing so graphic occurred to her for the next bill, and she read with a dry mouth. "Bill five addresses our limited energy resources. We are proposing more rapid expansion of solar and wind power as alternatives to natural gas for heating and fossil fuels for locomotion. Automobile companies will receive tax incentives to experiment with new ways to economize the internal combustion engine. Since this will benefit each of us in healthier air and a more tranquil city life, we're proposing to pay for this program with a one-cent-a-gallon increase in the gasoline tax."

She expected pandemonium, but the reporters now sat like hostage statues, several with eyes rolled toward the ceiling. The cameras would transmit the negative atmosphere.

She was losing them. Embarrassing the committee. Their ideas were so sound, so well-thought-out, so essential to a decent future. Why hadn't she written a speech worthy of them? Her throat ached with the need to speak the right words, but they disappeared in the jangle of nerves between her brain and her mouth.

"Bill number six also addresses phasing out the automobile as we know it. We propose recycling the old vehicles into small farm machinery..."

She droned on, reading now. Mortified. Already she knew this was a failure, and she wished she could just disappear in a flood of tears. She clenched her jaw to stop the hot buzzing behind her eyes. The work was too important to give up now. She straightened her shoulders and finished the last proposals on international birth control measures and the establishment of a new cabinet post, the Secretary of Population.

Emma laid her notes aside, breathed deeply, and spoke from the heart, trying to salvage something. "Ladies and gentlemen, we are the most powerful country on earth. The richest. And the most wasteful. We are the greatest user of natural resources. We can no longer afford to be the renegade consumer on an Earth in danger of death. We must not only show the world that we care about the future, we must lead the way into it so that there *is* a future for everyone."

The reporters were on their feet and she focused on them now, but waved them back into their seats.

"Those are the eight recommendations of this tireless committee. They will be spelled out tomorrow in your local papers and in our website, www.future.gov, along with the dollar figures on revenue from savings, taxes and fines, and the expenditures for education and retraining programs. We've studied these figures for months. They will work. Other than the gasoline tax, we don't envision any new taxes to pay for the transition.

"But *transition* is the key word here. In the years ahead we *must* change our thinking and our way of living. If we fail to consider our descendants, we will leave them a world denuded of green, depleted of energy, and devoid of breathable air—hideous to inhabit.

"These proposals are designed to help us make that transition without throwing millions of people out of work in the next century as our population peaks and declines." Emma looked into the cameras with all her passion for the Earth. "Please study them carefully and see where you fit into them. If you are caught in one of the retraining areas, can you find it in your heart to say, 'Hard for me but necessary for my grandchild'?"

She paused for a few seconds. "I timed this speech earlier, ladies and gentlemen. It lasts seven minutes. In that time *eleven thousand eight hundred fifty-five* children were born into our world, *nine thousand two hundred seventy-three* of them into poverty and hardship. In the same span ten years from now *seventeen thousand five hundred* children will be born to worse conditions if we do not apply the brakes now.

"If you can support any or all of these proposals, President Greer and I ask you once more to let your senators and representatives know. I thank you."

By the time she felt Paul at her side, all the reporters were clamoring to be heard, their hands flapping in the air.

Emma started to point to McClain, but Paul stopped her and bent toward the microphone.

"May I say one thing before we begin answering questions?" he asked.

Emma moved aside and he looked into the cameras. "I support these bills with all the conviction of a recent convert. I believe you, the people, have the right and the duty to pressure your representatives to pass legislation which you know is necessary. I hope you will do that. I'm sending them to Congress as eight bills rather than one so that at least parts have a chance this year. Though I hope they will all pass, I will alter slightly any that fail and send them back as often as it takes, for as long as I'm president."

The reporters' hands shot up again. Paul moved to let Emma back at the microphone.

Before Emma could recognize anyone, Jules Blanchet jumped up. "Don't go away, Mr. President," he called, his voice oily with sarcasm. "This question's for you. You *know* the Catholic Church is going to fight you on the birth control items. Just how do you plan to get these bills past your former colleagues?"

"The Vice President did not recognize you, Mr. Blanchet. Normally, I'd ask you to do her the courtesy of waiting your turn, but in the interest of letting her get on to more pertinent questions, I'll answer you. In the first place, I have no intention to call *any* Church into a national debate on *any* issue. That would violate my firm belief in separation of church and state. However, if I should find myself in private conversation with my 'former colleagues,' I would ask them to consider the conditions of the world when the church was founded two thousand years ago. No doubt its rules were appropriate at the time, but some of them are no longer viable on an earth suffering from over-population. There are morals and values that are desirable for all times. Perhaps all religions should decide which those are and focus on them rather than ones that are inappropriate, even destructive, in the twenty-first century.

"In the second place, no church has a direct vote in this, but the people do. It is to them that I appeal as thinking citizens in a troubled world."

Paul turned away from the podium without waiting for a re-action from Blanchet.

Emma watched him sit down again and turned to field oth-er questions. She strained to keep her focus on the skeptical reporters, but her mind kept returning to Paul. Never in her life had she known anyone she respected so completely. He knew how to relate to the people.

And she didn't. She'd failed Paul, she'd failed the committee. She'd failed Mother Earth. Feeling hopeless, she called on Royce McClain.

Two hours later Emma stood at a chopping block in the White House kitchen, hacking glumly at a pile of green onions. Paul and Danny, chefs for the evening, were poking about the cupboards for a salad bowl. They'd tried to reassure her about the speech. Even Laurel, who'd come out of hiding when no more threats were made on Danny, had told her it was a great success.

Right. Which was why the evening news had allotted five full minutes to Jaubert's raving about "pie in the sky" solutions to a problem that didn't exist, offered by a political party so juvenile that its national symbol ought to be the diaper.

A box of rice appeared inches from her face and she jerked her head back in surprise.

Laurel rattled the box. "Look what they gave me. *Pre*cooked rice," she said, glaring disdainfully at the offensive item. She turned back to the men. "Surely you could have found some Louisiana rice somewhere in this provincial city."

"You're probably right," said Paul, "but I told the staff to use plain stuff unless it was for a state dinner or something."

Laurel put her hands on her hips. "You mean you don't consider us a state dinner? I'm cut to the quick!"

"You're family, all of you," said Paul, looking at Emma.

Heat rose to her face and she bent over the onions. She watched Laurel sidle up to Danny, shake the rice at him, and put her arms around his waist. How could she do that? How could it be so easy? So natural? As if she were absolutely sure her touch would always be welcome.

It would be so comforting to go to Paul and let him hold her when she felt so bad. Why couldn't she trust him with her feelings? Because he was white? No. If he were as Indian as Crazy Horse, she couldn't just walk up to him and assume he'd welcome her in his arms, even knowing he loved her. Because love always died. And his surely would when he got tired of her wanting him so badly but fearing they'd hurt each other.

Danny and Laurel stood with his lips against her forehead and her hands resting on his chest. They melded into a single unit of peace for a minute.

Emma swallowed hard. It was possible for two people to become one. Just not possible for her.

Danny arched back from Laurel and shook his finger at her, grinning. "You're distracting me, woman. I have work to do." He dragged a large metal container from under the sink, sloshing a little of the water on the floor. "At least these aren't precooked crawfish. I had these flown in out of my own pocket for the occasion. No taxpayers involved here."

Emma dropped her knife and went to look in the container. "My God, they're alive."

"Not for long," crowed Danny. "That water boiling yet, Paul?"

She stared at him. "What! You don't mean you're going to throw them live into boiling water?"

"No other way," said Paul, dragging the container toward the stove, where a spicy steam already rose from a huge pot. "I guess it is pretty cruel, but the results..."

"No! I can't bear the thought of it. I'm not eating those things."

Laurel patted her on the shoulder. "Well, there's plenty of salad and French bread. You don't have to eat them if you don't want to. But right now, how about coming with me? I left my recipe for bananas glacé upstairs in that yellow room and I feel really weird running around this house by myself."

Out of the corner of her eye, Emma caught Laurel motioning with her head from the container to the pot as they shut the door.

Two more hours later Emma stared over her healthy portion of salad and bread at three plates of steaming crawfish *etouffée*. "I don't know how you can eat that, knowing what you did to those poor little animals."

Paul gave her one of those smiles that melted her very skeleton, and the desire to be in his arms nearly knocked her from her chair.

"Well," he said, "there's only one way to find out how we could eat it, but we'll leave that up to you."

All three of them looked at her expectantly.

She was grappling with her need for Paul, but she made the struggle look like indecision over the food.

"You have to admit, it smells wonderful," said Laurel.

"Yeah, but still..."

"Mmm," moaned Danny, chewing ecstatically.

The others joined him.

The smell was, in fact, driving her crazy. "Okay, just give me a little of the sauce and rice." At least it would get her mind off him.

Paul shoved aside a curly pink crawfish tail and put a forkful in Emma's mouth. She concentrated on her taste buds, chewed, and swallowed. She opened her eyes to the eager faces of her friends. "Uh-huh."

Paul, Danny and Laurel looked at each other and forked up three more mouthfuls of the *etouffée*.

"Is this the dish you talked about when we were on the way to California?"

Paul nodded, his mouth full.

She frowned. "I guess there's not *really* much difference between eating the sauce made from the animals and eating the animals themselves, is there?"

Paul leaped up and served a plate of *etouffée* for her.

At eleven they settled in the East Sitting Hall for the evening news. Most of the half hour was devoted to the Emma's speech, comparing it with Paul's State of the Union Address, which commentators had called concise, absurdly short, or appropriate to the accomplishments of the administration, depending on their bent. Hers they called a hodge-podge of radical nonsense or the freshest ideas to hit the Hill in decades. After the first commercial the news turned to reactions, spearheaded by Clive Jaubert.

He sat at his desk overlooking the reflecting pool and the Washington Monument, looking healthier than he had in months. He seemed to be fighting down a fit of glee. "I can only repeat what I said after Mr. Greer's State of the Union Address: this administration is a sorry attempt at justifying living in the White House, *at taxpayers' expense.* It's offering us government of the weirdoes, by the weirdoes, and for the weirdoes. These hare-brained schemes will wreck our economy and make us the laughing stock of the entire world." His face contorted in a blatant attempt to stifle a sneer. "Those two..." he rolled his eyes around, as if a word usable on public airways might appear, "...persons in the executive branch of our government want to throw millions of unborn children to the wolves with their welfare program; they want to throw millions of workers into bread lines; they want to kill the lumber, construction, automobile, and oil industries; and they want to control the internal politics of other countries." Jaubert triumphantly counted off the horrors on his fingers. "The man isn't even God-fearing, for God's sake. Well, like I always say, what can you expect from an atheist?"

The commentator looked startled and coughed behind his hand.

Jaubert stared at him. "Yes, indeed, I did mean just that, sir. The man is the Anti-Christ in my book, and his woman, our so-called vice president...," Jaubert's voice turned sour with irony, "...is nothing more than his concubine. Given their way, they'll plunge us into certain ruination. I won't let that happen." He turned and faced the camera directly. "My fellow Americans, someone must go into the breach. Tomorrow, I will personally call for the no-confidence vote that Mr. Greer promised would make him resign; however, I will demand the vote for the both of them. We must excise these two political tumors before it's too late. I beg you now, you good Christians of America, call your congressmen and let them know you've had enough of this misbegotten regime. You want clear, strong, leadership again, to keep our families strong and our country moving forward."

The commentator's eyes grew large. "You're actually going to demand the resignation of both the president and the vice president, Senator Jaubert?"

"Yes, sir, I am."

"And that would make *you* the new president."

Jaubert leaned forward in his chair. "Yes, it would. I am willing to shoulder this burden, no matter how difficult, if it means..."

Paul grabbed the remote, swung it hard while punching the off button, barely controlling the desire to throw it at the screen. "That..." No word vile enough came to mind.

"Sanctimonious swine," Emma filled in for him.

"Self-serving bastard," cried Danny.

"Mealy-mouthed monster," Laurel said between clenched teeth.

"Ambitious felon. Sneaking, two-faced liar," added Paul.

"What do you think will happen?" asked Laurel.

"The only thing I know for sure is that I personally will deliver these bills to Congress tomorrow so early they'll be registered before Jaubert even puts in an appearance on the Hill. Then they'll have to consider them and take action no matter what happens to us. I hope."

"Do you think he can get a majority for a no-confidence vote?" asked Danny.

"Very likely."

"Your approval rating was at 33% the last time I heard," said Laurel.

Paul sniffed loudly. "Well, I guess we know what'll happen if that's any indication."

Emma leaned toward him. "I don't think a man like Jaubert can carry it off. Don't you think most people see through that veneer of piety to the ambition? Isn't it clear how repulsive he is?"

"Probably not to millions of the religious right," said Paul.

The same feeling of jumping off a cliff he'd had when he ran from the church came over him, with the added certainty of failure. He sighed. "I guess I can go back to selling shoes. I was good at *that*. But not before I do my best for these bills."

CHAPTER FIFTY SEVEN

Paul shoved aside a stack of documents he'd just signed or vetoed so Jaubert wouldn't get his hands on them. He left the desk and stared through gray drizzle at a bed of tulips lining the colonnade. Their heads looked shriveled and dry, even in the rain. Their red petals lay on the ground, slowly going back to earth, their season over, like his presidency.

He'd have to start looking for another job. Right. Who was going to hire a dishonorably discharged president?

He knew what Emma would do. The knowledge hung like an anvil around his neck. He had to find a way to keep her, but she was so set on parting when their term was over.

A door opened behind him and he felt her presence before he turned.

"What a dreary April shower," she said, joining him. "I'll take Wyoming thunderstorms any day over this. At least they're hit-and-run."

Just like her feelings for him, he thought. He put his arm around her and felt her body hesitate and then relax against him. "Yeah, but I bet you have three or four days of snow at a stretch."

"Okay, you're right." She shrugged out of her coat, laid it over a chair, and drew him toward the fireplace. "How'd it go this morning?"

"Well, I took the bills over to the Hill at the crack of dawn. The minute Jaubert's staff arrived, I handed over the bills with 'priority' stamped all over them in red. I made his secretary give me a timed receipt for them, so Jaubert can't say he didn't get them till after he'd started the no-confidence call. Every telephone in his office was blinking on every line when I left." He drew her to him again.

"Does it take a two-thirds majority to put through a no-confidence vote?"

Paul heard the question but his focus was on the feel of her. Her body merged to his like a limb that had been missing. Now. He should say something now about staying together, but certain rejection dried up the words. "Uh, two thirds? No idea. It's not spelled out in the Constitution. But if they get a majority, I'll resign anyway."

"I guess I will, too." Emma heaved a sigh that was half sob. "We tried so hard, Paul. I just did such a bad job with that speech."

He pulled her closer. "No, you didn't. Anyway, Jaubert would've pounced on us if you'd given the finest speech in history. He was just looking for the excuse."

"Well, that much is true. I tried to reach Brent to see how he thought the bills would do, but his phone was busy all day."

"I called Elijah this morning. He's coming by in a few minutes. Maybe he knows some political avenue that'll get the bills through."

Emma's face brightened. "If they kick us out, maybe Elijah will run against Jaubert next time."

Paul shrugged. "Who knows. I don't think there's much 'if' about what's going to happen, Emma. You'd better steel yourself for the worst. Jaubert has the pull and the polls on his side. We've had a year's run at it, and that's more than we ever expected. But if you want to know the truth, I can't wait till all this is over. I hate being president. The constant scrutiny, the temptation to abuse the power for something I know is right. When it's over..." This was his chance. His saliva turned to sand and no words came through.

Emma waited a second and then grinned at him. "Now you almost sound like the old Paul again."

"What do you mean?" he managed.

"You've changed a lot in the last year, don't you know that?"

Paul sighed. "Well, at least I've gotten more accustomed to the surroundings." He swept his arm around the Oval Office. "Just as I have to give them up. That's a nice irony."

"No, look at the way you handled Blanchet at the press conference yesterday. It was a brilliant answer. You were wonderful. A year ago, you'd have let him badger you. And in other ways, you've become more...more presidential."

Paul tapped her lightly on the nose with his finger. "Thanks for the compliment. It means a lot."

"Do you know when the no-confidence vote will be?"

"Jaubert hasn't deigned to let me know, but I'd guess before the end of the week. Early next month at the latest. I'll call a press conference as soon as I know. You can speak, too, if you want."

Norma knocked and announced Elijah Jackson.

After they'd exchanged a few pleasantries, Paul steered them toward the sofas. "Let's all have a seat. Elijah, thank you again for all your work on the Transition Bills."

"It was my pleasure. And my awakening. Everyone on the committee felt it was an eye-opener."

"Do you have a sense of how the vote on them is likely to go?"

Elijah took a chair at the end of the sofa. "No, Mr. President…"

"Paul."

"Yes, sir, Paul. No, sir, I couldn't say at the moment."

"How are the people leaning?"

"Hard to say. Most of the calls and e-mails are about the no-confidence."

Paul slumped with disappointment. "They're more interested in political scandal than in the future of the whole planet."

"If it's any consolation, I think the no-confidence will be close. Jaubert's using every ounce of clout he has. No doubt the oil companies are pressuring him more than ever since your aquifer bill got out of committee. Still, a no-confidence vote is a radical move, and a lot of people simply don't like Jaubert, both of which give you a little advantage; but I just can't call it."

Paul pulled himself to the edge of his seat. "Elijah, I don't think there's much doubt how the vote will go. What I'd like to do is leave here knowing you'd get these bills through somehow."

Elijah reared back, as if Paul had suggested something distasteful.

Paul raised his hands, palms out. "Whatever a congressman can legitimately do, of course."

Elijah relaxed. "I'll do everything I can. After all, I helped write them."

Emma sat upright, her eyes wide. "What if you were a member of the Earth Rights Party?"

Elijah let out a laugh that choked him and made him cough. "Now there's a case of political suicide, and I'm up for reelection next year."

She sighed and slumped back into the sofa. "Of course. I apologize, Elijah. It was a stupid idea. So we're left with just Brent to carry on."

Elijah stared vacantly at her for a moment. "All I can do for you is keep pushing the bills and hope for the best." He stood then and took his leave, a distracted frown on his face.

Paul and Emma went to the House and started up the broad staircase.

"Well, I guess that's that," said Emma.

Paul fought down the same sense of failure. "Emma, we sowed good seeds. Maybe they'll sprout. At least it'll all be over in a week."

"I know, and Elijah will help where he can."

Paul took a deep breath. Now. He'd broach the subject or die trying. "What'll you do when they oust us?"

She hesitated on the stair, and when she answered, her voice was heavy with sadness and something else that Paul couldn't name.

"Go back to Big Sleep, I guess. Try to pull the tribe together and get that buffalo ranch going again. Or find some other venture. What about you? Are you really going back to selling shoes?"

"I don't know." But then it came in a flash. "Maybe I'll teach school on some Indian reservation in Wyoming." He watched her out of the corner of his eye.

Emma stopped dead with her feet on two different steps. Her face paled. "That's nothing to joke about, Paul."

"Who said it was?"

Torn emotions raced over her face and her breathing flattened. She turned and ran back down the stairs.

CHAPTER FIFTY EIGHT

On the first of May, Clive Jaubert stood on the steps of the Capitol, concentrating on the reporters and cameras surrounding him. Much as he hated them, they were his megaphone, his transport to the top. He breathed deeply and freely, the way he would when Greer and that squaw were out of his way.

"Well, that's why I arranged the roll-call vote," he said, "so that Greer cannot possibly doubt the low esteem in which the good citizens of this great country hold him."

"And you really expect to force his resignation?"

"Of course. I have every confidence in the outcome. No sane American wants this..."

He spied Elijah Jackson coming up the steps. His face drained and his stomach soured. What the hell was Jackson doing here? He was supposed to be home for some kind of family celebration.

"Wants what?" asked an obvious rookie reporter.

Jaubert waved the question aside to end the interview, stepped out of the circle, and waited for the black representative to reach him. "Glad you could be here, Elijah," he said.

Elijah stared him down. "Sure you are. No doubt that's why you set the vote for today. But don't give it a moment's thought. This is more important than my granddaughter's birthday."

"Oh, were you home in Texas?"

Jackson glanced at the clutch of reporters. He grinned and said loudly, "As if you didn't know. I guess you didn't arrange the return of Waters and Giordano from Hawaii for the vote today, either."

Jaubert glanced back at the reporters. Damn hyenas, still hanging around with their ears turned to the wind of a scandal. He raised his voice for their benefit. "I merely scheduled it today in hopes that everyone would be here."

"Right." Elijah moved away from him and walked in alone, a few steps behind Brent Howards. Jaubert turned his back to the cameras and let a shudder of distaste pass through his body. "Well, there go Greer's two votes," he said aloud, leading the media pack into the Capitol.

Paul sat in the Oval Office with Petersen, staring at the television set backed up to the fireplace.

Ed reached over and held his arm. "You're going to rub that thing raw, Mr. President."

Paul stared down and realized he'd been working the scar again. "Thanks, Ed." He slid both hands under his thighs to keep them still, but he could still feel the tingle in the scar that was about to become the symbol of another failure.

Jaubert hadn't seen so many representatives present for a vote in his entire career. Several stood in the aisles and scratched their heads, trying to remember where they sat. When he finally banged his gavel, almost every chair was taken.

"As we're all aware," he began, "Paul Greer assured the nation at his inaugural speech that if the country demanded a no-confidence vote through us, he would resign. I believe the country is fed up with not only him, but Vice President Light in the Lodge, as well." He allowed only the slightest disdain to creep into Emma's name. "Therefore I have finally given the country a chance to do what the Supreme Court should have done in the first place. I call on each of you to stand and vote according to the requests of the majority of your constituents, and rid the country of this misbegotten presidency. Please note that a yea vote is for no-confidence in the President and the Vice President."

Jaubert waited a moment to let the drama of the vote sink in. He took up the list of names himself and began the roll call. "Aandahl of Wisconsin."

"Yea."

Of course, that huge payment for dumped surplus cheese. "Aberle of Vermont."

"Yea."

Yep, that vote lined up nicely after the go-ahead to the lumbering lobby. "Alban of Washington."

"Nay."

Jaubert's lips thinned and his eyebrow twitched. Shit. He hadn't expected a nay vote so early in the alphabet. "Alberts of Maine."

"Yea."

"Allen of Utah."

"Yea."

For the rest of the A's, Jaubert struggled to keep his face straight.

The last A stood, voted yea, and sat down again quickly.

"Bethune of Florida."

Sally Bethune stood and looked around timidly. Her voice was barely audible in the crowded room. "I'm one of the new representatives from the Earth Rights Party, and I believe in President Greer. I vote nay."

Jaubert looked intently at the wispy woman. She flushed and sat down hard. Several congressmen swiveled to look at her then turned back with barely concealed smiles. Well, at least no one took her seriously. He continued the roll call through the G's, all yeas, trying to keep the triumph from his voice before the call was finished.

"Hebert of Louisiana."

"Yea."

"Howards of California."

In the last row, where Jaubert could hardly see him, the prissy little rep stood so quickly that his chair banged into the wall behind him. Even in the dim light under the balcony, his face glowed red. "I have more confidence in Paul Greer than I have in anyone in this room," he said in a shaky voice, and Jaubert felt the shadowy eyes focus on him. "I vote nay." Howards sat down again quickly as every head in the room turned toward him.

With great effort Jaubert ignored the slur. "Huberto of New Mexico," he hissed through clenched teeth.

"My constituency is split right down the middle. I abstain."

"Ibarra of New York."

"Yea."

"Innsmann of Minnesota."

"Yea."

"Jackson of Texas."

Elijah stood slowly and waited until all eyes in the room were on him. "We could set a dangerous precedent here, Mr. Speaker. We should not dismiss President Greer, the *duly*, if strangely, elected President of the United States, so easily. Nor Ms. Light in the Lodge. I have the greatest respect for both. I believe strongly in the president's programs to effect change and avert global catastrophe. Further, I have checked my constituency on this matter and on the matter my reelection next year, which is assured. Therefore, I am now announcing my membership in the Earth Rights Party for the next two years." He turned to address the other representatives. "I urge the rest of you to join me in voting nay."

A few seconds of astonished silence were followed by an uproar.

Jaubert forgot himself entirely and banged his gavel, shouting, "You can't do that, Elijah Jackson."

Elijah's big bass voice quashed the room into silence. "I beg your pardon, I have just done it. I know the strength of our government lies in its two-party system, which assures a clear majority for one party. However, I believe a third party can be useful for a time in pressuring two blindfolded major parties into doing what the people need."

Another clamor rose, and most of the representatives were on their feet.

Jaubert shrieked, "You're out of order!" His words were lost in the din. He banged louder. The handle on the gavel broke off in his hand, bouncing the mallet off the podium.

Elijah raised his arms and flapped his hands to calm the representatives.

Stillness settled over the room slowly as they sat down again.

Jaubert clenched his jaw. He had to move on, get more yea votes into the proceedings. "No more outbursts like that," he shouted. "We'll never get through." He looked at the list again. "Janssen of Minnesota."

Every eye turned to Janssen, in the back row, two desks from Brent. "Earth Rights Party. And proud of it. Nay."

"Jaubert, Louisiana. Yea. Jilkins, Oregon."

"Nay."

"Josten, South Dakota."

Josten stood, but his answer was long in coming. "Yea."

"Judd, Rhode Island."

"Nay."

"Klingmann, Michigan."

Klingmann stood, still tallying something on a sheet of paper. "My constituency is split down the middle, too," he said, "but I personally agree with my respected colleague from Texas that we should not set a precedent of dumping a legally elected official so lightly. I can find no wrong in his actions, and if we don't believe in his views, all we have to do is vote them down. I vote nay."

A thoughtful mood settled over the room. Jaubert looked quickly through the next few names. He needed a few certain yea votes immediately to counteract the effect of Jackson and Klingmann. "Lovell, West Virginia."

"Yea."

"Now just a minute, Jaubert, you skipped me," yelled Kolb.

"And me," yelled Kriezka. "And I vote nay."

"Me, too," said Kolb, "and you just pushed me off the fence with that trick."

"What do you mean by that? I thought I was finished with the K's. I apologize to my learned colleagues." Jaubert bowed in their direction and looked down at his list again to cover the reddening of his face. He could hardly bring himself to read the next names. He knew they were not his friends. He dared not skip any more.

Paul and Ed Petersen watched the proceedings in the Oval Office.

Paul stared at Jaubert's attempts to pull the vote back to his side. "That's it, isn't it?" he asked, reeling with disbelief. "The roll call's only half over and he's blown it."

Ed was jubilant. "Even he knows he's pushed too far. The rest of the vote will go against him."

The camera swung quickly to the floor, where Elijah Jackson was slowly rising.

Paul stood and laid a hand on the television set. "I wish I were there right now to shake the hand of that good man. What an incredible sense of timing."

Jackson moved deliberately out of his row, up the aisle, and out of the room. Brent followed, then Bethune, Janssen, Kolb, and Kriezka. Jaubert glanced darkly at them as he read off the next names. The station took a commercial break, and when it returned, several others were walking out. Jaubert had reached the P's and was looking sick. The screen shifted to the studio and a commentator said, "Our experts are certain at this point that Clive Jaubert, who has apparently committed the political blunder of his career, can no longer pull the votes he needs to put the President back in shoe sales and the Vice President back in her office on the reservation."

Paul and Ed shook hands and cuffed each other on the shoulder.

"I have to call Emma," Paul said. "Give me a minute before Norma sends in the next appointment, please, Ed."

When the door closed, he glanced at the scar again. It seemed diminished.

He dialed Emma's private number, desperate to share the moment with her, but fearful, too. He hadn't heard a word from her since he'd suggested following her to Wyoming.

CHAPTER FIFTY NINE

In the President's Dining Room, Paul regarded his guests, Emma, Elijah, and Brent, who sat huddled around the table despite the warm air coming from the ancient heating vents. Outside, a gust of the howling February sleet storm badgered the windows, sending an icy tremor tracking down his spine.

He passed the tureen of steaming potato soup around the table. "A little more to warm you from the inside out?"

Emma took it without allowing her fingers to contact his, leaving him with a sense of loss. The touch would have warmed him more than the soup. For months now she'd avoided him when she could and kept her distance when the duties of office threw them together. But he always saw the sadness and longing in her eyes. Now she kept her eyes on the tureen and set it in front of Elijah.

Elijah patted his perfectly flat stomach. "Before I take any more of this, please tell me there's not some heavy main course coming."

"Nope, just fish and green salad," said Paul, getting up and stepping to the sideboard to keep from reaching across the table and touching Emma. As he passed behind her, his hands stiffened in desire to lift aside the long black hair and kiss the back of her neck. Tonight, when the others left, he'd make her talk to him, no matter how she shrank from him. "Anyone for another cup of tea?"

When no one answered, he sat down again and took up the yellow note pad next to his knife. No matter how queasy his determination made him, he was still president with the evening's agenda to attend to. "Okay, where were we? The rapid transit bill passed by a hair. Elijah says Emma's bills one, four, and eight will get out of committee next week; the rest got buried somewhere."

Brent held his teacup in front of him, his fingers around it for warmth. "I don't get it," he said. "They're letting out the education bill, they'll probably give you a secretary of population, and they'll recommend the proposed greenbelts to replace slums. The greenbelts are the most distant results of these bills and hinge on two and three. What's the matter with their thinking?"

Elijah smiled. "Now, see, this is where I have a leg up on all you neophytes," he said, shoving his soup bowl aside. "Bills one, four and eight don't directly affect anybody at this point. The rest of them mean the real changes, the ones that scare the people."

Emma sighed. "I'm glad at least the education bill's on its way. How soon can we get television spots and printed ads out there after it passes?"

"A couple of weeks, I would think," said Brent.

Paul watched the young man who'd come so far since that first meeting in the Oval Office. "Brent, you want to be population secretary?" he asked.

Brent flushed and laughed. "I'm at least a prime example of not having too many kids. But no thanks. They'd never approve me."

The others glanced at Paul and then stared into their soup.

Paul's shoulders sagged at his own thoughtlessness. "I'm sorry, Brent, I said that without thinking."

"Actually, it was pretty funny." Brent looked around the table. "It's okay to laugh."

The others tried, but the gaffe had gone flat by that time.

"What about Danny?" asked Emma.

She was looking at him now, and the ache was in her eyes.

Clenching his hands together in his lap, Paul answered, "Nepotism."

Emma pulled her sweater tighter across her chest. "True. Gordy would love to do it."

"Who's Gordy?" asked Elijah.

Everyone laughed.

Brent said, "Chairman of your own new party."

Elijah grinned. "Good thing I'm black. You'd all see me blush."

Emma sat up straighter. "Someone from The Population Connection?"

"That sounds like the best idea," said Elijah.

Paul made a note on his pad. "Okay, how do we get the other bills exhumed?"

"We make about a million phone calls," said Elijah.

Paul rolled his eyes back. "Ugh, my favorite pastime. And it runs the whole political system."

When the meeting broke up around nine, Emma started to bundle up and leave with Brent and Elijah.

Paul grabbed her coat before she got the second arm in the sleeve. "Emma, could you stay a few minutes longer?" He hardly heard his question above the thrum of his heart.

She tensed but stopped with her back to him and watched Brent and Elijah step into the elevator. Her body jerked as she grabbed the coat sliding back down her arm.

He moved closer but kept his hands in his pockets. "Come, we'll take another cup of tea into the Sitting Hall."

"No more tea, thank you." She walked ahead of him, dropped her coat on a chair, and stood by the fireplace.

Paul crossed around her. He started to lift her head but saw her tense again. He dropped his hands to his side. "Emma, look at me, please."

When she raised her head, her eyes were hard as two chips of obsidian and her lips drawn thin.

"It's been so long," he started.

The muscles around her eyes softened and her chin quivered. "I have to do this," she said, her voice hoarse and ragged. "Don't make it any harder, please."

"Why do you have to? Talk to me."

She bit her lip and swallowed hard. "All right. I owe you an explanation." She took a deep breath. "You said you'd follow me to Wyoming, Paul. I can't let you do that. You saw my life when you came out for the funeral. That's why I let you come. It was a lot worse than you imagined, wasn't it?"

"I saw a bleak setting and a tragic situation. And yes, it was worse than I imagined. But if you wanted the setting to change my mind about you, it didn't."

She searched the ceiling as if a convincing argument were printed there. "I have to go back to that life. You don't. You wouldn't be happy in my world. You can go anywhere and do bright and happy things."

"Emma, that setting and the plight of your tribe aren't your life. Your life is *in* you, it's the willing struggle to make things right, to take on an entire world and say, 'There are things more important than our petty desires and wasteful habits, and we

442

need to change them.' That's what you are; that's what I love. Will love until I die. If I don't love what you have to cope with, perhaps it's my destiny to help you make it right."

Tears filled her eyes and ran down her cheeks. He fought down the desire to grab her and hold her so tight their bodies would merge into one.

Slowly, she shook her head. "I just ca..."

He put his finger on her lips. "Don't say no. There has to be a way to work it out."

A long time passed. Bit by bit, the rigidity in her body dissolved and left her head bent low. She whispered, "I try so hard, but I can't imagine my life without you, Paul." She put her forehead against his chest. "Sometimes I think everything we go through together, every cabinet meeting, every set-back, every small triumph binds us together like Siamese twins. I don't think I can survive the separation when this is over." A sob tore from her chest. "I don't want to lose you, but I'm so afraid I'll make you unhappy. I'm miserable just thinking about it."

He stroked the back of her neck and pulled her to him. "Will you at least talk to me about it? I know we'd have to find a way to live that'd make both of us feel useful, but we're intelligent people. If we put our heads together, we can come up with something."

He felt her start to shake her head against his chest. He put his hand on her head and held it still. A long time passed.

Slowly, Emma nodded, but as she lifted her head, his lips found hers and touched them so lightly that he could whisper directly into her, "I love you Emma."

She sobbed and threw her arms around his neck.

CHAPTER SIXTY

Clive Jaubert closed his office door and locked it, his back to the marble columns of the Capitol halls.

"Jaubert," a loud, grating voice demanded behind him.

He jumped, jerking his hand so wildly the key remained in the lock. He yanked the key out and wheeled around.

The man facing him wore a tailored gray suit with a diamond studded gold horseshoe in his black tie. He fixed Jaubert's eyes with the calm intensity of a cobra. "We're going for a walk."

"I'm not going anywhere with you. Who the hell do you think you are? What do you want?"

A page hurried by and the man smiled broadly. But his eyes never changed, and he said calmly, "You do not want to cross me. Let's go."

The man grabbed his arm like a tourniquet and steered him out of the building. They walked silently down the long steps and crossed to the Mall, where cherry blossoms lay as white petals and brown mush under their feet.

He slowed their pace and said, "I represent the interests of the people you've let down."

Jaubert's heart fluttered in fear. He had to get rid of this man. The Mall was filled with joggers, dog-walkers, and the usual tourists. He couldn't afford to be seen with anyone connected to... "Krieger?" he whispered. "He's not supposed to contact me. We agreed on that years ago. Why is he doing this?"

"Because in three years you haven't done a damn thing to stop Greer. The aquifer bill is about to come out of committee. You were supposed to block it."

"You have to get out of here. Tell Krieger I'm doing all I..."

The man tightened his grip and kept shoving him down the walkway under the shower of petals. "Shut up and listen. Krieger didn't send me."

"Then who...?"

"I told you to shut up. You will not let that bill through. My clients' interests are not served if it passes."

The blood rushed from Jaubert's face and hit his heart like a fire hose. "The gambling..."

The man jerked him out of the way of a jogger. "*Shut up.* You will do as I say now."

Jaubert felt his shackles rise and jerked his arm away. "You can't order me around. I'm the Speaker of the House. I don't care who you are, you can't control the whole political system."

The man gave a hearty laugh, but his cold, fixed eyes never left Jaubert's. "For now. But I can and will control you—the biggest cog in the wheel, the consummate public servant, the white knight of the people—as long as there's a big reward in it for you and somebody else does the dirty work."

Jaubert puffed out his chest, but the man jabbed a finger into it.

"Your political career's about over, Jaubert. Krieger's been... well, let's just say he no longer controls anything. He won't be funding you again, and without support from my clients, you won't even get nominated. They're rich, they're powerful, and they're nervous. They don't like being nervous."

Jaubert postured. "I don't care who they are. They can't bring me down. I've got enormous popular support."

"You used to. And they have an ace you might remember. The one Krieger thought he had."

Jaubert looked at the man, the muscles below his eyes pinching his skin into tight little folds as he tried to assess what might be coming. How much did this man know?

"He bought you the very first election. Without his help you'd still be doing legal legwork for Sun Oil."

"You don't know that. And he doesn't either. I was a good lawyer."

"You were as mediocre as they come. And even Krieger's so fed up, he's ready to let that story leak."

"I'll deny it. It's his word against mine, and you can just bet who the people are going to believe."

"Especially when they find out that you took the funds for your first three campaigns from the pension fund of Sun Oil workers."

Jaubert stopped in his tracks. "That's not true," he yelped. "He may have, but all I did was..."

"It doesn't matter what you did. Krieger can prove you embezzled the funds." The man reached in his suit coat and brought out a plain white envelope. The opening in the jacket revealed a brown strap over the shirt and the handle of a revolver.

Jaubert's heart stopped and then beat wildly.

The man grabbed Jaubert's hand and slapped the envelope against his palm.

Jaubert tore the envelope open. What slipped out was a newspaper article with the date three weeks away. The headline read:

SUN OIL PENSION FUND IN TROUBLE

Jaubert's hands shook as he scanned the article. It claimed documented proof of his using the pension for his campaign funds. "You can't do this. It isn't true." Even to him, his voice sounded like a panicky whine.

The man smiled. "Of course we can. You know how amazing computers are. We generated archive documents in Louisiana that prove it. But not to worry, Jaubert. This will never see the light of scandal unless the aquifer bill gets out of committee," the man said. "It'll appear the day the bill gets to the floor. And Krieger made tapes of your conversations way back then, which have been edited into undeniable evidence."

Jaubert's pulse throbbed in his temples. He couldn't have known back then that the oil industry would join the gambling cartels because of the aquifers. It wasn't his fault, but things had gone too far now. These Nevada people were desperate and they occupied a whole different level of ruthlessness. They could ruin him. "I've kept the bill in committee for a year and a half," he whined. "I'm doing everything I can. Tell them that, for God's sake."

"Well, in your politician's way, maybe you think you are. It just isn't good enough, is it?"

Jaubert let the question go unanswered.

"So they sent me up to give the whole situation a boost."

"What do you mean?"

"We're going for the throat. We want the vice president."

The words punched him in the stomach and he could barely whisper, "You want her how?"

"Wrapped up in a nice package with an invisible ransom note tied to it. 'You want to see your red-skin lover again, rescind the aquifer bills.' Greer's not stupid. He'll get the picture."

Aghast, Jaubert dropped the envelope and the article. His internal organs melted into his pelvis; his bones turned to rubber.

"Are you telling me you want to kidnap the vice president and use her for extortion?"

"With your help."

"That's insane. Do you have any idea how transparent that is? How many guards there are on her? Nobody kidnaps a vice president. It can't be done. And I certainly won't help. Nothing doing."

"You don't have to be in on the snatch. You just have to set up a scenario so we have access to her. Get her where she's accessible to us. We'll take care of the strategy."

"Are you crazy? How do you propose I do that?"

"Jesus, Jaubert. What *are* you good for? Come up with something." The man picked up the article and held it in front of his face, shaking a couple of cherry petals from it. "This news item isn't their last resort, so don't even fantasize about warning Greer or the Secret Service. We've got you under surveillance."

Jaubert rubbed at a hot and constricted area of his chest. He looked up at the stranger. His voice came out as a pleading whisper. "The bill isn't out of committee yet. Tell him I'll find a way to kill it before it ever reaches the House."

"So much the better. They want the vice president anyway. Insurance. I'll be in touch in forty-eight hours. Make no mistake. By that time, you *will* have a plan. Otherwise, my clients are not likely to wait to release this. And that'll be the least of your worries." He patted Jaubert on the cheek and walked away.

Jaubert ran back to the Capitol like a small boy about to wet his pants. He'd lose everything. He wouldn't be able to show his face anywhere in the entire country if they ran that story. They might as well go ahead and kill him.

Five minutes later he was on the phone in his office, struggling to keep his panic out of his voice. "Giordano, Jaubert. How's it look for the committee vote on that bill Greer wants out tomorrow?...That close? Look, Giordano, it can't get out to the floor, you hear?...Never mind that. You realize what'll happen to our chances if it gets out ...I know that, but we thought the same thing about the housing bill, and the welfare bill, and those ludicrous bills the vice president dreamed up. If we don't stop this idiot, it's not just me that's going down. We've been bedfellows too long...I'm not threatening, it's just..." He listened for several minutes, growing paler. The line went dead and the dial tone droned in his ear. His mouth fell open and he stared at the receiver. "Constituents!" he spat at it, and "You put them above me? You don't dare dump me, you slimy son of a Wop." He threw the humming receiver across the desk. The telephone flew after it, and both crashed to the floor.

He got up and paced for a minute. "Damn fool, Giordano, not even the chairman. Josten, I'll work on him." He retrieved the phone and dialed the chairman of the committee.

CHAPTER SIXTY ONE

In her bedroom in the Vice President's House, Emma stepped into her black loafers while holding the telephone to her ear. "Paul?"

"Hi, sweetheart."

The smile she heard in his voice sent a rush of pleasure from her ear to her toes. Grinning back at him, she tucked the phone between her chin and shoulder while she shrugged into a jacket. "You always manage to give off such warmth, you know that?"

"No, I don't give off a single calorie if I'm talking to...say... Rutherford."

Emma laughed. "Okay, to me, then. I like it. It always comes through."

"I can't think how it'd come through right this minute. I'm in a stew over the aquifer bill. As usual."

"Yeah, I heard about the postponement. A whole week. Again."

"If we don't get it out soon, the debate will last until next year. Who knows what the new president will do with it? Unless, of course, it's Jaubert."

"Speaking of the lout, I just got a call from him. He wants me to meet him in half an hour."

"At ten o'clock at night? Whatever for?"

"He wants to talk about a compromise that'll get the bill out. He said he was too busy all day to see me but tonight he's making a speech to a group of high-schoolers in front of the Lincoln Memorial and wants me to meet him there."

"If he wants to talk about the bill, he should come to me."

"I told him that, but he says I'm harder to convince, and if he can win me over, you'll follow along."

"Strike three hundred against Jaubert. Look, that's no reason to haul you out in the middle of the night."

Emma slung her purse over her shoulder and headed down the hall. "I know. I should've insisted that he come here, but this is so important. I'd do almost anything. It'll be the first time I've met with him one-on-one, and I'll talk myself hoarse to convince him."

"Jaubert's a lost cause, Emma, and this is too fishy. Let me go."

"I'm already on my way out. Don't worry."

"Of course I'm going to worry. Take the whole squad of gray-suits, okay?"

"Oh, Paul, it's a public place. And this is not some cloak and dagger mission."

"Emma, please, do it for me."

"Okay, okay. I promise."

"And call me when you leave him."

"Will do."

From the top of the stairs, Emma called, "Get the whole posse, Shirl."

Shirl loped out to signal for three sedans to make up the cavalcade.

After he hung up, Paul paced and paced in the Oval Office. She should have let him deal with Jaubert. But that was Emma. Bull-headed as a gator just out of hibernation.

Jaubert. Why was he *always* such a thorn? What was he up to this time? Maybe she was right. Maybe there was nothing sinister about it at all. Still, sinister or not, she ought to be guard-ed, and lately she'd been finding ways of keeping the gray suits at a distance. Lord knows, it was stifling to have them hound-ing your every step, but she shouldn't leave herself open to risk. He should call Wes at the FBI. And Dave at Secret Service. He reached for the phone and hesitated. She'd promised to take the guards. He paced the length of the office and back again. What if she'd already sent them off shift early, one of her favorite tricks? He picked up the receiver. She'd be furious. Okay, let her be furious. At least she'd be safe.

From her seat in the middle car of the cavalcade, Emma was star-tled to see the area around the Memorial cleared of cars. Red cones and orange and white barricades surrounded it. At the entrance there was space for one car to pass through.

Shirl looked at her in the mirror. "This ain't right, Ma'am. Ah'm puttin' up this glass, jus' in case."

When the partition between the front and back had whirred shut, she added over the loudspeaker, "An' I shore wish you'd'a let one of them other guys ride with us."

Emma's heart stuttered. "It's just like Jaubert, Shirl, to have the whole place barricaded for his speech. But keep your eyes open. Have the others check things out first."

Shirl radioed the other agents.

Already Emma could see Jaubert waddling down the stairs of the monument toward them. At the other end of the area that had been sealed off a car sat facing them. Probably Jaubert's.

The three security cars rolled to a stop in a tight chain. The agents stepped out of the other cars. Immediately, the area was fogged in a white smoke. The agents went down, trying to find a target, their guns jerking though the smoke before they lost consciousness.

Shirl was already trying to maneuver the car to get out.

Emma grabbed her purse and searched for her cell phone. Why hadn't she listened to Paul?

"Damn, too close," cried Shirl. She threw the car into reverse and slammed into the car behind, but it was too late.

A dark figure in a gas mask ran toward the car. He pried open the corner of her door with a crowbar just enough to shoot something inside. The white smoke filled the front of the car.

Shirl choked, grabbed her gun, and shoved at the door. The second it was unlatched, the figure jerked it open.

Shirl tried to aim. Her hand wobbled. The man grabbed her arm and yanked her from the car. He struck her on the head, threw her to the side, and unlocked the rest of the doors.

Others were there now, also wearing gas masks. Arms reached in. Gloved hands grabbed Emma by the arm and jerked her out of the seat. She came out fighting and screaming, but the dissipating smoke choked her. The cell phone flew out of her hand. Her fist found ribs and she heard a grunt. She found a rubber mask and tore at it. A hand pushed at her face. She opened her mouth to bite it but instead of fingers she got a wad of cloth. Someone slapped tape over her mouth. Another cloth clamped over her nose. She clawed at the hand. Liquid in the cloth burned her nose, inside and out. Her muscles began to weigh at her. She went down.

The car parked at the end of the steps shot forward.

As they shoved her into the back seat, she heard Clive Jaubert's voice in a loud whisper, "Hey, you're supposed to make it look like you beat me up."

She hoped they obliged. The car jolted forward and she fell backwards; she heard the screech of tires as if from a great distance. Her mind went dark.

CHAPTER SIXTY TWO

S till in the Oval Office, Paul was moving his eyes across the newspaper spread out on the desk, but his mind was on Emma and Jaubert. It didn't feel right, and he should have made those calls the second he hung up. He glanced from his watch to the phone for the tenth time in half an hour. How long would it take before she gave up on Jaubert?

The phone rang, startling him. So soon?

"Emma?"

"Mr. President, this is Dave Carling. The vice president has been kidnapped."

Paul leaped from the chair. "What? What happened? Didn't I tell you to send a detail?"

"I did, sir. I'm on my way to the House right now."

Paul slammed down the phone and buzzed for Ed to come in. Before Ed arrived, Paul whipped himself through every level of hell. He should have made her stay away and gone himself. He should have called Dave sooner. He should have cowed Jaubert into complete submission when he had the chance. She was gone because he'd been too stupid to protect her.

And beyond the guilt was pain. He balled his fist against his chest, squashing shirt and tie into a rumpled mess. They might as well have sliced out his heart and taken it with her. Without her he was only half a human being.

When Ed heard the news, his face drained of color, but he rushed out of the room again without a word.

Ten minutes later he ushered in Dave Carling, head of the Secret Service. With him was Shirl Wainwright, a scuffed and embarrassed strung bean, towering above him, swaying, her face pale and her bloodshot eyes slightly slued. She and Dave started talking at once, but Shirl's twang overrode him.

"Mr. Presiden', Ah am so sorry. You put her in mah charge, and I shorly did let you down." Only one of her eyes focused on him, but tears ran from both.

Paul charged past Dave and grabbed her by the arm. "What happened?"

"They took her, sir, an' Ah didn' even get off a shot at 'em. I shoulda known they was comin' for her, that car parked goin' in the wrong di-rection like that."

"Who took her, for God's sake, woman."

"Ah don' know, suh, the one come at me, he was wearin' a gas mask."

"Where were the other agents?"

Shirl's face reddened. "All in the other cars, Mr. Presiden', like she told 'em." She looked at the floor. "Soon's they opened their doors to check things out, they got gassed. They went down tryin' to fight, sir."

Paul closed his eyes and tried to calm himself. "Okay, Shirl, tell me the whole thing."

"We drove up and, like Ah said, there was this other car settin' there. It didn' have no plate on the front, or Ah woulda memorized it. After the others got gassed, I tried to drive her away, but we was blocked between the other cars. Then somebody pried open the door and got some of the gas into the front of my car, too. I came out fightin', but my eyes was watering, and I was already losing it. This guy with the mask knocked me out. Soon's Ah come to, ah tol' 'em, you take me right to the White House to tell the presiden', cause it's mah fault, sir, an' don' you go blamin' her, y'hear?"

"Did the car have a plate on the rear?"

"Ah don' know, suh, Ah never got a look. But Ah know what kind it was, 'cause Ah know cars. It was a '94 Cutlass, gray or dark blue, hard to tell in the light 'round the monument."

"Be sure the FBI gets that. Was Jaubert there?"

"Yessir, standing on the steps, an' he started right toward us. When Ah come to, they was tendin' him, too."

"Did you hear any voices you'd recognize?"

"No, suh, nobody said a word."

"Have you had your head looked at?"

"No, sir, like Ah said, Ah had 'em to bring me right on here."

"Go check in at the hospital, Shirl, and if they don't keep you, be here first thing in the morning."

"Ah'm gonna be here no matter what, sir. Ah ain' gonna let you down again."

Shirl left and Wes Schmidt arrived with Ed through the same opening of the door.

Paul turned to Dave. "Where were your men?" he shouted, barely able to control his anger, though he knew he should direct it at himself.

Dave turned back from watching Shirl leave. "I sent them out the minute you called, sir. They just didn't get there in time."

"I want them working with the FBI on this."

"Yes, sir."

"Jaubert set this up."

Ed Petersen frowned. "Jaubert and kidnapping? It doesn't fit, Mr. President. It's not his way. It's stupid. Besides, he'd never get that close to his own dirty work."

"Even under pressure?"

Ed shrugged. "Not unless someone has a whole trainload of dirt on him."

"Can you doubt that?"

"No, but it'll take an archaeological dig to unearth it."

Wes opened a small notebook. "He got beaten up in the incident."

Paul stifled an impulse to cheer. "Serious?"

Wes shrugged. "We don't know yet. He's in the hospital."

"Have him cuffed to the bed and question him the minute he's able to talk."

Wes slipped his notebook back in his coat pocket and started for the door. "We have the scene cordoned off, Mr. President, and if there's so much as microscopic evidence, we'll find it."

"Worry about the scene later, Wes. Right now, I want Emma found. According to the agent who was with her, the kidnappers were wearing gas masks, the car was a dark '94 Cutlass with no plate on the front."

"I'll get right on that, Mr. President."

"Get the D.C. police on it, too, Wes. Immediately. And have my private lines tapped for the time being in case the kidnappers make demands. I'll sign an order for that."

Wes nodded and left with Dave.

Paul paced the office, his arms folded hard across his chest. He tried to keep the fear out of his voice. "I need to do something, Ed."

"There's nothing you can do but let the others handle it, sir."

"What kind of people have the nerve to kidnap the vice president? Where would they take her?"

"I have no idea."

Paul stopped and faced the curtains behind the desk. "I'm in love with her, Ed."

"Yes, sir, I know."

"Help me think. No, I ought to send you home. You've been here since dawn."

"I'm staying, Mr. President. As a friend, Paul."

Paul turned toward him, blinked and swallowed. "Thank you, Ed." He went back to pacing. "What do we start with?"

Ed sat down on the sofa. "I guess we can assume who's behind it—Jaubert's oil constituents."

"Kidnapping the vice president? I can't see them plotting anything so brazen. They buy the political machine to get what they want. More likely the Nevada interests. And we can assume they want the same thing."

"There's an outside chance it was just a daring kidnapping for ransom."

Paul ran his hands into this hair and pulled. "If it were, they'd have called by now."

"I doubt anyone would call the White House, Paul. Maybe there'll be something by courier or the plain old mail in the morning."

"Let's put ourselves in their place. Whatever their reasons..."

Ed sniffed. "Money."

"Right. They desperately want unlimited access to the aquifers. This Krieger with Sun Oil has the closest ties to Jaubert, but every time the FBI tries to investigate data about him, the information is blocked. Wes has the best hacks in the Bureau working on it. I know Danny said the gambling cartels were using what he called a computer Mafia, who could gain access to anything. Once they get in, they alter data to suit their purpose. This is going to make following the money almost impossible."

"Then we batter away at the human side of it. Who would agree to kidnap such a guarded, public figure? No one in his right mind would try it."

Paul sat down on a sofa and stood again immediately. "Someone too stupid to know better or too professional to be intimidated. Terrorists, maybe."

"We'll know more when we get the ransom demand."

"If we get one."

Ed looked up, surprised. "You think there's any doubt?"

"Well, if it was the gambling people, they'll probably assume I know what the motive was and not bother. We get a lot less to go on that way, too."

"You're right."

"If that's the case, let's hope the kidnappers they hired were stupid, not professional."

"So all we're likely to have is Shirl's description of the car."

Paul searched desperately for a strategy. "Get Caitlin to notify the media that we're asking all area residents within a...say... three hundred mile radius to help find the Cutlass. Be sure there's a picture of one on all the channels."

Ed used the phone on Paul's desk.

When Caitlin had promised to get right on it, Paul paced again. "Where would you take a kidnapped vice president, Ed?" he asked. "You know D.C. better than I."

"Well, if I were stupid, I guess I'd find some dark, abandoned place, the basement of a building scheduled for demolition, like in the movies. If I were smart, I'd take her to some place where no one would expect it, like back to the vice president's house or the reservation. And if I were professional, I'd already have her on a plane out of the country, or out to sea."

Paul stopped. "Out of the country. That makes the best sense to me. Get Wes to check every airport within a hundred mile radius for private planes that took off any time after 10:30.

And have them get the helicopter ready, will you? We can check on boats."

"Paul," Ed said, reaching for the phone again, "I've already shut the House down. You know you can't leave here in a crisis."

Paul growled through his clenched jaw and rolled his head in frustration. "What I really want is to get my own car and scour this city looking for her."

"I'd go with you if it were possible. I'll stay with you."

"Ed, I can't tell you what it means..."

Ed touched his shoulder. "I understand. I'll have them bring some coffee."

CHAPTER SIXTY THREE

Emma's mind shrank from the pain of a grinding black headache. She forced herself into consciousness and sent a message to her hand. Somewhere very far away something moved at the end of her body but met a restraint and flopped back into inertia. She opened her right eye a slit. A thousand pinpoints of light shot into her head and slammed full force into the headache. She groaned. The groan lowered to a continuous low hum that didn't stop when her voice did. An engine.

She sank back into darkness. Again the headache intruded, but her mind was clearer. Her tied hands came up and touched her lips, sore where the tape had been ripped off. She tried her eyes again, opening both slightly and waiting until they adjusted to the many lights.

She was in the cockpit of an airplane. To her right a fish swam by outside a small round window. Her head jerked back and set off another wave of pain. She tried to put the airplane and the fish together. She looked left. The pilot wore a ski mask. He turned and looked at her but said nothing.

"Where am I?" she tried to ask. Her tongue, thick and revolting, turned the question into a croak.

The pilot pointed a gloved finger at a gauge on his controls. It showed depth of 100 feet. He pointed at her little window and a television monitor between the two seats. She was in a small submarine. She froze in terror. This was no bunch of amateurs that had kidnapped her. They were desperate and had resources. They wouldn't stop at killing her. Paul would be frantic. Paul. She nearly sobbed but forced herself into control.

"Where are you taking me?" she asked more clearly, trying to sound authoritative and dangerous.

The pilot stared ahead. To his left a small clipboard partially covered his window. With effort, she focused on the forms clipped to it. The clip covered part of the heading, but she read Sun O....

Anger settled in and drove the last fuzziness from her head but did nothing for the headache. Emma looked around. This was not a military submarine; it was barely large enough for two people. Above her was the escape hatch. The pilot was paying her no attention. She began to watch his actions and study the controls. He was not a large man. If she could hit him... Right. Then she'd know exactly what to do with a submarine.

He drew back on a lever and they tilted upwards. When the gauge registered fifteen feet, the pilot cut the engine and a clank sounded against the side of the submarine, followed slowly by three others. The submarine surfaced into bright sunlight alongside a ship. Emma's heart sank. She had been out for at least eight hours. She was eight hours from safety and from Paul.

The pilot took a second mask from the floor and yanked her closer. With her tied hands, she tried to scratch him, rip the mask from his head.

He got his hands around her throat. "Don't make me kill you," he whispered harshly.

She sank back and let him pull the mask over her head. Now all she could see was ribbed fabric. Her breath left a patch of moisture below her nose.

The submarine rocked, swinging through the air. She heard the squeak as he turned the hatch wheel. She was lifted out and set down onto the swaying deck. Hands turned her and propelled her from behind. A hand on her shoulder guided her. When it pressed down, she stopped. Two hands moved her foot over a ledge and down a step while two others held her upright. The boat lurched, she fell against a wall and pitched forward, throwing the person below her down the steps. They landed in a heap at the bottom of the short flight. In the confusion that followed, she reached up and yanked the mask from her face. It did her no good. The two men who grabbed her both wore masks, one of them the pilot. They picked her up, untied her hands, shoved her through a door, and locked it. She fell onto a bunk along the wall. The ceiling light showed nothing at all in the cabin but a tiny bathroom. There was no porthole.

For two days the ship rolled through rough seas. After a third day in quieter waters, they hooded and bound her again. They shoved her into a smaller boat, along a jetty, across sand, and into another room, its only furniture a bed draped with mosquito netting.

The one window in her new quarters was boarded on the outside, leaving only cracks between the boards and a couple of knotholes, through which she could see water and a palm tree. An adjoining bath, windowless, contained toiletries she might need. The room was stifling, and the fan on the ceiling did little to stir the muggy air.

Paul hurried with Ed from their hasty breakfast to the Oval Office. "I don't believe for one minute that Jaubert was so injured he needs all this time in the hospital, Ed. Have him brought here the minute he's released, to the Cabinet Room. And have his attorney there. I don't care what day, what time, or what else happens to be on my agenda. And I want the entire table full. Get Wes to bring several other FBI agents that Jaubert's never seen before, get a few men in uniform with their chests full of medals, and have a court reporter sit right next to him, taking down every word."

"Yes, sir."

"I want to intimidate the hell out of that bastard. This time we'll get something out of him. And get Shirl. Poor thing, she's about to kill herself trying to make up for it. Maybe when she sees him, it'll jog some memory."

"Right. Did they find the car?"

Paul nodded. "And one hair that was Emma's. Wes said the Cutlass was bought for cash at a used car auction, but there were no prints in it other than the previous owner's and people related to her. Not even Emma's, which means she must have been unconscious when they put her in it." He choked. "A single hair, Ed. I'm going crazy with worry. How could they snatch her like that and disappear without a trace?" Paul clenched his teeth, blindly striding along the colonnade, fending off visions of Emma lying in a pool of blood. "Do you think they'd harm her, Ed, kill her?"

"Absolutely not, Paul."

"I keep telling myself that'd be the wrong move on their part, but I'm so damned scared they will..."

"We're going to find her, Paul."

"They don't want that bill out. The committee vote is coming up. If they vote the bill out, that might already mean the end of her usefulness to them."

"No, it wouldn't. There'd still be the House vote, and that won't come up for at least a month."

"They couldn't risk keeping her that long. I could call Josten and ask him to postpone the vote from day to day till we find her, buy some time, but that just knuckles under to them. And Emma'd be furious. Oh, God, she even said the last time I talked to her that the bills were more important than she was. She might as well have said, 'Don't negotiate with them over me.' It was almost as if she knew."

"The vote isn't until Friday. Let's hope she's found by then."

Two evenings after she'd been imprisoned, Emma stood with her ear to the door, listening as usual. By now, she knew their routine. There was always a man was on guard in the next room. Occasionally she heard a male voice speaking alone, in Spanish. Since she heard a second voice only when a servant rolled in her meal cart, she assumed there was a telephone there. The servant and the guard always exchanged a word or two. Then the guard's key scraped in the lock, the door opened, and they came in, both in masks, always silent. She had to get to that telephone and call Paul. The thought of Paul made her heart ache and squeezed tears into her eyes.

She pressed her ear against the wood and forced herself to concentrate on how to help him find her. She had no idea where she was. It was a tropical place, where mosquitoes plagued her at night even with the netting around the bed. If Sun Oil was in on the kidnapping, she was probably somewhere on the Gulf Coast.

Anger rose to her throat again and she balled her fists. Outside the door she heard the cart roll in on its squeaky wheels, bringing supper. She leaped for the bed and curled up, facing the wall. She listened hard for a change in their routine. If there were only one of them, she might be able to hit him on the head with something and run for the phone, but she had no chance against two.

CHAPTER SIXTY FOUR

The ringing of a telephone sliced through Emma's light sleep and her eyes flew open. The telephone she surmised in the other room had never rung before but it was a cell phone ring, not a land-based phone. She leaped through the mosquito netting and had her ear to the door in a second. The voice was muffled and spoke Spanish, but it was loud. It kept repeating itself. Bad connection. Still, there was no mistaking the subservience in the words, and the acceptance of a command.

Footsteps followed and she started to bolt back to the bed. A word of annoyance accompanied the sound of keys landing on something near her door. And something more solid. The guard had dropped his keys. Maybe the phone, too. A door opened and closed. The room on the other side was still. Emma looked at her watch. It was nearly seven, when they always brought breakfast. She tried the door handle once, even knowing it was futile.

She ran to the bathroom, grabbed the towels, and rolled them up. She jerked back the cover on the bed and laid the towels at an angle to simulate legs drawn up. She laid the pillow next to them, poked it in the middle to make hips and shoulders, and threw the sheet over the dummy. There was nothing in the room she could use to fake her dark hair. She bunched the netting where it would hide the missing head from anyone coming in. She ran to the door, shaking her head at this oldest trick in existence. They'd never fall for it. She listened briefly. Already she could hear the rattle of the cart coming from outside the guard room.

She looked around wildly. There was not a single object in the room she could use to hit him over the head. The hairbrush was plastic, there was no chair, no dresser with drawers in it.

The door to the guard room opened. Emma rushed to the bathroom, grabbed the lid off the top of the toilet, and raced back to station herself behind her door. In a rush of adrenaline, she raised the heavy porcelain over her head and waited.

The servant stopped and muttered something in Spanish. Keys jingled. He fiddled with them, swore when the first few didn't turn in the lock. Emma leaned against the wall. She would not be able to hold the lid up much longer.

The door swung open. The cart rolled through it and stopped before the servant cleared the door. Emma heard him breathing and sensed him looking back for advice. The guard had not returned.

"*Señorita?*" he whispered, pushing the cart another few feet.

The toilet lid was about to crash on her own head. Emma bit her bottom lip and waited, her arms trembling under the weight.

The servant took a couple more steps forward, his attention focused on the very still figure on the bed.

Emma stepped out and brought the porcelain down, striking him on the crown of his ski mask. The lid slid down his back and smashed on the tile floor. He pitched forward, sending the cart crashing against the wall. He lay still.

Emma turned, stepped to the door, and listened. The phone. It lay on a small table inches from her hand. She flipped it open, ready to dial Paul's private number. Her fingers froze over the buttons. No signal. With a soft cry of annoyance, she turned slowly. There. One bar. Weak. She started to hit the area code for Washington. Wait. All the Spanish. Was she in a foreign country? If so, what did she dial for an international line? Assuming this phone would connect to international. She closed her eyes, pushing aside her anger over not having thought of this during the last three days. Desperately, she punched in numbers and then Paul's private line.

She glanced back at the servant she'd floored. He was not moving. The line she dialed was ringing, crackling through the bad connection. Voices were approaching from the hall. They must have heard the cart crash.

"Pick up, Paul, answer it," she whispered. She had to get out of the room. They'd lock her up again, possibly kill her. She punched the end button and then swore at herself. She should take it with her. No, if she were running away, she wouldn't be able to keep the phone on the signal. Frantically, she clicked it to redial, then laid it on the table with its antenna toward the weak signal, hoping the guard wouldn't notice it.

She raced through French doors that opened to the outside. Below the house there was a jetty, but no boat offered escape. She glanced terrified in both directions. To her left a stone wall closed in the terrace. To the right, past the boarded window, a set of stairs led down to a beach. She ran down them. By the time she'd run fifty feet on the sand, a man's voice was yelling in the guard room. She glanced back and realized that her footprints on the sand were a giveaway.

Thick stands of palm trees and underbrush lined the beach. She veered off the sand into the cover of the vegetation. She thrashed through sword-like grasses that cut her arms and hanging vines that tripped her, trying to keep the water in sight, dismissing visions of snakes and malarial insects. She was leaving a trail of broken plants, but if she slowed to be more careful, they'd catch her before she reached help.

The beach had curved as she ran, and she stepped out onto the sand again after fifteen minutes, looking back to the left. No one was in sight, but she could hear voices. This part of the beach was strewn with rocks and old coconuts. If she could use them as stepping stones, she could run in the water, where the small surf would cover her footprints. She'd surely find a town or at least another house just up the coast.

She stepped wildly from rock to rock, missing a few and turning her ankle as one coconut shell rolled out from under her foot, but she reached the water and began running away from the voices. Always the beached curved to the right. The yelling voices began to laugh and faded behind her. Emma glanced back. No one was following her now. It made no sense. She turned and ran on, and on.

Forty minutes later, she rounded a pronounced curve, stopped and hurried back into the trees. Before her lay a slight inlet. Across it stood a house with a low stone wall, and just past it, a trail of footprints that veered into the vegetation. Emma's heart sank. It was an island. Four men in head masks sauntered along the beach, heading toward her, occasionally poking about in the underbrush. It would not take them ten minutes to reach her. There was no point turning back. She could only head away from the beach and hope to find a place to hide. She looked out quickly and scanned the horizon. No other land was visible, nor any boats.

She ran back through the water a few hundred yards and then worked her way carefully inland, trying not to break the vegetation. She was climbing, but not by much. The island was flat. At best she would find some thick vegetation to crawl into.

She'd gone only a short distance when she came across a large wooden tank with a wide flange at the top, a giant rain barrel, the water supply for the house. On its downhill side, where the water leaked through the staves, the vegetation was rank and tall. Emma scouted it and found she could squeeze between the brush and the tank.

She looked down into the tank. She couldn't reach over the broad lip and get to the water, but if she took off her blouse and draped it into the tank, she could drink from a dripping sleeve. There were bugs and dead leaves floating in the water, but she'd drunk it in the house and not gotten sick. Probably it was filtered somewhere. She would wait till she was desperately thirsty before trying it. Instantly her mouth turned to hot cotton.

She turned and squeezed under the flange, surrounded by green stems and leaves and a few hanging fruits that she'd never seen before. Damn it, why couldn't this be a banana or mango island, even avocado. Her escape had been stupid, had brought her into more danger than if she'd stayed put. She should have waited. She might have had another chance at the phone, when she could wait for Paul to answer.

Paul. His name made her breath catch and tears burn her eyes. Paul, who gave her so much. Who asked so little in return. Who loved her. Whom she loved with every beat of her exhausted, terrified heart. And had never told him. It was the first thing she would say to him when he found her. If he found her.

CHAPTER SIXTY FIVE

From his seat at the Cabinet Room table, Paul heard Jaubert in the hall, spouting his usual bombast, and stifled the desire to run out and strangle him. He grabbed the arms of the chair and reminded himself of his promise to let Wes Schmidt handle the meeting.

"This way, gentlemen," said Wes, holding the door open.

Clive Jaubert stepped into the room, limping, his head swathed in a huge gauze turban, a large bandage across his chin, his left arm in a sling. His face, however, registered no pain, his eyes no confusion. Wardell Majors, his attorney, came in behind him. They stopped just inside the door when they saw the number of people in attendance. Jaubert's face paled. Majors' darkened.

Paul laughed inwardly without twitching a muscle of the stern glare on his face.

Wes prodded them from behind. "You will sit opposite the President, Mr. Jaubert. Mr. Majors, your seat is next to Mr.

Jaubert. The lady to your left, Mr. Jaubert, will keep a record of this interview."

"Just a minute, sir," Majors cried.

The court reporter's keys clicked softly.

Majors looked belligerently at the military figures Ed had situated around the table. "I'd like you to explain who all these people are and what right they have to be in on these proceedings."

Wes tsked with impatience. "Mr. Majors, I'm sure you know this interview concerns the abduction of the Vice President of the United States. As such, it is a matter of national security, especially as we suspect she may have been taken out of the country. That should explain the military. Others here are from the President's staff, the State Department, the FBI, Secret Service, and the CIA. Do you have any objection to their presence?"

"No," said Majors. His voice had shrunk, but he raised his head and expanded his chest.

Wes waited till the two sat down and slowly moved around the table to take the seat next to Paul. He leafed through a file folder, appeared to read several pages, knit his brow into deep furrows, and looked up to address Jaubert.

"Now, Mr. Jaubert, you called Ms. Light in the Lodge at..." Wes looked into the folder again, "...9:53 p.m. on the night of April 7. What was the purpose of that call?"

"Don't answer that, Clive," warned Majors.

"According to Mr. Greer, you told her to meet you at the Lincoln Memorial where you were speaking before a group of high school students. We'd like you to provide the name of the high school so we can confirm it."

"My client is Speaker of the House, for God's sake," said Majors. "You have no right to question his word."

Paul shifted angrily in his seat and opened his mouth. He snapped it shut again when Wes nudged him under the table.

Wes went on calmly. "Well, Ms. Wainwright here did not see any children at the crime scene. In fact, the only person she saw was your client." He addressed Jaubert again. "Nor are we able to confirm that you had any speaking engagements at all on April 7. So why did you lie to Ms. Light in the Lodge?"

"Don't answer," said Majors.

"No matter, Jaubert," said Wes. "We know there's a connection between you and the kidnapping. It's only a matter of time before we prove it. In the meantime, you might consider the consequences. There's a difference between cooperating with us now as accessory to kidnapping and facing charges later for whatever else might happen to Ms. Light in the Lodge, injury or worse."

Paul blanched.

Wes put his hand on Paul's arm.

Shirl Wainwright leaped from her seat against the wall behind Majors, her fists balled.

Paul glared her back into her seat.

"I can't tell you anything," bleated Jaubert. "I got beat up when they took her, too, you know."

Wes gazed skeptically at the turban and the sling. "Yes, well, that would be necessary, wouldn't it?"

Jaubert squirmed.

"All right, we'll move to another topic. We need you to tell us everything you know about Mervin K. Krieger. We know he was behind every political advancement you've ever made. And we know he and his gambling friends are using the services of computer mercenaries to alter records of all kinds to suit their purposes. How is Krieger involved in this crime?"

Jaubert opened his mouth.

"Don't answer that," interrupted Majors. "My client has told you all he's going to. And this line of questioning is irrelevant."

Wes thumbed through the folder and found a few pages to scan before the glared at the lawyer. "Mr. Majors, you may be sure we're checking your records, too. If we find any connection, however slight, to Sun Oil or Krieger or certain gambling cartels, we will examine every breath you've drawn since you were born on..." Wes glanced into the folder again, "...August 18, 1958."

Majors raised his hand and pointed angrily at Wes. "We will not stand for this intimidation, sir."

The door to the reception area banged open and Norma burst in. She handed Ed a telephone message and smiled at Paul. Ed glanced at the slip of paper and rushed around the table.

Majors slapped Jaubert on the shoulder and they both stood to leave.

Paul started to order them back in their seats, but Ed shoved the telephone message in front of him. He read the slip. "8:17 a.m. Call to president's line traced to island off coast of Venezuela, 64:53 W long., 12:88 N lat."

Ed grabbed an atlas from a side table and pinpointed at the coordinates.

Paul grabbed Schmidt's arm, forgetting Jaubert completely. "Get on this immediately, Wes. Find out who owns this island."

Wes jotted down the numbers and ran from the Cabinet Room.

Jaubert and Majors rushed out behind him.

Paul glanced at their backs, but they barely registered. "Ed, I need someone in here who speaks Spanish, and get Norma to connect this phone to the president of Venezuela immediately."

Ed picked up the phone.

"Mister President, Ah speak Spanish, suh," drawled Shirl.

Paul looked up. "That's right, Emma told me you did. All right, the minute the call comes through, tell him we believe the Vice President is being held on an island that may belong to Venezuela. We want permission to use whatever means are necessary to free her. Can you manage that?"

"Yes, suh." Shirl sat down in the chair Wes had vacated and started practicing.

"General Pierson..." Paul started, but the telephone interrupted him. He nodded at Shirl. She picked up the handset and listened.

"*Señor Presidente*," she twanged into the phone, "*Hola, yo soy la...la...una secretaria de la...del presidente de los Estados Unidos.*" She listened and looked quizzically at the phone. "No, *Señor*, no *es un*...joke, joke," she said with her eyes closed, searching memory, "Oh, yeah, *chiste, no es chiste, Señor...Sí, naturalmente, mi presidente está aquí, pero no habla español*...oh." She handed the phone to Paul. "He wants to speak to you."

Paul took the phone. "*Señor Presidente*, I'm sorry, I don't speak Spanish...Ah, yes, and very well, I might say. *Señor* Ramos, we have just traced a call which might have come from our Vice President. As you know, she was kidnapped several days ago...Yes, thank you for your concern, sir. The thing is, the call seems to have come from somewhere along your coastline...no, an island, if we have the correct coordinates. Mr. Ramos, I am asking your permission to send whatever forces are necessary to rescue the Vice President...I see, yes, just a second... 64:53 west longitude, 12:88 north latitude...It's reasonable to assume so, yes...Thank you, sir, I'll pass that along to our men... That's very generous, Mr. Ramos, thank you very much." Paul laid the phone back on the table. "General Pierson, President Ramos has agreed to let us land a force on the island, on the condition that his own Coast Guard, who know the area, accompany us. He'll find out who owns the property there before we arrive and have his air force check the area out. We can use the Caracas airport. He'll provide helicopters and pilots to the island. I'll fly down with our forces in the fastest plane you have..."

"Oh, no, Mr. President, I absolutely cannot let..."

"I'm going, sir."

"But, Mr. Pr..."

Paul stood up so forcefully that his chair toppled. "General Pierson, I am the President of the United States, your commander in chief. This is a direct order. The presidential helicopter will take me to the nearest base, where you *will* make room for me in the fastest fighter plane in my command. I am going to get Ms. Light in the Lodge, do you understand? Have a doctor in another plane, just in case."

Shirl plucked at his sleeve.

"And find a place for Miss Wainwright, also," he commanded.

Across the table Ed grinned at him and raised his hand in a grand salute.

"Yes, sir," said General Pierson.

"Yes, *sir!*" echoed Ed.

CHAPTER SIXTY SIX

For five hours Emma leaned against the dank boards of the tank, brushing away flies and mosquitoes and centipedes and the sweat that rolled down her face. Occasionally, when voices approached from the beach, maybe a hundred yards away, she froze until they faded again. They seemed to be searching half-heartedly. Well, no wonder. They knew she couldn't get away.

Now they returned, ran toward her, and stopped. There was nothing half-hearted in their voices this time. She heard the thrumming of a large helicopter. Rescue. Flooded with joy and relief, she stood without thinking and banged her head on the flange. It let out a loud, hollow protest. She crouched again and listened, hoping the men hadn't heard the noise over the rumble of the helicopter. She needed to get out on the beach and wave her shirt or something. But they were between her and the helicopter.

She waited for it to come closer, but the chopper kept its distance, and in a few minutes the voices started up again, this time with an edge of fear. They headed away.

An hour and a half passed with no return of the helicopter. She was hungry. Too bad she hadn't hit the man *after* breakfast. Now it was mid-afternoon. She looked at a couple of the fruits hanging nearby. They were all green. She pulled the largest one from the vine and squeezed it. Hard as a coconut. She looked up at the flange of the tank. She could smash the fruit on it to see whether the rind enclosed flesh she could eat, but the noise would probably bring the guards.

She cut into the green skin with her thumbnail and sniffed at the juice that beaded out. It had no smell at all. Probably still green. She put her tongue to the slit in the fruit skin and puckered at the bitter taste. She couldn't bring up enough saliva to get spit it out.

She pulled off her blouse, stood cautiously, and threw it over the lip of the tank, holding on to the sleeve. When she pulled it out, the other sleeve was wet to the elbow, with only one dead bug stuck on the cuff. She flicked it off, sniffed, then sucked on the dripping end, and spit the bitterness out. She put the blouse back on.

Another hour went by. Every leaf in sight had Paul's face on it. He was coming, she thought. She had to believe it. They would advise him against it, but Paul would come. If her call had gotten through. The chances of that were almost zero. Bad signal. Probably dialed wrong. She fought back tears when their humming in her ears made it hard to listen for the voices.

The voices! They were close; speaking both Spanish and English now. The men were beating the brush, chopping it away. Why were they suddenly so frantic? She shrank as far into the bushes as she could, cringing against the tank and ignoring insects and sweat. Something hit the other side of the tank, sending a vibration through the wood and water. They were hacking at the vines and bushes, throwing branches aside, clearing everything around the tank. Emma made herself as small as possible, wishing she'd worn a green blouse.

"*Aquí*," yelled a voice only inches away, and the hacking increased on her left. Hands reached in.

She scrambled to the other side, but now there was slashing from that direction.

Next to her, a machete chopped away her last cover and two of the men came at her.

She came out kicking and grasping for their masks.

They surrounded her, marched her back to the beach, and turned right. A small yacht lay at the jetty now. They were moving her. She tried to jerk her arms from her captors and run again, senseless though it was. She couldn't let them move her. Paul would never find her, even if her call had gotten through. She'd never see him again.

Suddenly the men stopped and stared out to sea. Several launches appeared on the horizon, cutting wide wakes toward the island, followed by a large gray ship. A helicopter was approaching. Emma raised her arms to wave; a man threw her down. She struck her head on one of the rocks that littered the beach.

One of the men shouted something in Spanish. Another grabbed her under the shoulders and pulled her into the trees.

"Leave her," screamed another in English over the beat of the helicopter, "She's dead." The man dropped her.

She opened her eyes and saw palm fronds flapping under the rotors. He'd come. Paul had come. It was her last thought before everything went black.

CHAPTER SIXTY SEVEN

Paul strained against the window of the pontoon helicopter, surprised at how small the island was. He'd visualized a tropical tourist resort. Instead, only one house was visible, a low, sprawling bungalow with a walled terrace facing the beach. As the chopper landed next to the jetty, he threw open the door and leaped up to the faded, warped boards. He could already see where they were holding her: a window overlooking the terrace was boarded over.

Weighted down by a bullet-proof vest, he raced for the beach. Behind him the chief of Secret Service yelled for him to stop. The Venezuelans were shouting, too, and Paul assumed they wanted to go first. He ignored them and rushed to the house.

At the French doors, he stopped at the side and peered into the room. It was empty. He ran through to Emma's room. Large shards of china lay on the floor, along with remnants of a meal that had bounced to the floor from a food cart. Emma lay curled up on the bed. He yanked the netting aside and his heart stopped. Had they cut off her head? He touched her shoulder.

It was a dummy. He'd fallen for the oldest trick in the world. But the kidnappers had, too. Emma had gotten out, made the call somehow. Had they found her? Killed her?

"Mr. President," said the chief of Secret Service behind him, "you have to let us do this. Stay back..."

Paul wheeled around and ground out between clenched teeth, "Don't tell me what to do, Dave, and don't get in my way. That's an order." He ran back to the first room.

"Clear," yelled a voice from the middle of the house.

Several others echoed that from different rooms.

"The whole house is clear," reported another.

Emma, Paul thought, feeling her presence as palpably as if she were in his arms, still fearing she was dead or near death. If she got out of the room where would she go? He ran back out the French doors. On the right footprints led into the brush; on the left more widely spread tracks led around the inlet. At almost the point where the beach curved out of view, someone had hacked at the bushes and strewn leaves on the sand. He ran down the steps and along the inlet, the entire Secret Service at his heels, along with the Venezuelans and an Air Force SWAT team in full regalia.

The path of slashed underbrush branched and curved through the jungle seemingly at random. The men spread out and started across the island.

"Mr. President," yelled someone.

Paul ran to where the officer stood at the side of a water tank, pointing at mashed brush under the flange. From there a path of broken but not slashed brush headed back toward the beach.

Paul followed it, running and yelling, "Emma, Emma!" He reached the beach and followed the footprints for a few feet before he found the tracks where someone had been dragged toward the trees. He could no longer speak. Fear massed in his throat. He saw her shoes, her still legs. So deathly still. The tap root of his life ripped away. He stepped forward, shoving broad leaves aside.

She lay with her shoulders pulled up, as if she'd been dropped there, her hair a tangle of sand and leaves. Her face was waxen.

He fell to his knees and put his ear to her chest. Her heart was beating and she was breathing lightly. Relief soared through him. He kissed her forehead, ran his hand over her hair. "Emma," he moaned, still fearful. "Please, Emma, don't leave me." Tears ran onto her dirty blouse. He lifted her limp hand from the sand and kissed it. She moaned and her eyes fluttered open.

"Emma!" he cried.

"Who are you?"

"It's me, love, Paul. I came to get you. I love you and I swear if I have to kidnap you myself, I'll never let you leave my side again."

A smile flitted across her face and was gone. "Where am I?"

Paul turned and yelled, "Doctor! Get that doctor over here *now.*" He faced her again and said, "You're on an island, sweetheart, you were kidnapped."

"Who are you?"

The following afternoon Paul ran from the Oval office to the White House and took the steps to the living quarters two at a time. He banged into the Queen's Bedroom, where Shirl turned from the bed and smiled at him.

"I tol' you Ah'd call you the minute she woke up," she said.

"Thanks, Shirl," he said, looking at Emma, hardly a ripple in the covers of the canopied bed.

Shirl left the room without making a sound.

"Paul." Emma's smiling eyes followed his face as he knelt beside the high bed. "Sit down," she said, patting the edge of the bed.

Paul sat gingerly, took her hand, and kissed it. "You're going to be all right. I had them move you here when the doctor said you didn't have to be hospitalized. I wanted to be with you when you woke up. I had Shirl bring..."

Emma put her arms up. "Come closer," she begged.

Paul inched forward. "I don't want to hurt..."

"Not feeling you next to me is what hurts. Just hold me."

He slid his hand under her head and his arm behind her back. Her arms went around him and he lifted her, supporting her head as he would a baby's.

"I love you, Paul."

His arms tightened und he buried his face deeper into her dark hair. "Emma," he choked.

"I love you with every cell in my body," she said. "I'm so sorry I didn't tell you before. It was my pig-headedness. And my fear of losing you."

"You'll never lose me, Emma." Paul released her enough to look in her eyes. He brushed tears from her cheek and blinked hard to control his own. "You remember telling me you felt we were being slowly cemented together?"

Emma nodded.

"You were right. When they took you, I felt as if they'd ripped away the entire front half of my body. And my heart. Everything ached for you."

"Would you still want me to be your wife?"

"I want you in any form I can have you, but if you'd be my wife, I'd be happier than I ever imagined. Please, marry me."

Emma let him support her and put both her hands on his face. "Please, marry me," she said.

CHAPTER SIXTY EIGHT

Paul unfastened his seat belt and glanced out at the June green landscapes slipping by. He stood up from the leather seat in Air Force One, stretched, and signaled Brent to join him in the conference room. More politicking to do, and he hated it as much as ever.

When they'd closed the door, he asked, "You want to go over your acceptance speech, Brent?"

"No, thanks, I've got it all memorized. And thanks for coming, Paul."

"I'm proud you asked us, and Emma is, too. You deserve this, Brent. You ought to have a lot more than a plaque on the monument to the victims of the quake. And you will someday. No one has done more to get California back on its feet than you. If they don't nominate you for governor in a few years, I'm going to want to know why."

Brent rolled his eyes toward the curved ceiling. "Perish the thought. My sister's going to be at the ceremony."

"Did you send your father an invitation?"

Brent nodded. "I don't know whether he'll come. Carol called him. She told him he if he didn't have a son any more, he didn't have a daughter, either."

"That's wonderful to have at least one family member so loyal to you."

Brent nodded again but looked away.

"Okay, son," said Paul. "Who's left that we might convince? Let's get at least one more on our side today."

Brent took a deep breath and pulled a small notebook from his pocket. "Whorley, Montana; Ziblich, Louisiana; Spaulding, Colorado; and Franks, Michigan."

"Michigan? Oh, yeah, no oil but cars. Okay, give me Spaulding. At least I spent some time in her state. You know Detroit, don't you?"

"I've been there to visit my sister."

"You take him. And talk to him about whatever freeways there are around the city as if you drove them every day."

"You want me to convince the senator from Detroit to vote for a bill that will phase out the internal combustion engine. Sure I will."

Paul sat down at one end of the table and pulled the telephone toward him. "Play up the retraining and the fact that manufacturers will be given incentives, you know what I mean. I'm on line one," he said. His shoulders drooped as he picked up the receiver. "God, I hate doing this."

"Me, too." Brent tucked the receiver under his chin and gave Paul the Washington number of Senator Spaulding.

Paul dialed. "Mrs. Spaulding? This is Paul Greer."

"Yes, Mr. President. I thought you were on your way to California." Mrs. Spaulding's gravelly, ancient voice was flustered and wary.

"I am, and still a little unaccustomed to having a phone at my disposal at thirty thousand feet. Mrs. Spaulding, could you spare a few minutes to talk about the aquifer bill?"

"I was on my way...well, yes, I guess so." Her voice conveyed more resignation than willingness.

"You know how long it took us to get it out of committee. It shouldn't take a year for the Senate to act on it after the House passed it. We'd like to see the vote before the end of the session. Are you still undecided or have you made up your mind?"

"I know how I'm voting. I'm afraid it's nay, Mr. President." Her voice actually emphasized "afraid."

There was something in her tone... Paul gripped the receiver harder. "Are you being pressured, Dorothy?"

"Well..."

Suddenly Paul knew there was someone with her, someone she didn't want to hear the conversation. "Dorothy, if you're being threatened, just say yes."

She was silent a minute and said, "I'm not sure."

"Well, if you ever are sure, please let me know immediately. We're not going to have our legislators threatened. Do you know where this is coming from?"

"Yes."

"All right. You get the name of the person with you to Ed Petersen."

"Yes, sir."

"Well, I don't want to add to your stress right now, Dorothy. I'll call you again. And I'd be very grateful if we could get these things passed this year."

Paul hung up the phone and growled at the air. So much for that bit of presidential influence. He dialed Wes Schmidt and told him to find out who was pressuring Senator Spaulding. He should make one more call, but Brent had the list.

Brent was still on the phone, swiveled so that his back was to Paul, but the hunch of his shoulders showed that his conversation was no easier. Paul grabbed the phone again and dialed Emma in Air Force Two. He got up and moved to the window farthest from Brent. "Hi, sweetheart," he said. "How's your flight?"

"Lonesome. I wish I'd taken Brent with me."

"We're still calling people. You know, I never can bring my-self to say flat out, 'I want you to vote for this bill.' I'm sure that's the mark of a sloppy politician."

"Maybe, but it's the essence of tact."

"Emma, the ones who're holding things up have their heels planted in concrete. We have almost no chance to get the rest of your bills voted on before the election."

"I know. Even *my* optimism has faded. I hoped they'd breeze right through in the ground swell of antagonism against the oil companies after the kidnapping."

"I guess it's really the automobile that's the sticking point. The only way we'll ever get an American out of his car is to make it more inconvenient and costly than any alternative."

"What are we going to do if Congress doesn't vote this year?"

"Let's just hope they do."

He sensed her hesitating.

She took a breath and said, "I've been giving it a lot of thought, Paul. How would you feel about running again?"

The question rang through him like a deafening gong.

After a minute of silence, she asked, "Are you still there?"

"Yes. Looking for a hole to stick my head in. I guess you realize there're about a million ramifications to that question."

"I know. I thought I'd go home and spend my life trying to counteract Earl's influence on the tribe. He's pushing harder than ever for the casino. But we've come so far. We can't quit now. Our work is too important."

Paul clenched his teeth. The gong was vibrating bells he thought he'd hidden in deep folds of his brain. "Damn, I wish we were together. I didn't want to discuss this with you at 35,000 feet, five hundred miles apart. To tell you the truth, Emma, this isn't the first time the thought of rerunning has entered my mind."

He heard her sharp intake of breath.

"Really? Why haven't you said anything?"

"Because I'm just not sure. Among other things, I don't want to wait four more years to marry you."

"Would we have to wait, or do you think they'd let husband and wife be president and vice president?"

"It can't be unconstitutional. I doubt the founding fathers foresaw women in political office of any kind. But I doubt we could win as husband and wife. Would you run? I wouldn't mind being your consort in the least. It should have been you in the White House all along."

Emma sniffed. "Oh, sure. The only person in D.C. who would have managed to force 'Madame President' out of his throat is good old Rutherford."

Paul laughed. "But *he* would have said it with such grace. That alone would've been worth the four years. But seriously..."

"No, Paul. I'd never be elected. Even if I weren't a woman and an Indian, the enormous rise in popularity is yours, not mine."

"Nonsense, the people have come to love you."

"I realize that, but they do love a hero. Your rescue mission was the stuff legends are made of."

The horror of her lying waxen and still on the beach shocked him again, and he wanted nothing more than to hold her. "Emma, sweetheart, I wish you were here."

"So do I."

He let the love he heard in her voice ease into his heart. "Anyway, you were the one who made the rescue possible. I didn't so much as bash a single head."

"Nevertheless, *you* could win. *I* couldn't. It's as simple as that."

"You know Cramner is going to quit as population secretary. Would you take that on?"

Emma gasped. "I'd rather be that than vice president. I'd quit and start this minute."

"What about your work, no, our work, with the tribe?"

"I'd squeeze it in somehow."

Paul shook his head. "Look, we're talking as if I'd already decided when I haven't. Truthfully, I'd rather be tied to the tail of this plane than go through it all again. On the other hand, when I left New Orleans four years ago, all I was doing was running with no idea of what I should run to. This is the last calling I'd have chosen. And certainly the last one I'm suited to, but now I'm in it, and maybe I can do some good. That's all I ever wanted. I just don't know. Of course, this discussion is moot, anyway. I'd never be elected."

Emma laughed. "Has it really been four years since I heard that? I love you, Paul. I plan to tell you that for the rest of my life. After all my pig-headedness and fear and determination to save the world, I've finally realized I'm just a human being who needs love, like every other. I don't know why I was lucky enough to run into the kindest man on earth. If you'd stayed in your church, they'd have made you a saint."

Paul laughed. "Thank you, sweetheart. And may I say whatever happy hunting ground your tribe believes in, you make it happier."

They smiled at each other in the sky, and both knew it from miles apart.

"You know," she said, "whatever happens, we at least planted some good seeds. They've begun to sprout, and whether we get to plant the rest or not, we can hope the next president will."

"I suppose you're right. At least it won't be Jaubert."

"Speaking of whom, have you been watching CNN?"

"No, we've been on the phone. What's new? He didn't break out, did he?"

"No, his testimony got Krieger convicted. They're going down together."

Paul let out a shout of triumph that made Brent swivel toward him. "What a relief."

"Run again, Paul. The country needs a good man."

Paul stared down at the country passing beneath him. "I'll think about it."

CHAPTER SIXTY NINE

Paul jumped up and rushed to the door of the Blue Room to greet Danny and Laurel, giving Danny his left hand to spare his bandaged right one.

"Come on in," he said when he'd hugged the very pregnant Laurel and slapped Danny's shoulder. He led them to the fireplace, where Elijah and Brent had stood up. "I think you all know each other from the convention."

Laurel took his right hand. "What'd you do to your hand? Are you hurt?"

Paul smiled as the memory of a painful metamorphosis rose and faded. "No, I had an old scar removed."

"Oh, I remember that scar. I always wondered where you got it." Her face reddened.

Paul guessed that her last confession to him was playing out in memory. It seemed impossibly long ago now.

She turned and pecked Danny on the cheek. "Well, if you folks will excuse me, I'll go check on Emma."

The men settled around the fireplace.

"Little brother, I'm proud of you," said Danny. "Who'd have thought you'd manage four years in the White House?"

Paul laughed. "*I* certainly didn't. In the beginning I just wanted to run after Hartsell and beg him to help me. Now I feel I made a dent in the country's problems and need to keep hammering away at them."

"You did great, Paul. You showed them all, and the country has a new feeling of government that cares." said Brent.

Elijah nodded. "We haven't had that in so long most people had forgotten what it was all about."

Paul felt his face go hot. "Thank you."

Danny reached over and poked Brent on the shoulder. "You should have seen him when I told him I'd nominated him. He..."

During the old story, Paul sat back and stared into the past, watching a confused priest bolt from the confessional and run from everything that had given him purpose, security, and identity. And then Danny had shoved him onto the last path he'd ever have chosen, and the only choice he'd had was to measure up to the impossible. He remembered the accident and himself sitting on the rock staring into the universe and wishing he understood his place in it. Now he nearly did.

Danny finished with, "It's hard to believe how much can happen in four years."

"Or what'll happen in the immediate future," said Elijah. "You nervous, Paul?"

Paul looked down at the red carnation pinned to the lapel of a presidential tuxedo. "Not even faintly. Just anxious to get on with it."

"Why didn't you do this sooner?" asked Danny.

"Partly because Emma was vice president, but mostly because at the time we thought it'd be a fitting last memory of the White House. I wasn't sure I'd run again, and neither of us thought I'd be re-elected."

Danny grinned.

The door opened and Rutherford stepped regally though it. "Gentlemen, the bride is ready."

The men made their way to the East Room. Paul stopped at the door and stared. The staff had festooned it with evergreen garlands and white flowers. Chief Justice Ward stood under an arch of evergreens. Laurel, Shirl, and Erlinda already stood in the front row near the windows. Danny joined them, while Elijah joined his wife on the other side. Rutherford seated himself discretely in the third row. The few other guests stood and turned to face the north entrance to the room. Brent waited at Paul's elbow as best man.

A single flute played a haunting, yearning melody.

Emma stepped into the aisle.

A gasp went up from the small crowd.

Emma was dressed in a snow white deer skin robe. The bodice and the top of the sleeves were covered with colorful beads in intricate designs. A row of fringes hung at the bottom of the beadwork. From each dangled a silver-beaded thong and a small white feather. The sleeves and the hem of the dress ended in fringes with silver cones that jingled as she paced the aisle in white, knee high moccasins. Around her head she had woven a crown of evergreen and white roses. She carried another white deerskin draped over her hands.

Stunned, Paul breathed in suddenly, but it was not the air of the East Room that filled his lungs. Emma had stripped away the White House, the city that surrounded it, and all of the white man's world. She came to him over the plains of Wyoming, the wind dancing in her hair and in the ripe, golden grasses waving at her feet. He sensed the openness, felt the wind on his face and the grass crushed into earth beneath his feet. The wind filled him again and again; each time he breathed in the realization that he finally knew what Emma knew.

Space and time, past and future extended out from her, and he was connected through her to all things, all parts of the ageless cycle of birth, life, and death. His youthful search for truth faded away and left him with the ultimate answer, the elemental rightness of man, woman, earth, and love.

Slowly, hardly conscious of his action, he took off the tuxedo jacket and dropped it to the floor. He untied the bow tie and let it fall from his hands. He slid out of his left shoe, then the right.

The vastness of space and time whirled about the small fragility of earth as he moved, man, through the ripeness to Emma, woman, his woman, child of the Earth, mother to his offspring, his small contribution to the cycle.

He reached her in the middle of the wind-swept, grassy aisle and stopped. They smiled. She unfolded the robe she was carrying and lofted it in the air in a single, fluid motion. It settled around his shoulders. She moved both hands to his face.

"I am your wife," she said, her eyes brimming.

He put his hands on her face. "I am your husband."

They stood transfixed in the swirling wind. Then the wind became the haunting flute, and they were in the East Room again, where all their friends were clapping. They turned and walked to the front, where Chief Justice Ward was waiting. Paul stepped over his jacket, a little disoriented.

"We've already witnessed an extraordinary marriage here," said Ward, smiling, dazed. "Any ceremony I might conduct would be superfluous. I now pronounce you man and wife."

Two hours later Emma and Paul stepped onto the platform for his inauguration. Though she'd been reluctant to do it, the others had persuaded her to leave the beaded robe on. Paul had put his clothes back on with the deerskin around his shoulders.

When the crowd that had gathered in the unusually warm sun saw Emma, a roar went up. She stopped and turned back to

Paul. He put his hands on her shoulders and turned her to face the crowd. "They're cheering," he said. "They love you."

She looked up at him and back at the people. She waved and the cheering grew louder. They took their seats.

"Ladies and gentlemen, President Paul Greer," the Chief Justice spoke into the microphones.

Paul stood and approached the podium. He waved at the people, the white bandage on his right hand an arc of triumph over his own demons and those of the country. A cheer rose again, and signs bobbed above the faces, so far away behind the barricades. He could read only one from this distance, stretched across several spectators in the front row. It read, "All *Right*.

www.ingramcontent.com/pod-product-compliance
Lightning Source LLC
Chambersburg PA
CBHW071629260626
47170CB00001B/27